3.00

Dear Reader,

We're thrilled that some of Harlequin's most famous families are making an encore appearance! With this special Famous Families fifty-book collection, we are proud to offer you the chance to relive the drama, the glamour, the suspense and the romance of four of Harlequin's most beloved families—the Fortunes, the Bravos, the McCabes and the Cavanaughs.

Our third family, the McCabes, welcomes you to Laramie, Texas. A small ranching town of brick buildings, awnings and shady streets, Laramie is the kind of place where everyone knows each other. The little town is currently abuzz with wedding plans—and no McCabe is safe from the matchmaking! The path to the altar may not be smooth for the McCabes, but their humor-filled journeys will no doubt bring a smile to your face.

And in August, you'll be captivated by our final family, the Cavanaughs. Generations of Cavanaughs have protected the citizens of Aurora, California. But can they protect themselves from falling in love? You won't want to miss any of these stories from *USA TODAY* bestselling author Marie Ferrarella!

Happy reading,

The Editors

CATHY GILLEN THACKER

is married and a mother of three. She and her husband spent eighteen years in Texas and now reside in North Carolina. Her mysteries, romance comedies and heartwarming family stories have made numerous appearances on bestseller lists, but her best reward, she says, is knowing that one of her books made someone's day a little brighter. A popular Harlequin Books author for many years, she loves telling passionate stories with happy endings, and thinks nothing beats a good romance and a hot cup of tea! You can visit Cathy's website, www.cathygillenthacker.com, for more information on her upcoming and previously published books, recipes and a list of her favorite things.

FAMOUS FAMILIES
the McCABES

CATHY GILLEN THACKER

Texas Vows: A McCabe Family Saga

HARLEQUIN®
entertain, enrich, inspire™

To Charlie—
For everything, always.

Recycling programs
for this product may
not exist in your area.

ISBN-13: 978-0-373-36512-8

TEXAS VOWS: A McCABE FAMILY SAGA

Copyright © 2001 by Cathy Gillen Thacker

www.Harlequin.com

Printed in U.S.A.

FAMOUS FAMILIES

The Fortunes

Cowboy at Midnight by Ann Major
A Baby Changes Everything by Marie Ferrarella
In the Arms of the Law by Peggy Moreland
Lone Star Rancher by Laurie Paige
The Good Doctor by Karen Rose Smith
The Debutante by Elizabeth Bevarly
Keeping Her Safe by Myrna Mackenzie
The Law of Attraction by Kristi Gold
Once a Rebel by Sheri WhiteFeather
Military Man by Marie Ferrarella
Fortune's Legacy by Maureen Child
The Reckoning by Christie Ridgway

The Bravos by Christine Rimmer

The Nine-Month Marriage
Marriage by Necessity
Practically Married
Married by Accident
The Millionaire She Married
The M.D. She Had to Marry
The Marriage Agreement
The Bravo Billionaire
The Marriage Conspiracy
His Executive Sweetheart
Mercury Rising
Scrooge and the Single Girl

The McCabes by Cathy Gillen Thacker

Dr. Cowboy
Wildcat Cowboy
A Cowboy's Woman
A Cowboy Kind of Daddy
A Night Worth Remembering
The Seven-Year Proposal
The Dad Next Door
The Last Virgin in Texas
Texas Vows: A McCabe Family Saga
The Ultimate Texas Bachelor
Santa's Texas Lullaby
A Texas Wedding Vow
Blame It on Texas
A Laramie, Texas Christmas
From Texas, With Love

The Cavanaughs by Marie Ferrarella

Racing Against Time
Crime and Passion
Internal Affair
Dangerous Games
The Strong Silent Type
Cavanaugh's Woman
In Broad Daylight
Alone in the Dark
Dangerous Disguise
The Woman Who Wasn't There
Cavanaugh Watch
Cavanaugh Heat

Chapter 1

It was a bad day and it was getting worse, Sam McCabe thought as he called all five of his sons to his study for an immediate accounting of what was just the latest event in a whole string of family catastrophes.

"Don't look at me. I don't know what happened." Will shrugged his broad shoulders. "I was out running. I wasn't even here."

No surprise there, Sam thought wearily. At seventeen, the only thing Will cared about was getting in shape for the upcoming football season. He was never around to help out or hold down the fort.

Sam turned to sixteen-year-old Brad, who was busy combing his immaculately tended brown hair and checking out his reflection in the glass-front bookcase in Sam's study. At Sam's glare, Brad pocketed his comb and offered his version. "Actually, Dad, I think it was hormonal. You know, one of those 'women things,' that made Mrs. Grunwald pack up her bags and walk out of here on such short notice."

"Hormonal," Sam repeated disbelievingly. And "no notice" had been more like it. Sam had been called out of an important business meeting to be told she'd already left and wasn't coming back—not now, not ever. When he'd tried to get an explanation from her, the irate woman had just said he needed to do something about his home situation and hung up.

Sam turned his attention to Riley, who at fourteen was definitely the most mischievous of his brood. And, unless Sam missed his guess, had probably been instrumental in pushing the retired lady-marine-turned-housekeeper to quit.

"I just don't think she's cut out to take care of growing boys," Riley explained with a remarkably sober expression. "You know. Given the fact that she never had any kids herself."

"Face it, Dad." Sensitive as always to what was going on behind the scenes, Lewis stepped forward, suddenly looking much older than his eleven years. "We were never gonna be happy with her here, anyway. Mrs. Grunwald just wasn't Mom."

And no one ever would be, Sam McCabe thought solemnly. Ellie had been one of a kind. But that didn't excuse what his boys had done here, chasing away their tenth housekeeper in six months. Not that they would ever come right out and admit that that was what they had done. No, they would continue giving excuses and shifting the blame.

Sam turned to Kevin, his youngest, and the only one of his five boys who hadn't yet put in his two cents about the latest episode in their lives. "What do you have to say about all this?"

Kevin ducked his head. Sam wasn't surprised his six-year-old had nothing to say about their housekeeper quitting. Kev hadn't talked much to anyone about anything since Ellie had died. In a way, Sam could hardly blame him. Since Ellie had died, the light had gone out of all of their lives, and with it the need to even *pretend* their world would ever be normal again.

Sam looked up to see John and Lilah McCabe in the doorway of his study. His aunt and uncle were not just a gifted nurse and doctor and founders of Laramie Community Hospital, they had been his lifelines to sanity this past year. They'd provided moral support and guidance when Ellie was ill, as well as helped during the dark days after her death.

Sam had moved back to Laramie to be closer to them, thinking more of a sense of family might help his boys adjust to the loss of their mother. And it had helped, but only to a point. The boys still didn't want a housekeeper, and indeed seemed to be doing everything they could to chase whomever Sam hired away.

After the ninth one had walked out on them, Sam had let his sons talk him into being responsible for themselves. Only to have Kevin end up in the hospital ER with a sprained wrist, numerous abrasions and a cut that needed stitches after a still-unexplained fall off the porch roof. So Sam had hired housekeeper number ten. Unfortunately, Mrs. Grunwald's take-charge style had not worked well on his boys. And now here Sam was again, relying on his favorite aunt and uncle to come and save the day, when what they really should be doing was savoring the first heady days of their long-awaited retirement.

Gently, Lilah interrupted. "Guys, we need to speak to your dad alone. So why don't you all see what you can do about cleaning up the kitchen?"

Sam waited until the boys had left, then shut the door to his study before turning back to John and Lilah. "Thanks for coming over. I don't know what I would have done if you hadn't been here."

Sam shook his head grimly, wondering what it would take to get a housekeeper who was reliable and responsible enough to handle all five of his boys even half as well as Ellie. "You'd think Mrs. Grunwald could have waited to quit until I got back from California." Instead, he'd had to cut short his Silicon Valley business trip and grab the first flight back to Dallas, then drive to Laramie, where John and Lilah had been holding down the fort, awaiting his return.

"We're glad to help you with the boys anytime, you know that," John said sincerely.

"But this is out of even our scope," Lilah added as if worried.

Sam didn't like the sound of that. It seemed as if John and Lilah were planning to quit on him, too. "What do you mean?" he demanded tensely.

John clapped a comforting hand on Sam's shoulder and led him over to the leather sofa. "Your aunt Lilah and I both grew up in large families and reared our own. So we know first-hand how chaotic households with a lot of children can be, even under the best of circumstances. But what's happening here, Sam, in the aftermath of Ellie's death, is not routine."

"Which is why we've arranged for Kate Marten to talk to you tonight." Lilah sat on the other side of Sam. "She'll be over as soon as she finishes with her grief group at the hospital."

Sam grimaced. "You know how I feel about that little busybody." He and the boys had barely moved back to Laramie a month ago when she'd started bombarding him with literature—none of which he'd read—and phone calls—none of which he'd bothered to return—about her professional counseling services.

Lilah and John exchanged a pointed glance. "We know you haven't given her a chance."

What would have been the point in that? Sam wondered, even more exasperated. "She's just a kid."

"No, Sam, she's not," Lilah said firmly as she patted his

hand. "And if you took a good look at her, gave her just a few minutes of your time, you'd realize that."

Sam shook his head and pushed to his feet. "Even if I wanted to meet with Kate—" *which I don't,* he amended silently "—I don't have the time. I've got my hands full with the boys tonight."

"No. You don't," John corrected. "Lilah and I are taking the boys to the ranch for the evening."

Lilah added helpfully, "That'll give you time to talk to Kate alone."

Sam knew his aunt and uncle meant well. It didn't mean they were right. "All I'm going to do is tell her I don't need her."

Lilah paused. "If that's really what you think, then tell her that face-to-face. But at least hear her out, and listen to what she thinks you and the boys need to get your lives back on track."

Sam knew what they needed—they needed for the damn cancer to never have taken hold in his wife's body. They needed their family intact, with everything just as it was. But none of that was possible. Much as he and the boys wanted to, they couldn't turn back the clock. They couldn't make anything happen any differently than it had. They couldn't bring Ellie back.

Sam was already two shot glasses into a bottle of Scotch when the doorbell rang. He was pouring himself a third when he heard the front door open, followed by the staccato sound of high heels crossing the foyer and heading his way. From beneath hooded eyes, he watched as Kate Marten paused in the portal, and squinted in his direction.

"Sam?" Her voice filled the dark room as she carefully made her way toward his desk. It was a you-can-tell-me-anything-and-I'll-understand kind of voice. Soft, seductive, incredibly pleasing to the ear—and the last thing he wanted to hear.

Sam propped his elbows on the desk and cupped his hands over his ears. The last thing he needed right now was Kate Marten's perky, professional presence.

Too late. As she neared he couldn't help but catch sight of a pair of long, slender, sexy legs that would have put a swimsuit model's to shame. Stopping his glance at her dimpled knees—he didn't need a woman this beautiful around, never mind one of her incredibly aggravating persistence—Sam felt a familiar bitterness seep into his veins. "Go away."

"Sorry," Kate responded with a nauseating amount of good cheer. "No can do, Sam."

Muscles tensing, Sam leaned back in his desk chair and lifted his head. Usually when he told someone to clear out, they went. Double time, when he used that particular tone of voice. Not pesky little Kate. She had to be—what?—thirty-one years old now, to his thirty-six—and still she pursued him with all the unending cluelessness and vigor of a love-struck teenager.

He glared at her, momentarily tabling his urge to punch something—anything—to smithereens. He didn't care if she thought she was helping. He wanted her gone. Now. For good. "Which of those two words don't you understand?" he demanded in a voice that wasn't anywhere near cordial.

"My vocabulary's fine, thank you very much." Kate smiled. "As for the rest…" Stepping closer yet, Kate leaned over in a drift of citrus scent and turned on his desk lamp. "I understand you all right—maybe more than you think."

Grimacing at the glow of the light hitting him in the face, Sam reached out and adjusted the shade so that the beam exposed less of him and more of her. She was dressed in a figure-hugging yellow dress that stopped just above her knees. The matching jacket clung to her breasts and fell away slightly at her midriff. Sam glared at her. Swore. He didn't want to be this physically close to any woman, never mind a crusading little innocent like Kate. "When did you turn into such a pest?"

Kate's lips curved into a wry smile. "If I were to believe what you think…the moment I was born." Her light blue eyes softening, Kate perched on the edge of his desk. "Why are you sitting here in the dark?"

Sam lifted his shoulders in an indifferent shrug. "My house. My choice."

"I see." Kate continued to regard Sam steadily.

Sam turned his eyes to the framed picture of Ellie, half buried in a pile of papers on his desk. "You don't *see* anything."

Kate lifted her manicured left hand—which sported a very nice diamond engagement ring—then let it fall back to her lap. "I might if you gave me half a chance."

"Then see this." Sam knocked back another shot of Scotch. He set the glass back on his desk with a thud and stared at her. "I don't want you here. I don't need you."

Refusing to back down in the slightest, Kate lifted her delicately arched brow. "What makes you think this is all about you?"

Stung, Sam shifted his gaze away from her, anything to avoid the faint hint of derision in her blue eyes. "What is it about then?" he asked gruffly.

"Your boys."

Sam lifted his glance to Kate's. Held it there with effort. "My boys are doing fine," he said flatly.

"Are they now?" Kate's goading smile widened as she casually reached over and recapped his bottle of Scotch. "I suppose that's why they've just chased off their sixteenth housekeeper in six months."

"Tenth." Before the little know-it-all could get any ideas

about dumping his liquor down the sink, Sam took the bottle from Kate's hand and set it next to him, well out of her reach. "Mrs. Grunwald was the tenth, not our sixteenth, housekeeper."

"I stand corrected," she conceded. "And if they're doing so fine, why did you get called back from California? From what John and Lilah said, that was an important business deal you were negotiating."

Not anymore, Sam thought, aware his quick exit and the client's need for an extremely speedy resolution to the problem had put his company out of the running. "Don't worry. There will be others." His business never had and never would hinge on any single deal.

"I'm not worried. I know how well your business has been doing. Unfortunately—" Kate hopped down from the desk and began to pace the study "—money doesn't buy happiness, does it, Sam?"

"You're on very thin ice here, Kate. So in other words back off."

Kate turned and looked at him as if she were pleased to know she was getting under his skin. She folded her arms in front of her and said, "You need someone to help you with the boys, Sam."

Sam lifted his glass in a mock salutation. "The lady wins a prize for that astute observation."

Ignoring his sarcasm, Kate edged closer, her arms still pressed tightly against her waist. "I am that person."

Sam poured himself another drink. "I thought I made it clear—I'm not interested in bringing them in for counseling."

"You know what they say," Kate replied. "If Mohammed won't go to the mountain, take the mountain to Mohammed."

"You're not coming here to counsel," Sam said flatly.

"How about I just sign on as your housekeeper then? Temporarily, of course."

Unable to resist, he goaded her. "What happened? The hospital fire you?"

The last thing Sam needed was Busybody Kate underfoot twenty-four hours a day. Never mind that he knew how his five boys would react to having someone as pretty as Kate living in the house with them. All five of them would have crushes on her in no time. A complication he also didn't need.

"On the contrary," she retorted pleasantly, standing so close he could take in the alluring fragrance of her hair and skin. "We've had so much success we're expanding the department. The second grief counselor started last Thursday."

If she hadn't been badgering him, charging in repeatedly where she so clearly was not wanted or needed, Sam would have congratulated her. As it was, he let the opportunity pass, and took another sip of his Scotch. "What does that have to do with me?" He studied her, wondering what he could do to incite her to leave and never come back.

Kate pulled around one of the straight-backed chairs from in front of his desk and positioned it so it was two feet away, facing him. Then sat. "You've got four weeks until school starts again."

Four weeks with the boys home every day, able to get into plenty of mischief, while he was at company headquarters in Dallas, struggling to not let any more business opportunities go down the drain.

Had it just been him, Sam could have done with the lost opportunity and income. But he had two hundred and fifty highly qualified e-commerce consultants working for him. If his company went under, the lives of his employees and their families would be thrown into chaos, too. Sam wasn't about to let that happen. Not if he could prevent it.

Still sipping his Scotch, he watched her gung-ho expression over the rim of his glass and waited.

"Meanwhile," Kate continued, "I've been so busy build-

ing up my program at the hospital I haven't taken any sig-
nificant time off in two years and I've got five weeks of
vacation coming."

Wariness quickly replaced Sam's willingness to listen.
The muscles in his jaw clenched as Kate sank into the chair
and crossed her legs.

"And you're proposing what exactly?" he demanded with
a curious lift of his brow, irritated to find he'd been paying
more attention to her knees than what she'd been saying.

Kate smiled at him as if her solution were the most natural thing in the world. "That I move in here with you and
the boys until school starts and or you find someone to take
over the job permanently."

Sam would have liked to think this was all a goofy im-
pulse on Kate's part, but he could see by her overeagerness
that it was not. The earnest little do-gooder honestly thought
she was helping here. "Why would you want to do that?" he
asked impatiently.

"A lot of reasons." Kate turned her hands palm up. "Your
parents are gone now, so they're not available to help you,
and you never had any siblings."

Sam forced a smile through stiff lips and, for his beloved
aunt's and uncle's sakes, returned with a politeness that was
even more strained, "But I do have an aunt and uncle right
here in Laramie. Not to mention all four of their sons and
their new wives." That was, in Sam's view, plenty of family.

"John and Lilah are leaving tomorrow evening to go to
Central America to do medical relief work for several weeks.
Or had you forgotten?"

Sam had been so wrapped up in his own problems he
had forgotten.

"I've no doubt Shane, Wade, Travis and Jackson would
be happy to help you. Only problem is, they've got jobs and
responsibilities of their own."

Sam frowned at Kate's holier-than-thou tone. "And you don't?" he countered, doing nothing to mask his disbelief.

Kate straightened her spine indignantly. "I worked as a high school guidance counselor before I worked at the hospital. As it happens, I know plenty about working with kids. But there are other reasons I want to help you out, as well."

Sam released a long, exasperated breath. He was sorry he'd ever let her get started on this pitch. "Such as…?" he asked, disinterested.

"Our families have known each other forever. And in Laramie, we help each other when circumstances warrant it."

That was true, Sam thought, but only to a point. He reached for the bottle of Scotch. "You're forgetting the fact your father despises me."

Twin spots of color appeared in Kate's fair cheeks. "What happened between you two was a long time ago," she countered.

Sam poured himself another shot. "I'm betting your dad hasn't forgotten or forgiven."

Beginning to look a little annoyed herself, Kate replied, "That's not the point."

With an economy of movement, Sam set the uncapped bottle back on his desk. He regarded her steadily. "Isn't it?"

"Ellie used to baby-sit me when I was a kid. Did you know that?"

Sam shrugged. As far as he was concerned, that was of no significance. "She used to baby-sit a lot of people around here."

"Yeah, well…" Kate's voice took on a tremulous, emotional quality Sam liked even less. "Ellie was especially kind to me in the months after my brother died, and I've never forgotten it." Kate paused and looked down at her hands. "I've been thinking—maybe this is the way I'm supposed to repay her kindness."

Which was, Sam knew, exactly how Ellie would have seen it. Hadn't that been one of her favorite sayings? One kindness begets another. He sighed again, more loudly, wondering how he had ever allowed himself to get into such a mess. *Now he was going to have to do what Ellie would* not *have wanted him to do: turn down Kate's offer of help.* Aware Kate was waiting for him to say something, Sam finally allowed, "Ellie was a good person."

"The best." Kate's eyes shimmered suddenly. Her voice grew even huskier. "Everybody loved her, Sam."

But not as much as me, Sam thought, knowing as much as everyone still missed Ellie their grief was nothing—*nothing*—compared to his and the boys'. He looked at Kate. "The answer is no," he said flatly.

Her eyes widened with disbelief. "Why not?"

Sam swore silently. She was really going to torture them both by making him do this. He didn't want to put her down. But, damn her, she'd left him no choice. "Because you've never been married or had kids of your own," he told Kate, giving her a look that immediately relieved her of any responsibilities, any past debts, she thought she had here.

"A fact that will be remedied soon enough," Kate interjected, wiggling her left ring finger.

Sam blew out an aggravated breath. "The fact you're getting married to Craig Farrell later this fall changes nothing, Kate. You still know nothing about being a mom."

"Maybe not," Kate conceded, clearly hurt he didn't think her capable. "But I know plenty about being a friend."

What little patience he had fading fast, Sam shoved a hand through his hair. He wished Kate would just give up and go home. "My kids have friends," he told her gruffly. "They *need* a disciplinarian."

A fact that, to Sam's consternation, did not faze Ms. Kate Marten in the least. "If you think I can't bring order to your five rowdy boys, think again, Sam. I worked as a camp counselor five summers in a row. I was an athletic trainer for my father's football team all four years of high school. *I can handle your boys, Sam.*"

Sam rolled his eyes. "That's what Mrs. Grunwald said. And she was a marine. They drove her out in two weeks." Sam shuddered to think what his kids would do to someone as well-intentioned but as hopelessly naive as Kate Marten.

Kate shrugged and continued to regard him like the dynamo she thought she was. "All that proves is that she wasn't the right person for the job," she persisted amiably.

Sam took in Kate's dress-for-success clothing and carefully selected jewelry. With her soft honey-blond hair falling about her shoulders in a style that probably took hours every day to maintain, she looked as though she belonged in an office, not a kitchen or a laundry room. "And you are?"

"You're darn right I am." Kate looked at him steadily. As she continued, her voice dropped a compassionate notch. "Furthermore, I can help you, too, Sam."

Now that grated, Sam thought. To the point it really shouldn't go unrewarded. "How?" Sam asked sharply, eyeing her with a brooding stare designed to intimidate.

"By giving you someone to talk to."

Finally, he acknowledged silently, they were down to the tiny print at the bottom of every contract. "What are we talking about here?" Sam asked in a deceptively casual voice that in no way revealed how truly annoyed he was with her. "Some sort of informal grief counseling on the side?"

"Yes." Kate beamed her relief that he was catching on. Her blue eyes gleamed with a mixture of gentleness and understanding. "If that's what you want, certainly I'd be happy to help you with that."

Sam drained the last of his Scotch. Setting his glass down with a thud, he got slowly, deliberately, to his feet. What was it going to take, he wondered, to get people to stop trying to examine his private pain and leave him alone? What was it going to take to get people to let him grieve, in his own time, in his own way, at his own pace? He'd thought if he left Dallas—where he and Ellie and the kids had made their life together—and returned to the town where he and Ellie had spent their childhoods, that the people would be kind enough, sensitive enough, to just leave him and the kids alone to work through their grief however they saw fit. Instead, everyone wanted to help. Everyone had an opinion. Everyone had some method of coping they wanted him and or the boys to try. Leading the charge of the "Laramie, Texas, Kind Friend and Neighbor Brigade" was Kate Marten.

Sam had tried ignoring her. Been rude and unapproachable. He'd even—for a few minutes tonight—gritted his teeth and tried to reason with her. To his chagrin, all he'd done was encourage her.

And that, Sam knew, as he stood in front of Kate, would not do.

To make everyone else cease and desist their well-intentioned yet misguided efforts to snap him and the boys out of their grief, he would first have to make Kate Marten back off. As disagreeable as he found even the idea of it, Sam knew of only one surefire way to do that.

"If that seems like too much at first, we can just—I don't know…be friends," Kate continued a little nervously, finally beginning to eye him with the wariness he'd wanted her to all along.

"Suppose I want more than that?" His idea picking up steam, Sam reached down, took Kate's wrist, and pulled her to her feet. Ignoring the soft, silky warmth of her skin beneath his fingertips, and the widening of her astonished blue eyes, he danced her backward to the wall. "Then what?"

"Um—" Kate swallowed as she tried and failed to unobtrusively extricate her wrist from his iron grip. "We could get into other areas, too."

Sam smiled cynically at the sheer improbability of that ever happening. Aware his plan was working, he said gruffly, "You're not getting it." Sam caged her with his body and braced an arm against the wall on either side of her head.

Her expectant look changing to one of alarm, Kate tried and failed to push past him. "Not getting what?" she asked, still smiling, albeit a lot more nervously now.

"That's not what I want from you, Kate," Sam murmured as he slanted his head over hers. Telling himself this was for both their sakes, Sam let his gaze slowly trace the contours of her face, linger hotly on her lips, before returning—with all sensual deliberateness—to the growing panic in her ever-widening eyes. "That's not what I want from any woman."

Fear turned to anger as he leaned impertinently close. "Sam…" Kate warned as she splayed both her hands firmly across his chest and shoved. Again to no avail.

Now that he'd found something that would work to rid himself of her, Sam wasn't going anywhere.

"This is the liquor talking," Kate continued in her pious counselor's voice.

Knowing he would have to become a real bastard to remove Kate and her damnable interference once and for all, Sam merely smiled. "I'm not that drunk," he said, his voice taking on a menacing tone. "Yet." Before the evening was over, for the first time since the night of Ellie's funeral, he would be.

"You don't have to behave this way." Kate lectured him with a mix of compassion and desperation. Ignoring his obvious disillusionment, she insisted stubbornly, "I can help you."

Sam shook his head. Kate was wrong. She couldn't help. No one could. The best thing anyone could do—the only thing—was leave him the hell alone. The sooner Kate Marten understood that, the better.

"The only thing I want is this." Grabbing her roughly, Sam lowered his lips to hers and delivered a short, swift, punishing kiss meant only to inflame her anger and vent his. "And this…" His hands moved from her shoulders to her breasts in a callous way he knew would infuriate and frighten her even more than his brief, bruising kiss. Ignoring her muffled cry of dismay and shuddering breaths, Sam forced her lips open with the pressure of his and deepened the contact.

"Are you willing to give me that, Kate?" he demanded contemptuously, shifting his hands lower still. "Do your professional services…your unending sympathy for me and all I've been through extend that far?" He kissed her again, harder, more relentlessly than before as his hands slipped beneath her dress and closed around the satiny softness of her inner thighs. "Or are their limits on what *you'll* take, too?" he taunted, wanting her—needing her—to share some of this pain she had so cruelly dredged up.

Breathing hard, Kate shoved him away from her. Hauling back her hand, she slapped his face. Hard. "That's for kissing me, when you know I'm engaged," she spouted angrily, fire in her eyes. "And that—" Kate kicked his shin even harder than she'd slapped his face "—is for the grope."

"Got to hand it to you, Kate," Sam drawled, mocking her, even as shame flowed through him at his behavior. Limping, grimacing, he let her go. "You haven't lost your fighting spirit." *Nor your aim.* Even through the numbing haze of alcohol and grief, his face stung and his shin throbbed even worse.

"Too bad I can't say the same for you." Hands propped on her hips, she regarded him with unmitigated disgust.

Ellie would have hated this. Hated what I've become….

Pushing the guilt away, Sam went back to his bottle. He

tipped it up, drank deeply. "You don't know anything about what I've been through," he said roughly, wiping his lips with the back of his hand.

"But I will, Sam," Kate promised. "Before all is said and done, I will." She surveyed him with one last contemplative glance, then turned on her heel and stomped out of the study.

Sam followed her into the foyer, the Scotch he'd consumed doing nothing to abate his misery over either losing Ellie or this latest debacle in his life. "Leaving? So soon?" Since Ellie's death, he'd been empty inside. Dead. Now Kate, with her endless prodding and pushing, had made him cruel, too. He wouldn't forgive her for that, any more than she was going to forgive him for the pass.

Kate shot him a look over her shoulder, anger flashing in her eyes. "Go to hell."

Can't, Sam thought miserably, *I'm already there.*

Not about to apologize for what he'd known would happen all along if he spent any time alone with her, he shrugged. "I told you it wouldn't work."

Kate gritted her teeth. "Only because you're behaving like such a self-centered jerk."

"What can I say? You bring out the best in me." Ignoring the hurt in her eyes, Sam forced himself to not feel guilty, to not take anything of what he'd said or done back, no matter how unkind it was. He hadn't invited her here. He hadn't asked her to stir up his pain to unbearable, unmanageable levels. She'd ignored all his signals to the contrary and barged in here at her own risk. What she had gotten was her own damn fault. Not his.

"The best or the worst?" Kate returned sharply. "'Cause if this is as good as it gets from here on out, I'd sure hate to be one of your sons."

Sam had never slapped a woman—he never would. But she made him want to slap the daylights out of her. Another first. "Get the hell out." Sam scowled. He jerked open the door, took her by the shoulders, and shoved her stumbling across the jamb. As soon as she'd cleared the portal, he slammed the door behind her, and didn't look back.

There were some people it was best just to stay away from. Starting now, Kate Marten topped his list.

Chapter 2

Footsteps clattered across the floor, not stopping until they were precariously near. "I had a feeling this was going to happen."

Sam McCabe groaned. That voice again. Do-gooding. Soft. Persistent. He struggled to bring himself out of his stupor, felt the sledgehammer pounding behind his eyes, and decided it wasn't worth it. Sighing, he headed back into the blissful darkness of sleep.

Feminine perfume teased his senses. A small, delicate hand touched his shoulder.

"Rise and shine, big guy."

Knowing full well who it was without even looking, Sam moaned and tried to lift his head. He swallowed around a mouth that felt as if it were filled with cotton and tasted like the bottom of a garbage pail. "Go. Away."

"You keep saying that." The low voice was laced with amusement. "Don't you know by now it's not going to work?"

Realizing the only way to get rid of the busybody was to face her, Sam grimaced and lifted his head as far as he could—which turned out to be several inches above the desk. Feeling as if he were going to throw up at any moment if he moved even the slightest bit in any direction, he struggled to open his eyes. Kate Marten was standing beside him, dressed much the same as she had been the night before, in some sort of dress-for-success business suit. Her hair fell in a gentle curve of silk to her shoulders, before flipping out and up at the ends. Her fair skin glowed with good health and just a hint of summer sun. Worse, unlike him, she looked and smelled like a million bucks.

"Do you know what time it is?" she asked with a sweet, condescending smile that made him want to throttle her all the more. Not waiting for him to answer, she replied for him. "Seven-thirty."

Sam groaned again, even louder and, using his hands as levers, pushed his head up a little more. The last thing he wanted to be doing in his hungover state was noticing what a pretty face Kate Marten had.

"Do you know what time John and Lilah are due to bring your boys back this morning?" Kate Marten continued in a bright cheery voice that grated on his nerves like fingernails on a chalkboard. Her long-lashed light blue eyes arrowed in on his. "Eight-thirty. That gives you an hour to look halfway sober. Unless of course you want your boys to see you this way."

Sam regarded her with unchecked hostility. Damn her not just for seeing him this way but for coming back...after what he'd done. He turned his glance away from the determined tilt of her chin. "I thought you would have learned your lesson last night," he mumbled, cradling his pounding skull between his hands. Hell, if putting the moves on her as crudely and rudely as possible hadn't chased Miss Respectability of

Laramie, Texas, away, he didn't know what would. He'd been damn sure his actions would send her running as fast and far away from him as possible, never to return again, or he sure as shooting wouldn't have grabbed her and kissed her in a way neither of them was ever likely to forget.

"That works both ways," Kate retorted. "How's your shin?"

It still hurt like the dickens where she'd bruised it. But he wasn't telling her that! "None of your damn business." With a groan, Sam sat up all the way.

"I'm not afraid of some bad behavior, Sam. In my line of work, I see that all the time."

Sam narrowed his eyes at her skeptically, taking in her finely arched brows, pert, slender nose and nicely curved lips, before returning to her wide-set, light blue eyes. "You get kissed and groped?" Sam didn't know why, but the idea that Kate might have been manhandled that way by anyone else rankled.

"No, you were the first," Kate said, crossing her arms against her waist in a way that accentuated the curves of her breasts beneath her sophisticated-yet-oh-so prim-and-proper dress. "No other patient has ever lashed out or acted out his grief and anger in quite that way. Not that I'm all in a tizzy about it, since I know darn well that what happened last night happened only because you were drunk."

Sam had news for Kate: he hadn't been that drunk when he'd made the pass. If he had been, he wouldn't be able to remember it nearly as well as he did. He wouldn't have had to spend half the night, and another quarter of the bottle of Scotch, trying to obliterate the soft, sexy feel of her lips or the responsiveness of her slender body as it molded sensuously to his. Because the last thing he had wanted last night was to get aroused. The last thing he had wanted was any proof he was still alive. When he had made that pass at her, he had just been angry, and looking for a way to vent.

Sam glared at her, wishing she would just go away. And stop acting as if she had something to do with the mess his life had become since Ellie died. "I'm not your patient."

Kate looked at him as if she wished he were her patient. "I think before all is said and done I'm going to end up helping you and your boys."

"That's going to be hard to do if you never see us."

"Oh, but I will see you, all of you, all the time, starting tomorrow afternoon."

Sam tensed. "How do you figure that?"

Kate circled around the desk. She leaned against the edge, arms still folded in front of her. "Because you're going to let me move in here until you find a suitable housekeeper for the boys."

Sam blew out a contemptuous breath and tipped back in his swivel chair. "Dream on."

Ignoring his hostility, Kate crossed her legs at the ankles and continued sweetly, "And you want to know why you're going to do that…?"

Sam knew the sparring was juvenile. But he couldn't help himself. Maybe because Kate was the first person in a very long time who wasn't tiptoeing around him, oozing nauseating amounts of sympathy and pity. He rubbed a palm across the stubble on his face, and drawled in a voice meant to annoy, "I can't wait to hear."

"Because if you don't, I am going to tell Lilah and John about your love affair with the bottle as well as the very uncalled-for kiss and grope last night."

Sam glared at her menacingly. He didn't want to think about the way he'd tried to scare her off, his reaction to her soft body and softer lips—the fact he'd gotten turned on for the first time since Ellie's death.

"And you know what they'll do if that happens, don't you?" Kate continued, oblivious to his pain. "They'll cancel their trip to South America, and lose this chance to do medical missionary work."

Sam knew how long his uncle John and aunt Lilah had been looking forward to that. This had been several years in the planning and was the culmination of a lifelong dream. He couldn't do that to them. They deserved better.

"Not to mention," Kate continued, "their month-long second honeymoon trip to New England in October to see the fall colors. It would be a lousy thing to do, depriving them of those two trips. And even in as bad a shape as you evidently are, you wouldn't want to do that. Now would you?"

Sam didn't need Kate reminding him how much John and Lilah had done for him and his family. For the past ten years or so, they had filled the void left by the deaths of first his and then Ellie's parents. They had been "parents" to him and "grandparents" to his boys.

"I'm not asking my aunt and uncle to cancel anything," Sam snapped.

"You and I both know John and Lilah won't leave town unless they are sure you and the boys are going to be taken care of in their absence. And right now, for that, I'm your only option."

Unfortunately, that was true, Sam thought. His cousins were all busy with their own lives, careers, families. As for housekeepers, they'd already run through quite a few. Finding another one was not going to be easy, given the bad rep in the state his boys had conjured up for the family. None of that, however, meant Sam wanted Kate's help. He glared at her, resenting the position she'd put him in. "I know you mean well, Kate. But you living here will never work."

"We'll never know until we try," she said practically, at that moment looking every inch the determined grief counselor she was. "So what's it going to be, Sam?" Her fingertips curled impatiently around the edge of his desk. "Are you going to give me a chance to help you and your kids before this turns into the kind of crisis you can't come back from, or do I call John and Lilah now and tell them you are in worse shape than even they realize?"

Sam didn't answer that. He didn't have to. No one, not even the busybody Kate Marten, needed to tell Sam how important it was to shield his family from the way he'd given in to the pain and frustration and bottomed out the night before. Bad enough that Kate had been there to witness his behavior firsthand. Fortunately, he thought wearily, his kids hadn't been around to see it. And by the time they got back from John and Lilah's, there would be no evidence that anything had happened any differently than any other night.

He met Kate's stare head-on, his anger under tight control. "I'm going to take a shower." He gave her a hard look, making it clear he expected her to be gone when he returned. Then he dragged himself out of his chair, up the stairs, and into the privacy of the master bedroom suite he'd shared with Ellie on trips back to Laramie. Sam's throat ached as he glanced at the huge four-poster where he and Ellie'd made love many times and he still slept. *I love you, Sam,* Ellie had whispered every night before they went to sleep as she cuddled close. *I love you so much.* He would murmur the words back without really thinking about what they meant, what she meant to him. Scowling, Sam shook his head. He'd had so much, for so long, and he'd taken it all for granted.

In the hierarchy of things to be done, Ellie rarely if ever took the time to see to her own needs. She was always busy seeing to everyone else's. Had he just paid attention to those first signs, her sluggishness and unexplained weight loss. If he'd just insisted she go in for a physical, instead of letting her put it off... Instead, he had believed her when she said it was probably nothing. And by the time they discovered the tumor on her ovary, the cancer had spread. He'd known it was bad, but he still hadn't believed she was going to die. Nor, when it came down to it, had she. After all, she was so young...just thirty-two when her illness was discovered. She had her whole life ahead of her, a husband to love and sons to raise. She'd been as certain as he that she would beat the disease. Realizing now how foolish and naive they had been, Sam shook his head and stripped down to his shorts. Leaving his clothes on the floor where they lay, he headed into the bathroom to shave. A glance in the mirror did nothing to lift his spirits. He looked even worse than Kate had indicated or he'd expected. His face was haggard beneath the stubble of his beard, his eyes puffy and red, the corners of his mouth drawn in an expression that revealed just how miserable he felt inside. There were harsh lines on his face; a grim look in his eyes. He hadn't slept more than three or four hours a night in months and the strain showed in his gaunt, tired appearance. Kate Marten was right about one thing, Sam thought as his lips twisted in bitter gallows humor. He was a hell of a role model for his sons.

The regret inside him mounting, for all the times and ways he had failed his family, Sam picked up the can of shaving cream. Scowling, he spread the foam over his face and began to shave. He needed to start eating right and to get a decent amount of rest every night. But even as he thought it he knew: even if he hadn't been drinking last night, he probably wouldn't have slept. The insomnia was just one more thing he didn't know how to deal with. It had started during the first days of Ellie's illness, when their days and nights were filled with worry. *This couldn't be happening to them... her tumor wasn't really malignant...her cancer hadn't really metastasized.* And even if it had, nothing was going to happen to her. Not with all the specialists he had flown in, the strings he and his uncle John McCabe—one of the most respected and well-connected family doctors in Texas—had pulled to get her the very best of care possible, the most up-to-date, comprehensive treatment.

After all, their lives had been charmed up to that point. Sam had professional success beyond his wildest dreams, he and Ellie had a lively, loving family that was the envy of all their friends. They had money and clout. And Sam hadn't been afraid to use it to help his wife. But none of it had done any good in the end. Through endless rounds of surgery, radiation and chemotherapy, Ellie's cancer had continued to grow and spread. She'd gotten weaker and thinner by the day. And all Sam could do was be strong for her and the boys. Behave as if everything was going to be fine, even when he and Ellie had been told by the doctors that she had very little time left. He'd wanted to level with the kids immediately. Prepare them for what was to come. Ellie had resisted—vigorously. "I don't want them grieving while I'm still here," she'd told him emotionally. "I want our last days together to be full of love and laughter and joy. Not weighed down with unbearable sadness."

So Sam had prayed hard for a miracle and pretended she would survive, even when he knew her lungs ached with every breath and her pain required larger and larger doses of painkillers to keep it manageable. When the boys had entered her sickroom she had smiled and been the mom they needed and depended on. Only with Sam, in the last few days of her life, had she let down her guard and told him the truth, that the suffering she felt was getting to be too much. She felt so unbearably weary. Weak. Sick. It was time to move on, Ellie had whispered tearfully as he'd held her in his arms, crying, too. She was beginning to *want* to move on. And quickly after that, she did. Slipping away from them peacefully in her sleep. Leaving him to face their boys' wrath—at having been misled about the terminal nature of her illness—alone.

It wasn't easy seeing the disillusionment and disappointment every time he looked into his sons' eyes, Sam thought as a single tear slid down his cheek. Harder yet realizing just how much of their family's happiness had centered around Ellie. His family and friends kept telling him the numbness, the disorientation, the relentless anger over Ellie's fate would go away with time. But it hadn't, Sam realized as the spasms shook his body and a harsh racking sob rose in his throat. Instead it seemed to get worse, Sam thought as he sank helplessly down onto the cool tile floor, buried his head in his arms, and wept the way he hadn't, even on the day of her funeral. He'd loved Ellie so long and so much, he wasn't ever going to get over this.

Chapter 3

The football team had just started running drills Saturday morning when the black Jeep Wrangler pulled into the parking lot on the other side of the chain-link fence. Mike Marten frowned and glanced at his watch. Whoever it was, was late.

Seconds later, a lanky six-foot-plus kid strode through the gates and down the clay running track that rimmed the football field. He carried himself with an accomplished athlete's confidence and was dressed in a T-shirt, running shorts and athletic shoes. Mike Marten didn't have to see his dark buzz-cut hair, good-looking mug or familiar blue eyes to know who it was. The seventeen-year-old kid had arranged to see Mike that morning, through Laramie High School's front office and Mike's assistant coach Gus Barkley, and he was the spitting image of his dad.

Will McCabe tensed as he neared. "Coach Marten?"

Mike nodded, and tried not to let the gut-deep resentment he still felt for the kid's father affect his treatment of Will as the two of them shook hands. If there was one thing he prided himself on when it came to his work, it was his fairness to every one of his players.

"I'm Will McCabe. I called about getting a tryout for the football team."

"Right." Mike nodded, forcing himself to put his personal feelings aside. "You played quarterback at your school in Dallas?"

"Varsity, last two years," Will confirmed with a man-to-man glance at Mike. "I didn't get much playing time my sophomore year, but last year I started every game."

Zeroing in on the pride in the kid's voice, Mike blew his whistle and waved one of his running backs over. He nodded at the sidelines. "Grab a football. Let's see what you can do."

Mike put them through a series of increasingly complicated passes. Given his obvious tension, he had expected Will to start out nervously and maybe get better as he went along. Instead he started out great and continued at the same level, no matter what Mike asked him to do.

When the rest of the team finished a series and took a water break, something that had to be done frequently in the summer heat, Gus Barkley came over to the sidelines to stand beside Mike and watch. He shook his head in awe. "Man, that kid's got an arm. Speed and accuracy, too."

All should have been qualities Mike welcomed. That was hard to do when every time he looked at Will, he saw Sam, and by association, Pete.

Gus frowned, seeming to read Mike's mind. Gus, too, had worried about the potential for animosity between Sam McCabe's son and Mike. Mike had assured him it wouldn't be a problem. Now that it was happening, he wasn't so sure. Especially when the loss he felt had returned—at the mere sight of the kid—like a sucker punch to the gut. Mike frowned. He thought he had buried all that years ago, along with Pete.

"Want me to get him outfitted with some gear?" Gus asked, the anxiousness in his eyes contrasting to the easygoing camaraderie of his voice.

"Not until after I talk to him." Mike motioned Will over to him and Gus, and let his running back know, with a nod in the other direction, that he could take a break with the other players. Will trotted over. He looked at Mike hopefully.

"No guarantees about starting or anything else," Mike warned gruffly. He didn't care how naturally gifted a kid was. That went for Will and everyone else. "Whatever you get on this team, you earn. And you haven't earned anything yet. Got it?"

Will nodded and, to his credit, kept his composure despite Mike's underlying message that this was not going to be easy. Will was not just going to be "given" a slot as starting quarterback on Mike's team.

"You're also going to need a physical before I can let you on the team," Mike said, turning away from the disappointment in the kid's eyes. Obviously he had expected to be praised for his performance on the field. In fact, had probably been used to that in Dallas. "Assistant Coach Barkley will take you inside the field house and get you the forms. You can come back when you've gotten them filled out, and not before."

Will knew if he wanted to get a football physical fast, he'd have to arrange it himself. He could hardly ask his dad to do it, he was so preoccupied and out of touch with what was going on with the rest of the family he might as well have been on a different planet.

Of course, it hadn't always been that way, with him and his brothers left to fend for themselves for practically everything. When his mom was alive all any of them had ever had to do with a problem was go to her. She'd be on the phone and two minutes later everything was all fixed. Didn't matter what it was, Mom had known what to say and do to take care of it.

That had changed when she'd gotten sick, of course. But even when she was really suffering there at the end, she'd call the shots, while his dad stood around, helpless to do anything except comfort her physically and fly in more specialists.

On the domestic front, his Dad hadn't a clue. And thanks to the succession of ridiculously bad and bossy housekeepers, he still didn't. Will knew the reason why his dad wanted those idiotic ladies there. It made it easier for him to go off to work and forget all about the rest of them, the way he always had before Mom died.

Only it wasn't like before, Will thought as he turned his Jeep Wrangler into the hospital parking lot. Life was hell. Home was worse. The best he could do was try to make this year as bearable as possible by finding a girlfriend and playing football. Then go to college and never look back. Maybe never even come back.

Jackson McCabe was waiting for Will, as promised, in his office at the hospital. Young, handsome, successful and newly—happily—married, Jackson was everything Will wanted to be when he grew up. "Thanks for doing this for me, Jackson." Will handed over the forms. "I know it's a Saturday morning and you're a surgeon not a family doc, but I really need this physical right away. Otherwise, I can't show up for practice Monday morning with the rest of the team."

"Not a problem." Jackson gave Will a look that let him know he understood how chaotic life had been for him and his brothers since their mom had died and that he didn't mind the last-minute call one bit. He ushered Will onto the scale. "What are second cousins for, anyway? Besides—" Jackson shifted the metal weights on the bar until it hung perfectly in balance at one hundred and eighty seven. "I know what a stickler Coach Marten is for the rules."

"That's right." Will stood perfectly still while Jackson measured his height. "You used to play on the L.H.S. football team, too, didn't you?"

"A couple years after your dad." Jackson paused to jot down Will's weight and height on the form. "I sure did."

Appreciating the way Jackson treated him—as a man instead of a kid—Will walked with Jackson into the adjacent exam room. Figuring Jackson was enough of a straight-talker to tell him the truth, he asked, "What did you think about Coach Marten?"

Jackson checked out Will's ears and throat. "He's an excellent coach. Tough. Demanding. A little blustery at times, but don't let that worry you. His bark's worse than his bite, if you know what I mean. By the time you finish playing on his team, you'll know the sport inside and out. And probably a lot more about yourself, as well."

Will watched as Jackson jotted down some notes on the paper, then fit a blood pressure cuff around Will's arm. "What do you mean?"

Jackson took Will's blood pressure. "This is going to sound like one of those really hokey sports metaphors, but it's true." Jackson paused to look Will straight in the eye. "Coach Marten doesn't just teach you about football—he also teaches you about honesty, integrity, responsibility and commitment. Playing on his team changes a guy—for the better. If you let it."

Funny, Will thought. Jackson, never a guy to wax eloquent about anything, was speaking almost reverently about Coach Marten. His dad hadn't mentioned any of this. In fact, his dad hadn't looked all that happy about the prospect of Will playing on Coach Marten's team. Though, as usual, he'd done nothing to discourage that or any other extracurricular activity his kids wanted to pursue.

Puzzled, Will slipped off his T-shirt so Jackson could listen to his heart and lungs. He breathed in and out as directed. Something was going on here that they weren't telling him, just like when his mom had died. Damn it all, if they were deliberately keeping something from him again, he was going to be pissed.

He looked at Jackson curiously. "Did Coach Marten and my dad get along?"

Jackson tensed slightly as he unhooked the stethoscope from his ears. "Why would you ask that?"

Gut instinct. Something was off here. Will just wasn't sure what. "I don't know," he said slowly, doing his best to put all the little signs together to come up with something. "Usually when I do something around here that my dad or mom did when they were a kid, people get all nostalgic or something. Coach didn't."

Jackson sat on a stool. Suddenly he looked as if he had the weight of the world on his shoulders. "Maybe he just wanted you to feel like you were there under your own steam, not as a relation to anyone else," Jackson finally said.

And maybe, Will thought, the bitterness that had been with him since his mother's death rising up inside him once again, there was something else they weren't telling him. Something he had every right to know.

Kate spent Saturday afternoon conducting two back-to-back grief groups and the evening juggling her schedule and calling her associates at the hospital to let them know she would be taking her accumulated time off to deal with a personal emergency. She waited until Sunday afternoon to tell her parents where they would be able to reach her, starting that evening. Her mom hadn't said much when they spoke on the phone. But fifteen minutes later, both her parents were on the doorstep of her apartment, which was located on the second floor of a big white Victorian that had been converted into four separate dwellings, each with its own outside entrance.

Kate's mom, a homemaker with gray-blond hair and pale blue eyes, had obviously been baking. She still wore her blue denim chef's apron over her coordinating shorts set. Kate's dad, wearing a burnt-orange Laramie High School knit shirt, shorts and coach's cap, had a roll of antacids in his hand. A big bear of a man, he was known for his blunt speech, admirably strong character and often brutal honesty. He was also still extremely protective of "his little girl." Part of it was that he didn't want anything to happen to Kate. He'd already lost a son and he didn't want to lose his one remaining child. The other part was his protectiveness of women in general. He just wasn't sure members of the fairer sex should be out on their own, without a man to watch over them. Hence, he couldn't wait for Kate to marry her intended, Air Force Major Craig Farrell. But that wasn't going to happen until much later in the autumn. Right now, at the beginning of August, Coach Mike Marten, and his loving, dutiful wife Joyce, apparently felt they had a problem on their hands. As Kate suspected, it didn't take her father long to get to the point.

"I don't want to hurt your feelings, honey, but this is the dumbest idea you've ever had."

Out of respect, Kate tried to not roll her eyes as she continued moving around her apartment, packing up a few of her things. "Thanks for being so supportive, Dad."

Mike sighed, lifting his burnt orange coach's cap off his head and running his hand through his short salt-and-pepper hair. "You're a professional woman," Mike declared, replacing the cap low across his forehead, "not a domestic hire."

"Meaning what?" Kate interrupted, not about to let her

dad talk her out of doing what she knew in her gut had to be done. "I can't help out a friend?"

Mike Marten looked at her steadily. "Sam's not your friend."

Leave it to Dad to hit the nail on the head in two seconds flat, Kate thought. "Ellie was, when we were kids."

"But you rarely saw each other," Mike pointed out.

"Only because she was so much older than I was and she moved to Dallas after she married and then I went off to college. That doesn't erase all the kindness she showed me both before and after Pete died." At the mention of her brother, her father's face turned to stone. "Is it really so wrong of me to want to return the kindness?"

Silence fell between the three of them as Mike looked to Joyce for help. Joyce nervously wrung her hands together. There was nothing she hated more than family discord of any kind. She would do or say whatever she had to do to try to keep the peace. "I think what your father is trying to say, sweetheart, is that we don't understand why you have to move in there in order to help Sam McCabe and his boys."

Even as Kate had rued telling her parents where she could be reached for the next few weeks, she'd known there had been no avoiding it. It would have been worse had they found out any other way, and in a town as small as Laramie, they would have found out. "There are a lot of reasons. Number one, the boys are too much for Sam to handle on his own. Kevin's accident proved that."

"So let him hire a housekeeper," Mike interrupted.

"He's hired ten," Kate spouted back, beginning to resent her father's protectiveness as much as she loved him as a parent and a man. "They've all quit within a matter of weeks."

"And what makes you think you're going to do any better?" Mike demanded impatiently, peeling another antacid tablet off the role and popping it into his mouth.

Kate grinned and offered her father a disarming smile. "The fact that I'm your daughter and you taught me to never be a quitter."

Mike's brows knit together. "Don't try to charm your way out of this, Kate. I have serious concerns here."

Kate sobered immediately. She sat on the edge of her bed. "So do I, Dad. Sam's boys are in trouble." So was Sam for that matter, but Kate figured it was best to not get into that just yet. One thing at a time, and Sam's boys were first on the priority list.

Mike shrugged, not unsympathetic to Sam's plight, just more realistic—in his view, anyway. "So let 'em come to the hospital for your help like everyone else who can't handle things on their own."

Kate ignored the faint hint of derision in her father's voice. Mike, not only one of the premiere football coaches in the state with more state championship experience than anyone else in the Triple A division, was a staunch believer in survival-of-the-fittest theories. He approached every life situation as though it were a game to be strategized, played and won. In his view, there was no room for failure of any kind, and only the weak needed counseling. Unfortunately his "survivor strategies" very possibly cost Kate's older brother his life, which was something her own family was still trying to come to grips with.

"Sam doesn't believe in any kind of therapy or grief counseling for the kids," Kate said quietly, putting her own hurts aside.

"Well, I can't say I blame Sam there," Mike Marten muttered.

"Mike." Joyce gasped.

"Oh." Mike looked sheepish. "You know what I mean."

Kate surely did. If her mom and dad had only believed in counseling, her brother might have talked out his feelings instead of acted them out. If only her parents had gotten help at the first sign of trouble with Pete, instead of trying to ignore his problems, maybe Pete wouldn't have felt so misunderstood and behaved so recklessly. And maybe the three of them wouldn't have suffered for years after Pete died. Knowing there was no way to change the past, only ways to deal with it honestly and openly and move on, Kate had eventually resolved her feelings about her family's tragedy. She wasn't sure her parents had yet, or ever would without the appropriate help, which they were determined not to get.

Watching as Kate closed the suitcase containing her clothes Joyce said gently, "I know you feel like you owe John and Lilah McCabe a lot for helping you start your grief and crisis counseling program over at the hospital."

Not to mention what she owed Ellie, Kate thought, for all the times she had cried on Ellie's shoulder the year after Pete died.

"But can't you just help them out in some other way?" Joyce continued.

"Such as?" Kate asked impatiently, wishing her parents were not so difficult about this.

"Maybe you and I could just act as general coordinators for them, to help get them through this emergency. We could enlist other women to cook dinner for them. Find someone else to clean the house on a regular basis. Teenagers to babysit the little one in Sam's absence."

Kate wasn't surprised by her mother's suggestion. Joyce believed in community service, though she would avoid becoming too involved in anything that might turn out to be emotionally painful or difficult. Mike was the same way. Even when Kate's brother had died, her mom and dad had simply toughed it out and expected her to do the same. They'd never talked about the accident, except to declare Pete innocent and apportion blame for Pete's bad judgment on others.

They'd never shown or talked about their feelings, or allowed Kate to do so with them, either. Grief, uncertainty, despair, angst, sadness were not allowed in her family. In her family you moved on, period. And you avoided like mad anything that might tempt you to do otherwise. In her family, you were part of the team or you had no place there. And Kate was perilously close to getting benched. At least temporarily.

But she couldn't worry about that. She had to concentrate on Sam's boys. She had only to look at them to know they were suffering exactly the way she had suffered for years after Pete's death. Everyone was telling them everything was going to be fine—when it wasn't. Everyone was pretending things were fine—when they weren't. If it continued, the boys would start to think the problem wasn't the tragic situation they'd found themselves in, or their unresolved feelings about their mom's death. They'd begin to believe there was something wrong with *them* because they weren't dealing with their grief. They had enough to contend with, just losing their mother and their previously happy family life, without adding the burden of low self-esteem, anxiety and depression, too. Sam and his boys needed her and the help she could provide—whether they realized it or not. What they didn't need was another temporary solution like her mother's, which was no solution at all.

"Assume you and I could work out the cooking and cleaning and all that by some round-robin system, Mom, the bottom line here is child care. Do you really want to put teenage girls in the house while Sam's not home, knowing he's got three teenage boys there already?"

Joyce paused, thinking hard. "Maybe the little one could go into day care?"

"That would work for Kevin, sure, as long as Sam doesn't have to travel. But then you've still got the other four unsupervised, and believe me, you don't want to leave those boys without round-the-clock guidance the rest of the summer." Not the way they were acting out. "But not to worry, Mom, Dad. Sam's still looking for a housekeeper. As soon as he finds one, I'm out of there." In the meantime, she'd try to figure out the best way to help each of the boys. Maybe they would get to know her and regard her as a friend, eventually becoming comfortable enough to talk to her on an informal basis. Kate didn't care about being paid for her services. She just wanted to help the boys deal with their feelings so they could get on with their lives. If she ended up eventually helping Sam, too, all the better.

Mike sighed as he popped yet another antacid tablet into his mouth. "I still don't see why this is your problem, Kate."

Maybe it wouldn't have been, Kate thought uncomfortably, if what the boys were going through wasn't so close to what her family had suffered. Like Sam, her parents had ignored the warning signs about her brother, when he first began acting out his unhappiness. They had reassured each other and everyone else it was just growing pains, when even Kate— at age twelve —had been able to see that it was much more. Her brother had died as a result of that naiveté. She didn't want to see it happen again. Not to anyone. And especially not to Sam McCabe's family who had already suffered such a devastating loss.

"Sam has family in the area," Mike continued.

"Yes, he does, and they're all being too easy on him, cutting him too much slack because of what he's been through." Kate felt for Sam, too. But she wasn't afraid to confront him.

Kate's dad sighed, shook his head. "You should never have gone and gotten that Ph.D. in clinical psychology. You should have kept your job at the high school. You should be spending your time helping kids get into college—" A task Kate knew her father considered much more practical, respectable and laudable "—instead of pushing your way into situations you have no business getting involved in."

It was Kate's turn to sigh as she packed her toiletries into a tote. "I became involved, Dad, when I was asked to talk to the boys at the hospital after Kevin's fall off the porch roof."

Mike gave Kate a stern look. "And your involvement ended when he was sent home, with little more than a sprained wrist and a few stitches."

Joyce laid a restraining hand on Mike's arm. "Honey, we don't want to fight about Kate's choice of careers. That's not why we came over here."

"Why *did* you come over here?" Kate asked, exasperated.

"To make you see that moving in with Sam and his boys, even for a few days, is a mistake."

He was beginning to sound like Sam.

"First of all, you don't owe that man anything, and neither do I. Maybe if he'd been there for your older brother the way a best friend should have been, I'd feel differently, but the way it is…I don't."

Tension stiffened Kate's shoulders as the conversation veered into dangerous territory. She folded her arms in front of her and squared off with her dad. "Pete's death was not Sam McCabe's fault."

"And I suppose what he did to Ellie that year wasn't his fault, either," Mike countered sarcastically.

Kate flushed. "Sam loved Ellie, Dad."

"He ruined her reputation, Kate."

Just as Mike now feared Sam would somehow ruin hers, Kate thought. "Maybe for five minutes," Kate allowed, remembering how the scandal had rocked the town initially. Kate went over to the bureau and got her brush. "Once they were married, I don't think anyone cared."

"Nevertheless, he proved he can't be trusted around innocent young women."

"Dad, I'm thirty-one years old," Kate said wearily as she caught her hair in a French twist and pinned it in place.

Mike's face softened. "And still as sweet and innocent as the day is long, thank God."

Kate was silent. She had lost her virginity to her fiancé a long time ago, but her father would never accept that she was not a kid anymore. No, as far as Mike Marten was concerned, she was still daddy's little girl! Wondering when it was going to get easier to deal with her dad, she slipped her hairbrush into her tote bag and regarded her dad steadily. "I'm old enough to take care of myself."

"That won't stop a man like Sam McCabe from making a pass at you," Mike warned grimly.

He already has. Pushing the memory of Sam's lips and hands away, Kate turned back to her suitcase. "There are going to be five boys there as chaperones. Sam is not going to do anything in front of his sons, especially when they are so clearly grieving the loss of the mother they loved so much." Otherwise, she probably wouldn't be able to stay over there, given what had already happened between her and Sam.

"I still think you ought to concentrate on your upcoming marriage to Craig and let the McCabes take care of their own."

Kate wondered how her dad would feel if she were involved in the solution. Would he at long last be really and truly proud of her? As proud as he'd been of Pete at the height of Pete's high school football career? Even as she wondered she knew the only thing her dad was likely to respect her for was becoming Craig's wife—and providing a few grandchildren for him and her mom to love. Mike was desperate to carry on the family name, and had even talked Craig into naming their first son Marten Michael Farrell.

"It may just be for a couple of days, at most a few weeks."

Gently, Joyce asked, "What does Craig think about this?"

Kate shrugged. "I didn't ask him."

"But he's your fiancé," Joyce protested, upset.

"That doesn't mean he controls my life," Kate countered stubbornly.

"Honey," Joyce said, aghast, "this is the kind of thing… moving into another man's house…that a young woman should discuss with her fiancé."

Kate knew Craig wouldn't mind. She grabbed her laptop computer and headed for the door. "I'll tell Craig what I'm doing the next time I hear from him," she promised.

"When will that be?" Mike asked, exchanging concerned looks with Joyce.

"I don't know. I never know." That was one of the frustrations of being involved with a military man. "Soon." She hoped.

"I'll tell you one thing," Kate's dad said as he carried her suitcase and tote bag down to the car for her. "That Sam McCabe better appreciate what you're doing for him and do right by you or he's going to find himself answering to me."

Chapter 4

Late Sunday afternoon, Sam summoned his boys to the living room to tell them Kate Marten would be taking care of them temporarily.

"Starting when?" Will asked, belligerent as ever.

"She'll be here any minute," Sam said. And he was dreading it.

"Why'd you wait so long to tell us?" Riley demanded at once.

Because I was hoping she'd come to her senses and change her mind, Sam thought. He gave his most brashly outspoken son a stern look. "I'm telling you now." Not that she'd be here more than a day, anyway, Sam reassured himself. Once Kate had refereed a few fistfights and put up with temper tantrums, surly moods and nonstop rowdiness, she'd understand what it was really like to ride herd on five boys twenty-four hours a day, seven days a week. She'd want out. And no one, least of all him, would blame her for packing up and going back to work at the hospital, where she belonged.

"It seems to me—if we really want a total babe like Kate Marten to help us out for the next few weeks—that we should be doing the opposite and really cleaning up our act." Brad pulled mint breath freshener from his pocket, sprayed some in his mouth, then paused to check his reflection in the mirror.

Sam frowned. It was exactly this kind of thing he sought to avoid. He did not want his home life turning into some sort of B movie with a bunch of underage kids lusting after the "baby-sitter." "That's enough," he warned. "I don't want anyone coming on to Kate Marten or calling her a babe, even on a lark. She's a nice woman." If ill-advised, Sam amended silently to himself. "And she deserves your respect."

"Just not yours?" Riley guessed, his shiny silver trumpet dangling from his fingertips.

Sam tensed. "What do you mean?"

Lewis stopped fiddling with his hand-held video game long enough to say, "We get the feeling you don't like her."

Sam felt the eyes of all five of his sons upon him. "It's not that," he said uncomfortably.

"Then what is it?" six-year-old Kevin asked in frustration as everyone turned to him in amazement. Since Ellie's death, he rarely spoke.

Noticing the peanut butter and jelly on his hands, Kev attempted to clean them off by wiping them on his shirt.

"Are you afraid she's gonna get on your nerves by asking you how you're feeling all the time and stuff like that?" Riley blurted.

There was that, Sam thought. Kate, being the do-gooder she was, probably wouldn't hesitate to try to force some counseling down his throat. He had news for her—it wasn't going to happen. Here, or at the hospital. He knew how women liked to talk things to death, but there was nothing talking about Ellie's passing managed to do except bring him and the boys more pain. They'd already had enough pain the past year to last them a lifetime. He wasn't signing any of them up for any more. Once Kate understood that…well, Sam had no doubt she'd find some other family to "help."

"Nah, Dad can handle that. Dad doesn't want her staying here cause he's afraid we'll fantasize about her," Brad said.

It was, Sam thought, a little more complicated than that. Made more difficult by the callous pass he had used to try to scare Kate away. If his ploy had worked the way he had intended, he wouldn't be dealing with Kate or her well-intentioned but unwanted meddling again. Unfortunately, it hadn't worked, and now every time he looked at her they'd both be reminded of what he had done. And neither of them needed that.

Lewis, who at almost twelve had yet to discover girls, frowned and looked disgusted. He adjusted his glasses on the bridge of his nose. "Yuck. I would never fantasize about someone as old as Kate!"

"You say that now," Brad replied with a smug wink, "but we haven't seen her in her nightie, yet, either."

Sam grimaced at just the thought. He watched as Kevin slid under the coffee table to play with his toy cars. "Kate Marten is not going to be running around here in her nightie," he said firmly.

"We saw all our other housekeepers in their bathrobes," Brad pointed out.

"Yeah, but they were all over fifty and none of them looked anywhere near as 'babe-a-licious' as Kate," Riley added.

Sam did not see what the big deal was about Kate. So she had a trim figure that curved in all the right places, slender legs that looked good in high heels. There was nothing extraordinary about the honey-blond hair that fell to her shoulders. He saw hair that soft and silky all the time. As for her face, any prettiness Kate had on that score—and he reluctantly admitted she had some—was canceled out by her boldly assessing manner and the unflappable determination in her light blue eyes. Sure, she had full, kissable lips. And a softness about her that made a guy want to do his best to protect her even though he knew from the sassy look in her eyes and the confident way she carried herself that it wasn't at all necessary. But none of that made up for the way she had judged him to be a total screwup as a father and forcibly inserted herself into his private life. And it was high time his boys realized it took more than a slender waist and a pair of breasts to make a woman worth going after.

Six-year-old Kev came out from beneath the coffee table. "I like Kate. She was nice to me at the hospital. She wasn't all mean and bossy like Mrs. Grunwald and the other baby-sitters."

Will looked bored as he tossed his football from hand to hand. "Who cares who comes to stay here?" he asked insolently. "I'm out of here."

Sam stopped his oldest son before he could depart. "Oh, no, you're not. When Kate gets here, we're all going to be here. We're still a family, remember?"

Will gave Sam a look that reminded Sam that wasn't quite true. They hadn't really been a family since Ellie's death. She'd been the center of love and warmth in the family and the glue that held them together. Without her here to care for them, they were all kind of lost.

"Look, Dad, if you don't want Kate staying here—and we can all tell by looking at you that you don't—how come you don't just come right out and tell her that?" Brad asked.

Sam figured the boys didn't need to know about the way he and Kate had already squared off about this. That was between him and Kate. "Because Kate really wants to help us out here and thanks to the unmitigated encouragement she's been getting from Aunt Lilah and Uncle John, she's not going to stop pestering me until I let her try."

Lewis studied Sam thoughtfully. "But you don't think she'll last."

"It's not that I don't appreciate the sentiment behind her actions," Sam said carefully. "When someone wants to help you out of the goodness of their heart, it's important to appreciate the thought behind the gesture. What Kate doesn't realize—" Sam looked at the dirty dishes and fast-food wrappers littering every conceivable surface throughout the entire downstairs, including the living room "—is that she doesn't have the life experience to be able to handle all the cooking and cleaning and organizing around here and ride herd on all you boys simultaneously." Only Ellie had been able to do that, Sam thought. And she'd done it with such style, warmth, wit and love that everyone else who'd tried to fill her shoes, even partway, had paled by comparison and failed miserably.

Will gave Sam a faintly accusing look as he finally sat. "So why didn't you just tell Kate Marten she's getting in over her head, and find someone else to move in?"

Sam let out a frustrated breath. "I tried." He knew from the moment it was suggested that it wasn't going to work out. But Kate hadn't accepted that. And here he was, Sam thought, still having to deal with Kate. His four older sons exchanged speculative glances, forcing Sam to explain further as he picked up some clothes off the floor and clumped them together on the piano bench. "Look, I know her," Sam muttered, picking up a few empty soda cans, too. "We grew up together. I can try talking to Kate Marten until I'm blue in the face and it's not going to matter one whit until she figures it out for herself. However…" Sam sighed. "Once Kate's here for a few days—" if it even took that long, Sam amended silently "—she'll realize she wouldn't wish this job on her worst enemy. By then, I'll have found another housekeeper for us. Kate'll be able to leave, knowing she did her part to help us survive in the interim, and everyone's happy." His aunt and uncle would be satisfied Sam had given Kate a chance, and Kate could move on to her next do-gooding project. And best of all, *he'd* be rid of Kate and her interference once and for all.

"Gee, Dad, don't think you have to sugarcoat it for us," Riley retorted glibly.

Sam shrugged and continued just as bluntly, "We gotta face facts here, guys. Collectively, you boys have *not* been easy on the help."

The boys exchanged disgruntled looks. "That's 'cause we don't like them," Will growled finally, standing and looking immensely irritated at being forced to stick around.

Abruptly, Sam realized he was missing a son. "Where did Brad go?" he demanded irritably. How was he supposed to have a family meeting if one or another of the boys kept running off whenever he turned his head?

"He's where he always is, upstairs on the phone with a girl," Lewis said.

Will paced aimlessly, tossing his football around. "He's in a panic cause he's only got one date so far tonight instead of the usual three."

Irked to find even the smallest details of his life unmanageable, Sam strode to the front of the house and bellowed up the stairs, "Brad, get down here now!"

Footsteps rumbled across the third, then the second floor. Reeking of aftershave, Brad appeared at the head of the stairs, the phone glued to his ear. "But, Da-ad..."

"Now, Brad!" Sam ordered.

Outside, a car door slammed. In tandem, the boys rushed to the window and peered out. "Kate's here—" Lewis reported, looking happy to see her.

Brad stopped checking his reflection long enough to look out the window. He let out a wolf whistle. "Man, oh, man…"

"Brad…" Sam warned.

"We're serious, Dad," Riley added, his jaw dropping open in amazement. "You ought to see her."

That was just it, Sam thought wearily, the dread inside him increasing by leaps and bounds. He didn't want to see Kate. At all.

Kate knew Sam and his boys were desperate for help the first time she'd met with them at the hospital after Kevin's accident. That impression had been reinforced when she'd come to the house to talk to Sam alone. Kate had been hoping Sam and the boys would clean up a bit before she arrived. They hadn't.

Technically, of course, the contemporary Victorian home with the slate-blue paint, white trim and dark gray roof, was one of the largest and loveliest homes in Laramie. Or at least it had been when Ellie was alive. Sam had inherited the place from his folks. But it was Ellie who had, over the years they'd lived in Dallas, made it into an elegant summer and holiday retreat for the family.

A waist-high white-picket fence placed just inside the sidewalk that ran along the street framed the large square lot. Live oak trees shaded the front yard. Low-lying juniper and holly bushes edged the porch. The flower beds had been filled with an astonishing profusion of Texas wildflowers that bloomed year after year with little care. Some, like the Texas bluebonnets, bloomed in early spring. While the Indian paintbrush, shasta daisies, scarlet sage, rocket larkspur, baby's breath and pink evening primrose bloomed all summer long and into the fall.

A rope-hung swing with a wooden seat hung from one of the trees. On the wide shady porch that adorned the front and both sides of the large, three-story Victorian home, were comfortable groupings of cushioned wicker furniture. Ellie had worked hard to make it warm and welcoming.

Kate shuddered to think what Ellie would make of the unkempt condition of the home now. The grass was thick with weeds and hadn't been cut in several weeks. Bats, balls, bikes, skateboards, lacrosse sticks, a soccer ball and goals were strewn across the front yard. Worse than the disarray, was the air of neglect. Spiderwebs clung to the porch ceiling. A wasp's nest had started atop one of the shutters. The glass had been broken out of one of the old-fashioned porch lamps and the windows were covered with a thick layer of dirt and smudges. And that was just the outside. Knowing the inside was in even worse shape, Kate squared her shoulders, shoved her sunglasses atop her head and rang the bell.

The front door opened and Sam's boys filed out en masse. Despite the fact they were still grieving Ellie's death intensely in their private moments, all were glowing with good health and physical strength and tons of somewhat misguided energy. They were an intelligent, handsome group of boys, with Sam's dark hair and Ellie's soft eyes.

Kate greeted them all in turn. Although they'd been happy enough to speak with her at the hospital during the aftermath of Kevin's accident, to her dismay they did not seem anywhere near as enthusiastic to see her now. Probably because she was going to be the family housekeeper, aka Hired Gun, for the next few days.

Tension radiated from Sam McCabe as he stepped out onto the porch.

He was wearing neatly pressed olive-green slacks and a sport shirt in a slightly lighter hue. His face was clean-shaven and his short brown hair had been combed away from his face in a no-nonsense style that mirrored the look on his ruggedly handsome face. His dark brown eyes were shadowed with a fatigue that seemed months old. In previous summers his face had always been tanned. This year he looked as if he hadn't spent a second outdoors. His lips pressed together thinly, Sam continued to regard Kate in a way that was meant to intimidate.

"Now can I go?" Will asked Sam impatiently.

"No," Sam answered his oldest son, his implacable gaze totally centered on Kate's face. "No one leaves here until after dinner."

Kate had been hoping Sam McCabe would greet her with more enthusiasm than he had shown when she had pressured him into letting her help out. Obviously, she conceded silently, that wasn't going to happen.

Sam gestured at Kate. "I'll show you around," Sam said, leading the group back into the house. "Then I've got some work to do."

"I'm hungry," Riley complained loudly.

"Kate will get you guys dinner in a few minutes," Sam promised.

"Okay, but not take-out again," Riley interjected. "I'm sick to death of it. That's all we ever have for dinner when one of the housekeepers quits."

"And whose fault is that?" Sam asked, abruptly wheeling around and looking at his sons. A guilty silence fell all around. Having subdued them all for a moment, he turned back to Kate. Wordlessly he took Kate's elbow and steered her inside. "I want this to be a strictly business arrangement, so I'll pay you what I've paid all the other housekeepers as long as you're here."

Kate tensed in surprise. "It isn't necessary for you to do that. I'm doing this as a friend."

"It's the only way I'll let you stay."

He didn't want her friendship, Kate noted with disappointment.

"All right," Kate conceded, trying to not feel hurt. "If you insist."

Sam escorted her briskly up the stairs to the second floor. They passed Kevin's and Lewis's extremely messy bedrooms—a kid's bathroom, which was also a royal mess. As they headed for the stairs leading to the third floor, Kate pointed to the closed door on the left. "What's in there?"

Sam stopped just short of her. They were close. Too close. "Master bedroom and bath. It's off-limits."

Kate took a step back. "To just me or the kids, too?"

His glance narrowed. The unhappiness that had been part of his face for months now deepened. "What do you think?"

That was just it, Kate thought, she didn't have a clue. And Sam wasn't helping her to understand him.

Sam led the way up to the third floor, where Riley, Will and Brad bunked. Their bedrooms and the spacious bath were equally messy. "Are the boys responsible for their own rooms?" Kate asked as she looked around.

"To a point," Sam said. "Someone else usually vacuums and dusts."

"Their rooms would have to be picked up first."

"You're beginning to catch on to the problem."

"You can't just tell them to clean up?"

A shadow passed over Sam's eyes and the lines of fatigue around his mouth deepened. "You really don't know much about rearing kids, do you?" He gave the stinging words a second to sink in, then continued. "In any case, as our temporary household manager you'll be expected to ride herd on the boys 'round the clock."

"What are you going to be doing?"

"Working. From home tonight, but I'll probably go into my office in Dallas first thing tomorrow morning." Sam brushed by her, inundating her with his masculinity and rapidly led the way back down the two sets of stairs to the first floor. Bypassing his study and the formal dining room—which were both at the front of the house, on either side of the foyer— he escorted her through a living room with comfy-looking sofas. Kate couldn't help but notice that sometime in the last ten minutes, mud had been tracked inside. Ignoring the mess on the floor, Sam led the way past a screened-in sun-porch off the family room to the dream kitchen with every built-in, top-of-the-line appliance imaginable. "I'll give you some money to buy groceries in the morning. In the mean-time…" He gestured at the polished black-granite counter-tops and open cherry-wood cabinets. Here, too, dirty dishes and trash covered every surface. The floor was sticky. "You better use what's here to rustle up some dinner for the boys."

Kate nodded. Having apparently decided to not wait for her to fix anything, Riley came out of the laundry room on the other side of the breakfast nook. He was eating a pickle and drinking milk straight from the container. Brad looked ready to go out for the evening and was reeking with co-logne. Will was putting on his running shoes. Kevin came toward Kate. Shyly, he slipped a Matchbox car in her hand, then stood close to her while Lewis picked up a discarded burger wrapper next to Kate's foot, wadded it up and dropped it into the overflowing kitchen trash bin.

"When are we gonna eat, Kate?" Riley prodded, helping himself to another pickle from the big jar on the counter. "I'm starving."

"As soon as possible," Kate said, wondering where to start. Not even in summer camps had she encountered such a dis-organized mess.

"I can help you, if you want," Lewis piped up shyly.

Happy at least one of Sam's sons was into being helpful, Kate dug in her pocket and handed over her keys. "Thank you, Lewis. I'd appreciate that. Would you mind getting my bags out of my car? And bring in my laptop computer, too, please."

Sam's lips compressed. He leaned against the counter and folded his arms across his chest. "Why do you need your laptop?"

"E-mail—it's our main way of communicating when Craig is stationed overseas."

Looking happy to be able to help, Lewis went off to do Kate's bidding. The other boys, perhaps fearing they would be enlisted to help out, too, drifted off in all directions. Kate turned to Sam, already mentally rolling up her sleeves. "Before I start cooking, I want to get this place straightened up," she said.

"Fine." Sam regarded Kate impatiently. "But before you do that, let me show you where you're going to bunk." Sam led the way to the small bedroom and bath on the other side of the kitchen. "This is the guest suite. As you can see, you have your own TV, phone, bedroom and bath."

Lewis came rushing in, her suitcase and laptop computer in tow. He set both down on the floor, then asked, "Did you need those boxes of wedding books and stuff, too?"

"I sure do." Kate smiled and watched as he ran back outside.

Sam arched a brow in Kate's direction. "I'm using my vacation to plan my wedding," Kate explained as they headed back into the kitchen.

He lounged against the counter and folded his arms in front of him. "When's the date?"

"Sometime in the fall or maybe over the Thanksgiving or Christmas holidays. Craig and I haven't actually set a date yet."

His brows drew together in a frown. "Why not?"

Kate flushed, feeling abruptly self-conscious as she met Sam's eyes. "It's not that easy," she said, wishing Sam suddenly didn't sound so much like her parents. "Craig has to get permission from his superiors to take time off."

"So why hasn't he already done that?" Sam prodded, difficult as ever. "Given the fact you've been engaged for... what?" he asked impatiently.

"Three years now," Kate said, beginning to feel a little bit defensive despite herself. "And it's complicated."

Sam shrugged. He obviously didn't think so. "Seems to me if you and Craig really wanted to do this, nothing, not even the U.S. military, would stand in the way."

"Thanks for the insight," Kate said, annoyed he had so quickly and easily gotten under her skin.

"Any time." Sam shrugged.

"And for your information," Kate continued, "we're going to set a date when Craig comes home on leave the weekend after next." She paused, knowing now was as good a time as any to inform Sam of her plans. "I'm going to need that time off, by the way, if you still haven't found someone suitable to care for the boys."

"I'll have found someone by then," Sam vowed flatly. He sent her a hard, warning look. "In the meantime, I meant what I said, you're here as a temporary household manager and baby-sitter and that's all."

Back to that again. "I promise I won't run any group therapy sessions," Kate said dryly. She wouldn't promise she wouldn't be available to listen, if either Sam or his boys decided they wanted to talk.

Sam regarded her sternly. "Just so we understand each other."

"Oh, we do," Kate replied. *Maybe more than you'd like, Sam McCabe.*

A tense silence fell between them. Sam turned and started to head out. "I'll be in my study, working," he said over his shoulder.

"Wait just a minute." Kate hurried ahead and inserted herself between him and the doorway. "I'm going to need your help as well as the boys', Sam."

Sam looked at her suspiciously.

"Whether you're paying me or not, you shouldn't expect me to clean this up alone," she said practically. "All six of you made this mess. All six of you should help clean it up."

Sam's shoulders tensed. Kate knew what he was thinking: she'd been here five minutes and already they were arguing about where the lines should be drawn. Nostrils flaring, he leaned toward her in a deliberately intimidating manner. "Let's get something straight. I don't do housework, and I don't run interference between you and my boys."

"You mean, you won't back me up on this," she surmised, not giving an inch despite the way he was physically crowding her, and pushing her back out of the doorway.

Sam shrugged, letting her know it wasn't too soon for her to see how things were going to be. "You wanted to run the show around here. Now's your chance." Brushing past her, he stalked off.

Knowing what she did in her first few minutes on the job would set the tone for her entire stay in the McCabe household, Kate gathered the boys into the kitchen for a meeting. While they listened with varying degrees of attention, she explained what she had planned.

"There's only one problem with that," Will announced as soon as Kate had concluded, looking more than a bit surly as he worked with two hand-held weights. "As I mentioned earlier, I've already got plans for the evening."

"So do I," Brad interjected, then resumed talking on the phone.

Wordlessly, Kate reached over and took the receiver from

Brad's hand. "He'll call you back after he's finished his chores," she said into the receiver, then cut the connection.

Brad's mouth gaped open. "Hey! You can't do that!"

Riley grinned, enjoying his brother's discomfiture. "Looks like she just did."

Will looked at the list of chores Kate had scribbled. "I don't do bathrooms—ever!" he said with a scowl.

"Don't look at me. I'm not scrubbing anything!" Brad said.

"Then that's too bad," Kate said as she cut the jobs into little slips of paper and put them into the newly christened Job Jar in the center of the table. She folded her hands in front of her calmly. "Because none of you will be getting out of here anytime soon."

It was time this group started behaving like a family, Kate had decided. And the first order of building a team was to identify and then embrace collective responsibility. Then to work together to make things happen. Without either of those things, there could be no real caring for each other or pride in or acknowledgment of all they still had in the wake of Ellie's death, which, whether they realized it or not, was plenty.

All four older boys exchanged anxious looks. "What are you talking about?" Will demanded.

"As long as I'm in charge here, the rule is, you do your chores before you go anywhere. So each of you four older boys pick two tasks and get busy. Meantime, I'll get supper going. And Kev here can help by picking up all his toys and putting them away and setting the table."

As Kate opened the refrigerator door to see what was on hand, she could feel the McCabe boys' eyes staring at her as if she'd grown two heads. She perused the shelves crammed with junk food and wilting produce and forced herself to not think about how much easier this would have been if Sam had been in here with her, pitching in, too, and setting a good example for his kids.

He wouldn't be here during the day tomorrow, anyway, so they might as well get used to listening to her now—while he was still on the premises to witness her success at handling them. Because if this was a test, from both him and his boys, she was determined to pass it. She turned around and smiled at them, using the same matter-of-fact tone of voice she'd heard her father use with his football teams countless times. "You heard me, guys. Get moving."

All three older boys—having completed their chores in the most unhelpful manner possible—stared at the platters of hot dogs, macaroni and cheese, baked beans and cut-up fruit Kate had put on the kitchen table. "You've got to be kidding," Riley said.

"This is kid food," Will scowled. At seventeen, he did not see himself as a kid. "I don't see any hot dog buns," Brad complained.

"There aren't any," Kate told them, not about to apologize for the meal she'd put together.

"Well, I can't eat a hot dog without a bun," Brad announced grimly.

"We have bread," Kate offered. It had been stale but not moldy and she had freshened it as much as she could by warming it in the microwave.

"Bread is not the same as buns!" Brad pushed back his chair with a screech.

"Mom made her mac-n-cheese from scratch." Riley scowled and pushed the bright orange pasta around with the tines of his fork.

So did Kate, when she had the resources. Since she hadn't, she'd used the mix in the pantry.

Riley frowned and held his nose. "Did somebody put onions in the baked beans?"

Okay, so it wasn't going smoothly so far, Kate reassured

herself firmly, but this was only the first meal and she was only two hours into the job. It would get better as soon as she acclimated.

Lewis returned, his glasses sliding down his nose, his hands stuck in the pockets of his jeans. "Dad says eat without him," he reported with a deeply disappointed sigh as he slid into the chair next to Kate. "He's busy."

The boys exchanged unhappy glances. "No surprise there," Will muttered.

Clearly they wanted their dad to join them. So did Kate. Thinking maybe that would help the boys feel better, like more of a family unit, she murmured, "I'll see what I can do."

"Better not bother him," Lewis warned, looking worried.

"I'll just be a minute. You boys can go ahead and start putting food on your plates," Kate said. She went to the study. The door was shut, as it had been earlier. She knocked.

"What?" Sam demanded in an irritated voice from the other side.

In for a penny, in for a pound, Kate thought as she pushed open the door.

Sam shot her an annoyed glance then went back to his computer screen. "I already told Lewis I don't want to eat now."

"Sure now?" Kate prodded lightly, "we're having all your favorites." And then proceeded to name what was on the menu.

Ignoring her, Sam continued to stare at the chart on the computer screen in front of him. "I'll get something later."

Kate edged closer. On the shelves behind his desk were a variety of framed family photos taken over the years. Some had been taken on vacations, others on birthdays. And there were a couple of formal portraits, too. In all of them, the Mc-Cabes appeared to be a close-knit group. And in all of them,

Ellie, a hauntingly beautiful brunette, with delicate features and light green eyes, stood at the center of the group.

Realizing what she was looking at, Sam spun around in his chair. Suddenly his dark brown eyes were cold as ice. "Didn't the boys tell you the rule? When I'm in here working, I'm not to be disturbed! And you aren't to be in here, either. I don't want you in here cleaning, or reading a book, or even opening a window, whether I'm here or not. Got it?"

Kate got it, all right. She didn't need her Ph.D. to realize this wasn't just about maintaining his privacy. By effectively fencing himself off from his sons at home, just as he did at work, Sam McCabe had made himself damn near inaccessible to his sons much of the time. No wonder they were all acting out. He didn't even show up for meals when he was actually present. But figuring it was too soon to get into all that with any hope of success, Kate concentrated on the things they might be able to discuss with a little more success. "What about your laundry?" Kate asked.

Sam grimaced and turned back to his computer. "I send it out." A muscle worked in his jaw as he slanted her yet another aggravated glance. "You just get the boys organized and back on schedule and we'll all do fine."

"I can do that," she acknowledged quietly. "Maybe even eventually be their friend if I'm here long enough, but I can't be their mom or their dad, Sam. Only you can do that. And right now, those boys of yours want a *parent* eating dinner with them."

A grim silence fell between them but once again Sam made no move to join them. Instead he snapped defensively, "My relationship with the boys has not changed since Ellie died."

If that was true, it was a pity. But Kate didn't think it was. Kate glanced again at the framed photos of happier times, when Sam and Ellie both looked very much engaged in their children's lives. "Those photos, Sam, say otherwise."

"He's not coming, is he?" Lewis said, frowning unhappily.

"No." Kate put on a cheerful face and worked to hide her disappointment. "He said he'll grab something later." She took her place at the head of the table, between Kev and Riley.

Dinner was a silent affair. The three older boys, still angry about their chores, merely picked at their food. They bolted the moment they were excused from the table, muttering disparaging comments just loud enough for Kate to hear. Lewis did his best to enjoy the meal Kate had prepared, but after the way Sam had shut them out, he didn't seem to have much of an appetite. Only six-year-old Kevin ate heartily, getting as much on him as in him. "If you want, I can watch Kev for a while," Lewis offered as Kate began to clear the table.

"That would be great, Lewis." Kate smiled. "Thank you."

She was nearly finished cleaning up the kitchen when Sam walked in. Doing her best to hide the discouragement she felt about the way things were going thus far, she said, "I made up a plate for you."

As he opened the refrigerator door, Sam gave the food a dismissive glance. "I'll get it later." He took out a cold beer and a single serving of string cheese. "I just put Help Wanted ads in all the major Texas newspapers."

Kate closed the dishwasher and tried not to think how easily his six-foot-four frame dwarfed her own five-foot-seven inches. She tilted her head, studying him. "You're not going through an agency this time?"

Sam shook his head, his dark eyes grim. "Been there, done that," he said, sounding exhausted.

"In other words, you've been blacklisted."

"Something like that, yeah," he said dryly.

"Doesn't surprise me."

Tensing visibly from head to toe, Sam twisted off the beer cap, and tossed it into the trash. "Why?"

"Oh, I don't know, maybe because the three older boys are just a tad hostile," Kate said sweetly. *And so are you.*

"I thought they liked you," he remarked.

That was the irony of it, Kate admitted reluctantly. She and the boys had started off fine…at the hospital. Had Sam only consented to bring them there for group counseling, she and the kids might still be communicating fine. But he hadn't. She'd had to go to them. Invade what was essentially hostile territory. As a result they'd gone so far backward in the trust department it was going to take days to recover lost ground. This could have been avoided, had Sam welcomed her into their home and their lives, or even given his boys the slightest hint he thought she might be able to help them deal with losing Ellie. Instead, he had worked to make things that much worse, and succeeded.

Aware Sam was still waiting for an explanation, Kate struggled to contain her frustration. She knew she had come on strong, but it had been necessary. The boys needed to know they couldn't walk all over her the way they had their previous housekeepers. They had to know that even though their mother was gone, there were still rules.

"I think they did like me until I tried to come in and take Ellie's place."

Sam's expression hardened as he took a swig of beer. "No one can do that," he warned grimly. "However, I will find someone who can run the house."

"And until then?" Kate challenged, knowing, even if Sam didn't, the boys needed much more than clean clothes, good food and a tidy environment to get over the loss of their mom.

Sam glared at her and took another long drink. "What's your point?"

Finding it awkward to talk about something so intimate when he was standing all the way across the kitchen, Kate stepped toward him and lowered her voice. "When was the last time you and the boys did something together as a family, Sam?"

"I don't know." Resentment glimmered in his eyes. "Why?"

"Are you telling me it was so long ago you can't remember?"

"I'm not telling you anything," Sam said stonily, pushing away from her, "except to mind your own business."

"So we can't even talk about the boys?"

He straightened, towering over her, intimidating her with his height and weight and strength. "You got that right."

"What about Ellie?" Kate persisted, deliberately pushing his buttons, to bring his emotions closer to the surface. She edged closer, mimicking his kick-butt stance. "Are we allowed to talk about her?"

"Ellie's gone, Kate," Sam said, the edgy expression on his face intense. "No amount of talking is going to bring her back."

No wonder the family was such a wreck, Kate thought on a beleaguered sigh. Not only had they all suffered a major loss, they were following Sam's lead and keeping all their grief locked deep inside.

Sam took a long drink of his beer. He wiped his mouth with the back of his hand, letting her know with a glance they were changing the subject—now. "I have to be out of here early tomorrow."

Kate ignored the curtness of his voice and the feeling that he didn't want her—or any other woman—in his house any more than his three older sons did. It wouldn't be easy living in such a hostile environment, even for a few days. "How early?" she asked.

"4:00 a.m."

Kate waited, but to her mounting frustration no explanation was forthcoming. Was this typical of his schedule? she wondered, as she turned and headed back to the sink. Something being enacted just for her behalf? Part of the "test" he was expecting her to fail? Or a once-in-a-while occurrence? He gave her no clue. Because he seemed to be expecting some reaction from her, she utilized the most professional response that came to mind. "Do you want me to get up and cook breakfast for you?" Is that what he wanted from her?

Sam did a double take. Obviously not the reaction he had been looking for. "No," Sam said as he helped himself to some whole wheat crackers.

So you're not going to make this easy on me, either, Kate thought as she fished the dishrag out of the sudsy water and wrung it out with both hands. "When do the boys get up in the morning?" she asked as she began to wipe down the kitchen table.

Still ignoring the dinner plate she'd made for him, Sam polished off the crackers, drained the rest of his beer, and reached for another long-necked brown bottle. "Generally, the older four sleep as late as they can, since it's summer, although that will change starting this week when their extracurricular activities kick into full pre-season throttle with daily rehearsals and stuff. Kev gets up around seven-thirty—like clockwork."

"I'll set my alarm for six, then," Kate promised, briskly wiping down the already-wiped black granite countertops. Finished, she flipped the cloth back into the sink and wiped her hands on a towel. "If Kev needs me before that, wakes with a bad dream or something, and you're already gone, will he know to come to me?"

"I'll tell him when I tuck him in." Sam paused to twist open his second beer. "As for tomorrow specifically, I don't know what any of the boys has on the agenda. Although Will may have said something about an early football practice...."

"I'll find out and handle it," Kate promised.

Sam lapsed into a brooding silence. Kate looked into his face and read his unease. Odds were he was thinking about her inexperience in the homemaking arena, worried she couldn't handle his crew. She'd prove him wrong if it was the last thing she did. And once she conquered that, she'd win his confidence as a professional therapist and start to work on their grief.

Late Sunday evening while Mike was over at the high school working on the physical training program and practice schedule for the entire season, Joyce Marten spread sample styles of wedding invitations across her dining-room table.

She was determined Kate would have the most perfect wedding Laramie, Texas, had ever seen. She had promised Kate that she and Kate's father would "take care of everything," from the invitations to the reception. She didn't want her daughter worrying about anything during what should be the happiest time of her life. Joyce knew what it was like to have parents who weren't the least bit interested in their child's life.

Joyce had grown up in a chaotic, two-career household where the only thing that could be absolutely counted on was the constant bickering between her two very strong-willed, domestically disinclined parents. Early on, Joyce had decided she was not going to let that happen in her own adult life. When she married Mike and had his children, she made homemaking—instead of an outside career—her priority, ensuring their home was a cozy, warm and welcoming place where hot meals and clean sheets were to be counted on. She did whatever she needed to do to keep the peace between Mike and herself and the kids. It wasn't easy, given Mike's overprotective attitude where his kids were concerned. He felt he knew what was best for them in every situation and no one was going to tell him any different.

But Joyce had managed just fine, keeping everyone happy and healthy and reasonably content, until the summer before Pete's senior year of high school. Then, for reasons she still didn't completely understand, everything had fallen apart. Tension between Pete and Mike escalated day by day until Pete's death. And Joyce had been powerless to stop it.

She saw the same potential for family conflict arising from Kate's involvement with Sam McCabe and his boys. Mike still resented Sam for his role in Pete's death. He felt, more than anyone, that Sam had had the potential to prevent the accident, and hadn't. In Mike's mind, Sam was part of the reason Pete had died, and the last thing Mike wanted was Kate under Sam's roof, even temporarily.

But how to get Kate out of there without causing a rift between herself and Kate, Joyce didn't know. Especially since Kate was every bit as headstrong as her father. She couldn't just tell Kate not to do it. Mike had already tried that and it hadn't worked. And now Kate was, if not angry at her father, at least very exasperated and upset with him. Joyce couldn't get Mike to change his attitude, either. If she even tried, they would end up having an argument. So here she was, Joyce thought, powerless and caught in the middle again. And all this with Kate's wedding coming up....

Outside, Joyce heard a door slam. Seconds later Mike strode in the back door. "I drove by Sam McCabe's place on the way home," he reported gruffly, coming into the dining room where she was working. "Kate's car is parked out front."

Joyce put down a lovely ivory parchment invitation with a filigreed gold leaf design. "I don't know why you're surprised about that," she said gently. "Kate told us this afternoon she was going to do this, whether we approved of her actions or not."

Mike sat at the table, opposite Joyce. "I was hoping she would change her mind when she found out how much we both disapproved of what she's doing. Failing that, I hoped Craig would be able to talk her out of it." Mike shook his head disparagingly. "What's wrong with that boy, anyway?"

The last thing Joyce wanted was for Mike to find fault with Craig who, up to now, anyway, had been very high on Mike's approval list. "I'm sure he just trusts her judgment," Joyce said gently as she picked up a pale blue invitation with embossed wedding bells on the front and navy ink.

"There's a difference between trusting your woman and handing her over to another man," Mike replied sagely.

Joyce paused to give Mike a level look. "Craig is not handing her over to Sam."

Mike took off his coach's cap and set it on the table. "He may as well be."

"Kate's not going to do anything to disrupt her upcoming marriage to Craig."

Mike leaned forward urgently, elbows on the table. "I'm not saying it would be deliberate. But let's review facts here. Kate loves helping people. She loves being needed and knowing she's making a difference. And God knows, Sam McCabe needs help with his kids in the wake of Ellie's death. That's why he moved back to Laramie. You put Kate there for a couple weeks, when she's on vacation and should be off somewhere with Craig—" Mike snapped his fingers and looked all the more disgruntled and upset. "Kate could get emotionally involved with Sam and his boys before she knows what is happening."

Joyce pushed her own uneasiness away. "She probably will get closer to all of them. That doesn't mean Sam is going to try to steal her away from Craig and marry her himself."

"But he might take advantage of her."

Under normal circumstances Joyce would have said that was impossible. But these weren't normal circumstances, Joyce admitted silently to herself as she began gathering up her things. Kate wasn't doing this on a professional basis, but as a friend of Ellie's, and that put a personal emotional tilt on the situation that would not have been there otherwise. She had been away from Craig for more than nine months now. And although Kate never complained about the long separations, Joyce could tell Kate was finding them increasingly hard to take, which in turn made her not just lonely but vulnerable in a way her daughter had yet to admit.

There was also the secret crush Kate had had on Sam McCabe when she was just a kid. Mike didn't know about that. And, Joyce was pretty sure, neither had Sam. But Joyce had seen the way Kate's face would light up whenever Sam came over to toss the football around with Pete. The way Kate had hung on Sam's every word or deed. Unfortunately, because he had been a good five years older than Kate, Sam had never seen Kate as anything more than Pete's pesky kid sister. And then, when Pete had died, Sam had stopped coming around altogether.

Other crushes had followed. And eventually Kate had started dating Craig. But a girl never forgot a first crush. And that was what worried Joyce. But, figuring Mike was upset enough without knowing any of that, Joyce rose and carried the stack of sample invitations to the rolltop desk in the corner of the living room. Mike followed her and, still brooding, watched as she put everything away.

"Kate is not going to let Sam use her to ease his grief," she said firmly, doing her best to soothe Mike's fears. "She wouldn't let anyone do that. She's got too much self-respect. Plus, they'll be well chaperoned by the boys."

"I hope you're right," Mike sighed.

Joyce closed the distance between them. She turned her face up to his and fanned her hands across his chest. More than anything, she wanted this new tension in her family to just go away. "I know I'm right," she said with quiet confidence.

"And how is that?" Mike demanded gruffly, taking Joyce all the way into his arms. He looked down at her, smiling just a little as he waited for her reply.

Joyce leaned her head against Mike's chest, loving the warmth and strength and smell of him. "Because starting tomorrow, I'm going to be keeping an eye on the situation there, while I help Kate with her wedding plans. And before you know it, Craig will be home on leave, too." Those two things combined would work to keep Kate's heart focused firmly on her own future. Joyce was sure of it.

"Will?" The urgent whisper sounded outside Will's bedroom door.

"Are you up? Come on. Let us in."

Will groaned at the sound of Brad's and Riley's voices. He wasn't asleep yet but the last thing he wanted to do was be bothered by those two troublemakers. He rolled over and put the covers over his head, feigning deafness.

Too late, the lock gave under the persistent fiddling from the other side. His bedroom door eased open. Lewis and Brad and Riley tiptoed in, flashlights in hand, whipped back the covers, and hunkered down beside Will's bed. "We're having a secret meeting," Riley announced.

"Yeah, and we need you to come." Lewis sent Will a pleading glance.

Will had an idea why Lewis wanted him there. He wanted someone to talk some sense into Brad and Riley, because while Lewis liked to be part of the "group" he didn't like to get chewed out or grounded. And whatever mischief Brad and Riley were concocting for Kate Marten's first night under their roof was probably going to cause both things to happen, Will thought. Dad would hit the ceiling. And some—if not all of them—would end up on some sort of restriction. Will had had enough of that the past six months to last him a lifetime. Even when he'd had nothing to do with it, he'd ended up getting blamed just because he was the oldest. He glared at the three of them. "Next person who unlocks my door is going to get a fist for breakfast. Now get out of here."

Lewis looked disappointed. Brad and Riley remained unperturbed. "Fine. Be that way." Brad shrugged, already heading for the door.

"Yeah, your loss," Riley warned. "You're going to miss some fun." Together, they eased from his room as stealthily as they had entered.

Will flipped onto his stomach and pressed his face into the pillow. He wished he could have some fun. But now that he was living in Laramie, there wasn't much chance of that. All of his friends were back in Dallas.

He could have vetoed the move here. Persuaded his dad they should stay in Dallas. But he hadn't because he was tired of seeing the pitying glances of his friends and teachers, tired of being reminded everywhere he went, in everything he did, that his mom had died. And he'd known, with his senior year coming up, and all the senior activities scheduled that it was only going to get worse.

He wasn't the only one feeling the pain. It had been just as bad for his brothers and his dad. So once school was out, they'd taken a vote and decided to move back to Laramie, to their house there. To see if that was any better.

In a sense it was. In Laramie, he really felt part of the Mc-Cabe clan in a way he never had in Dallas, and Will liked being closer to Aunt Lilah and Uncle John, their four sons and their families. It gave him a sense of belonging he hadn't had since his mom had died.

What he didn't like was the way he was constantly being compared to his dad. Since they had moved back here at the beginning of July, Will had been told he looked like his dad, acted like his dad, and as far as some people were concerned, might as well have been his dad "at that age."

Will just didn't see it.

Okay, so there was some physical resemblance. He had seen pictures of his dad at seventeen. Admittedly, they did look a lot alike. But any similarities ended there. Will couldn't have cared less about computers or business or any of that. He wasn't going to grow up to be a workaholic who knew more about what was going on at work than he did in his own home. And he sure as heck wasn't going to get so wrapped up in any one woman that he couldn't seem to function without her. There was a place for females in his life. But no female was going to be his life. Any girlfriend he had from this point forward would just have to understand that.

Meantime, Will sighed, looking at the clock and seeing another half-hour had passed, he had to get some sleep if he was going to be worth a damn at practice tomorrow. Knowing there was only one way that would happen anytime soon, Will got up and went to his closet. He reached for the duffel bag beneath the pile of clothes and magazines and brought it out just far enough to get what he needed before he headed back to bed.

Chapter 5

Kate woke to find the sun streaming in through the curtains. She sat up with a start and glanced at the clock. The digital display flashed four-fifteen. Damn, she thought, tossing back the covers. Her first full day taking care of the boys and the electricity was out. Odds were, six-year-old Kevin had been up for hours. Anxious to make sure everything was under control in the rest of the house, she grabbed her robe, belted it around her, and went to the bedroom door.

Though she could see the door was unlocked, the handle still wouldn't budge. Frowning, Kate tried again to no avail. It was definitely stuck and she had the sinking sense it was no accident. So the boys were giving her a welcome of their own, hmm? Amused but far from defeated, Kate grabbed a pair of denim shorts, a T-shirt, and sneakers. She dressed hurriedly, put her hair up in a ponytail, then went back to try the door one last time. It still wouldn't budge. Which left only one way out. Her bedroom window.

Kate went to the curtains and opened them. She lifted the window, then the screen. Ducking her head, she swung her leg out over the wide wooden sill. She groaned in dismay as something soft, thick and squishy plastered the inside of her thigh. Almost afraid to look, Kate touched a finger to the gooey mess. Peanut butter. *Oh, nice, boys, nice.*

Well, a little peanut butter had never hurt anyone, Kate told herself sternly as she wiped what she could off with the flat of her hand, then smeared it on the sill, figuring that was going to have to be cleaned, anyway. And she knew by whom! Her heart thudding in her chest, she used her hands as leverage and lowered her sneaker-clad feet onto the ground beneath her. Kate swore again as her ankles stuck to the surprisingly wet ground cover.

Knowing by now there had to be something there, too, Kate looked down at her feet. She was up to her ankles in leaves and—oh, God—was that…maple syrup that had been generously slopped all over the ivy? She touched her finger to it, then lifted it to her face and cautiously sniffed. Yes, it sure was.

"Funny, boys," Kate muttered as the Texas summer sun shone down on her head. Telling herself she had been a camp counselor for six years and could certainly handle this, Kate made her way out of the ground cover and onto the stone pathway that curved around the house, her shoes smacking irritatingly with every step. She made her way down the sidewalk to the garden hose. Using the flat of her unsticky left hand, she removed as much of the remaining peanut butter from her inner thigh as she could, then took off her shoes and rinsed off her feet and ankles. She did not want to be barefoot when she confronted the boys, but she had no choice.

Aware she did not have a house key, as Sam had neglected to give her one, Kate leisurely made her way around to the front door. It was locked. She rang the bell. No one answered.

Sure by now she was being watched from somewhere—the boys would not have wanted to miss this!—Kate glanced around behind her and saw nothing. No one in the trees or in the cars. Kate went around to the garage. It, too, was locked up tight as a drum. Kate headed for the back door off the laundry room. It was unlocked. Which meant what? she wondered. Another booby trap?

Determined not to be caught unawares this time, she edged it open. Then waited just outside the doorway. Again, not so much as one breath was heard. "Okay, guys," she called in a firm but cheerful voice as she gingerly stepped inside. As she did so, a bucket above her upended, pouring at least a quart of white flour onto her head.

Kate sneezed several times, and thought, but couldn't be sure, she heard a chorus of muffled male giggles. "All right, guys, you've made your point," Kate announced as she dusted the flour from her face.

Heading for the kitchen, she went straight to the drawer beside the sink and brought out a clean dishtowel. Still standing in front of the sink, she reached for the spigot, turned the water on and was promptly drenched from neck to waist by the sprayer hose beside the faucet. Screaming in surprise, Kate jumped backward away from the still-spraying hose on the sink ledge. This time she heard lots of laughter. Kate swiftly moved around to shut off the water.

Okay, this was the place where she was supposed to scream and threaten and lose it, Kate concluded thoughtfully. No doubt that was what all the other housekeepers Sam had employed had done. But not her, Kate thought as she studied the rubber band the boys had wrapped around the handle of the sink sprayer, pressing the lever into an on position and guaranteeing that whomever turned on the water next would be drenched. They might have gotten her four times in a row. But this was one situation where they would definitely not have the last laugh.

Her plan already forming, Kate tiptoed back out of the house and headed for the driveway. Will's Jeep was gone—he was probably at football practice. But Brad's car was still there and it was unlocked. Kate lifted the hood and did a little quick handiwork, then dashed around to the side of the house, out of view. Seconds later the front door opened. Stealthy footsteps padded out onto the sidewalk. "Hey! The hood on my car is up!" Brad said.

"And that's not all!" Riley noted grimly. "She took the distributor cap!"

"That's it," Brad vowed passionately, upset to have his social life interrupted yet again. "We're gonna have to—"

"Gonna have to what?" Kate taunted as she came around the side of the house and gave Brad and Riley a good squirt with the garden hose.

"Show you who's boss!" Riley shouted, followed with a rebel yell as he and Brad whipped loaded Super Soaker water pistols from their belts, confirming Kate's guess that their earlier pranks had just been a warmup to their much-anticipated grand finale. Still whooping, they let her have it. Kev and Lewis—who'd been lingering uncertainly on the front porch—jumped out to join the melee.

Grinning, Kate gave back as good as they gave her, even as they all dashed around madly and soaked each other from head to toe. If she and the boys were going to have it out, they might as well do it now. And maybe that was just what these boys needed, a rousing fight with their new sitter. Fortunately for her, she had an endless supply of water—they didn't.

"Run for the house!" Lewis directed, taking charge as the Super Soaker pistols emptied. "She can't get us there!"

"Want to bet?" Kate shouted as she merrily gave chase, still spraying them madly all the while. The boys shrieked and howled and stumbled over one another as they scrambled up on the porch, climbing over the railing that edged it in an attempt to get to safety.

"Cowards!" Kate teased as she ran up the front steps and joyously squirted them again. Dashing forward, she put herself between them and the front door. Still aiming the hose at the boys, she effectively kept them from getting inside. And that was when she heard the powerful motor of Sam's limo pulling into the driveway.

That quickly, everyone froze in mid-mischief, the laughter dying in their throats, the smiles fading from their faces. Kate lowered the hose as Sam stepped out of the rear of the vehicle. Ever so casually, he leaned back toward the car, and said something to his driver through the open window. The driver nodded, backed out of the drive, and drove away, while Sam started for them, his lips set, his eyes hard.

"Oh, man, are we in for it now," Brad groaned, wiping his forearm across his drenched brow.

And that, Kate thought glumly, water dripping down her face as she watched Sam coolly and methodically close the distance between them, just about summed it up. Suddenly she felt as if she'd been transported back to the Old West and it was high noon in the middle of the street. She was the cowboy—or girl—in the white hat that everyone was relying on to get them out of the mess they were in. Sam was the much-feared gunslinger.

A muscle working in his jaw, Sam stopped just short of her.

Kate smiled with as much charm as she could muster and, garden hose still in hand, stepped off the front porch. The boys may have started this, but the fact they'd been caught whooping it up red-handed was just as much her fault as theirs. "So, Sam," she said cheerfully, as if such a riot as this were to be commended instead of denigrated. "What brings you home this early?"

"Instinct," Sam retorted grimly. "I had a feeling something might happen." His eyes ruthlessly swept the group before returning to Kate's. "Just what in blazes is going on here?" he demanded furiously.

The boys exchanged uneasy glances, and much to Kate's surprise, couldn't seem to wait to leap to her defense. "We were just horsing around, Dad," they claimed, surprising Sam, too.

Seeing no point in involving Sam in what was essentially a power struggle between her and the boys, Kate inserted glibly, "And now that we're finished—"

"Boys. Inside. Now!" Sam commanded. Hands braced on his waist, he regarded them all sternly. "Unless I miss my guess you have a lot to undo in there."

Uh-oh. Work fast, guys, Kate thought.

She turned to go, too. Maybe if she lent a hand, things wouldn't look so bad.

Unfortunately, Sam moved with her, blocking her way. "Oh, no, you don't."

Aw, heck.

His hand curved over her shoulder, grabbing a fistful of drenched pale blue cotton. "I want to talk to you."

Sam waited until the boys had all gone inside before he continued. "What do you think you're doing?"

"Having a little fun?" Kate said cheekily. Unfortunately, the irony in her voice was lost on him.

"This was precisely the kind of behavior I had hoped to avoid by having you stay here."

Abruptly aware her shirt was clinging damply to her breasts in a way that was much too revealing, Kate grabbed a handful of fabric and pulled it away from her body. "If you don't mind, Sam, I'd like to change clothes..." Maybe by the time she was dry, she'd have figured out how to handle him.

He remained much too close to her. "I do mind," he said, his brown eyes boring into hers. "What possessed you to get down to their level?"

Kate decided to put some distance between them and moved away from him to replace the distributor cap on Brad's Mustang. "Maybe because I wanted to pass initiation," she said over her shoulder. She paused long enough to see his eyes soften, his posture relax. "You don't look surprised," she said as she replaced the hose at the side of the house.

Sam sighed, looking no less unhappy but a little less fierce as he told her, "They've put everyone who's worked for me through some kind of test, though never to this extent." His glance traveling over her from head to toe, he continued to regard her with disapproval.

Kate noticed the long smear of peanut butter on her inner thigh, and did her best to wipe it off. "It's a good thing I had so much experience at summer camp, then, isn't it?"

"Only one problem with that, Kate," he said, his voice a husky mix of frustration and fury. "I don't want my home turned into a summer camp."

"News flash, Sam," Kate countered, unable to resist tweaking him just a little. "It already is one. But that can change. This place can be a home again instead of a battle-ground if you'll just give me a chance to really get to know you and your boys." Once she had their trust, they could move to tackle the family's grief. Either one by one or all together.

Sam frowned and, obviously curious to see what other damage had been done, started to walk toward the back of the house. "I don't know what good socializing will do if you can't make them mind you when I'm not around."

"Meaning what?" It was all Kate could do to repress a sigh of exasperation as she followed him, simultaneously doing her best to keep him out of harm's way and any other booby traps she had yet to discover. "You'd prefer to have them cared for by someone who knows nothing about them?"

Sam looked frustrated and didn't answer. Abruptly he spotted the peanut butter smeared on the ledge beneath her open bedroom window, frowned and started toward it. "What the heck?"

"Sam, don't go there," Kate warned, putting up a hand.

Too late. A swearing Sam had already stepped into the syrup-drenched ivy. Before he could extricate himself, Brad, Riley and Lewis came filing out the back of the house.

"Uh, sorry about that, Dad," Brad said. "That trap was meant for Kate."

Sam frowned. "I thought I told you boys to clean up."

Riley interrupted, "First we want to tell you something, Dad."

"Since you won't let us stay unsupervised the rest of the summer…" Brad hedged.

"You're darn right, I won't." Sam scowled. "*Especially* after today."

Lewis shot a pleading look at Sam. "We want Kate to stay."

Sam stared at his boys as Kev came out to stand beside his brothers. "After all this," Sam repeated in disbelief, dragging a hand through his rumpled hair, "you decide you like Kate?"

Riley and Brad cringed comically. "I wouldn't exactly go that far, but we…we, uh, could probably get along if we had to," Brad allowed quite specifically. "And we sorta do, don't we, Kate?"

Knowing this was as much of either a surrender or a mea culpa they were likely to give, Kate said amiably, "That's what I've been trying to tell you guys."

Sam's face hardened. "The question is why would Kate

want to stay after the way you boys have behaved this morning? Why would anyone?"

"Oh, lighten up, Sam," Kate interjected breezily. Hands on her hips, she regarded the boys with a victorious smile. They'd made real progress here this morning. The boys had vented a considerable amount of emotion. They probably all felt better, even if they had little understanding as to why. But they'd get to that eventually. In the meantime they had learned Kate was not going to abandon them or Sam. "They're not going to do it again," Kate said.

Sam pivoted to face Kate. He looked at her as if she hadn't a brain in her head. "How do you figure that?"

"Because we reached an understanding this morning, didn't we, boys?" Kate said as the attention of all four boys riveted back to her. They knew now that she could and would give back as good as she got.

The boys nodded sheepishly at Kate.

"Fine," Sam sighed, apparently realizing all over again what few choices he had at the moment. "But I'm warning all of you. If this or anything even remotely like it happens again, you're all going to have me to deal with."

As soon as she and the boys got cleaned up, Kate called a meeting. They met at the kitchen table, around glasses of orange juice and milk and cereal and cinnamon toast. As they finished eating, Kate handed out pencils and pieces of paper. "Okay, I want you each to write down your five favorite meals."

Once again she met with resistance from Brad. "Why? You're not even going to be here all that long."

"It doesn't matter," Kate replied practically. "If we can develop a rotating menu that makes you all reasonably happy, then whoever your dad hires can just continue using the system that I am going to set up for all of you."

They regarded her suspiciously. No one wrote anything down but Lewis, who neatly penciled in his name across the top of his paper. Kevin, who was too young to know how to write, drew pictures on his paper.

"Look, let's face it…" Kate paused, stared each of the boys straight in the eye, and continued gently, "No one can take your mom's place in your lives. No one should even try. Because what you and your mom had was very special." At that, the guys all nodded their agreement. "It's just not ever going to be duplicated." Kate paused to give them an understanding look. "But does that mean no one can ever come in and do your laundry or cook you a meal again? I don't think so."

As they thought about a life without Ellie, their faces could have been carved in stone. Their hearts, their feelings, were every bit as fiercely guarded and locked away as Sam's. Kate just couldn't let them stay that way. She had to find a way to get through to them, if only because she knew it was what Ellie would want. "What do you think your mom would want for you guys now?" Kate asked quietly. "Do you think she would want you to be living like this…chasing one housekeeper off after another? Or would she have figured that if she weren't around your dad would have immediately hired someone who would come in and do the kinds of things that needed to be done to keep a household running smoothly?"

"She would have wanted Dad to hire someone," Lewis said.

"Would she have expected you to be nice to whomever your dad hired?" she asked, the look she gave them reminding them that she had known Ellie, too.

They all hung their heads in shame. "She would've expected us to be nice," Riley admitted grudgingly as he glowered at Kate. "But she never made us do chores."

Kate blinked in surprise. "Never?"

Lewis pushed his glasses up. "Mom did everything." All

the boys nodded their heads in agreement. Bolstered, he continued speaking for the group. "She said that was her job. Ours was schoolwork and sports and stuff like that."

Kate didn't think Ellie had done her kids any favors by letting them off the hook that way, but that was neither here nor there, given the circumstances and the out-of-control way the kids had been living for months now. Refusing to back down in her quest to get the boys to take more personal responsibility for the family's living environment, Kate said, "Did she let you throw your stuff all over the place?"

Guilty flushes all around. Which was, as it turned out, all the answer Kate needed.

"So in other words," she continued, "when your mom was around, the house was never one huge mess."

Lewis sighed. "She made us take all our stuff to our rooms and keep our rooms neat, otherwise she'd come in and straighten up for us."

Kate could tell from the way he said it and the looks on their faces that none of the boys had liked having Ellie straighten their rooms her way, going through their things when they weren't around. Which in turn would have been powerful motivation for the kids to keep their rooms straightened on their own. "And after she died?" Kate asked curiously.

Shrugs all around. Brad said, "Dad didn't care if we cleaned 'em up or not."

"I like mine messy," Kevin piped up abruptly, wanting to be noticed, too. Everyone turned to him in surprise. Pleased Sam's youngest had decided to participate more actively, Kate smiled at him. "Okay, so maybe there should be some compromise on that score now that you guys are helping to make and enforce the rules around here," she allowed.

"Like what?" Riley challenged.

Knowing all the while that no team or family could thrive

without a certain amount of discipline, organization and group effort, Kate said, "Like your rooms can be as messy as you want as long as they're not a health hazard, as long as you keep the main areas of the house fairly neat. And that means everyone picks up after themselves. You dirty a glass, you put it in the dishwasher. You drop a box of cereal on the floor, you clean it up."

"And if we don't agree to that?" Brad asked suavely.

Kate shrugged. "Then I get out the Job Jar again and we all pick chores and we end up picking up after ourselves and each other, anyway. It's up to you." She regarded them steadily. "What do you want to do?"

It didn't take them long to decide. "Clean up after ourselves as we go," Brad sighed.

"Okay. Next is a sign-in, sign-out sheet." Kate got up and moved to the bulletin board beside the telephone. "I'm going to put this paper on the bulletin board, and if you're going somewhere, I want you to put down where you can be reached, when you left, and when you'll be home."

Lewis pushed his glasses up. Unlike Brad and Riley, he looked more puzzled than annoyed. "Why do we have to do that?"

"So your dad and I can keep track of you more easily."

Brad and Riley exchanged aggrieved glances. "Do we still have to ask permission if we want to go somewhere?" Brad asked.

Kate nodded firmly. "Yes." She didn't want to deny them any request that was reasonable, but she wanted them to go through the procedure, to get used to behaving as one caring, cohesive unit again. And part of that was learning to care for and look out for each other instead of it being an every-person-for-himself household.

"Even Will?" Riley asked.

"Even Will," Kate said.

"Well, have fun telling him when he gets home from football practice," Brad said. "'Cause he is not going to like these new rules."

"You let me worry about Will," Kate said, even though she knew they were right.

Lewis studied her, his head tilted slightly to the side. "Is this therapy?"

"No." Kate grinned, knowing therapy was almost easy, compared to trying to bring order back into Sam McCabe's out-of-control household. "It's just plain common sense that you guys should be able to use to your advantage long after I'm out of here."

Sam came into the kitchen. From the look on his face, Kate had the feeling he'd been standing there listening to all of them for quite a while. Was it her imagination or was he just a little less disapproving of her than he had been earlier?

"Want to join us?" she asked cheerfully. "We're in the process of setting up some ground rules. And I'm also taking dinner menu requests. Speak now or forever hold your peace."

Sam's body language and expression were both aloof. "I just want some coffee." He went over and poured himself a cup.

As the boys regarded Sam, the mood in the room went from borderline cooperative to tense and unhappy. Although no one said anything, Kate could feel the boys silently willing Sam to participate, to help them become more of a family again, but he was either not attuned to their emotions or unable to fulfill their needs in that respect. But that didn't mean she had to give up. Again, Kate tried to engage Sam in what was going on with the family, on any level she could. "Lewis and Kevin and I are going to the grocery," she told Sam pleasantly. "Do you want us to pick you up anything there?"

Sam opened his billfold and pulled out several hundred dollars in cash. "Whatever you get will be fine," he said and, coffee in hand, exited the room.

Chapter 6

At eight-thirty on Tuesday evening, Joyce came over to discuss wedding plans with Kate. She had a carryall stuffed with brochures over her shoulder and a rectangular cake carrier in her hands. "I brought a Texas sheet cake over for the boys."

"Thank you. They'll love that," Kate said, holding open the door and ushering her mom inside. The traditional chocolate-buttermilk cake with pecan frosting was one of her favorites, too, which her mom knew very well. Kate set the cake on the kitchen counter, then escorted her mother to the adjacent family room where she had already placed a pitcher of iced tea and a plate of sugar cookies.

"No problem. I was baking one for our neighbors, anyway, so I figured I might as well put two in the oven and bring you-all one, too." Joyce paused as she caught sight of the illuminated screen on Kate's computer. "I'm not interrupting anything, am I?"

"I was just catching up on my e-mail while I was waiting for you to get here. Would you like some iced tea?"

"That'd be lovely, thank you." Joyce set her bag of wedding brochures down and looked around at the clean, orderly surroundings. "It's awfully quiet," Joyce said.

Clearly, Kate thought, this was not what her mother had expected, and if she'd come over either Sunday evening or Monday morning, she would have found a much different environment. Kate gestured for her mother to take a seat. "Will is at football practice. Brad and Riley are out with friends. Kevin is asleep and Lewis is upstairs playing on his computer, in his room."

Looking as pretty as always in a long, flowing floral print dress and matching pastel flats, her gray-blond bob a fluffy halo around her face, Joyce asked in a low, worried voice, "What about Sam?"

Figuring she could e-mail Craig later, Kate shut down her computer. "Sam hasn't come home from work yet."

"Has he found a new housekeeper yet?"

"Not to my knowledge." Kate added lemon and sugar to Joyce's tea and handed it to her. "I know he's looking. He's placed ads in all the major Texas and Oklahoma papers."

Joyce took a delicate sip of tea. "What about Craig?"

Tensing at the unspoken implication, Kate offered her mother a sugar cookie. "What about him?"

"What does he think about you living here?"

Kate had known this would continue to be an issue with her parents, even if it wasn't one with her fiancé. She looked at her mother calmly. "Craig thinks it's great that I'm helping out, Mom."

"He said that?" Joyce said, stunned.

"On e-mail. Yes, he did." Kate studied her mother, then grinned at the absurdity of it all. "What? Did you expect him to be jealous?"

"Well…" Joyce fingered the pearls around her neck. "Actually, yes, since he is your fiancé and the two of you haven't seen each other for almost nine months."

It was all Kate could do to not roll her eyes. Sometimes her parents were so old-fashioned. "Well, that will change shortly. Craig's coming home in ten days, Mom."

"Did you get the knock-'em-dead dress you ordered from Jenna Lockhart?"

Kate thought about the dress and matching jacket that was so outlandishly sexy she wouldn't want her parents to ever see her in it. Or even get a look at it. "I picked it up last week."

"You haven't forgotten your appointment to try on wedding dresses at Jenna's boutique?"

"Thursday morning, nine o'clock."

Realizing those plans were continuing as scheduled, Joyce began to relax. "Before we talk about the wedding, I wanted to tell you that your father and I are planning a welcome home party for Craig at the house."

"He'll like that."

Joyce removed an elegant leather-bound day-planner and pen from her purse. "He's getting in on a Friday night, right?"

"Yes, and we've already made reservations at a really nice hotel in Dallas." Kate watched her mother flip through a calendar crammed with social and charitable activities to the appropriate page. "So we won't be driving back to Laramie until early Saturday afternoon," Kate cautioned.

"Do you think his parents are going to want to come up from Corpus Christi for that?"

"I'll ask, but I doubt it. They're going to be on vacation until the day before he gets back in the U.S.—they booked a cruise months ago—and I know his mom is planning a party there for us also."

Joyce sighed wistfully. "I wish they still lived in Laramie. It'd make things so much simpler."

"Yes, it would, but they wanted to live on the beach when

they retired, and they're happy there, so we'll just visit both places. After we have a night to ourselves."

"That's probably best. You two need some time alone after such a long separation."

Kate studied her mother. "Anything else on your mind?" There seemed to be something.

Twin spots of color appeared in Joyce's cheeks. "I may as well tell you. I heard there was a big free-for-all over here yesterday morning."

"Things aren't perfect. The boys would still rather be un-supervised, but since that's not going to happen, they've more or less given up on trying to chase me away. For the moment, anyway." And that, Kate knew was a first step toward let-ting another woman into their lives. Something they had been unwilling to do on any level—the love and loyalty to Ellie was that fierce.

To Kate's annoyance, her mom remained skeptical of any progress Kate had made. "And Sam?" Joyce asked.

Kate helped herself to a sugar cookie. "What about him?"

"He's been so moody. I don't ever remember him being that way."

Kate nodded, acknowledging this was so. "He misses his wife terribly." To the point he still couldn't bring himself to join the boys for dinner. Last night because he had been closeted in his study, involved in conference calls with the California company and his own staff from 5:00 p.m until nine. Tonight, because he had chosen to once again work very late. Kate had pondered Sam's aversion to eating a sit-down dinner with his kids, and theorized doing so probably was just too painful a reminder of Ellie and the way things used to be. It was something he was going to have to get over, for all their sakes. But it was going to take time.

Joyce's eyes clouded with worry. "I just don't want him taking out his grief on you."

"I have very thick skin, Mom," Kate explained gently. "I have to have one to be able to do what I do over at the hospital. When people are trying to come to terms with a tremendous loss or calamity in their lives, they lash out at whoever is closest as well as at anyone who tries to help them face their feelings. And because I run a grief counseling program, that's often me. I don't take it personally."

"I'm glad to hear that, honey. Because I wouldn't want you to get hurt by all this, or overly involved."

Kate didn't want to be hurt, either. As for becoming overly involved with Sam and his kids...well, she just wouldn't let herself do that. Kate reached over and patted her Mom's arm. "Mom, will you relax? I'm a professional. I know what I'm doing. Now, let's talk about the wedding."

"Good idea. I've compiled a preliminary guest list of people your father and I would like to invite."

Kate scanned the pages her mother handed her, stunned. "Mom, there have to be over two hundred people here."

Joyce nodded. "I'm thinking the final tally will be around five hundred or so, give or take."

Having more or less expected as much—there was nothing her mom liked better than a great big party—Kate said carefully, "I had in mind something much more intimate, Mom."

"Honey, you only get married once. You and Craig should make a big deal of it!"

Kate offered the most practical argument of all. "It'll be too expensive to have that many guests, Mom."

Her mom waved away her concerns. "You let me and your father worry about the budget. You just worry about making this the happiest day of your life."

Kate had a hard time seeing how her wedding day was going to be the happiest day of her life when she and her mother were at odds about everything from the place the ceremony was going to be held to the type of reception she should have. Knowing it would serve no purpose to argue with her mother, however, until she had Craig there to weigh in on the process and back her up, Kate put off making any hard and fast decisions about anything for another ten days.

"I feel like we haven't accomplished anything," Joyce said as she prepared to leave.

They'd done one thing, Kate thought. They'd figured out just how much there was to do. But sensing her mother didn't want to hear that, she said, "We narrowed the style of invitation down to four."

"Which reminds me. We're going to have to get those ordered as soon as possible."

That was going to be hard to do until she and Craig selected a date and booked a place for the ceremony and the reception, Kate thought. "Maybe we should just worry about selecting my dress first," Kate said. "After all, that's probably one of the important things."

"If not the most important thing," Joyce agreed.

"So I'll see you Thursday morning, at Jenna's boutique?" Kate said.

Joyce nodded and kissed Kate's cheek. "You've got a date."

Lewis came tromping down the stairs shortly after Kate's mom had left. He spied the rectangular cake carrier on the kitchen counter. His face lit up. "Hey, is that my birthday cake?" Not giving Kate a chance to reply, he rushed over to investigate. "I thought everybody forgot it was tomorrow. I'm usually the invisible kid around here. But…" He lifted the lid on the cardboard box and immediately deflated, his slightly uncoordinated legs and arms going still. "Hey. There aren't any decorations."

"That's because it's not your birthday cake," Kate said, improvising quickly to spare Lewis's feelings, because he'd been right on the money, everyone had forgot his twelfth birthday was tomorrow. "It's just a Texas sheet cake my mother made for you boys. She thought you might like it. Your birthday cake is coming from Isabelle Buchanon's bakery. I'm to go over to Main Street tomorrow to pick it up." *I'll call Isabelle tonight, to arrange it.* Knowing this was the kind of fib that could be excused, Kate continued, "It was going to be a surprise, but now that you're in on it, maybe you better confirm for me your favorite flavor just so there are no mistakes."

Lewis's eyes lit up excitedly behind his glasses. "Chocolate, with vanilla icing and chocolate sprinkles."

"Whew!" Kate pressed a hand to her chest. "I'm glad we got that right!"

With the intensity of the budding intellectual he was, Lewis studied her. "You really ordered a cake? Dad really didn't forget?"

"He didn't forget," Kate replied firmly, hoping like hell it was true, because the last thing she wanted to do was to lie to Lewis on Sam's behalf about something like that. "I didn't know your birthday was coming up so very soon, but once your father mentioned it… Hey, you know I'd go all out to make the day a really happy one." And she would, Kate vowed. Even if she was up all night making the arrangements.

Lewis grinned, thoroughly trusting her about that much. "Are you going to tell me what's going to happen tomorrow, or is it going to be a surprise?"

"A complete surprise." To Kate, as well.

"Are you even going to give me a hint?"

"I'll leave that decision to your dad," Kate decided. First, she and Sam would have to talk privately about when, where and how to celebrate.

Lewis linked his fingers together and rested them on top of his short, rumpled, dark brown hair. "When's he going to be home?"

"He said it would probably be after ten. I know he's still

working very hard on the California bid. Tell you what. If you want to go back upstairs and play on your computer some more, I'll let you know when he does get home."

"Okay. This is so cool. I wasn't even sure I'd have a birthday celebration this year, on account of mom and everything. After all, we didn't celebrate Dad's or Will's birthdays because everybody was just too sad to have a party."

Kate's heart broke at the revelation. "Well, not to worry, sport," Kate soothed, patting Lewis on the shoulder. "You're going to have one," she promised, "and it's going to be the best twelfth birthday ever."

As soon as Lewis went back upstairs, Kate took her cell phone and went outside to call Sam. She reached his office easily, but that was as far as she got. His assistant answered the phone, put her on hold, and came back and said Sam was busy. Kate countered it was important, she really needed to speak to him. Once again she was put on hold. The assistant came back on and said unless it involved smoke, blood or a similar life-threatening emergency, it would have to wait until Sam got home, because he was in the midst of delicate negotiations.

Kate decided it could wait. If only because she wanted to see the look on Sam's face when she told him to see for herself whether he had remembered or not. She was hoping he had. But given what had already transpired she was not betting on it.

"You may want to call Kate Marten before you head home," one of Sam's administrative assistants said as he was getting ready to leave the office. "She sounded…well, you should call her back."

"Did she say what it was about?"

"No. Just that it was about one of the kids and it was urgent."

"But didn't involve smoke, fire or illness," Sam stipulated.

"Right. No one was hurt or sick or anything, and the house hadn't burned down. I made sure of that."

Sam had no intention of talking to Kate until he got home. He assumed the boys had gone back to giving her a hard time. Since Ellie died, they never behaved for long. Especially Riley and Brad, who could usually be counted on to cook up some sort of mischief together. Or Will, whose "senioritis" and indifference to the family, in general made him hard to deal with. But none of that necessitated bothering him at work, Sam thought. And Kate needed to learn that. He looked at his assistant. "Do you have those housekeeper résumés for me to look at?"

"Sure thing." She snatched up a thick manila folder. "I contacted agencies in Oklahoma, Missouri, Arizona and New Mexico, just like you asked. This is what they sent. Plus, here are the responses to the newspaper ads you've been running in the Texas papers. As you figured, the Texas employment agencies weren't interested in sending anyone else out."

"Thanks." Sam went to the front of the building, where his limo and driver were waiting, and climbed into the back. He ate his dinner—a steak sandwich from the carry-out down the street—on the ride home, and perused the résumés. Most of the applicants were wrong for the job right off the bat—he could see that from their résumés or letters of recommendation. He needed someone flexible, with great problem-solving skills, and enough energy to keep up with his boys. Someone who wouldn't call him repeatedly, like Kate Marten. Someone who wouldn't lecture him or get under his skin the way she did. By the time he arrived home, he had five prospective candidates. He put their résumés aside. He would have one of his assistants call them in the morning and start setting up interviews in Dallas. The sooner he replaced Kate Marten, the better.

And that sentiment was confirmed double time when his limo pulled into the driveway well after twelve-thirty and he saw she had apparently waited up for him. Portable phone pressed to her ear, she was pacing along the side porch, talking.

Sighing, Sam said good-night to his driver and got out of the car. Dreading whatever it was Kate wanted to discuss with him, he headed up the sidewalk to his house.

Kate glanced at Sam, then turned her back and walked farther away from him. Her tense words carried through the silent night. "But you said it was okay." She paused. "My father's opinion should not have anything to do with this. No, Craig, I'm not going to change my mind." Her spine stiffened beneath her short-sleeved, mint-green blouse and matching casual skirt.

Sam didn't know what she had been doing earlier in the day, but right now she was barefoot and stockingless. Her honey-blond hair was caught up in a clip on the back of her head, her lips missing the usual carefully applied lipstick. She gestured to Sam to stay right where he was, then turned her back on him and continued speaking into the phone in a clipped voice that radiated both anger and hurt. "I'm sorry you feel that way. I'll talk to you later. Sam's here now. *I have to go, Craig.* Goodbye."

She cut the connection then swung around to him, the portable phone still cradled in her hand.

"You didn't have to end the call on my account," Sam said, already heading inside the house. He set his laptop computer and briefcase down next to the front hall table, where the day's mail was stacked and waiting. "You and I could always talk tomorrow."

Kate's chin shot up as she brushed past him and returned the hall phone to its base. She glared at him as he flipped through the day's mail, taking only what he needed or wanted to read and leaving the junk for someone else to disperse. Kate slapped her hands onto her hips. "No, we need to talk now!"

Sam shot a glance at the living room, which looked like a disaster area, with a dozen or more of her videotapes and cases strewn across the floor. Catching the direction of his gaze, Kate wheeled around and headed for the VCR, which was playing some sort of homemade movie of a local country and western band. She punched the button to stop the tape. Sam could see that Kate was spoiling for a fight. He wasn't sure it was with him, though. Craig seemed to be the one she wanted to deck. Unfortunately, Craig was on the other side of the earth.

As a rule, Sam liked to let people handle their own problems without interference from him. And yet here was his chance to get under Kate's skin, the same way she'd been getting under his, by barging in where he had no business. Maybe if the shoe were on the other foot for once, Sam decided, she would realize how it felt to have her private life and feelings pried into, and cease and desist from his. It was worth a shot, anyway.

"So what's going on?" he prodded as Kate sank to her knees and began to match up music videos and their cases. "Trouble in paradise? Did you two have a fight or what?"

Kate scrambled up off her knees, half a dozen videos in her arms. "If you must know, my father sent Craig an e-mail, telling him that he and my mother thought it was a very bad idea for me to be living here, even temporarily. Something ridiculous about how it might look to people. As if anyone would think there was something going on between you and me!" she fumed, dropping the cases into a box before going back for more.

"Pretty ridiculous, all right," Sam agreed, even as he

couldn't help but notice her sexy, bare legs. "Besides, I thought Craig was okay with you staying here."

Kate frowned. "He was until he learned my father and mother were upset, and now he wants me out of here, pronto."

"You told him how you feel?"

"That I wanted to stay, yes." Kate swallowed as she hunted around for the case for the last tape.

"And...?"

Kate lifted up the skirt of the sofa and peered beneath it. "He still doesn't care."

"Seems to me your feelings about something should be a lot more important to Craig than your parents'," he said, wishing Kate would quit slithering around on the floor like that. Didn't she know it hiked up her skirt to an unladylike degree?

"It's complicated." Her voice was muffled. And defensive.

"Not that complicated." Sam turned to the prodigious notes Kate had made on every one of the music videos she had watched. "Craig is marrying you, not your father."

Kate grabbed the missing case with a triumphant cry and, still clutching it in one hand, struggled to her knees. Breathlessly, she snatched up the lone remaining video and swiftly mated the case and tape. "My father was a mentor to Craig when he was growing up."

Sam pointed to the clip in her hair, which was hanging sideways and about to fall all the way out. "He was a mentor to me, too, and you don't see me falling all over myself to please my former football coach."

Kate set the tape on her lap and reached for the dangling hair clip. "My dad gave Craig the courage to apply to the Air Force Academy, when his own parents didn't think he had a chance in heck of getting in."

Sam shrugged. "Your father helped a lot of kids get into a lot of colleges. He helped a lot of guys dream big. None of them is marrying you."

Kate glared at Sam resentfully as she twisted her hair up, then clipped it. "Are you saying Craig is just marrying me because he likes my dad so much?"

Are you? More aware than ever that Pete's younger sister was in need of some brotherly "enlightenment" on this score, and Pete wasn't here to give it, Sam shook his head in a noncommittal manner. "I am just pointing out that Craig's first allegiance should be to you, Kate." Craig wasn't a kid anymore, trying to please his coach, or in this case, his future father-in-law. His loyalty needed to be to Kate. First, foremost and always. "Craig shouldn't be talking to you about doing what your dad wants," Sam continued firmly. "Craig should be talking to your dad about what you want. He should be going to bat on your behalf with your father, not the other way around."

Kate shot to her feet. "Craig does defend me to my father," she returned hotly.

If that was so, Sam applauded it, because Kate needed someone to stick up for her with her father, to keep Mike from running roughshod over her the way he had with her brother Pete. Unfortunately, Sam didn't think Craig was doing that. Now or at any time in the past. Because there was something in Kate's eyes that said he had struck a nerve.

"And, anyway, that's enough about my problems," Kate said, seeming desperate to change the subject. She looked Sam square in the eye. "It's time we talked about yours…."

Sam regarded her with a mixture of contempt and exasperation. "Kate, I'm tired."

So was she, Kate thought, as well as irked he had blown off her attempt to reach him so they could discuss the birthday plans she was making for his son, but that didn't change anything. There was a sensitive young man who was counting on them; she wasn't about to let Lewis down, late hour or not. "Do you know what date it is?"

Sam braced his hands on his waist and continued to regard her in hostile silence. "August first." He spoke as if he could barely contain his temper.

Kate pushed on, anyway. "And tomorrow is…?"

Guilt flashed across Sam's face as he muttered a short, self-deprecating oath. "It's Lewis's birthday." His eyes filled with regret. He obviously felt bad he hadn't remembered.

Gently she said, "I had to go ahead and make some plans. I hope they're okay." She really wanted and needed Sam's involvement in this, and so did his sons.

Sam went back into the front hall, snatched up the mail, his computer and briefcase and headed into his study. "Lewis is the one you have to please." He switched on his desk lamp and, still standing in front of his desk, tore into one envelope after another. "Did you talk to him?"

"I thought I'd run them by you first." She followed him over to his desk and, feeling more than just a tad unwanted, stood there opposite him. Certain he was listening to her, even if he wouldn't look at her directly, she continued. "Will, Brad and Riley are busy at school tomorrow with various extracurricular activities, but Lewis and Kevin are free, so I thought I'd take them to Fredericksburg. They have an excellent military museum that has all sorts of war relics, including planes and tanks and even an old submarine. After we take the tour, we can have lunch in one of the local restaurants."

Sam looked up with approval.

Kate hesitated. "I didn't know if you wanted to join us for that…"

The relief in his eyes fading as fast as it had appeared, Sam shook his head. "I've got to work."

Kate nodded. "I figured that would be the case so I made plans for the evening, as well."

"What kind of plans?" Sam asked gruffly, beginning to look irritated and impatient again.

"I booked a section of the restaurant at Greta McCabe's dance hall for dinner tomorrow evening. I invited the rest of the McCabes and told the older boys they can invite friends and or bring dates. I didn't know if you wanted to do anything with only you and the boys this year, but—"

"That won't be necessary," Sam interrupted brusquely as he loosened the knot of his tie and sank into the chair behind his desk. "What you have already done sounds fine."

Kate took a chair in front of him, and crossed her legs at the knee. "I didn't know what to do about presents."

"I'll have my assistant take care of that tomorrow." Sam regarded her brusquely. "Anything else?" he asked in a short, clipped tone.

As far as he was concerned, Kate thought, their conversation was already over. Probably had been before she had even entered the room. "Just one more thing." Kate's heartbeat picked up as she regarded Sam steadily. Even though she knew Sam was likely to take offense at it, she knew this had to be said. "Lewis thought everyone had forgotten his birthday. I told him that wasn't so." An ache rose in Kate's throat as she continued with difficulty, "I thought he'd suffered enough hurt this year, without feeling like he didn't matter, too. Which, by the way, is exactly how he does feel."

Sam went very still. "He told you that?"

Kate nodded. "He said he's usually the invisible kid around here. I thought you should be aware he feels left out."

"And for that you're blaming me?" Sam attested angrily, getting to his feet.

Kate stood, too, and leaned across the desk toward him. "You're misunderstanding what I'm trying to say here, Sam."

His expression hard and unforgiving, Sam remained where he was. "Oh, I think I read you right," he said curtly. His eyebrows slammed together. "The boys are not happy. And you think it's all my fault."

Going into battle with her would not only stop Sam from examining just how "abandoned" his sons really felt, it would give Sam a good and necessary outlet for his anger. Her. She wasn't about to make it that easy on him. "They lost their mom," she said evenly, working to keep their conversation on task.

"Exactly." Sam looked at her with such loathing her skin went clammy. "And that's never going to change."

"But, Sam, if you'd just talk to—" Kate tried again.

Sam grimaced and looked at her with all the intensity of a soldier facing down the enemy. He came across the desk until they were nearly nose to nose. "It wouldn't hurt any less, Kate," he said icily. "And if you think it would, you're wrong."

"Why do you have to take offense at everything I say about this?" she demanded, furious.

"Maybe because you're wrong?"

Aware they were suddenly standing much too close, Kate took an involuntary step backward. It wasn't far enough. She could still feel the heat of his fury emanating from his skin.

"I am not!" Kate said.

Sam's glance hardened all the more. "If you don't like the way I do things, you're welcome to leave at any time."

"And that wouldn't bother you a bit, would it?" Kate retorted, hurt. Wondering, even as she spoke, why she had ever thought there was even an outside chance he might be grateful for what she was doing to help him get his and his boys' lives back on track. Sam barely saw her, never mind acknowledged what she was doing for them, and for Ellie. He wasn't about to meet her—or anyone else, it seemed—halfway.

In answer to her question, Sam said, "I'm looking for

someone else as we speak. As soon as I find that person, you're out of here." His eyes raked her with contempt and the disdain in his low voice made her want to cringe. "So it really doesn't matter what I feel about you or anything else. Does it?"

Chapter 7

"**D**ad forgot. I know he forgot," Lewis told Kate as they sat in Greta McCabe's Lone Star Dinner and Dance Hall at six-fifteen the next evening.

"He probably just got stuck in traffic," Kate soothed, glad they had chosen such a locally popular, family friendly place to have the party. Once a garment factory, the large brick building had been turned into a restaurant several months back by Shane McCabe's wife, Greta. She'd gone all out to make sure the local residents had a place to kick up their heels in style. In the center of the large establishment was a polished oak dance floor. The high-beamed ceiling was exposed, the walls painted white. Four raised dining areas, walled off by a rustic cedar railing, surrounded the spacious dance floor. The kitchen was at the rear of the building. To the left of that, was a raised play booth for a DJ, complete with a state-of-the-art sound system that even now was playing only the very best of country music. The food was plentiful and good, the atmosphere lively and fun. It was impossible to come here and not have a good time. "You know it's an hour and a half drive from his office to here," Kate continued.

"Maybe he's just not coming." Lewis continued to worry as he adjusted his glasses on the bridge of his nose.

Brad and Riley both gave Kate looks that said, *We knew this was a mistake, even attempting to depend on Dad.* Even six-year-old Kevin looked a bit morose as he sat with his chin resting on his clenched fist while he wordlessly pushed a Texas Rangers' patrol car back and forth across the blue-and-white gingham tablecloth. Knowing something had to be done to reassure the kids, Kate stood. "I'm going to call Sam on his cell phone to see if he's on his way."

"You're assuming he's even left the office," Riley said glumly.

"He probably hasn't," Brad concurred.

Kate hurried off, determined to prove them wrong. Grabbing her cell phone, she headed out back and dialed Sam's cell phone. Instead of ringing through, her call was automatically forwarded to his voice mail, which meant he was either in the car and on the phone, or not taking calls.

Greta McCabe caught up with Kate. A professional dancer and former Dallas Cowboys' cheerleader before she turned dance hall owner, she was also a gifted dance teacher with a huge heart and a sassy sense of humor. But she was most famous for taming—and recently marrying—John and Lilah's wildest son, Shane. "Where's Sam?" Greta asked curiously.

I wish I knew, Kate thought. "On his way, I think. Hope."

Greta cast a look over her shoulder, at the party area, which had been roped off with crepe paper and balloons. "The boys don't seem to be having a very good time."

Kate sighed, glad she had Greta to confide in. "They're afraid their dad isn't going to make it." And, truthfully, so was Kate.

"Sounds like they're desperately in need of some fun."

Kate nodded. She looked at her old friend. "You thinking what I'm thinking?"

"Absolutely," Greta nodded. "You see what you can do to get the party going, and I'll open up the dance floor a little early tonight."

Kate decided to do even better than that. She went around to the tables that rimmed the big dance floor. Before the first note of the Dixie Chicks sounded, the dance floor was half full with experienced line dancers. Once that happened, it was no problem getting Riley, Brad and their dates on the dance floor, too. Kevin even put down his toy cars long enough to look interested. It was the birthday boy himself who looked paralyzed...with fear or loathing, Kate couldn't tell. "What is it?" Kate asked as the lively strains of "Some Days You Gotta Dance" filled the hall.

Lewis flushed beet-red. "I can't... I mean, I never... I've watched but...I don't know how to..."

Kate clapped a reassuring hand on Lewis's thin, bony shoulder. "I'll teach you."

Lewis looked as intrigued as he was terrified of making a fool of himself. "I'll only goof up."

"Then I'll goof up, too." Kate shot him a teasing wink. "We'll make it look natural."

Lewis rolled his eyes, unable to completely prevent a grin. "Oh, man..." he groaned dramatically.

"That's the spirit!" Kate clapped Lewis on the shoulder again even as she reached for his younger brother's hand. "Kev, you come, too. If we're gonna have fun, we're all gonna have fun."

Greta met them on the dance floor. "We got two beginners, here," Kate said.

"Exactly what I was hoping to hear." Greta grinned, taking Lewis's arm in hers. "There's nothing I like better than teaching one of the McCabe boys to line dance. Kevin, you save a dance for me, too, all right, buddy?"

Kevin smiled shyly.

Thirty minutes and several dances with both Kate and Greta later, Lewis was kicking up his heels when Sam walked in the door. He had obviously taken the time somewhere along the line to change, because instead of the customary business suit and tie he wore to his Dallas office, he was wearing worn jeans, a pale blue Western-style shirt and boots. He carried a stack of presents in his arms. Sam started for Kate and Kevin, who were taking a break back at the party area. Kate stood as he approached and helped Sam with the presents. She noted Sam looked tired and stressed, despite his casual demeanor.

"Sorry I'm late," he said as they arranged the gift-wrapped packages next to the others.

"No problem." Kate said as Sam hugged his son Kevin hello, then watched as Kevin skipped back out to the dance floor to join his brothers. "The boys have been having a great time dancing. You ought to join 'em."

"No. Thanks." Grimacing unhappily at just the suggestion of kicking up his heels to the raucous Garth Brooks's tune, Sam said, "I'm not much for dancing."

Now, Kate wanted to ask, or just since Ellie died? Although she suspected she already knew the answer. Beginning to feel a little uneasy…Greta's Lone Star Dinner and Dance Hall looked like the last place Sam McCabe wanted to be, that or any other night, Kate continued enthusiastically, "We can eat whenever you want. The cake is in the kitchen, ready to go."

Sam turned to Kate. "Where's Will?"

Kate tried hard not to think about how unenthusiastic Will had been about attending the party. "Still at football practice. He'll be here a little later."

* * *

Will had never liked being singled out and criticized, but by the time he had attended his sixth "two-a-day" in the grueling August heat, he had figured out that for him that was all football practice at Laramie High School was going to be about. Every third word out of Coach Marten's mouth seemed to be "McCabe!" and it was never in a congratulatory context.

Wednesday evening's practice was particularly tough. The heat and humidity were brutal and Coach had them running from the get-go, moving rapid-fire from one play to another. And to his embarrassment, Will hadn't memorized them nearly as well as his teammates. He went left when he was supposed to go right. He threw center when he was supposed to pass back. By the time practice ended he was as frustrated with his unaccustomed screwups as his coach. And it didn't help to have Coach riding him constantly.

"Okay, one more play," Coach said, with a steady look in Will's direction. "And let's try to get it right this time."

The players lined up. Will shouted out the play, then took the ball from the center on the snap count and executed a five-step drop. Beautiful, Will thought as the rusher headed inside. Ball cradled securely in his hand, Will stepped first toward, then around the rush. Still looking downfield, Will reset his feet. Checking to make sure the receiver was open, he lifted his arm, adjusted his aim and prepared to throw.

"Stop thinking, McCabe!" Coach Marten bellowed impatiently. "And just do it!"

Coach Marten's chastising words ringing in his ears, Will hastily followed through on the pass. As soon as the pigskin left his fingertips, he knew he'd released it a split second too soon. Not surprisingly, the football landed just short of the receiver. Will swore silently as yet another of his passes went incomplete. He couldn't believe they were going to end practice on a failed play. And from the looks of it, neither could his teammates. He didn't know what was wrong with him. He'd been all thumbs today. It didn't help knowing there was a group of varsity cheerleaders at the other end of the stadium, practicing on the running track that rimmed the football field, who had witnessed his every screwup.

On the sidelines, Coach Marten shook his head, making no effort to hide his disgust. "Okay, that's it for today. I'll see you tomorrow morning. McCabe! Get over here!"

The players headed off the field, with Assistant Coach Gus Barkley. The team managers gathered up the equipment. The video manager for the team came down from the stands, his video camera in tow. As they all streamed for the locker room, Will ripped off his helmet and jogged over to the fifty-yard line where Coach Marten was standing, clipboard in hand. He braced himself for the tongue-lashing sure to follow.

Mike Marten looked at him. "You're thinking too much. The plays need to be as automatic to you as breathing."

Like he didn't know that?

"Have you been studying your playbook?"

"Yes, sir." Not that it helped all that much given that Coach Marten used an entirely different system of offense than what Will had been used to and had double the number of plays. Many seemed to be either the same or variations of plays his team had used in previous years. That gave the returning players a big advantage over Will, who'd had just two days to memorize them before practice started. Will had always been a quick study, but between the turmoil at home, his problems sleeping and the pressure of being the new guy on the team, he was having a hell of a time adjusting. Coach's constant on-field badgering wasn't helping.

Mike shook his head and continued grimly, "If you want a lot of playing time this year, you're going to have to do better. Right now, the sophomore on Junior Varsity is playing better than you are. Understand, I'm not saying you can't throw the ball. You can. In fact, you've got the best arm we've seen around here in years. But it's going to take more than raw talent to lead this team. Do you understand what I'm saying?"

Will was filled with shame. He wasn't used to failing. The fact he was trying so hard and still screwing up right and left made it all the harder to bear. Not that Coach Marten's criticism was totally without merit. The truth was his concentration hadn't been worth crap since his mom had died. Some days, such as the morning he tried out for the team, it was there, great as ever. Other times, like this evening, he was so rattled he could barely recall his own name. Not that it mattered. On the football field, you either had it or you didn't. It scared Will to think maybe he'd lost his ability to win. And judging from the highly pissed-off look on his face, Coach Marten wasn't exactly too thrilled about it, either. "I need to work harder," Will said finally when some response seemed required from him.

"A far sight harder," Coach said flatly.

The brunt of the lecture over, Will waited for some sign of encouragement that things would get better by week's end, or reassurance that he would find it easier to blend in with the team. Even an offer of extra help from the coaching staff while he adjusted to a different school and a different way of doing things. None came. Coach Marten just shook his head at Will again, looked at him as if there was so much more he wanted to say but wouldn't, and walked away. Will stood there, helmet dangling from his hand, sweat streaming from his brow into his eyes, watching him go. He'd never felt like more of a failure in his life.

"You're new around here, aren't you?" a soft sympathetic voice said behind Will.

Will turned, and saw a pretty girl with long golden-brown hair and dark brown eyes, some half a foot shorter than him.

She was dressed in burnt-orange wind shorts, a snug-fitting white T-shirt that had a megaphone and "Laramie High School Cheerleader" across the front, white athletic shoes and socks.

Not sure he wanted company after being chewed out by Coach Marten, he merely nodded in answer to her question.

"I'm Amanda Sloane." Ignoring his less than enthusiastic welcome, she held out her hand.

Will shifted his helmet to his left hand and clasped her hand in his. It was soft and small enough to fit in the palm of his. He didn't know why, but he felt better just talking to her, despite the way he had just humiliated himself in practice. "Will McCabe."

"I know." Amanda batted her eyes at him and smiled in a slow, sensual way that promised any guy lucky enough to get close to her a good time. "You're the new quarterback."

Remembering how bad he'd done at practice since joining the team, Will grimaced. "Not if Coach Marten has anything to say about it."

"Oh, don't mind him." Still looking him over from head to foot, Amanda waved Will's concern away. "Everyone knows he is always toughest on the good players. He wouldn't bother yelling at you so much unless he thought you were really going to be good. Which," she said firmly, batting her eyelashes at him again, "you are."

"Oh, yeah?" Will challenged, his pulse picking up at the distinctly sexual vibes he was getting from her. "How do you know?"

Amanda tossed her hair. "I looked up your stats from the previous three years on the Internet—I accessed them through the sport section archives of the Dallas newspaper. They were impressive."

So was she, Will thought as he took the time to look her over, too. He hadn't had anyone show this much interest in him right off the bat for a long while. Of course her interest probably came with a downside, too. She was probably only interested in him because she needed a new boyfriend and thought he was going to be the new quarterback for their team.

Her sexy smile widened. "Have you signed up for classes yet?"

Will shook his head. "Late registration isn't until next week."

She twirled the ends of her hair around her fingertip and looked at him thoughtfully. "Since you're a senior transfer they'll probably let you take whatever you want, but I should probably tell you who the best teachers are, anyway, so you can try and get in their classes."

"Thanks," Will said. "I'd appreciate it."

Amanda looked into his eyes. "Want to do it tonight?" she asked casually.

Will hesitated. Lewis's birthday party was tonight. He'd already missed several hours of the celebration, which was slated to continue to around eleven. He was supposed to go over to Greta McCabe's dance hall as soon as he'd showered and cleaned up. He'd been dreading it all day.

"I haven't had dinner yet. We could grab a pizza," Amanda suggested. "My treat."

Suddenly that sounded a lot better than any family weepfest, where they all sat around trying to look happy, pretending they didn't miss Mom when they did. "Sure," Will said, pushing aside the tinge of guilt he felt for ditching his family. Again. There were going to be so many people there, no one would miss him, anyway. "Just let me go in and get a shower and put my equipment away."

Amanda grinned. "Welcome to Laramie High School, Will."

Funny that she should be the first person his age to say

that. Will grinned back, aware he was suddenly happier and more excited about something than he'd been in a long time. "Thanks."

Will never showed up. And Lewis never really stopped looking for him. Hours later, they returned home one exhausted group. While the boys scattered, the older ones going off to walk or drive their dates home, Sam carried a very sleepy Kevin up to bed. Kate and Lewis brought the presents in, then Kate took the leftover cake out to the kitchen. Kate was just closing the refrigerator door when Lewis came up to Kate and offered her an impromptu hug that meant the world to her. "I want to say it was my best birthday ever," he said, a glimmer of sadness coming into his eyes. "But I really can't."

"Because of your mom," Kate guessed.

"Right." That quickly, Lewis had tears glistening in his eyes. To his credit, he didn't even try to look away. "I mean, I had fun. I really did," he assured her thickly, "but…"

"You still miss your mom," Kate said softly, stroking his hair when he couldn't seem to go on.

Lewis nodded. The tears he'd been withholding poured down his cheeks. Kate took him all the way into her arms. She rubbed his shoulders, just the way his mother would have done. "Of course you do," Kate sympathized gently. "You all miss her and so does your dad. Especially days like today."

"Is it gonna get better?" Lewis moved back, so he could see Kate's face.

Kate nodded. "Yeah. It will. It's just gonna take time. Meanwhile, let yourself feel what you need to feel. Don't try to keep anything buried deep inside you."

"But if I—" Again, Lewis choked up and couldn't go on.

Kate studied his worried expression. "Are you afraid your brothers will make fun of you?"

He nodded anxiously and kept his eyes pinned on her

face. Sensing he needed physical as well as verbal comfort, Kate pulled him in close to her side, and walked them over to the kitchen stools, so he could sit beside her, and they could talk more comfortably. "If they did, honey, it would only be because they didn't understand…because they haven't gone through anything like it themselves. It's nothing for you to feel bad about. What makes you feel bad is when you're sad or lonely or scared and you don't talk to anyone about it."

Lewis bit his lower lip anxiously. "You mean, like a shrink?"

"I mean, like anybody," Kate corrected gently. "Your dad, me, a teacher or guidance counselor, even a family friend. Heck, you could pour out your problems to that stove over there or write them down in a journal and you'd end up feeling better because you took 'em out and dealt with them instead of letting them fester inside and make you miserable. And of course, you've got your uncle John and aunt Lilah, who are always ready and willing to listen anytime you need to talk, too. Don't forget about them."

Lewis frowned. "They're in Central America, though, doing that missionary stuff."

"But they'll be back in another week and a half." The same time as Craig. "In the meantime, I'm here and so is your dad," Kate said gently.

Sam appeared in the doorway. Ducking his head so his dad could not see his tears, Lewis swiveled around on the stool. Sam gave Kate a fierce look only she could see, clearly blaming her for Lewis's distress, then said to Lewis cheerfully, "Hey there, sport, want to go up and see if we can't load that game software onto your computer?"

"Sure, Dad." Doing his best to hide his tears, Lewis rubbed his knuckles across his cheek and dashed up the back stairs.

"I'll be right there," Sam called after him. As soon as

Lewis was out of earshot, Sam turned back to Kate, and snapped, "Did you upset him?"

"No," Kate said in a slow, measured tone, ignoring the accusing look in Sam's dark brown eyes and the way his constant questioning of her motives and actions hurt her. "I comforted him." There was a huge difference.

Tension simmered between them, stronger than ever before. "Then what was that about?" Sam demanded gruffly.

"He turned twelve today," Kate said quietly and emphatically. "It was his first birthday without his mom. He misses her. Of course he's sad, Sam. Everyone is." Because they couldn't help but wish Ellie were there, celebrating right along with them. But that wasn't happening and never would again. It was hard enough for an adult to accept; it was even harder for children, who were still very impressionable.

Without a word Sam turned away and headed up the stairs after his son. Kate wasn't happy about the abrupt way he ended the conversation, but she wasn't surprised. And she sure wasn't going to call Sam on the way he evaded his feelings instead of dealing with them, lest her words spark an argument and ruin what was left of Lewis's birthday. Besides, she knew she wasn't going to be able to talk Sam into opening up to her, any more than John and Lilah McCabe had. If and when that ever happened, and right now Kate wasn't sure it ever would, it would be because he wanted it to happen. And for no other reason.

In the meantime he would go on, teaching his sons by example. And everyone here would continue to emulate his strong, silent behavior and hold all their feelings inside, no matter how much it hurt, or how self-destructive that method of coping was. Until something happened, the dam burst, and the family fell apart even more, or one of them acted out in a way Sam couldn't ignore.

Kate wasn't sure she'd still be around to see it, when something finally woke Sam up to what was really going on here and brought him to his senses. Realistically it could take months or years for things to come to the kind of crisis that Sam could not find a way to rationalize and ignore. On the other hand, it could happen the very next day. Sadly, Kate thought, there was just no way to predict when and where. All she knew for certain was that one day the crisis would come.

Sam knew what Kate wanted from him, but she wasn't going to get it. He had survived Ellie's death by sucking it up and being as tough as he needed to be, and he'd taught his boys to do the same. He wasn't going to apologize for that. Their combined toughness had gotten them through the past six months. Yeah, there had been dark days, and even darker nights where they had all suffered, and Sam was sure there would be some in the future, too. In the meantime, Lewis was the son most like Ellie. The one who might not be tough enough. Lewis had a hard enough time as it was, coping with the loss of his mom. Sam was furious with Kate for encouraging Lewis to wallow in his grief on his birthday, of all days. Today Lewis should have been happy, period. And Kate should have encouraged him to concentrate on that instead of poking and pinching the wound.

"I'm sorry, Dad," Lewis said when Sam went up to join him. He was already seated at his computer desk, loading his game CD onto his hard drive. His face was red and he was staring hard at the computer screen.

Sam pulled up a chair and sat beside Lewis, amazed as always at his son's prowess with anything computer-related, even at such a young age. "Sorry for what?" Sam asked gently. As far as he was concerned, Lewis—the one kid in the family who could always be counted on to behave—never had anything to feel apologetic about.

"For acting like a sissy." Lewis wiped his nose on his

sleeve and kept his face averted in obvious embarrassment. "I didn't mean to cry. I just couldn't help it."

Sam knew that feeling. Realizing how much shame his son felt over the way he'd broken down, Sam abruptly felt like the unfeeling ogre and poor excuse for a father that Kate deemed him to be. "It's okay." Sam patted Lewis's shoulder awkwardly, unsure how to comfort him. "We all cry sometimes. We just can't do it all the time. You know what I mean?"

Lewis nodded as fresh tears threatened. "Why do you think Will dissed me by skipping the party?" he asked, his chin quivering. "Is he ashamed to be seen with me because I'm so nerdy?" His eyes were filled with hurt. "Or does he just not care about me at all?"

Sam reached over, took Lewis into his arms and hugged him fiercely. "Will loves you. We all love you." Sam rubbed his knuckles playfully across the top of Lewis's head as they drew apart. "And you're not nerdy."

Lewis sent Sam an irritated glance, sniffed. "Dad, I am."

"Being bright doesn't make you a nerd."

Lewis looked at Sam in exasperation. "But I'm not a jock, like Will, Dad. Or the coolest trumpet player in the jazz band, like Riley, or the star of school plays, like Brad. I'm a computer geek. That's all I can do. All I want to do!"

He said it as if it were the worst thing in the entire world. Feeling both sad and amused to realize Lewis had self-esteem issues related to who and what he was, which was in turn a chip off the old block, Sam said, "Well, my life revolves around computers, too, and that's all I want to do," Sam said emphatically. "Does that make me a geek and a nerd, too?"

"Well…" Lewis grinned as he thought about that. "No…"

"Then neither are you," Sam said firmly. "You are, however, twelve, and twelve is a tough age for anyone. Your voice changes, you go through puberty, and growth spurts…"

"I know all about that," Lewis interrupting, letting Sam

know with a glance that any further discussion of the subject was totally unnecessary. "Mom told me."

Which was something else Ellie had done. Had "the talk" with her boys, so that by the time Sam came along, prepared to do the same, they were already weary of the subject and convinced he, as their father, had nothing worthwhile to add. "Then you know this is a phase that will pass, and one day, too, you will be as tall and strong and sure about yourself as your older brothers are. You just have to give it time, and let yourself be who and what you are without worrying about what anyone else thinks. Okay?"

"Okay."

"In the meantime, we just have to hang tough, all of us, and keep on keeping on. Do you think you can do that for me?"

Lewis nodded and threw himself into Sam's arms again. Sam hugged him, hard. When he was sure Lewis felt better, he let him go. "You know, it's been a long day and you're looking a little tired—"

"Just let me play my game a little, Dad, and then I'll go to bed. Promise."

"Okay. But don't stay up too late," Sam said.

"I won't."

Sam headed back downstairs.

Kate was ensconced in a club chair, her legs curled up beneath her. She was fast asleep. She'd kicked her cowgirl boots off and they lay on the floor beside her, and she had more wedding stuff—satin ribbons and lace this time—across her lap. Her head was propped on her hand, her hair spilling across her shoulders. She looked vulnerable and sweet, nothing like the busybody she was. Despite the fact his mind and heart were so numb he had given up on the idea of ever making love to another woman again, his body was not getting the message. And it wasn't just tonight. Every time he walked in and saw her, he was aware of her. Too aware.

Behind him, the front door opened. Sam turned just in time to see Brad and Riley come in from their dates. They glanced at Kate. "What's she doing?"

"Sleeping, obviously," Sam said quietly.

"You're not going to just leave her there all night, are you?"

"Of course not," Sam said. Although he'd been thinking about doing just that. "I'll wake her up. You boys go on to bed."

"Sure thing. Hey, it was a pretty good party tonight, wasn't it?" Brad said.

"I haven't had so much fun since we moved to Laramie," Riley concurred.

Sam envied their ability to move on. Of the entire family, Brad and Riley were coping the best in the wake of Ellie's death. "I'm glad you boys had a good time."

"Lousy of Will not to show, though," Brad remarked.

"Yeah, I thought it was mean, too," Riley agreed.

"I'm going to talk to him about that when he comes in," Sam said.

Brad and Riley exchanged looks that said they didn't want to be in Will's shoes. "Yeah, well, 'night, Dad," Brad said.

"Good night."

Sam waited until the boys had ascended the stairs before he walked over to Kate. Her perfume, something citrusy and sweet, teased his senses as he neared her. He touched her shoulder. She started. "Go to bed," he said.

"Can't." Kate yawned and stretched in a way that only emphasized the fullness of her breasts beneath the soft cotton fabric of her dress. "I'm waiting up for Will. The way he hurt Lewis's feelings was inexcusable, and someone needs to talk to him about that."

Clearly, she had no faith Sam would have thought to do so on his own. "I'll take care of that," Sam said.

Kate looked at him, considering. The front door opened again and Will walked in. To Sam's annoyance his eldest son didn't look the least bit guilty or contrite. "Where have you been?" Sam demanded angrily.

"Forget that," Will replied disrespectfully. Ignoring Kate entirely, Will looked at Sam as if he despised him with every fiber of his being. "Did Coach Marten get you a football scholarship to U.T.-Austin?"

Sam went still. "Where did you hear that?"

Will advanced on Sam, fists knotted at his side. Frustration glittered in his eyes. "Is it true?"

"Yes."

"And you turned it down?" Will asked incredulously.

Sam nodded wordlessly in reply, even as he noticed the smear of lipstick on Will's neck and could smell perfume clinging to his skin.

"Why?"

"Because I decided I didn't want to play college ball," Sam said calmly.

Will clamped his lips together mutinously. "And Coach Marten was pissed."

Sam had only to catch a glimpse of Kate's pained expression to know that she recalled her father's emotional reaction to his decision every bit as well as he did. Mike Marten hadn't just been pissed off. He had been bitter, angry, hurt, disappointed and insulted. And he had stayed that way through the entire summer before Sam went off to college, Ellie by his side. For a while Sam had tried to make amends with him. When it became clear it wasn't going to happen—that Coach was never going to forgive him—he had given up and stopped thinking about what might have been and started thinking about his future, with his wife and kids and computers. Sam knew he'd made the right decision. He'd assumed that Coach would have figured that out over time, given Sam's extraordinary professional success. But apparently not, judging by Will's expression, Sam thought, aware he was now as deeply disappointed in Mike Marten as Mike Marten was in him. "What Coach Marten thought was not important," Sam said.

"The hell it isn't!" Will interrupted. He stomped farther into the room and threw his car keys down on the hall table. "I'm playing on his team now, Dad. Or at least I'm trying to. The way he's riding me…" Will stopped, shook his head. "Well, it all makes sense."

Sam's eyes narrowed. It had never been like Will to complain. "What do you mean, the way he's riding you?" he demanded, suspicious.

Will's expression hardened with resentment. "He's on my case all the time. I didn't understand why. Coaches have always been glad to have me on their team. But not Coach Marten. He acts like he doesn't even want me there. Thanks to Amanda Sloane, I finally understand why. It's because he thinks I'm just like you."

Sam blew out a breath. "I'll talk to him."

"Don't bother." Will prepared to head off.

Sam caught him by the shoulder and reeled him back. "Hold on a minute. We're not finished."

"Why?" Will spun around and glared at him. "Something else you forgot to tell me?"

Sam ignored the tightening in his gut and gave Will a narrow look. "You missed your brother's birthday party tonight."

Will shrugged, not caring, and not about to apologize for his absence. "I had a date," he said succinctly.

Out of the corner of his eye, Sam caught the look of frank disapproval and disappointment on Kate's face. He was feeling exactly the same way. Will hadn't exactly been a warm and fuzzy kid before Ellie died. He had always been one to keep his thoughts and feelings to himself. Ellie had been able to draw him out, to a point. Sam never had. Talking to Will about anything but sports was like talking to a stone. Still, Sam had to try. "You should have been there," he said flatly, recalling all too well how devastated and hurt Lewis had been.

Silence fell between them. The remorse Sam hoped to see on Will's face never materialized. Still, Sam waited, refusing to back down.

"So I'll apologize," Will said eventually.

"You'll do better than that," Sam reiterated sternly, aware he, too, was hanging on to his temper by a thread. "You'll find some way to make it up to him. Got it?"

Will nodded. "I got it," he said sarcastically. He shot a rebellious look at Kate, then another at Sam, before muttering cantankerously, "Can I go now?"

Sam dropped his hand back to his side. He'd won the argument but he still felt defeated. Maybe because he felt as though he hadn't dented the wall Will had built around himself since Ellie died. And he knew Will needed to let someone in besides the girl he had apparently been kissing. He wished like hell it would be him. "I'm disappointed in you, Will," he said, then waited for the impact of his words to sink in.

"Well, I'm disappointed in you, Dad." Abruptly, Will's voice trembled with emotion. "The least you could have done was tell me about the way you'd ditched your scholarship before we decided to move here."

Sam saw now putting Kate's father and his son together, even after all this time had passed, was just asking for trouble. "Do you want to go to school somewhere else?" Sam asked calmly.

"What?" Will blinked and looked at him as if he'd grown two heads.

"It's not too late to get you into a prep school in Dallas,

if that's what you want," Sam reiterated calmly. In fact, he was sure he could manage it.

"That's your solution to everything, isn't it?" Will said bitterly. He glowered at Sam as if he hated him. "Just run away." He shouldered past him and stormed up the stairs.

"You should go after him," Kate said, looking as deeply concerned as Sam felt.

Sam swung around to face her, furious she had been there to witness yet another of his failures. "And you should mind your own business."

Chapter 8

Sam hadn't been back to Coach Marten's office in the field house since the day he and Mike Marten had exchanged bitter, angry words over Sam's decision to turn down the college scholarship Mike had worked so hard to get him. Walking in, just after 6:00 a.m., the time of day Coach got to the field house to go over his plans for that morning's seven-thirty practice, Sam had a peculiar sense of déjà vu. A lot had changed: the paint, the conditioning equipment, even the athletic lockers that lined the walls. But Coach Marten hadn't. And neither had he, Sam thought, and that was the problem.

Mike was in his office, seated behind his desk, reviewing practice films when Sam walked in. "I know why you resent me," Sam said calmly, glad no one else was there to witness this. "I even accept it. I won't have you taking the rancor you feel for me out on my son."

Mike regarded Sam for a long moment. "Did Will complain to you?" Mike leaned forward and rested his beefy forearms on the desk. "Tell you I'm giving him an unnecessarily hard time?"

"No," Sam returned evenly. "But I could tell by what he said that's what has been going on."

Calmly, Mike reached for the remote. "Before you make an even bigger jackass out of yourself, sit and take a look at this. This is yesterday's practice."

Reluctantly, Sam pulled up a chair and sat. He watched for several moments in silence. Will fumbled, overshot and undershot the ball time after time. He was uncertain, slow and clumsy to the point even his teammates looked exasperated. Watching along with Sam, Mike shook his head. "I don't know what your son is thinking about out there on the field, but he sure as hell doesn't have his mind on what he's doing. Will's talented. But he's not going to be playing much this year unless he gets his head back in the game. So you want to tell him something, tell him that. I already have."

Mike clicked the remote and stopped the tape.

Aware he had indeed just made a very big fool of himself by rushing to defend his son before he knew all the facts, Sam stood. "One more thing," Mike said before Sam could even begin to formulate an apology. "Kate may be a grown woman but she's still an innocent in so many ways."

Sam tensed at the implied accusation. "What is that supposed to mean?" he demanded, slamming his hands onto his waist.

Mike regarded him steadily. "I want to make sure her virtue is safe."

"Her virtue," Sam repeated, both stunned and incensed.

Mike nodded grimly as he got to his feet, too, and squared off with Sam across the top of his desk. "I don't want you making a pass at her or seducing her in order to satisfy any of your 'needs.'"

Sam swore at the antiquated notion. He wasn't some lord of the manor looking to bed the help—especially when the help was Kate Marten! And still resentful of him or not, Mike should know that! "Sleeping with your daughter is the last thing on my mind," Sam said gruffly. But even as he said it, Sam knew it wasn't true. Ever since she'd moved in—hell, ever since the night he had kissed her to try to scare her away—he'd been aware of Kate as a woman. And the more she was around, the more comfortable she was in his house, the worse it got.

"I'm glad to hear that," Mike said grimly.

"But you still wish she wasn't staying with us," Sam stated, reading the look on Mike's face.

Mike acknowledged this was so with a shrug. "I know Kate feels for you and your family and what they've been through. But Kate's always had too much heart and too little self-preservation. I don't want to see her get hurt."

Sam did not see what that had to do with him. "I'm not out to hurt her," he said curtly.

"You already have just by getting her so involved in your problems." Mike shot Sam a narrow, warning glance. "As far as her mother and I are concerned, right now Kate should be thinking about only one thing—her upcoming wedding to Craig."

Kate was not about to miss her appointment to try on wedding dresses at Jenna Lockhart's exclusive boutique. So she'd enlisted Sam's cousin, Shane McCabe, to take charge of the boys for a couple of hours while she and her mother attended to that very important detail of her wedding. Kate started with a full-skirted satin dress, with a fitted, long-sleeved, high-necked lace bodice. The moment Joyce saw Kate in it, tears welled in her eyes. Jenna grinned and handed Joyce a box of tissues. "A little overwhelming, isn't it?" Jenna teased.

"Very," Joyce said happily, dabbing her eyes. Doing her best to compose herself, she looked at Kate, her lower lip trembling. "You're just so beautiful, honey. And so grown up."

And this was really happening, Kate thought, beginning to tear up herself. She was really going to stop talking about it and thinking about it and dreaming about it and marry Craig. She turned back to the mirror and took a deep breath. As lovely as it was, somehow the gown did not feel right. Kate bit her lip as she tried to think how to articulate her concern. "I think it's too…"

"Old-fashioned?" Jenna guessed.

Kate nodded. "Maybe something more sleek and sophisticated?" Something she'd feel comfortable in and Craig would really go wild over.

"Gotcha." Jenna took a sleeveless silk gown from the rack and helped Kate into that. Kate looked in the mirror. "Tell me what you're thinking," Jenna said as she caught the uncertain expression on Kate's face.

"It's so…plain. I almost look like I'm just going to a formal dance." She wanted a dress that would make her feel as special and cherished as she needed to feel as she walked down the aisle on that very special day.

"Okay. Let's try this." Jenna assisted Kate out of that gown and into the next. It had a fitted satin bodice, a portrait neckline that left her neck and shoulders bare, and a beautiful tulle skirt.

"I really like that one," Joyce said, beaming.

Again, Kate shook her head. "It just doesn't feel like me."

Over the next two hours Kate was in and out of almost three dozen gowns. Jenna quizzed her as she put on each one, asking what she liked, what she didn't. By the time they had exhausted her current inventory of dresses, Joyce looked worried they'd never find anything to please Kate, and Kate was exhausted and discouraged. Only Jenna seemed to take their failure to find "the gown" in stride. "Don't worry." Jenna patted Kate on the shoulder, after Kate got dressed again, and had taken a seat beside Joyce on the sofa. "This happens all the time. Brides rarely find the dress they want the first time out. It often takes quite a few shopping trips to find the dress of your dreams."

"That's the problem," Kate sighed. "I don't know exactly what the dress of my dreams is supposed to look like."

"No one does—until they put it on." Jenna zipped one dress after another into protective plastic bags.

"Actually, now that I think of it, it took me quite a few shopping excursions to find my wedding dress, too," Joyce soothed as she and Jenna exchanged understanding glances.

"I think I may know what you want now," Jenna said, turning back to Kate. "I've got a couple dresses already under way, and another I've just dreamed up that might fit the bill. Why don't I get those together and give you a call as soon as they are ready to try on?"

"Okay," Kate said, relieved. After all this time, after all this waiting and "making do," she wanted everything to be as wonderful and right as she had always dreamed it would be.

"In the meantime…" Jenna walked them both to the door. She laced a comforting arm around Kate's shoulders. "I don't want you worrying. We've still got plenty of time to find you the dress that's going to make your wedding picture-perfect."

"Hey, Kate. Do you know how to sew a button on?" Brad asked shortly after Kate had returned to Sam's and Shane had left. It was obvious just looking at him that he had tumbled out of bed and into the shower not too long ago. His eyes still had a not-quite-all-the-way-awake look and his hair was damp and scented with shampoo. He was wearing shorts, and had a loud Hawaiian shirt crumpled in his hand, a needlepoint-covered basket in another.

"Yes." Kate looked up from her perch on the front porch, where she'd been thumbing through bridal magazines, checking out the dresses, and keeping an eye on Kevin, who was riding his bike up and down the sidewalk in front of the house. She looked over at Brad, noting he hadn't bothered to shave and was sporting several days' growth of visible stubble. "Would you like to learn?"

Brad looked at her as though she had to be kidding. "No."

Kate arched a brow, letting him know that answer was not about to fly with her. "So find something else to wear. You've got plenty of clothes. Or wear it as is, with the button missing."

Realizing this was not a battle he was going to win, Brad released a put-upon sigh and continued rotely, "Okay, I'll learn. But you'll have to show me."

Kate patted the place beside her on the wicker settee. "Have a seat."

"So how'd the wedding dress shopping go?" he asked as Kate found a needle and some white thread. "Did you find a dress?"

"Nope. I tried on a lot but none of them was right."

"Bummer," Brad said with genuine sympathy.

"Yeah. I was disappointed. But I've got plenty of time." Kate paused to show Brad how to thread a needle and to find the place where the button had been. She got it started while he watched, then made him continue pushing the needle through the holes in the button to secure it in place.

"How long you been engaged, anyway?" he asked.

"Almost three years."

"Wow. That's a long time."

"I know."

"People must have been wondering if you'd ever get married."

Kate grinned. Leave it to Brad to hit the nail right on the head. "You've got that right." There had been some in town who had hinted that Craig should have been willing to give up his air force career to come back to Laramie and be with Kate, but she had never asked Craig to do that. As much as she loved living and working in the small Texas town where she had grown up, she knew Craig had always felt stifled there. While she had simply needed to help others, he had needed to achieve, to see the world, to do not just something important but something exciting and daring, something few people could do. And now that he had actually done that, he couldn't—wouldn't—just walk away from it, even when his commitment to the military was up.

His head tilted slightly to the side, Brad continued to study her. "So how'd you know Craig was the one you were supposed to marry?" he asked curiously after a moment. "Was there this lightning-bolt moment, like you see in the movies?"

"No," Kate recollected fondly. "It was more gradual. We grew up together and went to school together and were always friends. We started hanging out a lot on weekends when we were in high school, and then started dating before he went off to the Air Force Academy."

"But you didn't go to the academy."

"No, I went to college here in Texas."

Again, Brad looked stunned. "So you waited for him all that time?"

Kate hesitated. "It's not like we never had a date with anyone else. We both saw others from time to time, but in the end we always came back to each other." And Kate had been happy to do so. Life with Craig was familiar, safe. He wasn't volatile the way her dad and Pete and even Sam were. She dealt with enough turmoil and emotional upheaval at work.

She didn't want it at home, too. So, why, suddenly, since Sam had come back into her life was she feeling so restless, edgy, envious of the deeply passionate love he'd had with Ellie? She knew, even if Sam no longer did, that his relationship with his wife hadn't been perfect despite the depth of their love and the wonderful family they'd built. Sam was a workaholic. Ellie, for all her public show of coping, had often been lonely. And she'd told Kate as much more than once in the early days of their marriage. Having lived with Sam for a few days, seen what long

hours he put in at the office, and how wrapped up he was in his work, Kate could understand firsthand why Ellie had felt that way.

"What's Craig like?"

Passionate about his career, reckless enough to fly fighter jets. She loved his bravura and confidence, and his devotion to his country, the way he had always been, would always be, her friend. Her only complaint, if she even had one, was the lack of fire in the bedroom. And even that was understandable. They were together so infrequently, and when they were, it seemed there were so many people waiting to see Craig that they were almost never alone for very long. He had been her first lover, she had been his. Hence, neither of them was all that experienced in bed. But she was hoping the sexy-as-hell dress Jenna had designed for Kate to wear to Craig's homecoming next week, and the time alone they had arranged to have, would fix all that, and make her as completely, thoroughly irresistible to him as she had always wanted to be. In fact, she was sure it would.

Aware Brad was still waiting for her answer, Kate said, "He's very nice. He's an air force pilot."

"What kind of planes does he fly?"

"F-16's."

"Wow."

"Yeah. Wow."

"He must really be good if they let him fly one of those."

"He is." Kate acknowledged proudly. Deciding the button was now firmly sewed onto the shirt, she turned back to Brad. She let him know with a smile how much she appreciated his improved attitude. "Okay, now let me show you how to wrap the thread around the base of these threads, to make this button really secure...."

"What time will you need me again tomorrow morning, boss?" Sam's driver asked as he parked the limo in front of Sam's house.

"Five sharp," Sam said as he gathered up his laptop computer, briefcase and suit jacket. "I need to be in the office by seven."

"Okay. See you then." Looking happy he'd gotten off work at a reasonable hour for the first time in weeks, Sam's driver left.

Still feeling a little guilty for having left so much at the office undone, Sam headed up the sidewalk. To his surprise, the front door was locked. He fished out his key and let himself in. He walked through the downstairs, expecting to be confronted by the usual sounds of dueling televisions and stereos and boys fighting. Instead, the house was silent, devoid of even the slightest aroma. Sure dinner couldn't be over with already, he headed for the kitchen. The boys had been there. The evidence of their snacks and beverages was clearly evident in the dirty dishes and paper wrappers littering the counters. But there was nothing simmering on the stove, nothing in the oven. Beginning to be more than a little irritated, Sam searched the rest of the house and found no one was home. He sorted through the mail, then headed for his study. Finally, about eight-thirty, he heard the sound of a car in the drive. Sam moved to the window.

Instead of the casual clothes she'd been wearing around the house, Kate was dressed in a figure-hugging white dress with a matching jacket. High heels showed off her legs to spectacular advantage. Her sunglasses were pushed up on her head. Her bag looped over her arm, she was busy outfitting his son Lewis with her briefcase and laptop computer while she and Kevin both picked up several bags of groceries each. Lewis and Kate were still laughing and talking as they headed for the house, six-year-old Kevin tagging along wordlessly beside them.

Sam met them at the door. Kate's eyes widened in surprise, but she looked pleased to see him nevertheless. "You're home early," she said happily. "When did you get here?"

"Six-thirty. I thought I'd have supper with the boys."

Kate's jaw dropped. Immediately she understood and shared his disappointment. "Only no one was here," she said softly.

Once again, Sam found himself on the receiving end of Kate's compassion. Once again, he found himself not wanting it. Knowing full well it wasn't her fault, he was the one who had decided to "surprise" the family by coming home early and sitting down to dinner with them, Sam looked at Kate and said irritably, "If you'd let me know you would be late, I could have stayed at the office." As it was, he had wasted most of the evening, unable to concentrate fully, while waiting and wondering where everyone was.

An anxious look on his face, Lewis took Kev's hand. "Let's bring in the rest of the groceries."

"Kate and I will do that," Sam said firmly. The boys didn't need to hear what he had to say.

Kate smiled at the boys gently and, unlike Sam, still looking relaxed and happy and at ease, prompted cheerfully, "Yeah, why don't you guys go on up and finish the game you started earlier? You've got the diskette I gave you, right?"

"Yup. Thanks for taking us with you." Lewis gave Kate a quick, exuberant hug. "We had fun. Didn't we, Kev?"

Kev nodded shyly. He hugged Kate, too, then headed off with Lewis.

Kate headed back out to the car. Sam followed, close on her heels. "You could have called me to let me know you weren't going to be here," he said.

"I would have except our not being here didn't involve blood, fire or any other emergency that would warrant you taking a call from me."

At the reminder of the way he had refused her calls when he'd been hip-deep in crucial meetings, it was all Sam could do not to cringe. "You could have left a message."

Kate looked at him, her soft lips curved into a challenging smile. "Do you want me to do that next time?"

"I would appreciate it, yes." Sam pushed the words through his teeth.

"Okay, then, I will." Kate leaned into her trunk.

Sam tore his eyes from the fabric shifting gently over her slender hips. "Didn't you just go to the store?" he demanded.

"Three days ago," Kate affirmed as she took several bags of groceries and handed them to him. "Amazing, isn't it, how much growing boys eat?"

Ignoring the way her skirt hitched up her thighs, Sam watched as she reached back into the trunk and struggled to push two bunches of bananas and a big bag of oranges back into the sack before lifting them, too. "What's with all the fruit?"

Her arms full of groceries, Kate headed for the house. "The boys all need a lot of potassium in this kind of heat. Oranges and bananas are both good sources of it and they all like them. We were out of both."

Sam watched her long legs as she headed up the back steps in her short skirt. He didn't know how or why it had happened, but suddenly Kate was under his skin in a way no woman had been in a very long time. "You don't have to explain in such detail," he mumbled.

"I thought that was the point of the interrogation." Kate set the grocery bags down on the kitchen table and headed back out to the car. "You wanted me to explain."

Sam felt a muscle tick in his jaw as his pique with her built. He was used to respect from the household help. "What I wanted to see, Kate, were my kids. Only none of them was here."

Kate shrugged, "Then check with them on their schedules, so that next time you make a special effort to be home, they will be here."

Sam watched her transfer her groceries to one hand, then slam down the trunk. "Where were you?" he demanded. And why was she dressed that way? She was supposed to be taking care of his kids. Period. Not gallivanting around in formal business clothes.

Kate sent him an exasperated look and marched toward the house. "I had to go to the hospital for a meeting. Lewis and Kev went with me. While I did business, they played computer games in the conference room next to my office."

Sam moved ahead and opened the back door. "Have they had dinner?" he asked.

"Of course, they have," Kate snapped as she strode into the kitchen ahead of him, teetering slightly in her heels as she juggled to transfer the weight in her hands up onto the table. "As reward for their excellent behavior, we ate dinner at the Wagon Wheel restaurant, and then stopped by the grocery on the way home to stock up on everything we were running out of around here." Kate removed her sunglasses from the top of her head and set them on the counter. Her jacket came off next. She slung it over the back of a chair.

Her figure-hugging sheath exposed her bare sexy arms to tantalizing view.

Sam frowned. "I thought you were taking time off from the hospital."

Kate arched a brow his way. "Something came up." She began unloading groceries.

To Sam's aggravation, she didn't say what. "What about the older three—have they had dinner?" he demanded grumpily.

Her exasperation with him clearly mounting, Kate sucked in a breath. "Riley is eating dinner with the marching band—their practice goes until nine tonight."

"That late?"

"The next two weeks are considered their training camp. They practice from nine until nine, Monday through Friday."

Sam's brow furrowed with the depth of his concern. "That's a long time."

"Yes, it is," Kate explained patiently, "but it's the only way they can teach the kids the marching fundamentals, the music and the half-time show before school starts. Don't worry." She smiled at him in a soothing way he found even more irritating than the sarcasm she'd used on him earlier. "They're not outside all that time. They spend a good half of the time inside, in the air-conditioning. It's a very social activity as well as educational. The kids here love it, despite all the hard work. And I am sure Riley will, too."

Sam frowned as he realized he had practically invited that long drawn-out explanation, when all he was really trying to do was cut the conversation short, after first making sure his kids were okay, of course. "Did I say I was worried?" he demanded belligerently.

"No," Kate replied with the same maddening compassion. "You just look it."

Irritated she knew more about what was going on with his kids at any given moment than he did—never mind had the wherewithal to be nice when he was acting anything but, Sam snapped, "Where about Brad and Will? Have they had dinner?"

Kate went back to putting away groceries, her every move as feminine and graceful as the clothes she was dressed in. "Will is going to pick something up with the team, after football practice this evening—he can't eat and then go run in this heat, he'd get sick. Brad is having dinner with a friend at his house this evening." She paused, studying Sam openly as she put two cans of soup away. "If you're hungry...and don't know how to prepare yourself a meal...if *that's* what this is about..."

Sam released a provoked breath. She didn't just think he was self-centered and a bad parent. She thought he was incompetent, too! "I can make myself a sandwich, thanks," he returned bitterly.

Kate looked unconvinced as she slid the milk into the fridge. "Have you?"

"No." Sam pulled an enormous jar of pickles out of the sack. "I was waiting for everyone else to show up." He'd wanted to eat with his family. He'd wanted to talk to Will about how football practice was really going, and try to learn what was causing Will to screw up since joining Coach Marten's team. Was it just nerves—something Will had never suffered from before? Or something more? Something specific Kate's dad was doing? Sam didn't want to think it was the latter, but he also knew how much Mike Marten resented the fact that his daughter was living in Sam's house, helping out, even temporarily.

Kate carried an armload of canned goods to the walk-in pantry. She shot him a look over her shoulder, while struggling to put them away. "Do you want me to do it for you? Because if you do, I could—"

"No." Sam didn't want Kate doing anything for him. It

was bad enough having her here underfoot twenty-four hours a day, seven days a week, without her first trying to size up his mood and then cater to him the way Ellie used to do.

"Fine, then." Kate turned sideways to brush by him, her proximity inundating him with the delicate, womanly scent of her perfume.

The silence that followed was deafening.

Worse, Sam felt like the biggest jerk in the world for the way he was behaving.

Kate was doing a good job under extremely difficult circumstances, and instead of thanking her, the way Ellie would have wanted Sam to thank her, he was on her case constantly. Letting her know by look, word and deed that nothing she or any other woman ever did was going to be good enough to make up for Ellie's absence in their lives.

Sam released a weary breath and shoved a hand through his hair. He had to do better here. Had to. For the sake of the boys. For Ellie. For Kate. It was the least he owed any of them. He had been acting like a spoiled child and for the life of him, he didn't know why. He swallowed hard, and when she turned in his direction, he said, "Look, I'm..." *Angry all the time. Furious at I don't even know what.* He swallowed again and forced himself to go on. "I'm sorry."

Kate remained very still and said nothing, the look in her eyes willing him to continue.

Knowing he owed her this much, if not a hell of a lot more, Sam pushed on with effort as the ache of sadness and despair he'd felt for months now rose in his throat, choking him. "I was worried when I got home and there was no one here." He looked into Kate's eyes, wanting her to know it wasn't, and never had been, anything personal. That it wasn't her, it was him. Even when he didn't want to admit it, he knew it. "I didn't know where anyone was, and I just got worried, that's all." Sam shook his head, aware just how lame that sounded.

Understanding gleamed in her eyes, even as her low, sexy voice remained firm and direct. "If the kids had been hurt… if there was a problem and they needed you, I would call you, Sam," she said softly. "They would call you."

"I know that." Sam looked down and away as the unwanted ache in his throat grew.

"Then…?" Kate crossed her arms in front of her and remained where she was, though Sam could see—feel—that she wanted to come closer.

That was just it, Sam thought helplessly as he leaned back against the counter and she waited for his reply. He couldn't explain his bad mood. Except…seeing her come in like that, laughing and talking with the boys as they carried in groceries, reminded him of Ellie. Though Ellie had never dressed like that, unless she had a social function to attend. Ellie had never worked outside the house, either, juggled kids and career responsibilities. *He* couldn't seem to do it. He resented the fact that at least for a few hours, Kate had done it, and done it well.

"I thought you didn't want me to wait around for you to show up," Kate said finally.

Sam grimaced. "I don't." It irritated him when she did. Reminded him of the way Ellie had always been there, waiting for him, whatever time of day or night he had come in. She'd always had dinner waiting, eagerly listened to the events of his day. He didn't want Kate doing that, didn't want her doing anything that reminded him of Ellie and all he had lost. And yet when she didn't do that, when she didn't make him feel as if he mattered, he resented that, too. It made no sense. Just as his awareness of Kate as a woman made no sense.

"Okay, then what's the problem?" Kate demanded, clearly needing, wanting, to make sense of it all.

Not about to confess his physical yearning for her, Sam turned away abruptly. "Nothing. I'm tired. I'm hungry. I've had a long day." *And I want to take you to bed. Here. Now.* How sick was that? This was Ellie's home. Kate was engaged to be married to someone else. The last thing either of them needed was to get sexually involved with each other. And yet, there it was. The desire he'd discovered the first night she'd marched into his house to help him and he'd grabbed her and kissed her. The desire that no matter what would not go away. The desire that even now was working to keep him away, because this was not what he wanted to feel, and he was pretty sure, if Kate knew about it, she would not want it, either. What was he supposed to say to her? *I can't be in a room with you, I can't smell your perfume, without wanting to make love to you.* She might have come to help out, but she sure hadn't signed on for sex. And right now, sex—the oblivion, the release—was what hc wanted.

Aware she was still looking at him, trying to read what was in his heart and on his mind, and if she kept it up, he might just tell her, Sam said, "I'm in a bad mood, okay? What else do you want me to say?"

Something came and went in Kate's eyes. Abruptly, her demeanor became colder, less intimate, too. "Nothing," Kate said. "Absolutely nothing." And she walked away.

Chapter 9

Amanda Sloane was waiting for Will when he came out of
the field house after practice Thursday night. They didn't
have a date, but it was clear from the way she was looking
at him, that she wanted to go out with him again. Figuring it was either do something with friends or go home and
have his little brothers—or worse, Kate—pestering him, Will
headed straight for Amanda. She was wearing shorts and a
halter top. Her hair was in a ponytail. She had one hand on
her waist, her hips thrust forward in a provocative stance, her
head tilted sideways. She looked as if she was a model, waiting to have her picture taken. If Will hadn't been so lonely,
he would have found her glamour-girl pose a real turn-off.
But he was lonely, and she was the one girl in Laramie pur-
suing him, so....

Amanda smiled as he came nearer. "I thought you might
like to see where the popular kids hang out during the summer," she said.

Noting the envious looks of some of his teammates, Will

slid a hand around Amanda's waist. "Sounds good, as long as we stop somewhere first so I can get something to eat."

Amanda moved in close, and wrapped her arm around his waist, too. Grinning, she looked up at him. "No problem. We can even take my car, if you want."

"Nah," Will said, unable to help but note how good she looked and smelled. "I'd rather take my Jeep."

"Okay by me."

They stopped for hamburgers at the drive-in on the outskirts of town, then headed out toward Lake Laramie. Amanda put her hand on Will's thigh while he drove. By the time they found the spot, her palm had inched from down around his knee up to his groin. And from the way she kept glancing surreptitiously at his crotch, she had to know he had a hard-on that wouldn't quit. All they'd done the night before was make out a little in the car. Given the way she was coming on to him, Will couldn't help but wonder what she had planned for tonight.

"I think my mom told me about this place," Will mused as they got out of his Jeep and walked toward a large clearing next to the lake. The ground was covered with sand. Logs around the perimeter served as benches. A fire glowed warmly in the sunken pit in the center of the clearing. Some kids were dancing, some were talking, others were listening to music being played on a portable stereo. A couple of girls were roasting marshmallows over the fire, and feeding them to their boyfriends. Another couple was making out in the shadows. Will spotted several guys drinking beer. Everyone seemed to be doing their own thing, having a good time. Recognizing several players from the football team and some of the cheerleaders, Will lifted his hand in an indifferent wave. They nodded back, then went on with what they were doing.

Amanda nodded at an older guy Will didn't recognize standing in the corner, drinking beer. "That's R.J. If you need anything—beer, wine, whiskey—he can set you up. He makes a liquor run to San Angelo once a week. Or—" she smiled at Will seductively "—you can do what I do and…"

She took a small travel-size bottle of what looked to be mouthwash from the pocket of her shorts. "…drink some of this to get a buzz on."

Will stopped her before she could lift the little bottle all the way to her mouth. He didn't know if she was toying with him or showing off, but the alcohol in mouthwash was not the kind you drank to get high. If she wanted to do that she'd be better off boosting some vanilla extract or cooking sherry from the kitchen cupboard. "If you drink mouthwash it'll make you throw up."

Amanda twisted off the cap with a sly smile. "It's not mouthwash, Will."

It sure looked like mouthwash, Will thought, eyeing it warily. And the last thing Will wanted was to take some retching girl home in his Jeep.

Amanda dipped the tip of her index finger into the top of it and slowly sucked the liquid off. Then, her eyes still holding his, she dipped the same finger in and offered it to him by pressing it against his lips. "Have a taste."

Will inhaled. It didn't smell like mouthwash. It didn't smell like much of anything. He opened his lips and let her press her finger all the way into his mouth. He touched his tongue to the liquid. Felt the zing on his tongue. Definitely liquor. "What is it?" he asked. "Some sort of white lightning?" He'd never seen anything in the liquor cabinet at home that was blue.

"Vodka, with a dash of blue food coloring." Amanda lifted the little bottle to her lips and drank about a fourth of what was in there. "Want some?" She handed the bottle to him.

Will shook his head. "I'm okay." His dad would kill him if he drank and drove—it was the one rule his dad was hell-bent on enforcing, even in the wake of Mom's death. Besides, the last thing he needed was to wreck his Jeep or get hurt, as even a minor injury could put him out for the season.

Amanda took another sip then recapped the bottle and slid it into her shorts. She looked around to make sure everyone was watching—they pretty much were—then took Will's hand. "Let's go somewhere and make out."

Subtle, Will thought. Real subtle. But he let her drag him off into the woods that surrounded the gathering place next to the lake. "This all must seem so dull to you after growing up in Dallas," she said.

Will hated to break it to Amanda, but he didn't see a big difference. Sure, it was a little farther to the mall from Laramie, and there weren't nearly as many theaters or restaurants, but on the whole, from what he could see, the kids did pretty much the same things. Hang out. Play putt-putt and pool. Swim. See movies. Get something to eat. Besides, there wasn't any place he was really happy these days.

Evidently deciding they were far enough away from the others, Amanda stopped the forward trek and leaned against a tree. Keeping her grip on his hand, she dragged him closer. "Sometimes I am so bored," she whispered, and then she took his hand and laid it on her breast. She took her other hand and wrapped it around the back of his neck, guiding his head down to hers. "I just want to do something really wicked and wild and reckless!"

Will didn't really want the pressure of having to call and pay attention to her and see her all the time, but the feel of Amanda, so soft and warm and pliable, rubbing up against him—the sweet-hot taste of her—was too good to resist. He would do anything—anything—to be able to forget his mom dying and the mess his life was in. And being with Amanda this way, he learned swiftly, made him forget.

* * *

Kate's cell phone rang at three in the morning. Finding it where she'd left it, plugged in beside her bed, she picked it up and murmured a sleepy hello.

"Kate, honey, is that you?"

Kate's eyes flew open at the sound of her fiancée's voice. She sat up in bed, struggling to wake. Obviously he had gotten her e-mail asking him to call her much later—not this late—but hearing from him was better than not, especially since the last time they'd talked they'd exchanged words. Since then, he had apologized via e-mail for taking her dad's side and telling her to move out of Sam's. And she had apologized in a return message. But Kate knew she wouldn't feel that they had really made up all the way until they had talked again.

"Craig," she murmured happily, knowing if ever she had needed and wanted to hear his voice, it was now.

"I got your e-mail," Craig said, the smile in his voice as clear as the international connection. "Congratulations, honey. Winning the attention of the Graham Foundation is some coup."

Kate beamed at the pride in his voice. That was one thing she liked about Craig—unlike her parents, and now Sam, who had felt free to voice their doubts about what she was doing—Craig had always encouraged her heartily in her choice of careers. Kate leaned over and switched on her bedside lamp. Still basking in his praise, she sighed wistfully as she thought about the impromptu meeting that had taken her back to the hospital. "I just wish I could actually take them up on their offer to expand my grief counseling program to two other rural hospitals."

Craig paused, then clearly not understanding her point of view, said, "Why can't you?"

Kate shrugged and as she sat up above the covers, quickly

found herself shivering in the cool air blowing out of the vent above her bed. Kate clasped her bedcovers with one hand and pulled them up against her breasts. "Maybe because a little thing called our wedding and marriage just might get in the way."

Without hesitation, Craig empathized firmly. "I know how hard you've worked to create a program that will keep other families from suffering the way yours did after your brother died—how hard it was for you to get, and keep, funding. If this means even half of what I think it does to you, I think you should go for it."

Kate was tempted, especially when she thought of all the other families in crisis she could potentially help. But even as she considered it she knew she couldn't delay getting started on her future—her marriage to Craig—any more than she already had. Not if she wanted a family of her own. And she did. "You mean something to me, too, Craig," she said softly.

"Honey, I know that," Craig said gently. "Believe me, no one understands commitment to a cause greater than ourselves better than we military men. But I also know you've got to do what you've got to do," he said firmly. "And if that means waiting another six or seven months before we tie the knot, so you can use Graham Foundation money to expand your grief counseling program to two other rural hospitals, then I say do it."

Kate tensed, not sure why his willingness to sacrifice their own needs for the sake of her career, or his, suddenly rankled. In the past it had been one of the things she had loved most about him. "We're talking a minimum of a year here, Craig...maybe even longer..."

"Our love is strong enough to endure separations, Kate," Craig returned matter-of-factly. "It always has been."

"I don't want to wait anymore, Craig. I want to get married so we can finally be together all the time." She wanted to sleep by his side and make love every night. That wouldn't be possible when he was off flying missions or busy doing peacekeeping tours in hot spots around the world, but when he was stationed stateside it would be possible. And it was those very opportunities Kate didn't want to miss, certainly not for any career-oriented goals of her own.

"Honey, I know how you feel," Craig soothed. "I'm anxious to hold you in my arms, too."

Kate lowered her voice. "Are you?"

"Oh, yeah." Craig's voice was filled with a wealth of longing, both physical and emotional. His tone dropped a sexy notch. "You haven't forgotten I booked a room at the Mansion On Turtle Creek, have you?"

Kate closed her eyes dreamily. "No. Of course not." It was one of the most elegant hotels in all of Dallas and it would cost Craig a bundle, but it would be worth it, given the ultra-romantic homecoming and passionate reunion Kate envisioned for them.

"Good." Craig laughed softly, his anticipation evident. "Did you get that knock-'em-dead dress?" he teased.

Kate grinned, aware she had been building up his expectations on that score for months now. "You bet," she drawled. Besides being expensive as heck and designed by Jenna Lockhart, one of the hottest new clothing designers around, it was without a doubt the sexiest garment she had ever purchased in her life. Just thinking about the way it made her look had Kate feeling sensual, sexual and ready for action. She knew when Craig saw her in it he would quickly feel the same. And if not…she'd simply take off the dress and matching jacket and show him the equally expensive and to-die-for lingerie she'd bought to go under it.

"Just seven more days and I'll be there," Craig promised.

Kate closed her eyes. "I'm counting the hours, the days, the minutes…"

"Me, too, hon," Craig said, a smile back in his voice. "Listen, I gotta go. Love you."

Kate sighed and snuggled back under the covers. Before she knew it, all the waiting, all the loneliness, would be over. She just had to be strong a little longer. "I love you, too."

Chapter 10

Dinner over, dishes done, Kate was working on a counter proposal for the Graham Foundation that would allow her to implement two new grief counseling programs on an accelerated schedule that would not interfere with her wedding plans one bit, when the phone rang the next evening. She waited for Lewis or Kev, the only two boys home, to pick up one of the extensions. When they didn't, she caught it on the fourth ring. "Kate? Gus Barkley. Your dad would kill me if he knew I was calling you but I think maybe you better get over to the field house locker room."

"Why?" Kate demanded, alarmed at the concern in Gus's voice. The assistant football coach and friend of her father's for years was one of the most levelheaded men Kate knew. He wouldn't call her unless he had no other choice. "What's going on?"

"I'm not sure," Gus whispered on the other end of the line. "But I'm worried about your dad. Just get here as fast as you can, okay?"

"I'll be right there." Kate shut down her laptop, then grabbed her purse, cell phone and keys and dashed to the stairs. "Lewis—Kev—come here a minute!"

Within seconds, both heads popped over the banister. To Kate's dismay, the hyper-alert looks on their faces matched the terse, worried sound of her voice. Trying her best not to panic herself, or them, Kate looked them each in the eye and said calmly but firmly, "I've got to run over to the high school to do something for my dad. You two going to be okay here alone for a few minutes?"

They nodded. "Don't worry, Kate," Lewis reassured her when she hesitated. "I'll take care of Kev. He can come in my room and play video games with me."

"Thanks, guys. It means a lot, knowing I can count on you. You've got my cell phone number, Lewis?"

"It's on the bulletin board in the kitchen."

"Okay. Call me if anything comes up. I'll be back as soon as I can."

Her heart pounding, Kate drove the eight blocks to the high school. Cars were turning left and right out of the lot as the football team disbanded after evening practice. Knowing it had to be something serious for Gus to call her, she parked her car beside the stadium, made her way through the chain-link gate and headed for the field house. Gus was pacing around outside, hurrying the remaining kids along home, and watching for her. The moment he saw her, he made a beeline for her side. "Thanks for coming."

"What's going on?" Kate asked anxiously.

He wrapped a paternal arm around her shoulder and leaned down to whisper in her ear. "I think your dad's having chest pains."

Kate did her best not to panic. "Did you call an ambulance?"

"Are you kidding? He wouldn't care how long I've been

his assistant coach here, he'd have me fired. Not to mention that would be the end of our friendship. Besides, what if it's just indigestion, like he says?"

And what if it isn't, Kate thought, alarmed. "Did you tell my mom?"

"Just you. I didn't want to upset her if there was no cause. And I figured since you work at the hospital you'd know a little better what to do."

Kate had been trained in CPR, but that was little comfort to her now. "Where is he?" Kate asked quietly as they entered the field house. A couple kids came bursting out of the locker room and, nodding hello at Kate and Gus, headed for the exit.

Still guiding her down the hall, Gus spoke quietly into her ear. "He's in his office. The door's shut, but go on in. I'll be there as soon as I get rid of the rest of the team."

Not wanting to alarm any of the players, Kate did as Gus asked. She knocked once, let herself in, and shut the door after her. There were no windows in the room, and it took a moment for her eyes to adjust to the glare of the overhead fluorescent lighting. She dropped her bag onto a chair and moved toward him, not liking at all what she saw. Mike Marten was dressed in his usual burnt-orange coach's shirt, khaki shorts and hat, and he looked terrible. The air-conditioning was on full-blast, icy-cold air pouring from the vents, and he had unbuttoned the front placket on his shirt as far as he could, but he was still sweating profusely. His face was red and flushed. He had one hand pressed against his sternum, an uncapped bottle of water resting on his knee. With considerable effort, he lifted it to his lips and took a sip. "What are you doing here?" he growled from his perch on his desk.

Trying not to look as alarmed as she felt, Kate said, "Gus called me."

Mike let out a string of swearwords that blistered Kate's

ears and left no doubt how he felt about his assistant coach and best friend at that moment.

Ignoring Mike's temper, Kate said, "He's worried about you, Dad. And now that I see you, I am, too." *More than I can say.*

Mike sipped some more water and waved off Kate's concern. "It's nothing."

Kate touched his arm gently. It was cool and damp to the touch. "Let's have a doctor tell us that, okay? I want to take you to the emergency room right now."

Mike shrugged off her touch, glared at her. "I'm not going to the hospital, Kate."

"You're in pain."

"Damn right I am," Mike agreed, readily enough, still rubbing the spot just below his sternum. "I never should have eaten enchiladas for lunch."

"Is your ulcer acting up again?"

"That cleared up years ago. This is just acid indigestion, pure and simple." Mike wiped his brow with his hand. "I should have taken something for it earlier, but I didn't, and now I'm paying for it."

Kate studied her dad. "You really think this is heartburn?" she asked, not wanting to call in an ambulance unnecessarily any more than Mike wanted her to do so.

"Acid reflux," he corrected, handing over a prescription pill bottle for Kate's perusal. "Spicy foods, too much caffeine or acidic foods like tomatoes and jalapenos set it off. It feels like hell when it happens, but once the medicine gets to work, I'm okay."

Kate had to admit her dad was starting to look a lot better. "When did you take the medicine?"

"Ten, fifteen minutes ago."

There was a knock at the door, then Gus slipped inside. "Everyone's out of here." He shot Mike a concerned look.

Mike sent Gus an irritated look. "What were you thinking, calling Kate over here? Not that I don't think you should be out of Sam McCabe's house, anyway."

Kate tensed. "Dad…" Sick or not, she wasn't letting him run her life.

Mike looked at her, not the least bit apologetic. "Can't blame me for trying, Kate. You're making a mistake, getting involved with that man."

Kate spotted a white terry-cloth towel and handed it to her father. "Let's just worry about your problems for the moment. Did you tell John McCabe you were having trouble with your stomach again?"

"Who do you think called in this prescription for me?"

Kate glanced at the bottle, reading all the information she had skimmed over before. It was dated two weeks prior, ordered by the very recently retired John McCabe, and had no refills on it. "And he's not worried?"

Mike was silent.

"Dad," Kate reprimanded, feeling as if she had just grabbed a tiger by the tail because she and her dad disagreed on something.

Mike scowled. "Who died and made you my protector?"

Kate watched him loop the white towel around his neck and wipe his face. "Is that what you'd say to one of your players who needed medical help and refused to get it?"

"I did get it. I got the pills. I took one. Just not soon enough. Next time I'll know better than to eat enchiladas on a day that's been hotter than hades where my team doesn't perform worth squat."

Exasperated, Kate looked at Gus to see what he had to say. "It was a terrible practice," he confirmed.

Kate looked back at her father. He was still sipping water, but his color had returned to normal and he was no longer sweating. He did not seem to be in pain. "You're scaring me. You know that," Kate chided.

Mike shrugged his massive shoulders. "Then blame Gus. 'Cause he's the one who called you for no reason."

Kate and Gus exchanged looks. Though Gus was quiet, she could tell by the look in his eyes that he was still concerned. He just wouldn't dare say so to Mike. Kate turned back to her dad, wishing for once he weren't so darn bullheaded. "I want you to make an appointment with Luke Carrigan," she said quietly but firmly.

Mike scoffed. "That kid?'

"He's not a kid, dad, he's thirty-something, and he's a fine physician, John McCabe said so himself, otherwise he wouldn't have turned his practice and all his patients over to him."

Mike wiped his brow with the hem of his towel. "Okay, okay."

"Okay what?" Kate demanded.

"Okay." Mike sat up a little straighter and began buttoning the placket on his shirt. "I'll get in touch with him."

"Soon…if for no other reason than so he knows what's been going on with you," Kate insisted. "Your history with your ulcer and all that."

Mike stood, put his hands on the small of his back, and stretched. When he'd worked out the kinks, and he took his time about it, he reached over, grabbed his coach's cap and put it on his head. He tugged it low across his forehead, removed the towel from around his neck, set it aside and then looked at her. "You've spent too much time at the hospital, Kate. You're beginning to talk like a medical doctor, which you're not," he emphasized bluntly before softening slightly once again. "You should come back to the high school, where you belong, and be a counselor here again."

Kate didn't know whether to kiss him or throttle him.

She did know she was glad he was okay. "I'm glad you miss me, Dad. But I'm happy where I am. Now promise me," she pleaded, not caring if she had to beg. "You'll make an appointment to see Luke."

"Okay, okay." Mike gave up the argument if for no other reason than to get rid of her.

Kate stood on tiptoe and kissed his cheek. "I love you, you know that."

Mike nodded and turned away. Sentiment was not his thing. Kate knew her dad loved her dearly, despite all his gruffness, even though he had never come right out and said so, and generally pretended he was above all overt displays of affection.

Kate smiled at Gus. She suspected he was going to be getting heck from her dad for days to come about the way he'd panicked. "I gotta go. Thanks for calling me, Gus. And no matter how much bluster and bull he gives you, don't hesitate to call me again if this happens."

Gus nodded. Grinned. He turned to Mike. "Glad you're feeling better, Coach."

Mike responded by swearing, vigorously, again.

"Kate!" Sam yelled Saturday morning. "Come and get Kevin! I'm trying to work here."

Wincing at the degree of pique in Sam's voice, Kate rushed to the hall outside Sam's study. Sam was standing there, an irritated scowl on his face, a stack of jelly-smeared transparencies in his hand. He had already showered and shaved, and was dressed in olive-green khakis and a black polo shirt that emphasized his broad shoulders and expansive chest. Kevin slouched beside him, looking both guilty and hurt at the way he was being pushed away.

"I've got to finish this presentation and he needs some supervision," Sam continued brusquely, nodding at his son.

Kevin was still in his pajamas. He had finished his meal and surreptitiously left the table while Kate was busy getting breakfast for the other boys. Consequently, she hadn't had time to wipe the six-year-old's hands and face, and they were smeared with a sticky combination of chocolate milk and pancake syrup.

"I'll get him cleaned up," Kate promised.

Before she could take him by the hand, Kevin made a beeline for the dining room. He pushed aside the elegant satin covered chairs, getting syrup all over them, too, and climbed beneath the table, settling down where no one could easily get to him. Instead, they would have to coax him out.

Sam frowned at Kate as he took in her muted-rose sheath dress. "Why are you so dressed up?"

Realizing she was still holding her pearls in her hand, Kate fastened them around her neck as she patiently explained, "I've got a prenuptial meeting with our minister in thirty minutes."

Sam's glance narrowed. "Doesn't Craig have to be there for that, too?"

He sure should be, Kate thought. Shrugging at Sam, she replied, "My mom set it up. She's getting kind of antsy. Besides, Craig will be here next weekend and we'll both meet with Reverend Baxter then." Kate couldn't wait. It would mean her wedding preparations were officially under way.

"Then who is going to watch Kevin this morning?" Sam demanded, looking more annoyed than ever.

Kate gestured helplessly. "I thought maybe you—"

"Oh, no," Sam interrupted with a resolute shake of his handsome head. "I've got way too much work to do. Besides, that's why I hired you, remember? So you could take care of things like this for me? And I wouldn't have to worry about it."

"But you're here," Kate said a little desperately.

Sam shoved a hand through his short, sable brown hair. "I can't get anything done when he's underfoot. Besides, it's easy enough to see he needs some attention."

Yes, Kate thought, Kevin did need some attention. But he didn't need it from her. He needed—and wanted—it from Sam.

Realizing that wasn't going to happen, not this morning, anyway, Kate turned to Lewis. "Don't look at me," he said immediately. "I've got plans for the day. Josie and Wade are giving me my birthday present today, remember?"

Actually, Kate hadn't known about that.

"They're going to teach me all about the oil business," Lewis continued excitedly. "I get to ride to Houston in Wade's chopper, and visit a refinery, and go wildcatting for new oil with Josie, and even have dinner at the private club where all the Texas oil men and women like to eat. It's gonna be my best birthday present ever, and I won't be back until tomorrow afternoon."

Brad and Riley who'd come into the front hall outside Sam's study to see what all the commotion was about, made faces at each other. "Some birthday present," Brad muttered jealously.

"Yeah, sounds like geek city to me," Riley agreed.

Sam looked at them sternly. "Guys—"

Too excited about the weekend ahead to care, Lewis blew off their teasing with a shrug. "They're just jealous."

You got that right, Kate thought, taking in the resentful looks on Brad's and Riley's faces. They wanted some of that special attention, too.

"Oh, who the heck cares!" Will shouldered his way through the group loosely assembled outside Sam's study. "I'm going to football practice." Will shot an angry look at Sam—who had come down on him, hard, the night before, for coming in an hour after curfew. Kate had been in bed by

then, but she had heard bits of it, and the confrontation between Sam and his oldest son hadn't been pleasant.

"Which is just one more place to get yelled at for no reason," Will finished bitterly.

Sam clamped a hand on Will's shoulder, halting him in
midstride. "I had a reason for reprimanding you last night
and you know it. Furthermore, I want you back here as soon
as practice is over, and you're to give me the keys to your
Jeep the moment you get here. Understood?"

"Dad..."

"I mean it, Will. You're on restriction the rest of the day.
It will help you to remember to keep track of the hour and
come in before curfew the next time. Got it?"

"Got it," Will said sullenly. He shot an angry look at Kate,
then turned back to Sam. "Can I go now? If I'm late—" he
pointed at Kate "—her dad is going to ream me out but good."

"Go," Sam said.

The phone on Sam's desk began to ring. He swore softly
at the interruption on his business-only phone line. "I've
got to get that. Meanwhile, someone needs to keep an eye
on Kevin. Got it?" Not waiting for a reply, he stepped back
inside his study and shut the door behind him.

Kate shot a glance at Kevin, who was still crouched beneath the dining-room table. There weren't enough hours in
the day to tend to the emotional needs of all the kids, even
with Sam's help. And that she didn't have. She turned back
to Brad and Riley. "How about it, guys? Can one of you help
me out here for an hour or so?"

They were already backing out the door after Will. "Sorry,
Kate, we got stuff to do."

"What stuff?" Kate asked, following them suspiciously.
The boys' telephone had been ringing off the hook all morning. Different girls every time. All of them asking to speak
to either Brad or Riley.

"We've got big plans for tonight," Brad explained, backing out onto the front porch.

"But you will be here for dinner."

"Why?" Riley demanded.

"Because it would be a good chance for you to eat with your dad," Kate said.

At the thought of some "quality time" with Sam, Brad and Riley perked up immediately. "He actually said he's going to have dinner with us tonight?" Brad asked, looking pleased.

"Well, no," Kate allowed reluctantly. But she was going to do her level best to see that it happened. "But he's working at home today and tomorrow and—"

"Forget it. It'll never happen," Riley interrupted with a disappointed scowl.

"Isn't that the truth," Brad said morosely as he fished his car keys out of his pants' pocket. "Besides, Riley and I already have plans to have dinner out tonight with some…er, um…friends."

"Girlfriends?" Kate asked as she stepped out onto the front porch with them.

Brad's wicked grin widened as he contemplated their secret for a moment longer. "We *could* tell you. But then we'd have to kill you."

"Yeah, what me and Brad are doing is top secret," Riley agreed with a mischievous smirk.

Oh, Lord, Kate thought, this was all they needed, given the grumpy mood their father was in. Hoping to put on the brakes, at least a little, she asked, point-blank, "Is whatever you're doing going to get you in trouble?"

"Don't worry," Riley replied breezily.

Now that was a tall order, Kate thought, and one she couldn't possibly keep, given the looks of choirboy innocence suddenly on their handsome faces.

"We're not going to be breaking any of Dad's rules. And

we will be home by curfew," Brad emphasized sincerely as they dashed down the steps to Brad's Mustang.

As Kate watched Brad and Riley drive away, she found their promise small comfort. Those two boys were definitely up to something. She just didn't know what. And at this point, she wasn't sure she really wanted to know.

"You're late," Joyce said with a frown as Kate and Kevin rushed into Reverend Baxter's office some fifteen minutes past the scheduled time.

Given the way Kate's morning had been going, she was lucky to get there at all. "I know, Mom, and I'm sorry," Kate apologized hastily. "I didn't realize Kevin was going to be coming with me, and we had to get him ready, too." Unfortunately, Kevin hadn't been very cooperative, so dressing him and trying to get him cleaned up had been difficult to say the least.

"I thought Sam was going to be home this morning."

"He is, but he's also tied up on some important business calls." Kate settled Kevin onto the sofa between her and her mother and opened his plastic case of toys. Kate looked up with a smile, reading the look in her mother's eyes, the one that said she shouldn't be working for Sam and staying under his roof in the first place. "But it's going to be fine. Kevin brought his snap-together building blocks with him, so he and I are going to play quietly while we talk. Right, Kev?"

Kevin looked at the adults in the room forlornly and did not reply. Joyce and Reverend Baxter both shot concerned looks at Kate. Clearly, they wanted to know what had been going on to make Kevin look so dejected and upset. "It's a long story," Kate said evasively, not about to get into *that* in front of Kevin. Feeling as if she had been operating on maximum speed all week, she continued breathlessly, "Why don't we just get started?"

"Good idea, Kate. And, as it happens, we have a surprise for you." Reverend Baxter picked up the receiver and punched a button on his phone as Kate took some blocks from Kevin's box and fit them together. "What's going on?" she asked.

Joyce and Reverend Baxter just smiled as he put the receiver to his ear. Seconds later, Reverend Baxter said hello, then pushed another button on the base of the phone. "Kate, honey?" Craig's voice filled the room. "Are you there?"

Kate broke out in a smile. Finally, a surprise that morning that she liked! "Craig! Hi!" Kate bubbled over with delight. This was great. Now Craig could be "there" with them, too, just the way he should have been.

"I'd like to introduce you to my base chaplain," Craig continued cheerfully from the other end of the international connection as Kevin took his blocks and got down onto the floor to play with them there.

The next several minutes were devoted to a four-way discussion of how to best incorporate military and civilian traditions into their marriage ceremony. Craig wanted to wear his full dress uniform. He also wanted the saber ceremony at the conclusion of the church service. "Kate, are you in agreement with all that?" the base chaplain asked.

"Yes." Kate smiled as she reached over and squeezed her mother's hand, then continued speaking into the phone. "I am. I can't think of a better way to start off our marriage than for Craig and I to pass under the arch of military sabers." It was romantic and exciting, and very much in keeping with what Craig was all about.

"Another nice touch," Reverend Baxter added, "albeit a strictly civilian one is to include, along with the saying of the traditional vows, a more personal testament from Craig and Kate."

"You mean…you want Craig and me to say something

about how we feel about each other?" Kate suggested, surprised.

"Yes, exactly!" Reverend Baxter beamed. "It can be as formal or informal as you like, but I think it's wonderful for the bride and groom to put their feelings into words at such an important time, and then share it with everyone who is there to witness their marriage. It adds a very personal and special touch. And it's quite romantic, too."

"I think it sounds wonderful!" Joyce said happily.

Unfortunately, Craig didn't share Kate's mother's enthusiasm. "I don't know, Reverend," Craig hesitated. "That doesn't really sound like something I would do."

To Kate's relief, Reverend Baxter did not look either surprised or disappointed by Craig's reluctance. "You don't have to decide today," he soothed. "It's just something to think about."

"But what would we say?" Craig interrupted. To Kate's embarrassment, he was beginning to sound a little testy and defensive. "I mean…I could say I love her," Craig continued uncooperatively, "but wouldn't that be kind of lame?"

No, Kate thought, beginning to get a little irked and a lot embarrassed by Craig's recalcitrance. *It wouldn't be kind of lame. It would be sweet and wonderful and romantic.* But obviously Craig didn't see it that way.

"It doesn't have to be anything overtly mushy," Reverend Baxter stated. "It could be a simple recounting of the day you fell in love with Kate, or the moment you asked her to marry you, or the moment you knew you *wanted* to marry her. You could read a poem. Cite a brief passage in a book, or even from a movie that has particular meaning to the two of you. It's just a way of personalizing the ceremony, to make it uniquely about you, as well as to allow the guests to share in the very special love and affection you two have for each other."

"Well, I don't think I can do it," Craig said grimly on the other end of the phone connection, digging in stubbornly. "I wouldn't know what to say or where to begin."

Heat started in Kate's throat and moved up into her cheeks.

"It's not like people don't know how we feel about each other," Craig continued defensively. "Of course we love each other. Otherwise we wouldn't be getting married. Beyond that, there's nothing else to say."

Silence fell. Joyce exchanged uneasy looks with Reverend Baxter. Kate was so embarrassed and hurt by Craig's unromantic attitude, she wanted to crawl under a chair and stay there. "Maybe Craig and I should talk about this alone," she said, trying to sound cheerful.

"Good idea!" the base chaplain boomed on the other end.

"Very well. Meanwhile," Reverend Baxter said, "as long as we have you both on the line, we still need to set a date…"

Chapter 11

"Well, that couldn't have gone any worse," Kate said, excruciating moments later after she and Kev had said goodbye to her mother—who had stayed behind to talk to Reverend Baxter.

Kev looked over at her wordlessly from his side of the passenger seat. Clearly, Kate thought, he didn't understand a lot of what had been discussed in the five-person telephone conference, but he knew enough to realize that the end of the discussion had been full of tension, much of which had been caused by Craig. Only six, Kevin also seemed to sense that Kate, who'd gone into the meeting feeling frazzled, was now more upset than ever.

"Yes, I am upset, but it's nothing for you to worry about," Kate explained, smiling at him. She reached over and patted his knee, "I am just having a really really bad day." She switched on the ignition and turned on the air conditioner to full-blast. As she leaned over to help Kev with his seat belt, the cell phone in her purse began to ring.

"Probably Craig, calling to apologize," she said. Which, given the difficult way Craig had just behaved, he really needed to do. "Hello?"

"Kate! It's Jenna. I'm glad I caught you."

Hoping this at least was going to be good news, Kate said, "Hi, Jenna. What's up?"

"I finished the wedding gown I think may be just what you are looking for. I'm booked solid for appointments all afternoon, but if you want to come over to the boutique now, and take a look, maybe try it on, I can fit you in. Otherwise, we'll have to make it sometime next week."

This may be just what I need to turn my day around. "I'm just a few blocks away, Jenna, but I've got Kevin with me—"

"No problem," Jenna interrupted cheerfully. "He can play with Alexandra's toys out in the showroom, if he likes."

Jenna had the dress waiting for Kate when she arrived, and to Kate's bliss, it was everything Jenna had said it was. Even on the hanger, it looked perfect. Kate couldn't wait to try it on. "Kev, you want to come back to the fitting room with Jenna and me and watch me try on the dress?"

Kev looked at her expressionlessly, then said abruptly, "I'm hungry."

Kate's pleasure at hearing Kevin actually articulate his needs out loud—something he could do but usually chose not to these days—was muted by the difficulty of his request.

"Oh, dear," Jenna said, looking over at Kate. "Food is the one thing that I don't have and I don't allow in the shop. Expensive merchandise, you know."

"It's okay." Kate knelt to talk to Kev. She knew she could handle this. Besides, trying on the dress would not take long at all. But she did so want to try on this dress, and Jenna had made it clear this was the only time Kate could do so until next week.

Kate looked into Kevin's eyes and told him softly, "You have been so patient this morning, Kevin, and I appreciate it so much. Thank you."

Kevin's lower lip shot out. He seemed to know what was coming next.

"I promise you, it's just going to take a couple of minutes for me to try on this dress. And then I'll take you to any restaurant in town that you want to go to, and you can have whatever you want for lunch, okay? But first I do have to try on this dress," Kate said firmly, letting him know with a glance there was no debating that. "Now, do you want to come back with Jenna and me?"

Kevin refused to answer Kate's question. Instead, he walked over to the child-size table and chairs Jenna had set up in the corner of the showroom. He sat and picked up a stuffed dinosaur and a toy car and, ignoring both her and Jenna, began to play.

Kate got his attention long enough to show him where she was going to be—right around the corner and down the short hallway to the fitting room—if he needed her, and then went on with Jenna. Hurriedly, she shimmied out of her dress and with Jenna's help stepped into the bridal gown.

"Oh, wow," Jenna said as Kate stepped up on the pedestal.

"Wow is right," Kate said, spinning around and gazing at herself in the three-panel mirror. "You are right," Kate said breathlessly. "This is absolutely the dress for me." The off-the-shoulder gown was spectacularly beautiful. It had a closely fitted, Alençon bodice beaded with pearls, layers of English-net skirting which was also trimmed with Alençon and pearls, long, closely fitted sleeves, and a detachable cathedral train. It made her look and feel as elegant and feminine as she had always wanted to look and feel on her wedding day.

Jenna grinned, delighted. "I thought it would be just the

thing. Let's try on a few headpieces so you'll get the full effect."

She handed Kate a headpiece trimmed with Alençon and pearls, and a long tulle veil. "Now it's really perfect," Kate sighed, content.

Jenna was already reaching for another. "Let's try on a few more, just so you can see how different they all look."

They tried on several different styles of tiaras, with both short and long veils. All were contenders, as far as Kate was concerned. Then they tried a picture hat. "Not me," Kate said firmly as she studied her reflection in the mirror. "Not at all." Even though it did go with the dress and conjure up visions of a beautiful English garden.

"How about a simple floral wreath, or better yet, a little baby's breath on a comb?" Jenna asked, holding up both for Kate's perusal.

Kate had just put a wreath of white satin flowers in her hair when the front door to the boutique slammed. Loudly. Kate and Jenna looked at each other in alarm. "Kevin," they both said at once. And then seconds later Sam McCabe came charging in.

He was breathing hard. His face was all red, his eyes accusing.

"What are you doing here?" Kate gasped, her hand automatically going to her throat.

Sam stared at her for a long, uncomfortable moment, the set of his mouth as hard and uncompromising as his eyes. "I might ask the same question of you," he said, very coldly taking her in from head to toe.

Kate flushed, her heart knocking wildly in her chest. She didn't know what was going on with Sam, exactly. She did know, from the way he was looking at her, that she was at the center of it.

A muscle clenching in his jaw, Sam looked at Jenna. "Do

you mind if Kate and I have a moment alone? That is, if she can spare a moment when she's obviously so busy trying on wedding dresses."

"Um, sure." Jenna looked as confused as Kate by Sam's sudden appearance and deeply sarcastic tone. "I'll just go out in the showroom with Kevin."

Sam grimaced. Turning back to Kate, he gave her another sharp, unforgiving look, before saying to Jenna. "He's not out there."

"What?" Kate and Jenna said in unison, stunned, disbelieving.

"He's at Isabelle Buchanon's bakery, finishing a peanut butter and jelly sandwich and a chocolate shake," Sam informed them grimly.

Kate and Jenna exchanged uneasy glances before looking back at Sam. "How do you know that?" Kate climbed down off the pedestal on shaking legs.

"Because Isabelle just called me to come get him!" Sam shouted furiously, towering over her. He leaned down until the two of them were nose to nose. "Isabelle couldn't figure out how Kevin got there, but she knew I would never let him go wandering around town alone. So, figuring something was wrong, she phoned the house to let me know where he was. Fortunately, she kept him with her until I got there, and she is going to continue to keep him there until I go back for him!"

"Oh, my word." Kate covered her face with her hands, thunderstruck. Kevin had never wandered off before. What had he been thinking? What had she been thinking! He'd said he was hungry! She knew what a tough morning he'd had. That he was unlikely to come to her—or anyone else—with any complaint. Why hadn't she anticipated something such as this might happen? Why hadn't she absolutely insisted he come back to the fitting room with her and Jenna, or better yet, put off trying on the dress until some later time?

Jenna looked at Kate and Sam uneasily. "You know what? I think I'll just let you talk this out alone." Jenna backed out of the room. She had a panicked, remorseful look on her face.

"You do that," Sam muttered. He turned back to Kate, fury etched in his face.

Guilt closed like a vise around her heart. She couldn't believe she'd lost track of Sam's youngest, even for a moment. Kate had never felt lower, or more inept, in her life. Moving closer yet, she whispered helplessly, "I am so sorry, Sam." She knew she had given Sam one hell of a scare, and obviously let down Kevin, too. "Kev was supposed to be playing with the toys in the showroom. I thought—"

"And I thought I could trust you!" Sam stormed right back.

"You can!" Kate countered, hurt. Surely Sam could see this was a most unusual circumstance, one that would never ever happen again. But apparently not.

"Like hell I can!" he said.

Tears filled Kate's eyes as she realized how completely and utterly she had failed both Kevin and Sam, in allowing this to happen. "It won't happen again," she repeated firmly. Damn it all. She wouldn't let it.

"You're absolutely right it won't," Sam agreed, dark eyes flashing. "You're fired."

Short of chasing after Sam in the wedding dress she was now determined to buy, and causing even more of a sensation than she had by losing track of Kevin, there was nothing Kate could do but watch him leave. As soon as the boutique door slammed, Jenna came rushing into the fitting room.

"Oh, Kate, I am so sorry."

"It's not your fault," Kate said as steadily as she could. "It's mine." She'd gotten so caught up in her desire to have a wonderful wedding, to find the perfect gown, the one that would make her feel the way she wanted to feel, she had lost track of what was important.

"Let me help you get out of that dress," Jenna said.

"By the way, I do want this dress," Kate said as she slipped on the dress she had been wearing when she'd walked in.

"You don't have to make a decision today," Jenna said evenly. "Especially after what just happened. You can think about it."

"Nope." When it came to her wedding, Kate had done far too much thinking and procrastinating as it was. She had spent too many years engaged, waiting for the "big day" to finally arrive. "I'm buying it today. And I'm purchasing the very first veil I tried on, too." Determinedly, Kate wrote out a check.

"You'll need to come back for a fitting," Jenna cautioned. "We have got to get the hem right."

Kate nodded. "I'll call your assistant next week and schedule a time. Meanwhile—" Kate slung her bag over her shoulder "—I've got to talk to Sam."

Jenna sighed. "Lots of luck."

"Thanks," Kate said. Judging by the look on Sam's face when he'd left, she was going to need it.

Sam was in his study when Kate returned. Kevin was curled up next to Sam on the leather sofa, sound asleep, a stuffed animal held tight in his arms. Music from Will's stereo drifted down from the third floor.

Seeing Kate, Sam eased himself away from the sleeping Kevin and walked over to his desk. He picked up a check and headed straight for Kate. Taking her by the elbow, he led her into the front hall and shut the door behind him. "Here's your check." He shoved it into her hand. "I'll expect you and your things out of here in the next ten minutes."

Kate's jaw dropped open in astonishment. She knew Sam

was angry with her. He had every right to be. She also knew this was something they could overcome. "At least give me a chance to make it up," she pleaded quietly, determined to not let her stay with them end the way every other household manager's had—in dismal failure.

Sam quirked a sardonic brow in her direction. "Why? Losing Kev once wasn't excitement enough?"

Kate stiffened her spine indignantly. "I didn't lose him. He slipped away from me. And I told you, it won't happen again. I'll make sure of that."

In Sam's study, the phone rang. Sam swore beneath his breath. "Do something about that—" he pointed to the third floor "—while I get the phone in there."

Hoping she could get there before the pounding rock music woke Kev, Kate headed for the stairs. She raced up first one flight, then the next and rapped on the door. "Will! Turn it down, would you?"

No response.

Which wasn't surprising, Kate thought. He probably couldn't hear a thing over the thudding bass. "Will!" she knocked again, pushed open the door and gasped at what she saw. Kate backed out into the hall.

Seconds later, Will stormed out of his bedroom, still tugging on his shirt. "What the hell's your problem?" he shouted. "Don't you know how to knock!"

Behind them, Sam came dashing up the stairs, his expression grim. He glared at Kate. "I thought I told you to make him turn that down!"

"I did," Kate said.

Sam shouldered past Will, and shoved open the door to his room. Sam backed out just as quickly as Kate had. He turned to glare at her. *You could have warned me,* his look said.

Sam turned back to Will. "Turn off the music—now!"

Will went inside. The music ended. He stepped back out

into the hall, Amanda clinging to his arm and hiding behind him. She ducked her head, avoiding eye contact with the adults. "I've got to go," she murmured to Will. Then leaving him to face Sam and Kate alone, Amanda dashed down the stairs. Neither Kate nor Sam made a move to stop her.

"What the hell was going on here?" Sam demanded of Will.

Will was silent.

Sam looked at Kate. "What exactly did you walk in on?"

Kate swallowed. "I think you should ask Will."

"I'm asking you. What just happened here?"

"I walked in on Will and Amanda."

"And?"

Kate turned bright red despite herself.

"We were making out, okay?" Will said, clenching his jaw.

Kate looked at him. "It was more than that, Will." She wasn't going to let him pretend it wasn't.

Sam looked very unhappy. "This is just great, Will. Exactly how I want to spend my Saturday afternoon."

"Don't blame me. It's all her fault. She's the one who barged in without knocking." Will pointed a finger at Kate.

"I did knock," Kate said. "You couldn't hear over the music."

"Well, then next time don't walk in!" Will shouted.

"That'll do, Will," Sam said sternly, commanding his eldest son's attention once again. "What were you thinking, disobeying me? You know you're on restriction."

"You said I couldn't go anywhere," Will protested heatedly. "You didn't say that no one could come to see me."

Sam seemed to be counting backward from ten in an effort to hang on to his temper. "Leaving that pathetic excuse aside for the moment—although I assure you I do plan to come back to it—you know we have rules about girls in the

bedrooms. We don't allow it here. Ever. In addition, you
know I expect you to be responsible for your actions, Will—"

"It's not like Amanda and I intended for this to happen,"
Will interrupted, clearly irked they had to discuss this at all.

Unable to keep quiet a moment longer, Kate said, "Will,
you barely know her!"

Will glared at Kate. "*That* would be none of your business, Kate," he said with barely contained fury. "And why
don't you lay off the Good Mother routine."

Sam grabbed Will by the shoulder. "All right. That's
enough. You apologize to Kate. Now, Will."

"Sorry." He didn't sound it.

Kate knew enough to back off.

Silence fell between them. Sam looked at Kate. "Maybe
you should go downstairs and wait for me there."

Kate didn't need to be told twice. She fled.

Miraculously, Kevin was still asleep on the sofa in Sam's
study. She spread an afghan over him, then went into the
living room to wait for Sam. He came down fifteen minutes
later, no longer dressed in the polo shirt and khakis he'd had
on earlier in the day, but in a suit and tie. As if on cue, the
limo pulled up out front. Kate looked from it to him. Still
looping a tie around his neck, Sam said, "I've got to go to
Dallas. One of the execs from California is stuck at the Dallas airport on an unexpectedly long layover and he wants to
get together. I'm going to the Admiral's Club to meet him."

Kate's eyes widened. "Why are you telling me?"

"Why do you think?" Sam shook his head in exasperation. "Because you have to watch Kevin."

Kate didn't know whether to be relieved she hadn't been
booted out, after all, or furious at his audacity. "I thought I
was fired," she reminded him less than politely.

"You are. But you're also hired back until I can find your
replacement." Sam peered at her from beneath lowered

brows. "You think you can manage this without losing my son again?"

"I think, if you mention that one more time, I'm going to deck you."

Sam almost—almost—smiled as he regarded her with something akin to respect. Clearly, sometime in the last few minutes he had come to the conclusion he needed her. Kate wasn't certain how she felt about that. But it was better than being considered extraneous and a royal pain, that was for sure. "What about Will?" Kate continued after a moment, beginning to panic. Given the morning they'd had, she was not entirely sure she was up to this alone.

"He's now grounded for a whole week," Sam reported matter-of-factly, quickly taking Kate for granted once again. "He's not to leave the house for anything but scheduled activities."

Kate folded her arms in front of her. She was convinced this was not going to be as easy as Sam thought it was. "Does he know that?"

Sam looked her square in the eye. "Yes."

"Did you talk to him about the rest of it?" Because she sure couldn't!

"Briefly," Sam conceded. The evasive look on Sam's face told Kate that Sam didn't intend to bring it up again. Will needed a long talk with his dad about that, and probably a lot of other things, as well.

Kate sighed, her frustration with both Sam and the situation mounting. "Look, Sam—"

"Not now, Kate." Sam grabbed his briefcase and hurried toward the door.

Feeling more like a harried spouse than the temporary household manager she was, Kate followed him to the door. She knew this wasn't really her problem, but it still felt as if it was. Which meant that everyone was right and she was getting too emotionally involved in the situation. All she knew for sure was that she was worried about all of them, especially Will and Kevin. And if Sam ever let himself stop to really think about what was going on she knew he would be, too. "When will you be back?" she asked, wishing like heck he wasn't going at all.

Sam shrugged. "I don't know. Late, probably," he said. Then he was gone.

"I need to go running. Are you gonna let me or not?" Will asked.

Kate looked up from the stack of library books on her lap. She glanced at the clock. "Now? Will, it's ten o'clock!"

"So?" Will sat to put on his athletic shoes.

"So, isn't that a little late to go jogging?"

Will shrugged. He pushed to his feet and began going through his stretches like the seasoned athlete he was as he continued to chide Kate defiantly. "It isn't going to make any difference to your dad, the football coach from hell. He wants us all running two to six miles a day, in addition to our regular practices. I didn't get mine in yet." Finished with his calf muscles, he began his hamstring stretches as he waited for her to make a decision.

"I don't know about this, Will," Kate said, unsure whether he was pulling a fast one on her or not. She knew her dad wanted the kids on his team to run daily—it was the best way for the players to condition themselves to the heat. But Will had had all day to do this. Instead he'd sulked in his room, refusing the dinner she had made him, Kevin and herself, and playing his stereo much too loud. "Your dad isn't home and you're supposed to be grounded." And she doubted Sam would appreciate a call from her about something like this.

"Fine." Will abruptly stopped limbering up and glared at Kate. "Then you call your dad and explain to him why I can't run tonight. Because I'm sure as hell not going to—he'd kick me off the team for sure if I did that."

Will was probably right about that, Kate thought. Her father was not one to accept excuses. "You promise me this isn't a ruse?" She looked Will straight in the eye. "That all you're going to do is go out and run and then come straight home?"

Will shook his head and looked away for a very long moment. Finally he turned back to her and said with a sardonic smirk, "I'm not going to be having sex tonight, Kate, if that's what you're worried about."

Unprepared for the audacity of his remark, Kate sucked in a breath.

Happy he'd shocked her into silence, for the moment, anyway, Will shot Kate another disrespectful look, than headed out at a clip. The door slammed after him. Kate had no sooner picked up her book of love poetry again when she heard a car motor in the driveway. She went to the window, hoping to see Sam's limo. Instead, she noticed Brad's Mustang. As soon as he cut the motor, Brad and Riley vaulted out of it and stormed toward the house.

As Brad tromped furiously into the soft yellow glow of the porch lights, a chuckling Riley hard on his heels, Kate blinked at Brad in astonishment. "What in the world happened to you?"

Chapter 12

"What does it look like?" Brad grumbled, stomping past Kate. "I got lipsticked and perfumed by the girls, that's what!"

No joke, Kate thought, noting Brad, literally reeking of a nauseating mixture of perfumes, had been covered from head to toe with all colors of lipstick. She followed him to the kitchen. "Why would they do that?" she asked as Brad marched over to the sink and began splashing water on his face, making a mess all over the floor and counter, and doing little to get the color off his face.

"How would I know?" Brad scrubbed a dishtowel across his face, then bent to look at his reflection in the stainless-steel side of the toaster. He groaned, realizing all he'd done was make more of a mess of his face. "What's wrong with this stuff? It isn't coming off at all!"

"You're going to need a face cream to remove it. I'll go get some. Just wait here." Kate dashed down the hall, past the laundry room and into her bedroom suite. Returning moments later with tissues and a jar of facial cleanser, she handed both over to Brad.

"Is this stuff going to come out of my clothes?" Brad asked anxiously.

Kate nodded. "I'll show you how to take care of it."

"Just in case it happens again." Riley ribbed his brother mercilessly, chuckling.

Brad stopped painting his face with cleanser to glare at Riley.

Kate gave Riley a look, wordlessly telling him to cool it. "Because proper laundering techniques are something every successful bachelor needs to know," Kate corrected, playing peacemaker as she sank onto a kitchen stool. "Now start at the beginning and tell me what happened."

"Well, Brad had three dates tonight with three different girls," Riley began, raiding the fridge.

"Wait a minute. What did you have to do with any of this?" Kate asked Riley.

Riley grinned mischievously. "I helped him end a couple of them. I also ran interference for him when necessary, 'cause there are always glitches whenever you're doing anything this complicated, and I'm pretty good at thinking on my feet. Besides—" Riley shrugged "—this was a good way for Brad to show me how it's done 'cause I'm going to be dating in a year or so, too."

Kate shook her head, wondering where these guys came up with these lame-brained ideas.

"It's not like the dates were at the same time," Brad complained, anticipating what Kate was about to say as he tissued off the cream on his face. "I scheduled them one right after another."

"But the girls didn't like that," Kate presumed dryly as

Riley dumped salsa and Velveeta cheese into a bowl, and put it into the microwave to heat.

"I guess not," Brad replied sarcastically. "Because all three of them—Rose Aldridge, Anna Lisa Kennerly and Martina Wilson—jumped me behind the Armadillo putt-putt golf course and went at it. By the time I could come up for air, it was too late. I looked and smelled like this."

"Well, I hate to say it," Kate said sternly as Riley got the *chili con queso* dip out of the microwave, stirred it together and poured it on some crispy tortilla chips, "but you probably brought this on yourself, Brad, by messing with those girls' feelings in the first place."

"Hey! I didn't do anything to them," Brad protested as Riley got out two bottles of root beer and shoved one at Brad.

Kate looked at Brad sternly. "Rose and Martina and Anna Lisa probably feel like you led them on. And they were trying to teach you a lesson to not do it again."

Brad plucked at his lipstick-smeared shirt in disgust. "Couldn't they just have refused to date me?"

Kate watched him rub off most of the makeup and the gobs of cleanser. "I suspect that's coming, too," she said mildly.

"Great," Brad said, frowning all the more.

"Well, as fun as this has been, I've had enough entertainment for one evening." Riley handed over what was left of the chips and *queso* to his brother. "I'm going on to bed." Yawning, he exited the kitchen.

Brad grabbed the snack and a soda and started to walk off, too. Kate put a hand on his shoulder. "We still need to talk." Technically, Sam should be doing it. But since he wasn't here, and she was the one in charge, it fell to her. Sighing unenthusiastically, Brad shot Kate a look and sat. "Why do you want more than one date a night?" Kate asked matter-of-factly.

Brad shrugged and kicked back in his chair. Abruptly appearing as confident in his ability to *attract* girls as Brad

Pitt or Robert Redford, he munched on a handful of tortilla chips. "If you date one girl and then she leaves you, you're screwed. But if you have another girlfriend already waiting in the wings, it doesn't matter if she leaves you because you can just go on to the next one."

"What do you think your mom would've thought about the way you've been behaving?" Kate asked after a moment.

A mixture of grief and guilt flashed across Brad's face. Self-consciously he turned his glance away and admitted in a low, rueful tone, "She probably would have told me to treat the girls the way I wanted them to treat me. She was always big on the Golden Rule." Silence fell between them. Kate kept looking at Brad. Finally he looked back at her, too. "You want me to apologize to those girls, don't you?" Brad asked reluctantly.

"It's up to you." Kate shrugged, knowing Brad was old enough to make his own decisions about this, and then live with the consequences. "Just remember. Laramie is a small town. There's only a finite number of girls to date in the first place. You don't want to alienate them all with your Casanova antics. You live here now."

Brad let out a long, weary breath. "All right." He pushed to his feet with a great deal of drama. "I'll start making the rounds with my apologies tomorrow. Meanwhile—" he lifted his arm to his face and sniffed deeply of the nauseating mixture of perfumes "—I have *got* to take a shower."

Sam looked for Kate the moment he walked into the house that night. She was in her bedroom suite. The door was open. She was dressed in shorts and a loose-fitting cotton shirt that ended just above her navel. She had kicked off her sandals and was stripping the sheets off her bed. He paused in the doorway, not wanting to intrude, knowing they had to talk. Unable to help but appreciate how pretty she looked, even when she was obviously dead tired, he lounged in the doorway and waited until she looked up. "Did you give Will permission to go jogging?"

"Yes." She paused, the conflict she'd felt about that on her face. She met his glance, one adult to another. "I wasn't sure what to do, so I let him go."

Sam knew, in her position, he would have been hard pressed not to do the same. If Will was going to play football, he needed to be in the best possible physical shape. "How long was he gone?"

Kate gathered the sheets into a ball and tossed them into the laundry basket at the foot of the bed. "About two hours," she said.

"Twice the normal time."

Kate nodded. As she leaned across the bed to grab the pillows, her blouse rode up, giving him an unwanted glimpse of her midriff. Straightening, she turned to look at him. "I would've gone out to look for him but I couldn't leave Kev. He was asleep. And then there was a small crisis with Brad and Riley." Briefly she explained how his second oldest son had come to receive a modern, female version of tarring and feathering. "Anyway," Kate continued as she removed the cases from the pillows, "by the time I got done dealing with that, Will was slipping back in."

"I know." Sam frowned, thinking about the unsatisfactory nature of their too short conversation, and the nagging feeling that Will was still as defiant as ever, beneath his surface cooperation. "I just talked to him for a minute out in the driveway."

Still holding a pillow clasped in front of her like a shield, Kate paused and bit her lip. "Was I wrong to let him go?" She searched Sam's eyes. "Do you think he was up to something tonight?"

"I don't know." Sam sighed. "When my limo turned onto

the street next to this one, there was a car full of teenagers. It sped off pretty quickly. When we got a little closer to the house, I saw Will jogging up the driveway."

Kate lifted a speculative brow. "Coincidence?"

Sam shrugged. He didn't want to accuse Will unfairly any more than he wanted either himself or Kate to be played for fools. And like it or not, since they were both working to keep watch over his kids at the moment, he and Kate had to cooperate and share information over things such as this in the same way that he and Ellie used to. "Will'd obviously been running. He was drenched in sweat. But he also smelled like he had just used a heck of a lot of peppermint breath spray and I've never known Will to use breath spray before a run."

"You're sure it was the spray and not a mint?"

Sam nodded grimly, remembering. "I saw the little aerosol can in his hand." He had used it and tucked it into the pocket of his shorts just as Sam caught up with him.

"You don't think he was drinking, do you?"

Sam sighed. Again, he just didn't know. Times like this made him think he was not cut out to be a single parent and never would be. "Will looked and acted sober."

"But you're still worried about him, aren't you?" Kate said, shooting him a concerned look as she grabbed a clean pillowcase and slipped it onto her pillow.

"Yeah, I am," Sam said.

"Then that makes two of us," Kate said. She shook her head and sat on the edge of her bed, her bare feet tangled in the rumpled blankets on the floor. "Especially since a lot of this is my fault."

"Why would you think that?" Sam asked.

Kate sighed and shoved a hand through the mussed layers of her hair. "I haven't been able to establish any real rapport with Will. Plus, I really mishandled the situation today with him and Amanda."

Sam knew she was wrong to be beating herself up over that. She'd been shocked as hell to find Will with a girl on his bed. So had he. "You didn't know what you'd be walking in on." He stepped a little farther into her room.

"True, but..." Kate's voice dropped to a whisper and she stared at the floor.

"But what?" Sam moved closer yet. He had no clue what she was trying to say.

Kate jumped up from her perch at the end of the bed and grabbed one of the clean folded sheets. She went back to making the bed. "The truth is," she said with difficulty after a moment, "Will was right. I do try to mother everyone. It's one of the reasons I left my job as a high school counselor." Still avoiding Sam's eyes, she shook her head. "Sometimes kids need a friend or someone to look up to, not a stranger trying to act like a parent. And despite all the training and classes I've had in that area, I just couldn't do it, not with any degree of authenticity." She paused and looked up at Sam, before continuing honestly. "And I never could understand how teens could even think about going to bed with someone without first being in love with them. But some of them do." Kate gestured helplessly, her frustration about that evident, before she went back to fitting the contoured sheet on the bed. "Anyway, I knew that if I couldn't be as compassionate and understanding as the kids needed me to be, then I needed to get out of that job...so I did."

Sam thought back to his conversation with Mike Marten. *Kate may be a grown woman, but she's still an innocent in so many ways....* Aware he didn't really want to see that aspect of Kate change or see her become jaded, Sam asked, "Does your dad know that's why you left?"

Kate let out a brief, self-conscious laugh. "Mercy, no." She pressed a hand to her breasts. "What would make you think that?"

Sam figured Kate had enough problems without realizing that her dad was still running around trying to insulate her on that score. "Nothing," he lied. "I just wondered. I know he wants you back at the high school…"

"Well, it's not going to happen." Kate shook out a second sheet and added it to the bed. "I don't belong there," she said stubbornly, her mind made up about that much. "I'm a lot more comfortable dealing with people who need help overcoming grief. I've been there, lived it. I understand what a profound effect the death of a family member can have on a family. Whereas when it comes to teens and sex, I don't have a clue what that's about." Kate turned to Sam, incensed. "Can you imagine? I mean—" Kate took back the question as soon as it was out there. "Well, you and Ellie—"

"Had to get married," Sam supplied, having mercy on the fumbling Kate.

Kate flushed in embarrassment. "I didn't mean to say that."

"But you were thinking it," Sam said.

A silence fell between them that Sam had no idea how to bridge.

"Well, now I feel even worse," Kate said after a moment. "Why?"

Kate shook her head. "I just shouldn't have been so shocked. I shouldn't have been at such a loss as to the appropriate way to handle the situation with Will. I am an adult and a trained counselor, after all. And yet at the same time, the two of them have only had a few dates. For them to behave in such a reckless manner… I certainly never felt like that in high school—"

"But you were dating Craig then, weren't you?" Sam interrupted.

"Yes. But it was literally years before—" Kate broke off and started again. "All we did in high school was kiss good-night at the door. He was very respectful of me. That was one of the things I liked about Craig. That he didn't push me to have sex with him at any early age."

Sam found that hard to understand. Was Craig dead? Kate was a knockout. He and Ellie had always had passion. Maybe too much physical passion at an early age, but it had been one of their strongest bonds nevertheless. It was the one thing that had sustained them, even during the periods when the other aspects of their relationship hadn't been so great. Sam couldn't imagine marrying someone without that to build on.

"I was just surprised to see such passion in kids as young as Will and Amanda," Kate continued hastily. "And I handled it badly as a result. And in doing so, I made my relationship with Will—which wasn't all that great to begin with since we've established virtually no rapport between us—all the more strained. Now he's angry at me and he blames me for his being grounded. I guess I'm just afraid I've made the situation with Will worse, and that wasn't my intention." Kate picked up the clothes basket, and walked past Sam, out into the hall.

Sam followed Kate into the laundry room and watched as Kate stuffed sheets into the washer. "Don't kid yourself, Kate. Will would be having a hard time regardless of who was here taking care of him. He's seventeen. He's anxious to get out and be on his own. And he's sowing some wild oats."

Kate paused in the act of measuring out detergent. "I have to tell you, Sam, I think it's more than that," she said heavily.

"And I have to tell you, Kate" Sam said, his tone just as flat and meaningful, "I think you're overreacting."

Kate went to bed soon after that, and so did Sam.

By all rights, Kate should have been exhausted, after the day from hell in his household. He certainly was, and he hadn't even been home for most of it. But that night, Sam noted reluctantly, Kate Marten didn't seem to sleep much at all. The sounds started at three in the morning. The clink of a glass in the sink. The soft pad of footsteps across the kitchen floor. At four, he heard the hum of the washer again and later still, the rhythmic, rolling thud of the clothes dryer. At four-thirty, the opening and closing of the refrigerator door. At five-thirty, the aroma of coffee drifted up to the second floor.

Sam told himself it wasn't his business if Kate decided to forfeit her rest. But when he heard the back door open and shut at just a little before six, he knew he had to investigate. He found her in the backyard, kneeling next to the flower beds as the first pink light of dawn streaked the Texas sky behind her. She wore a loose-fitting denim work shirt over a snug-fitting T-shirt, jeans and sneakers. Her hair was braided and she looked younger than she was with no makeup.

"What are you doing up?" Kate said when she saw Sam standing there in a pair of jersey running shorts and a T-shirt.

"I might ask the same question of you." He sat on the porch step and began to pull on his socks and shoes. He figured as long as he was up, he might as well go for a run.

Kate rubbed her forehead with the back of one leather gardening glove, leaving a streak of dirt across her skin. "The flower bed needed weeding."

Sam knew it was a helluva lot more than that depriving her of sleep. "This isn't necessary, you know." He looked at Kate sternly. "You can call the garden center and have them send someone out to do it."

"I don't mind." Kate pursed her lips together stubbornly as she plucked out weeds and tossed them into a pail. "It relaxes me."

"I can see that," Sam said.

"Really." Kate continued weeding with a vengeance and refused to meet his gaze. "I'm fine."

Sam could go off on his run and pretend he had never

noticed her out here. But something in the defiant set of her shoulders, the troubled line of her lips, had him moving closer, instead of away. He stood and crossed to her side. Wary of waking the boys sleeping inside, he hunkered down beside her and asked quietly, "What's wrong?"

Kate lifted her chin and speared him with a haughty look. "What makes you think something is wrong?"

Sam nodded at her hand. "Maybe the fact you just yanked that flower out by the roots?"

Kate looked down and gasped at the geranium clutched in her hand. "I'm sorry," she murmured, her cheeks pinkening with embarrassment. "I'll just…put it back." She set it down gently and patted the dirt around it.

Sam put his hand on her wrist. It wasn't the flower he was concerned about. And now that the question was out there, he wasn't going to let it go unanswered, no matter how reluctant Ms. Kate Marten was to confide in him. "I repeat. What's wrong?"

Kate withdrew her wrist from his grip and sat back on her heels. Abruptly she looked as belligerent as Will on a bad day. "Nothing that concerns you."

Figuring this was going to take a while, he sat beside her in the damp, dew-covered grass. "That doesn't mean I don't want to know what's going on with you, or what had you walking the floor all night."

Kate's jaw set as she weeded in silence.

"Is this about what Will said yesterday or about Kevin?" Sam continued when she didn't reply.

Kate met his eyes, looking at him with utmost sincerity. "I never, ever should have lost track of Kevin. I can't believe…" She blew out an uneasy breath. "Well, suffice it to say I'm terribly ashamed about that and I'll never let it happen again."

Aware he'd been so furious and upset he'd never really

given her a chance to explain, Sam moved closer yet. "What exactly did happen there by the way?"

Kate sighed, suddenly looking as disappointed in herself as he had been with her. "I got a little too caught up in my wedding plans."

Sam studied her, not sure why he felt so protective of her, just knowing he did. "You've been caught up in planning your nuptials ever since you moved in last weekend, and it never interfered with your ability to take care of Kev or any of the other kids. What was different about yesterday?"

"You're very perceptive, aren't you?"

When I want to be, yeah, I am. And right now although Sam didn't begin to comprehend why it should be so, he wanted to understand what was going on with Kate. "You don't run a successful business without being able to pick up on subtle shifts such as this."

Kate rolled her eyes. "You're a pain in the butt, you know that?"

"So I've been told," Sam said, noting that Kate had grown into a much more complicated woman than he thought. "Back to yesterday...." he prompted, determined to have his questions answered.

"I was nervous about my meeting with Reverend Baxter. I didn't really want to go because Craig wasn't going to be there."

"Makes sense," Sam sympathized. He didn't understand why they'd gone ahead with the meeting, either. "Especially with Craig coming home next weekend."

"Yes, well..." Kate's voice trailed off in exasperation. "When I got there, I found they had fixed that by setting up a conference call with Craig and his base chaplain."

Sam nodded, impressed. "That was pretty smart."

"I just wish..." Kate stopped, bit her lip.

"What?" Sam asked, amazed at how pretty Kate could

manage to look on so little sleep, with a smudge of dirt across her forehead.

Kate bent over the flower bed and went back to weeding with a vengeance. "Well, it just didn't go very well, that's all."

Figuring he was going to have to tease it out of her, Sam grinned. "Why not? Don't tell me he still refused to set a wedding date."

"As a matter of fact," Kate said, finding no humor in the situation at all as she met Sam's probing gaze. "Craig refused to do just that, even after my mother, Reverend Baxter, and his chaplain at the base in Italy all urged him to do so over the phone."

"But not you?"

"I knew it was a lost cause." Kate yanked off her gloves, stood, and marched back over to the steps, where she had left a bottle of water. "I've been after him to do that for weeks now, so we could start solidifying some of the wedding plans. At least book the church and find out what caterers and reception halls are available, but he wants to wait and do it together, when he gets home, and I know how stubborn he can be once he makes up his mind about something."

No matter how it inconveniences everyone else, obviously, Sam thought resentfully, knowing Kate didn't deserve that. No woman did.

"Needless to say," Kate continued, uncapping the bottle and drinking deeply of the icy water, "my humiliation didn't end there."

"It didn't."

"Of course not." Kate paced, her unbuttoned work shirt flying open as she moved. "Craig refused to participate in a mutual testament of our love, too." Kate explained to Sam what Reverend Baxter had in mind.

"That doesn't sound so tough," he said when she had finished. What bride or groom couldn't relate some funny or tender anecdote about the person they were about to wed? Usually, people who had been together as long as Kate and Craig had tons of stories about each other.

"It really shouldn't be difficult at all," Kate agreed. "Especially when he could easily choose a poem or a part of a poem, or even a line or two from a popular movie if it summed up what he felt about me—us."

"But he didn't agree with any of those options," Sam concluded after a moment.

"Nope." Kate's eyes radiated the depth of her disappointment. "He said he loved me and beyond that there was nothing else to say."

Sam was no gushing romantic himself, but he thought where Kate was concerned there should be plenty else to say, especially for a guy who professed to be so head over heels in love with her he was going to make her his wife. Sam didn't love Kate. Hell, he was still just getting to know the woman Kate had become. And yet he could think of a dozen things Craig could talk about right off the bat. Her incredible pluck and courage, for instance. Her selflessness. Her compassion. The light in her eyes. The breathtaking nature of her beauty, inside and out. The way she had devoted herself to Craig, her patience in waiting for him while he'd gone off to the academy to pursue his dreams, and completed his pilot training. And that was just for starters.

Realizing abruptly that Kate was waiting for—wanting—his reaction to all this, Sam asked, "What do you want to do?"

Kate shrugged, looking hurt all over again, as she recapped her water bottle and set it aside. "It's not really up to me."

Yes, Sam thought as every protective instinct in him rose to the fore, it was. This was Pete Marten's kid sister they were talking about. The person who, though not quite yet successful, was doing everything in her power to help him and his boys put their lives back together, at great personal cost and sacrifice to herself.

"I can't exactly twist his arm," Kate continued miserably.

Sam didn't understand why Kate, who was such a feisty woman in her own right, would let Craig push her around this way. Not about to let her continue to make excuses, for Craig or herself, Sam looked at Kate steadily. "Pretend it is up to you. Pretend the decision about this one aspect of your wedding rests solely in your lap. What would you do, Kate?"

Kate sighed and dropped down next to Sam again. "I liked Reverend Baxter's suggestion. I'd like to say the traditional vows but also incorporate something personal of our own into the ceremony, too."

"So why don't you do that?" Sam persisted, encouraging Kate in the same way that he knew both Pete...and Ellie would have done. "If that's really what you want, why don't you just go after it?" *The same way,* he added silently, *you went after me and the boys when you were determined to help us.*

"You don't understand. It's not that easy." Kate clasped her hands together in her lap and looked down at them. "Craig has never been one to discuss his feelings. His parents are very reserved people. They don't express emotion in their family. They get along. I mean, they never fight. But they're also sort of formal. Growing up like that, Craig's not very comfortable in overt displays of emotion and affection. It doesn't mean he doesn't feel things. He just doesn't show it."

If you say so. In her zeal to make everything okay, it sounded to Sam as though Kate was rationalizing. Under the circumstances, he wasn't sure it was such a good thing.

Kate studied the look on his face and asked curiously, "What was your actual wedding ceremony like? I know you and Ellie eloped, but...I don't know much beyond that."

"We went to J.P. Randall's Bait and Tackle Shop."

"Your cousin Shane McCabe and his wife Greta got married there, didn't they?"

"Yep."

"Ellie went for that?"

Sam tried to not think about the disappointed look on Ellie's face as they'd entered the little store the day after she'd turned eighteen. "As much as anyone can, I guess, considering it's just a little grocery store that sells food and supplies to travelers and fishermen."

"Was it exciting, eloping like that?"

Nerve-racking had been more like it, Sam thought. "We were worried about getting caught. We just wanted to get it over with and get out of there."

Kate's face fell as she went back to working on the flower beds. "That doesn't sound very romantic."

"It wasn't, especially when compared to the big wedding Ellie had always dreamed about," Sam admitted reluctantly. But he'd made it up to her later, every way he could.

"You didn't have a honeymoon, either, did you?"

Sam shook his head. "Couldn't afford it. We lived with her parents that summer, and both of us worked two jobs, and saved our money before heading off to Austin in the fall."

"She helped put you through college, didn't she?"

Sam nodded. "She baby-sat for other kids as well as our own the whole time I was in school. I worked full-time, too, in addition to being a student. Those were hectic years."

"But good ones," Kate observed. "I mean, it was all worth it to you both in the end. The sacrifices you made, all the time apart. You were happy."

Was she talking about him and Ellie now? Sam wondered, studying Kate's hopeful, idealistic expression. Or was she really thinking about her and Craig? "Yes," Sam said, glossing over all the tough times early in his marriage. "It was."

Finished with the weeding, Kate took off her gardening

gloves and sighed. "I'm sure it will be for Craig and me, too." Her lips formed a rueful smile. "What happened yesterday was probably nothing. I am likely just having a case of the prewedding jitters. Craig, too. Once we're together again, everything will be fine. Meanwhile, I just need to calm down, be happy I've finally found my wedding dress—"

"You're going to wear the one I saw you in yesterday?"

"Yes. You did like it, didn't you? I mean, I've made the right decision, haven't I? Buying that one?"

"Oh, yeah," Sam said. Even as angry as he had been with her yesterday—and he had been plenty furious—he hadn't been able to help but notice how stunningly gorgeous she looked. How delicate and feminine and womanly. She was going to be one beautiful bride, and probably an equally devoted and understanding wife. He just hoped Craig Farrell appreciated her the way she deserved to be appreciated. Right now it did not sound to him as if that were the case.

Sam went back to California on Monday morning. Because he wasn't due to return from his business trip until the following Sunday or Monday and Kate was due to pick Craig up at the airport on Friday evening, they had had to make other arrangements for the boys during her weekend off.

Fortunately, Jackson and Lacey McCabe, who were staying out at the McCabe Ranch while John and Lilah were away, volunteered to take the boys for the weekend. Sam had been quick to approve the plan. Though Will didn't want to go—he wanted to stay in town with his friends, but since there was going to be no one to supervise him and he was still grounded—Sam made him go out to the ranch, anyway. Brad and Riley hadn't cared one way or the other—neither had had much of a social life since Brad had been lipsticked and perfumed. Kevin and Lewis, however, had been delighted to have the chance to ride horses and swim as much as they wanted.

By the time Kate's mother stopped by Sam's on Thursday evening to plan Craig's welcome home party, everything was all set. The only thing Kate had to worry about was her nerves. She wanted everything to go perfectly, and so, it appeared as Joyce went over her list with Kate, did Joyce. "We want you to have Craig at our house by three Saturday afternoon."

Kate smiled as she thought about the romantic reunion to come. "I promise we'll leave Dallas in plenty of time to get here, Mom."

"Do you think fajitas will be all right for the main course?"

Kate hesitated, knowing that could easily cause a problem. "Maybe we shouldn't have something that spicy, Mom. Maybe we should have something blander."

Joyce stared at Kate in surprise. "But Craig loves Tex-Mex! And you know that's the one thing he doesn't get when he is overseas."

"I know…" Kate hedged, feeling guiltier than ever about not telling her mother about her father's episode of acute indigestion the week before. "But he'll have traveled a long way and—"

"Your major has a cast-iron stomach and you know it, Kate." Joyce put down her pen and sat back in her chair. She folded her arms in front of her. "What's really going on here, Kate?"

Like it or not, for the sake of her father's stomach, Kate was going to have to fess up. "It's Dad," Kate conceded reluctantly. "He's having indigestion again."

Joyce began to look every bit as upset as Gus had predicted she would be. "Why didn't you tell me?" she cried, hurt.

Kate clasped her mother's hand, wordlessly imploring

her to calm down. "Because I didn't want you to worry, and there wasn't anything we could do until he'd seen the doctor, anyway."

"When is that going to be?"

"Tomorrow afternoon." Kate would have preferred her father see their new family doctor much sooner, but he had refused. And knowing she was lucky to have him go to their family doctor at all, she had finally backed off.

"Well, he must not be having much trouble," Joyce said finally, thinking hard. "Because he ate chili *rellenos* last night, and Cajun-style blackened redfish earlier in the week, and didn't seem to have any problem whatsoever."

Kate sighed her relief. Maybe her dad was right. "Well, maybe it was just a single case of way too spicy enchiladas and too much Texas heat, then. But just to be on the safe side," Kate proceeded cautiously, "maybe we should have grilled chicken for Craig's homecoming bash."

"Good idea." Joyce crossed out and added several things to her list. "I'll just have to rethink all the side dishes."

Kate's shoulders slumped. "I'm sorry, Mom. I didn't think about this." She had been so busy concentrating on the romantic aspects of Craig's homecoming, she hadn't given much thought to the practical.

"No problem," Joyce said, taking the abrupt change of menu in stride. "I haven't done my grocery shopping yet. And even if I had…well, nothing is too much trouble for Craig." Joyce smiled warmly. "You know how much we love him."

That, Kate did.

"Speaking of which, darling, you really have to do a better job of getting Craig to be more enthusiastic about the wedding arrangements. As soon as the two of you get that date set—and I want that done before you two return to Laramie on Saturday so we can announce it straight off at the party and get a church and reception hall booked—I want you to work on your personal testaments or vows. Reverend Baxter needs to know what they're going to be so the three of you can figure out how to best incorporate whatever it is you're going to say to each other into the ceremony."

Kate tensed. While she appreciated her mother's enthusiasm, there were times when her mom was a little too gung-ho about all the wedding details. "Craig hasn't agreed to that yet, Mom, and he may not."

"But you want to do this, don't you?"

"Well, yes." Kate thought it would be lovely and romantic and really make their marriage ceremony very personal and unique if Craig would say something sweet and romantic in front of everyone.

"Then tell Craig that!" Joyce ordered bluntly.

Kate flushed, embarrassed. "I don't want to argue with him, Mom. He's only going to be here for a few days." Even though Kate secretly still held out hope, she didn't honestly think there was much chance of getting Craig to change his mind about this. If he didn't want to do something, she thought on a resigned sigh, he usually didn't do it.

"Who said anything about arguing with him?" Joyce retorted coyly, putting down her pen. "I want you to *persuade* him."

Kate sighed. Her mother could lay on the charm thicker than molasses, but the Southern belle thing had never been Kate's way of dealing with whatever life threw her way. She supposed she was more like her father that way. She just liked to flat-out say what was on her mind and be done with it. She was also like her mother, though, in that she didn't like a lot of conflict in her personal life. Which left her between a rock and a hard place, because there was no way she was going to please everyone under the circumstances, least of all herself. "And if Craig won't be persuaded, then what?" Kate asked, exasperated.

Joyce frowned, clearly irritated Kate wasn't getting the message. "Now you listen to me, Kate. Marriage requires a lot of compromise. But it also involves getting what you need and want out of a relationship. If Craig hasn't given you what you want in regard to this wedding, it's because you haven't articulated just how vitally important his input and enthusiasm is to making this wedding as perfect and wonderful as you both deserve for it to be."

Kate bristled as she realized where this conversation with her mother—who avoided domestic conflict at all costs— was going. "You're saying Craig's uncooperative attitude last Saturday during that conference call was all my fault?"

Joyce sighed and tried again, more sweetly this time. "I'm saying you have to try harder to bring you and Craig closer together in all regards. Now is no time for you to be at odds with each other over anything, large or small."

But I am trying, Kate thought, frustrated her mother couldn't see it. That was why she'd spent all that money and gone to all the trouble to have a very sexy dress made for Craig's homecoming. Because for once, she wanted Craig to react the way men who'd been separated from the loves of their lives did in all the romantic movies. She wanted Craig to be so overcome with love and lust the moment he saw her he could hardly stand it. She wanted their first night together to feel like a preview to the wonderful honeymoon they were going to have in just a few months. She wanted to feel sure she was doing the right thing in marrying her high school and college sweetheart, and know in her heart that it wasn't just habit or fear of ending up alone that was keeping them together after all these years.

Chapter 13

She really had to hand it to Jenna Lockhart Remington, Kate thought as she strode confidently through the Dallas/Fort Worth airport early Friday evening. The dress Jenna had designed for Kate had already elicited dozens of appreciative male glances, and Craig wasn't even here yet! Better still, the sexy-as-all-get-out black cocktail dress, matching jacket, black stockings and high black heels gave Kate a sexual confidence she didn't usually feel. The truth was, after these long separations, she—as most military wives and fiancées—usually felt a little nervous and ill-at-ease with Craig. But with only a few days' leave, she couldn't afford to let the usual uneasiness after separation thing get in the way. She and Craig had to make the most of every moment they had together. And this time, Kate was prepared to do just that.

Ignoring the appreciative glances of the men around her, she paced back and forth in front of the windows and waited for Craig's plane to land. Finally, it did. There was the usual delay as people came through customs one by one. Her heart racing, Kate waited for Craig to emerge. And waited some more. A dozen passed her, then twenty, thirty and then her cell phone rang.

"Kate!" Craig's voice came over the phone, strong and loud.

"Where are you?"

"I'm still in Italy."

Stunned, Kate made her way to a deserted place next to the wall. She couldn't believe this was happening. Not after all their plans, all the months of waiting to see each other again. They were going to set a date for their wedding tonight! They had a fabulous hotel room waiting for them, champagne. "What do you mean you're still in Italy?" she repeated, crushed, hardly able to believe she had just driven two hours and battled Dallas's infamous rush-hour traffic for this!

"I'm not coming home this weekend," Craig went on, as if it were no big deal. "I'm sorry I couldn't let you know sooner."

"Why didn't you?" Kate demanded, fury bubbling up inside her. He'd had hours—hours!—to notify her and hadn't.

"Because it was a last-minute thing," Craig explained in a low, affable tone. "One of the other pilots' wives just had a baby. I flew his mission today so he could go home to see his wife and new kid. It was a last-minute thing."

"Surely someone else could have done that for him," Kate pointed out.

"Maybe," Craig agreed. "But I had promised him a long time ago that I'd cover for him when the time came."

"What about what you promised me?" Kate asked, barely containing her emotions. "You also said you'd come home to see me!" Did his word to her mean nothing? Was this what marriage to him was going to be like, with her always getting the smallest amount of his time and attention? And made to feel guilty or somehow less-than-charitable for even wanting that?

"And I will come home to see you, Kate," Craig promised, exasperated.

"When?" Kate snapped. She had been counting on this time together to renew and strengthen their relationship. She'd thought—hoped—he felt the same.

Craig sighed. "I don't know," he said, beginning to sound annoyed she wasn't being more understanding about his noble deeds. "I'll have to see."

Kate pressed her fingertips against the tension gathering in her temple. "Darn it, Craig, if you don't get here soon, if we don't complete the wedding arrangements, there's no way on this earth we can get married by Thanksgiving or Christmas like we planned."

"So we'll put it off a few more months and get married in the spring instead. It's not such a big deal. Listen, honey, I've got to go. I'll talk to you in a couple of days, okay?" The transatlantic connection ended.

Kate took the phone away from her ear and stared at the receiver in her hand. She couldn't believe it. She'd waited for months—gone to all this effort—and she'd been stood up!

Kate was in the kitchen when Sam came in. She knew it was him by the purring sound of the limo in the drive and the deliberate tread of his footsteps as he walked in and set down his belongings. Cursing her luck—wasn't there anywhere she could go tonight with any assurance at all of being alone?—Kate reached for a tissue and stayed where she was, knowing it was too late to run, anyway.

It wasn't long before he made his way to the kitchen. The minute he crossed the threshhold and saw her sitting there alone in the semidarkness, she saw the questions in his eyes.

What was she doing here? Where was Craig? Why had she been crying? What was she doing in that dress?

The hurt and the humiliation she had suffered that evening still far too fresh in her mind, Kate pressed her lips together defiantly. She knew what Sam wanted. She wasn't going to give it to him. "I don't want to talk about it," she told him flatly, her voice sounding belligerent even to her.

If she had wanted to talk about it, she would have gone home to her folks, or to any one of half a dozen girlfriends. She'd come back to Sam's because she knew that no one else was supposed to be home, and no one would think to look for her here, either. Had she gone to her apartment, had anyone seen her there, instead of at some posh hotel in Dallas neither she nor Craig could really afford, they would have known something was up. Or assumed Craig was with her. And stopped by for that reason, too.

Sam merely shrugged. "Don't mind me," he said dryly. Moving to the refrigerator for a glass of juice and some ice, he said, "It's just my house."

Okay. He had her there. Wishing she had taken the time to change—sitting there alone in her make-love-to-me-right-here-and-right-now dress only made her situation all the more ridiculous—Kate tossed out the only defense she had. "You're not supposed to be back here until Sunday."

Sam shrugged again. He lounged against the counter and sipped his juice. "I finished what I had to do and came home early." He looked at her steadily. "What's your excuse?"

Kate tensed. She wished she hadn't taken off her opaque black jacket and tossed it over a chair the moment she'd entered the house. Without it, she felt too exposed, too vulnerable to Sam's predatory gaze. She pushed back from the kitchen table, her shoes making a sharp staccato sound on the tile floor as she moved to the sink to dump her lukewarm tea. Tears burned behind her eyes. "I told you I didn't want to answer any questions."

"So sue me." Sam stepped alongside her so he could see her face and the unwanted moisture welling in her eyes. He leaned against the counter. "It's not going to stop me from asking them."

Kate released a slow, measured breath, turned and gave him a withering glare.

"Did you and Craig have a fight?" He studied her disheveled hair and tear-stained face with irritating thoroughness. "Is that it?"

Kate gritted her teeth and remained silent.

"That's it, isn't it?" Sam continued after a moment. "Craig said or did something to ruin your weekend together."

Not just our weekend, try our lives. Her heart pounding with a mixture of anger and exasperation, Kate stared at Sam. "Why is this so important to you?" And why wouldn't he just leave her alone?

He shrugged, once again the same old, indifferent, remote Sam. "Maybe I just want to know that the person who's going to be taking care of my kids is okay," he said finally.

The tears Kate had been withholding began to slip down her cheeks. Embarrassed, she turned away. The last thing she wanted was his pity. She suspected she was going to get enough of that from everyone she and Craig knew as it was. Her spine stiffened as she struggled to control the sob welling up in her throat. A sob that until now had gone unvoiced. "I'm fine, Sam," she choked out. *Or I will be just as soon as I pull myself together.* "All anyone else needs to do is leave me alone."

"Funny," Sam said sarcastically as he caught her arm and reeled her back to his side. He shoved his hand through her disheveled hair, forcing her face up to his. "That's what I used to say. Only I don't believe it now any more than you believed it when I said it to you."

Tears blurred her vision, even as her hostility toward him—toward everything—increased. "I don't need your kindness, Sam, simply because you feel sorry for me!"

Sam looked down at her grimly. "I don't have any niceness left in me, Kate. You know that better than anyone." His glance sobered abruptly. "But I still know a person in trouble when I see one. So if you want me to call someone for you, like your parents, or even drive you over there—"

"No," Kate said sharply, whirling away as her tears started anew. "The last thing I need is for them to tell me to forgive Craig and marry him anyway, because it's just not going to happen. Not after the way he stood me up tonight."

Sam stared at her, stunned, disbelieving. "When you say stood up—"

Kate shoved her hands through her hair, anger bubbling up, hot and vital, inside her. "I mean I drove all the way to Dallas to get him and then found out that he had decided at the very last moment that he wouldn't be coming home to plan our wedding, after all."

Sam's mouth hardened. All the sympathy left his eyes. "Then the loss is all his."

Yes, it was, Kate thought, glad at least Sam understood why she couldn't possibly marry Craig. "In fact," Kate said calmly, "in a way I'm relieved." And then the dam burst, the facade faltered, and she promptly burst into tears. And once the torrent started, she couldn't seem to stop it.

Sam swore.

As the loneliness and pain she'd felt for years took hold, another sob caught in her chest and then pushed its way up her throat.

"Ah, Kate—" he said as she smothered the unaccustomed sound with her hand and the tears ran down her face

and dripped off her chin. He looked at her, an unbeliev-
able amount of tenderness in his eyes "Don't," he whispered
softly. "Don't..."

The next thing she knew she was in his arms and he was
holding her against him, stroking his hands through her hair,
across her shoulders, down her back. She buried her face in
the hardness of his chest, wrapped her arms around his waist
and let him hold her and comfort her until at last her grief
was spent and her sobs began to fade. And then slowly, in-
evitably, everything began to change. His body grew harder,
hotter. And the pain of what had happened was superseded
by the trembling of her limbs and the quickening of her heart.

Slowly, Kate lifted her head and looked into Sam's dark
brown eyes. The hopes she had held for the future were over.
But there was now, Kate thought, her misery fading as Sam
cradled her head in his hands and lowered his lips to hers.
And there was tonight. And for once—for tonight—that was
all that mattered.

His kiss was searing and, she realized quickly, moaning
low in her throat, exactly what she needed. Kate wrapped
her arms around his shoulders and kissed Sam back with the
same wild, demanding need. She was tired of pretending she
could do without being touched, kissed, held. Tired of long
separations and the absence of tenderness in her life. She
wanted this closeness, this comfort. And most surprising of
all, she wanted...Sam.

Sam had thought Kate was unshakable. God knew she
had grown into one of the calmest, most capable women he
had ever met. It stunned him to realize he had been wrong.
Beneath her cool womanly demeanor her heart was just as
sweet and loving, as tender and vulnerable as it had been
when she was a kid. Realizing that made him want to protect
her from further hurt or injustice, just the way he and Pete

both had when she was a little kid. Which meant not doing what he wanted to do.

He lifted his head, breathing hard. "Kate—" *He wanted her so bad.* "We need to think about this." *We need to put on the brakes here before it really gets out of hand.*

She looked up at him as if she feared his rejection more than anything and slowly, defiantly, shook her head. "No thinking, Sam. Not tonight," she whispered, new tears glistening in her eyes as the vulnerability slipped back into her voice. "I've done far too much of that. Tonight I want to feel, and that's all I want to do. All I'm going to do." She rose up on tiptoe, wreathing her arms around his neck and pressing her breasts against his chest, reminding him that she had a need that—judging from some of the things she had told him—had never been met. Sam knew he shouldn't be the one to show her what it was her life had thus far been missing, what he suspected she might even think she didn't possess, or could ever even possibly understand. But even as he searched her eyes and warned himself to not go down that path, he could feel his reason slipping away. She was a beautiful woman and she needed. She was alone. So was he. They had both suffered a loss. What harm would there be in offering each other whatever comfort could be found?

And suddenly knowing she needed him, needed this every bit as much as he did, he threaded his hands through her hair, tilted her lips up to his and kissed her with a hunger he had never felt before. He kissed her until he couldn't breathe for wanting her. Then he picked her up and carried her down the hall to the bedroom and set her down beside the bed. She was trembling so hard she could barely stand. So was he. Their breaths were ragged as she slipped off her shoes and he unzipped her dress. He tugged the straps across her shoulders and peeled it away. The delicate fabric slid to the floor with a whisper, pooling at her feet.

Her transparent black lingerie left little to the imagination
and Sam hardened all the more at what he saw. Full, beautiful breasts spilling out of a tiny décolleté bra, pink nipples
poking at the cloth. A garter belt dipped well beneath her
slender waist and sexy navel before attaching to black thigh-
high stockings that made the most of her slender, sexy legs.
Lower still, a tiny scrap of cloth covered a golden nest of
curls. And everywhere, smooth satiny skin that begged to
be kissed and caressed.

She shuddered as his hands slid over her ribs and moved
slowly up over the satiny skin of her midriff to cup her
breasts. She jerked in a breath and closed her eyes as his
thumbs found and traced the pink nipples through the transparent lace. She sighed her pleasure and swayed against him
as her nipples puckered with pleasure, then turned her lips
up to his. She wrapped her arms around his neck once again
and kissed him with abandon. His muscles burning, knowing he was about to explode then and there, he tossed back
the covers, and eased her down onto the bed.

She lay against the pillows, regarding him with a mixture
of caution and need. Her lips glistening from their kisses,
her breathing rapid. Sam kicked off his shoes and, knowing
the only way to hold back was to remain as fully clothed as
possible for as long as possible, dropped down onto the bed
and stretched out beside her. Determined to give her what
she wanted and needed, determined to make the hurt she
had suffered fade away, he slipped an arm beneath her and
shifted her onto her side.

As they faced each other, he forgot about all the reasons
they shouldn't be together, all the reasons why she might soon
regret this, and gave himself over to the moment as surely
as she was giving herself over to him. Anchoring an arm at
her waist, he shifted her close and bent his head until their
lips met. She shuddered softly at the contact and opened her

mouth to his. The combination of her shyness and her need nearly undid him. Suddenly he wanted to make her his in a fundamental man-woman way that could never be disputed or undone. He gathered her closer yet and kissed her hungrily, softly, slowly, and then hungrily again, until she shifted restlessly against him, making a soft, whimpering sound in the back of her throat.

Knowing she needed more, he slipped first his hand, then his leg, between her knees, holding them apart. The skin of her inner thighs was satiny-smooth, and to his abiding pleasure, sensitive to the slightest caress. Over and over he stroked her, from the lacy bands at the top of her stockings to the edge of her transparent lace panties, until her hips took on a voluptuous rhythm and she strained against him, needing a more intimate touch. His own body throbbing, pushing him ruthlessly toward a climax of his own, he held back determinedly and eased his fingers beneath the cloth, slipping them between her delicate folds. Moaning softly, she surged against him. Dewy moisture bathed his fingertips. She trembled and, still kissing him raptly, caught him against her. "I can't wait," she whispered against his mouth, trembling with wanting him.

Aware she wasn't the only one having one hell of a time holding off, Sam shifted her onto her back, whisked her panties down past her knees, released the fly on his trousers and slid over her, into her. With a low, exultant cry, she rose up to meet him, arching beneath him, urging him not to restrain. And he didn't. He drove into her, into the tight wet heat of her, thrusting deeply, fully, until she exploded in a fury of heat and clenching pleasure. Knowing

he no longer had to temper his own reaction, knowing he no longer had to deny himself the pleasure of making her his, Sam climaxed right after her.

They held each other tight afterward. The only sound in

the room was that of ragged breaths and thundering hearts. Knowing his weight was too much for her, Sam eased away from her and rolled onto his back. Before he could do more than start to pull her back into his arms again, Kate shifted, sat up, and started to move away. Realizing reality had set in, and that she was about to run away as fast and far as she could get, and that it would be disastrous if she did, Sam caught her arm and pulled her back. She turned to him, a questioning look in her eyes, the wariness, the hurt back on her face. And suddenly Sam knew they couldn't leave things this way, either. "Don't go," Sam said quietly.

Kate wished she knew what to say or do in the wake of such an unexpected turn of events. But the truth was, she didn't. Maybe because hot, lusty lovemaking just for the sake of easing her loneliness was out of her realm. It always had been.

His expression curious, Sam propped himself up on his elbow. "I need to be with you."

That was the problem. She wanted to be with him, too. Too much. But for her it wouldn't be meaningless, mindless sex, no matter how much she told herself it was, or could be with Sam. The truth of the matter was, going to bed with Sam was more than just a meaningless roll in the hay, it was the fulfillment of a long-held adolescent crush she had never quite gotten over—a fantasy come true. The problem was, she lived in real life. The reality was, she was still—technically anyway, until she talked to Craig—engaged to someone else. And until she officially ended that— Maybe even after considering the way Sam still mourned Ellie…

Kate sighed. Aware Sam was waiting for some sort of response, some way to wrap this up nicely for both of them so they could both go away feeling good about themselves, she said warily, "I don't think it's wise." They had done this.

And it had been wonderful. More than wonderful, actually. But now it was over. They had their lives to consider. Their pride to consider. And hers had already taken a real beating.

Wishing her robe were somewhere within easy reach, she slipped on her panties and then perched beside him, in her far-too-sexy underwear, on the edge of the bed. Doing her best to pretend it wasn't such a big deal to be sitting with him like this, she turned her eyes to the floor and struggled to regain whatever equilibrium she could possibly recover. Curling her fingers into the rumpled covers on either side of her, she conceded, "You got what you wanted. I got what I wanted."

What more was there to say or do? She had known, going in, that this would be a one-time thing. But that moment of hurt, of vulnerability, was over. It had to be, Kate told herself sternly, if she was going to pick up the pieces of her life and go on. Because the last thing she wanted out of this was another broken heart or seriously damaged self-esteem.

"Not really," Sam stated, kicking off his trousers and shorts, instead of putting them back on. Next came his shirt, socks. "I mean, don't get me wrong. It was great as far as quickies go…" he said with a dark predatory look, "But the night is still young."

Kate flushed as he stretched out beside her, naked as could be. He had a beautiful body, athletic, sturdy, with smooth skin covered with swirls of velvety-soft dark brown hair. His chest looked even harder and broader without his shirt. Lower still, he was beautiful, too, so big and masculine.

"But what happened just now is hardly what I call making love," Sam said in that soft, seductive voice she was fast coming to love.

Kate studied him, trying to figure out exactly what it was in their lovemaking, in her, that he'd found so lacking. But all she could see in his face was a sort of matter-of-fact acceptance of the attraction between them, and an eager willingness to go the distance with her again, if only to further end the drought of physical intimacy they'd each endured. Knowing it would truly be disastrous if she allowed him to seduce her into making love with him again-she might do something really foolish such as embark on a hot and sexy rebound romance with him, or worse yet, maybe even start to fall in love with him—she swallowed and said, "We both climaxed. Didn't we?"

"Yes, Kate." Sam grinned, seeming amused she felt she had to ask. "We did. But we got there in a hurry." He kissed the inside of her wrist. "Probably because it had been so long for both of us. Unfortunately—" he took her arm and ignoring her passive resistance, pulled her gently down beside him on the bed "—I don't think what you needed and wanted tonight was something all that hurried."

You got that right, Kate thought, her heartbeat accelerating as he stretched out beside her and tucked one of his thighs over hers. What she had wanted…what she had looked forward to all summer…was a night of honeymoon-style lovemaking. Remembering how disappointed she had been when she'd learned the passionate marathon wasn't going to happen—not with Craig, anyway—it was all she could do not to weep. She studied Sam, as the heat of his body next to hers warmed and enticed her. "You're saying, given a choice, you would have done it differently…if we both hadn't been in such a hurry." Kate wished this was the one area of her life where she had more experience.

"Oh, yeah," Sam said, a mixture of satisfaction and anticipation in his low voice as he bent to kiss her temple, the slope of her neck. "I most certainly would have."

Kate forced herself to ignore the tingling generated by his lips on her skin. She could see what was going on, even if she didn't want to. Unable to deal with the emotional ramifications of what had just happened, and why, and how, Sam was instead dealing with the physical side of things. The damnable male pride that told him, as long as they had done this, it needed to be the best they'd ever had. For him, clearly, even though he had climaxed, it hadn't been the most stellar bout of lovemaking in his life. But then, she wasn't Ellie, Kate thought, depressed. She wasn't anyone with either the key to his heart or vastly sustainable sex appeal and bedroom talents. Kate looked over at him. "Well, that's just the problem, Sam," she said stiffly, holding herself as much apart from him as she was able, considering they were lying side by side on the bed. "I don't know how to do it any differently," Kate said. She only had one other person to compare him with. And with Craig, it had always been quick and efficient. Usually but not always without the orgasm on her part. After which, he immediately left the bed. Kate had never really blamed Craig for that. She had felt a little awkward then, too. Shy. Embarrassed. It had just been easier to get up, put on their clothes and pretend everything was fine. Even when she'd known, deep down, that it hadn't been.

Sam's eyes darkened with regret as he caressed and kissed the tips of her breasts through the transparent bra. "I was afraid I'd made things worse for you tonight instead of better." Casually, Sam unhooked one garter, then the other.

Not sure whether she was more embarrassed or aroused, Kate tried to block his hands. The only thing worse than a shameless roll-in-the-hay, in her opinion, was a second shameless roll-in-the-hay. Damn it all, there was a limit to just how much humiliation she was willing to take. "Sam, please… You don't have to do this, Sam," she protested breathlessly, damning the telltale moisture already gathering between her thighs.

"Don't you get it, Kate?" His expression more determined than ever, Sam slid his hands beneath her legs, and one by one, unhooked those garters, too. He traced the bare skin just above the lacy top of her stocking then bent and kissed her bare thigh gently. "I want to make love to you again. Now. Tonight," he whispered as he lifted her again and eased the garter belt away from her hips, down her legs, past her knees. "And before I'm finished I promise you, you'll feel the same way, too."

Helpless to resist such a slow, sensual assault, Kate watched as he slowly, lovingly, peeled off her stockings, panties and bra with such tenderness she couldn't help but feel deliciously sexy and wanton. When she was naked, he admired her with his eyes. "You are so beautiful," he murmured, his voice a low husky rumble in his throat. And the way he looked at her then—with such heat and passion— Kate knew that no matter what happened she would never doubt herself on that score again.

"So delicate." He kissed the tips of her breasts, making her aware of her body in a way she'd never been. "Feminine." He dropped a kiss across her navel. "Pretty." His lips touched the golden nest of curls, making her quiver in anticipation. Eyes smouldering, he laid her back against the pillows and, starting at the sensitive area just below her ear, kissed his way down the nape of her neck to her breasts.

"I never should have made love to you because I knew, going in, once would never be enough for either of us," Sam confessed as he traced her collarbone and circled the rounded globes of her breasts with the pads of his fingertips. His lips closed over the aching crowns, suckled gently, until she moaned and writhed beneath him, wanting—needing—so much more.

Kate had never felt anything so lush or sensual or wonderful as this slow, thorough loving. With a sigh of contentment and wonder, she let her head fall back and gave herself over to the experience entirely. She knew getting involved with Sam was emotionally risky, dangerous, but what was the point of resisting when they both wanted it so much? She moaned softly and shifted her legs as he made his way across her belly, kissing and nipping and kissing again. Going lower still, he maddeningly bypassed the nest of golden curls to start at her knees. Treating her as if she were the most precious of treasures, he made his way along the insides of her thighs with lips and teeth and tongue. Aware her heart was beating a little too fast, that she was feeling a little too vulnerable, she whispered his name.

He smiled, and slid up her body and kissed her again, hotly, rapaciously, until anything else she might have said, any questions she might have voiced, any doubts she might have raised, vanished once again. Her hips bucked and lifted and a delicious wanting hummed through her body. A wicked grin curving his lips, Sam slid his hands beneath her, possessively cupping her legs, parting her thighs. Treating every touch, every caress, as something to be savored indefinitely, he kissed his way back down her body. And this time, given the urgent need he'd created within her, there was no choice but to surrender to him, and his will, completely.

The next thing she knew he'd parted her delicate folds with his lips and tongue and took the hot, aching flesh into his mouth. She arched against him, beyond thinking, only feeling, unable to stop the sounds emanating from her throat as the pleasure overtook her in a white-hot wave. She trembled uncontrollably, tears of release slipping down her face, even as the dampness between her thighs flowed, and the emptiness within her, the ache, the need to be filled, to be part of something strong and solid and real, grew. Feeling more womanly, more powerful than she ever had in her life, she clutched his shoulders, shuddering, holding him close.

And he held her in his arms just as tightly. She wanted to make love to him, just as thoroughly. She wanted him writhing beneath her. But he was having none of it as he shifted her the way he wanted her, and slid up her body, again seducing her to acquiesce completely to his wants and his needs as he eased himself between her thighs, his shaft pulsing and hot between them. "Let me take you," he whispered between hot fevered kisses, pushing her knees up around his hips. "Just like this."

"Yes," Kate breathed, any inadequacies she'd ever felt as a woman fading permanently away. Her heart pounded as her body opened to accommodate his thick hot shaft. "Just like this."

She lost herself in the bliss of being possessed by him. The feeling of fullness, of being one with him, was overwhelming. Kate basked in the heat, the wonder of being with him this way at all, and then they were kissing again, straining against each other eagerly, driving each other wild. Their bodies twined together and Kate wrapped her arms and legs around him, her hips moving rhythmically in concert with Sam's.

The desire between them burned brighter, hotter, and she gave herself over to the sensation and with lips and tongue and hands, urged him on. Kissing him sweetly, then with a wildness she hadn't known she possessed, Kate ran her hands across his shoulders, down his back. He groaned as she cupped his buttocks in her hands. In answer, he thrust into her, harder, deeper.

"Kate," he rasped as they trembled with mutual need and their shuddering breaths reverberated with the pleasure ricocheting through them. The musky scent of their lovemaking filled the air as he took her to a place and pleased her in ways she had never imagined could exist. For long moments they hung there, on the brink, delighting in the unexpected but undeniable closeness and intimacy they had found. And then they were catapulting over the edge, soaring, surrendering to the sweet inevitability of it all. Holding each other close and slowly, ever so slowly, coming back to earth again.

Kate remembered falling asleep, wrapped in Sam's arms. Yet she woke alone. If it hadn't been for the rumpled, musky-scented sheets, the deliciously sated feel of her body and the clothing scattered around the room, she would have thought she had dreamed it all. But as she sat up, smelled the coffee already brewing and felt the tension and uncertainty welling up within her, she knew it had been very real. Deciding she couldn't face Sam until she'd had a shower, she headed for her bathroom. Fifteen minutes later, dressed in khaki camp shorts and a V-neck aqua T-shirt, her hair freshly washed and blow-dried, she ventured out into the kitchen.

Sam was sitting at the table, a cup of coffee cradled in his hands, a remote, brooding look on his face. Kate's heart sank as she realized he had most likely been sitting there for some time, thinking about Ellie, the only woman he had ever loved, probably wondering how she'd react to what they had done. Kate walked across the kitchen to the cupboard. With every movement she made, the headache she'd awakened with—the headache she always had after a good cry—tripled in intensity. "Morning," she said when Sam looked at her.

He nodded, watching as she retrieved a bottle of aspirin, opened it and shook two tablets into her hand. "Headache?"

Kate saw no reason to lie about it. Her body might feel as if it had received a world-class loving the night before, but her head was about to split wide open from the pressure in her temples. "Yes," she said, doing her best to ignore the increasingly wary look on his handsome face. Damn, but she hated to be just one more thing Sam McCabe would come to regret.

He narrowed his gaze at her, then got up, poured her a big glass of water and a cup of coffee. "Drink it all, along with the aspirin," he advised like the friend she had once wanted him to be—before she'd started working for him, before they'd been foolish enough to tumble into bed together. "You'll feel better."

Kate sipped obediently. "Thanks."

The awkward silence strung out between them, showing Kate just how hard it was going to be for her to keep working for him after what had happened. Was that what he was thinking about, too? "How long have you been up?" Kate asked, noting it was nine-thirty.

Sam turned his eyes to hers. "A couple of hours."

Which meant, Kate thought, realizing they hadn't gone to sleep until nearly five, that Sam had only had two hours' sleep at most. She'd had almost four. Deciding quickly anything they had to say to each other could wait until they'd both had more rest, as well as time to think about what they were going to say to each other, Kate said, "If you want to go back to bed..." Then realizing how her words could be construed, Kate forced herself to go on without blushing— much. "To catch some more sleep," she elaborated in a strangled voice. Suddenly she felt as shy and tongue-tied as she had always been around him as a kid.

Sam shook his head, nixing her suggestion, letting her know he was fine just as he was. He looked at her steadily, the determination in his eyes as evident as the caution in his voice. "We need to talk about what happened last night."

Chapter 14

Kate didn't like the way he said that. As if he had an ocean of regrets and a lot of second thoughts, and was equally wary about what the future held. But given the fact that she was still technically engaged to someone else and she had been temporarily taking care of his kids, she supposed he was right. Kate put on her game face…the one that didn't reveal anything of what she was thinking or feeling. "Okay," she said, taking a deep breath. "You first."

The doorbell rang. Once and then again. Sam swore. He put up a hand before she could move. "Stay here. I'll get rid of whoever it is and be right back." He headed off while Kate stayed where she was, her head still throbbing, and sipped her coffee.

There was a murmur of low male voices from the front hall, and then the tromping of heavy footsteps heading her way. Seconds later, Kate heard someone call her name. Then her dad burst into the kitchen.

Kate's glance widened as her father's narrowed. Of all the things she did not need this morning, a stormy confrontation with her father topped the list. "Craig called. He's worried about you. He thought you might still be upset and he asked me and your mother to make sure you were all right."

"I'm fine, Dad."

"You don't look it." Mike studied her critically. "You look like you've been crying."

Kate rubbed at the tension in her temples. Her headache had started to go away. Now it was back full force. "Yesterday was a bad day, okay?"

"Are you going to call Craig?" her dad questioned impatiently.

Not with you and Sam standing there, listening to every word I say, Kate thought.

Her dad frowned. "He needs to know you're okay, Kate."

"I'll take care of it," she returned quietly, letting her father know with a glance that whatever had or had not happened between her and Craig was her business not his.

Clearly hurt by the way she had excluded him and her mother, Mike Marten turned to Sam, who was standing in the kitchen doorway. "What about you?" Mike demanded abrasively. He looked from Sam to Kate and back again. "What are you doing here?"

Not in the least bit afraid to go toe-to-toe with Mike, Sam retorted flatly, "I live here."

"I meant with her—" Mike stabbed an accusing finger in Sam's direction "—Alone."

"We were talking," Sam said.

Mike looked around, his glance falling on the two coffee cups. Having reached a conclusion in his own mind about what the evidence meant, he turned back to Sam, his eyes gleaming shrewdly. "I knew her staying here would lead to trouble." He pushed forward aggressively, hands balled at his sides. "What the hell have you been doing to my daughter?"

Giving Sam no chance to answer, Mike rounded on Kate, looking like the vastly overprotective father he was and always had been. "Did he make a pass at you?" he commanded.

Kate flushed despite herself. This was a nightmare. "Dad, please—"

Mike clenched his jaw and rubbed at the tense muscles in the back of his neck. "You're telling me I have no reason to be concerned about you being alone with him?"

Kate gave her father a warning glance, letting him know he had embarrassed her quite enough. "I'm telling you I am a grown woman and quite capable of taking care of myself," she said icily.

Mike's jaw tightened. "All I know is he got one sweet, young girl pregnant without benefit of marriage!"

Knowing if she didn't do something soon this was likely to disintegrate into a brawl, Kate got up from the table and stepped between the two men. She directed a quelling hand at each of them. "Dad, for heaven's sake, Sam and Ellie were together for nearly twenty years."

Mike pressed his lips together and huffed. He braced both his hands on his hips. "Yeah, well…some things don't change." He glowered at Sam.

"What the hell is that supposed to mean?" Sam said, stepping around Kate, to square off with Mike.

Mike folded his arms against his bearlike chest and regarded Sam contentiously.

"It means you wouldn't be the first widower to try to obliterate his grief in the arms of whatever woman was handy. It means that if Kate and Craig had a fight last night, she was vulnerable. And instead of doing the decent thing and sending her home to her mother and me, where we could have helped her straighten things out with Craig, you kept her here and took advantage of her."

Aware this was the last thing she wanted or needed on the heels of her realization that she could not marry Craig, Kate interrupted with as much calm as she could muster. "Dad, no one said that!"

If there was one thing she knew, it was that Sam had not taken advantage of her. To lay that on Sam implied she hadn't known what she was doing. She had. And she'd done it, anyway. He might regret it this morning. In certain ways, she certainly did, because making love *without being in love* went against everything she believed in. But that changed nothing. And neither did this brouhaha.

Mike's expression was as hard and unforgiving as his voice as he continued to sagely size up the situation he'd walked in on. "No one *had* to say that, Kate," Mike said, his hand moving from his shoulder to his chest. "All I had to do was look at your face and see the way you've been crying to know what's going on." Mike stabbed an accusing finger at Sam. "He needs someone to take care of his house and his kids and it doesn't take a genuis to see that you've been doing a pretty good job. So he thinks if he seduces you, you'll forget all about your promise to marry Craig and will stay here with him and his kids instead. Sam McCabe doesn't care about you, Kate. But I do! And I'm telling you that you deserve to have kids of your own and to be someone's first and only love, not a runner-up or stand-in for someone else. So do not let this man muck up what you've got with Craig."

Sam glared at Mike. He looked as though he was about to lose it, too. "I am not—nor would I ever—use your daughter in that way!" Sam shoved the words through gritted teeth.

"Yeah, well, time will tell, won't it?" Mike flung back just as furiously.

Kate sighed.

Sam swore.

And Mike stiffened, groaned and clutched his chest.

Fear shot through Kate as she and Sam simultaneously moved toward Mike.

"Dad, what is it?" Kate asked, moving to support her father as his knees grew wobbly, sweat broke out on his face and his skin turned an awful pale gray.

"My…chest…" Mike whispered hoarsely, panic on his face, the argument forgotten in the wake of his near-overwhelming pain.

Together, Sam and Kate got her dad to the car. Sam drove while Kate got on the cell phone and called ahead to alert the ER they were on the way. She also called her mother and their family doctor, Luke Carrigan, to tell them both what was going on. The staff was waiting for them when they arrived five minutes later. Mike was immediately loaded onto a stretcher and rushed into a room for evaluation.

Sam stood and came over to where she was standing next to the windows in the reception area. "You okay?" he asked softly.

Kate nodded, knowing she had to be, even if she was only hanging on to her composure by a thread. She pressed the heels of her hands against her eyes to hold back the tears, but they came anyway. She was so scared. She hadn't felt this helpless or terrified since the night of Pete's accident.

"I'm sorry," Sam said, putting his arm around her shoulders. Abruptly, Sam looked as if he felt as guilty and as worried about Mike as Kate. "I didn't know Mike had a heart condition."

Kate shook her head, brushed the tears away and pulled herself together with effort. Now was not the time to break down. There'd be plenty of time for that later, if it came to that. Right now her mom and dad both needed her to be strong. She walked across the hall to the alcove that housed the beverage machines. Her legs were shaking, but at least she had a modicum of control again. "It's not your fault, Sam." If it was anyone's, it was hers. She should have made Mike see the doctor days ago. She should have brought him to the emergency room the night he'd gotten sick at the field house.

Swallowing against the ache in her throat and the weight of her own guilt, Kate reached into her pockets. Then realized in frustration that she not only didn't have any change, she hadn't brought her purse. "He's been having chest pains. He just wouldn't admit it."

Sam reached into his pocket and pulled out dollar bills. He slid one into the machine that contained the fruit juices, then gestured at the choices. "Push whatever button you want."

Kate made her selection, then started a little as the can loudly rumbled through the machine to the bin at the bottom. Sam reached down, got it, handed it to her, and then purchased one for himself.

Aware her legs were still pretty wobbly, Kate sat at one of the small round snack tables in the corner.

"Has this happened before?" Sam asked as Kate sipped her cranberry-apple juice.

Kate wrapped both her hands around the can. "Not too long ago, one night after practice. Gus was so worried he called me up and asked me to drive over to the field house. When I got there, I could tell Dad was in pain, but he shrugged it off, said it was his acid reflux acting up again. He'd already taken some medicine, and after a few minutes he looked and felt better."

Sam sipped his orange juice. "So he didn't go to the doctor."

Kate's glance strayed to the double doors that separated the treatment area from the reception area. "He was supposed to go see Luke Carrigan yesterday." She wondered if he actually had.

Joyce Marten rushed into the emergency area. Spotting Kate and Sam, she rushed over. Her eyes were swimming with tears and she seemed beside herself with worry. She took Kate's hands in hers and demanded urgently, "Where's your father?"

"He's back with Dr. Fletcher, the cardiologist, being evaluated, Mom. We can't go back. They'll come out and tell us as soon as they know what's going on. Luke Carrigan's on his way over."

"Did he have a heart attack?" Joyce asked, trembling.

"That's what they're trying to find out, Mom."

Noting Joyce looked pale, Kate helped her into a chair. Wordlessly, Sam got her a can of juice, opened it for her and pushed it into her hand. "I can't believe this is happening," Joyce said. "First Craig has to cancel his trip home and now this."

Dr. Fletcher strode out into the waiting area. He said hello to Kate and Joyce, both of whom he already knew, and introduced himself to Sam. "How is he?" Kate asked the doctor.

"Stable for right now," Dr. Fletcher said. "We gave him some medication and his chest pains subsided almost immediately."

"That's a good sign, isn't it?" Joyce interrupted, looking immensely relieved.

"It can be," Dr. Fletcher agreed cautiously.

But it wasn't necessarily in this case, Kate thought. "Was it a heart attack?" she asked.

"That we don't know," he told them honestly, then went on to describe and explain the tests they had run. "Mike's cardiac enzymes were normal. But his EKG was not, and that's reason for some concern. Which is why I want you to come back there with me, and help me talk some sense into him. We want to admit him to the hospital for a few days, so we can run some more tests. It's the only way we can absolutely rule out or confirm coronary artery disease. Unfortunately, Mike is resisting the idea pretty vigorously."

Sam took the opportunity to excuse himself. "I'm going to go out to the ranch to pick up the boys." Sam looked at Kate. "You let me know if there is anything I can do."

Kate had only to look at Sam to know she and her mom could count on him for whatever help they needed. She nodded, glad she had him to lean on. "Thanks."

Although she could feel him wanting to touch her, squeeze her hand—something—he merely looked at her. "No problem."

Feeling a little bereft, Kate watched him go.

Dr. Fletcher took them back to her father's room. Clad in a hospital gown, a sheet drawn up to his waist, Mike looked about as cuddly and happy as a grizzly, but his color was good and he seemed as strong and vigorous as ever. After the way he'd looked when they'd brought him in, pale and doubled over with pain, it was a vast improvement and Kate couldn't help but feel immensely relieved at the vigor with which her father began to complain.

"I told that nurse I want my clothes," Mike said, looking as if he were about to walk out of there with or without them.

"Wait a minute, Coach Marten," Dr. Fletcher said. "First, I want to explain to you and your family why we want you to stay with us a few days and have some tests done. The electrocardiogram shows that there may have been some damage done to your heart at some time in the past. We don't know when—"

Frowning, Mike interrupted, "Doc, I had all those fancy heart tests done when I had my ulcer. My heart was fine. Strong as an ox."

"Yes, I know, Mike," Dr. Fletcher said, "but that was over five years ago. A lot could have happened between now and then."

"And maybe," Mike argued stubbornly, "it was just my acid reflux acting up again and that EKG you just ran on me is what's all screwed up. After all, you said my cardiac enzymes are normal."

"That's true," Fletcher replied. "All we know for certain is that there's a difference between the EKG we took then and the one we took just now. It could all be artifact, from the way the leads for the EKG were placed during your previous test. Or it could be a result of some damage to your heart from an undiagnosed coronary disease. The only way we will be able to tell for sure what's going on here, is if you stay with us for a few days and consent to have all these tests."

"And if I don't?" Mike queried, more belligerent than ever.

Dr. Fletcher looked at Mike sternly. "I'm not signing you out of here. And neither is your family doctor, Luke Carrigan—I just spoke to him by phone. If you leave, it will have to be against medical advice."

"Fine. Then that's the way we'll do it," Mike said, already throwing back the sheet and swinging his burly legs over the side of the gurney. "Now either get me my clothes or I'm wearing this gown out of here!" he barked.

Kate spent the rest of Saturday with her parents. While her father rested, she and her mother each made dozens of phone calls to let everyone know the welcome home party for Craig had been indefinitely postponed. Once that was done, they took down the decorations Joyce had already put up and carefully packed them away for later use. Freezing what food they could, they took the rest over to their church for the Sunday evening potluck supper. Through it all, Joyce and Kate kept a careful eye on Mike. To their relief, he continued to feel fine, and by early evening, it was clear there was nothing more she could do for either of them. "Go home,

Kate," her dad said. "Enjoy the rest of your weekend off. And call Craig."

Looking calm and in control again, Joyce backed Mike up. "We'll be fine. In fact, it's been such a long day we'll be off to bed early."

Knowing her parents probably did need the extra sleep after the rigorous day they'd had, Kate went back to her apartment. By 10:00 p.m. she'd had a long bubble bath and was trying to decide whether to catch up on some work or to just go to bed herself when the doorbell rang. She looked through the viewer and saw Sam standing on the other side of her front door. He wore khakis and a short-sleeved slate-blue polo shirt. His hair was windblown, but his face was freshly shaven and he looked so handsome and self-assured it made Kate's heart race. Deciding she did not want her neighbors to hear whatever it was he had to say, Kate opened the door and ushered him inside.

"Where are the boys?" she asked as she closed the door behind him and then moved far enough away that she could no longer smell the soap and cologne clinging to his skin.

"The three older boys came back to town with me. They've all got plans for the evening with friends. Kevin and Lewis are still out at John and Lilah's ranch, with Jackson and Lacey. They're having such a good time out there, riding horses and swimming and barbecuing, they didn't want to come home tonight. So I told them I'd go back out tomorrow morning and spend the day with them there. John and Lilah are due back then, so it'll give me a chance to see them, also."

Too late Kate wished she had put on some shoes or a robe and done more with her hair than sweep it up in an untidy knot on the top of her head. She felt far too vulnerable in her skimpy pajamas. "Then I don't understand," Kate said as Sam advanced on her, a look of purpose in his eyes. A little uneasy to be alone with him this way again, she moved so the coffee table was between them. "Why are you here?"

He stopped, looked at her dead-on, and said gently, "I wanted to see you and to find out how your dad is doing."

Kate leaned a hip against the back of the sofa and although she appreciated Sam's concern about her father, especially after the way Mike had behaved toward Sam that morning, she did not invite Sam to sit down. "He's okay for now." Kate explained how her dad had checked himself out of the hospital against medical advice. "Luke Carrigan got Dad to agree to have the tests Dr. Fletcher wants done, but Dad won't do them until football season is over."

Sam's brow furrowed. "Is it dangerous to wait?"

"It could be if it's heart-related," Kate admitted with an unhappy sigh, unable to hide her anxiety over that. "But there's no budging Dad."

"Maybe he'll change his mind," Sam said optimistically.

Kate frowned. She wasn't going to harbor false hopes. "I doubt it."

Sam regarded her steadily. "Did he say anything else to you?"

Kate tensed. Aware exactly of what Sam was getting at— the argument that had precipitated Mike's attack—she nodded. "Yes. He wants me to fly over to Italy to be with Craig."

The corners of Sam's mouth turned down unhappily. "Are you going to do that?"

"No," Kate said, her mind made up about that. "My relationship with Craig is over. I've already purchased a wedding dress I'm not going to be able to wear. There is no way I'm spending thousands more on a lost cause. I've wasted enough time and energy on my relationship with Craig as it is." Besides, she knew Craig. If she went to him, he'd take it as a sign she still wanted to be with him, and she didn't.

Sam studied her face as he moved closer yet. "Did you tell your folks that?"

"No." Kate began to pace again, moving from the sofa to the dining nook to the bookshelves and back again. "I was afraid my dad would start having chest pains if I upset him. He and my mother didn't bring it up, either, probably for the same reason. Besides—" she shook her head, her mind made up about that much "—I've got to talk to Craig first to formally break it off with him before I tell my parents." It was bad enough she had confided her plans to Sam before talking to Craig.

Aware Sam was watching her carefully and listening intently to everything she said, Kate continued, "That's why I came home tonight." She met Sam's glance deliberately.

"I was going to call him, and end our engagement that way. And then I was going to send an e-mail to him, but when I thought about it I realized I can't really do that, either. It would be too much like a Dear John letter. And with Craig in the military, on active duty, flying missions that are dangerous to begin with... Well, I just can't be responsible for hurting him that way or messing up his concentration.

"This is the kind of thing that has to be done face-to-face, when he's on leave and has some time to deal with it before he gets back behind the controls of an F-16. Which means—" Kate took a breath and let out a long sigh "—I'm going to have to go on pretending that nothing's changed until I can convince him to come home and see me."

Sam did not look either surprised or disapproving of her decision. Which led Kate to wonder, just as she had that morning, what Sam was really thinking and feeling about what had happened between them. Her heart beat a little harder. She knew he had the power to devastate her. Still, she had to lay herself open to potential hurt and ask. "What were you going to say to me this morning before my father interrupted us?" she asked quietly, telling herself she was strong enough to handle whatever he said or did in the aftermath of their impetuous lovemaking.

"I don't think we should make love again at my house. There's too much of a risk of someone barging in on us, and it would be too confusing for the boys."

"Not to mention us," Kate replied with no small trace of irony.

Silence fell between them as her comment hung in the air. As she struggled to contain her disappointment, Kate balled her hands into fists at her sides. She hadn't even realized it, but she had begun to romanticize what had happened between them. And she knew better. Thinking that way would lead to heartbreak. Besides, she didn't need to be a bigger fool with Sam than she already had been with Craig.

Feeling more naive than ever, Kate turned away from Sam. "Look, Sam, my dad was right about one thing this morning." She forced the words over the knot of emotion in her throat. Gathering what was left of her courage, she swung around and met Sam's eyes. "What happened between us last night should never have happened," she continued, making no effort to mask the regret she felt for recklessly opening herself up to even more hurt. "I'm on the rebound. You're a recent widower. We've got your kids to consider. Technically, anyway, I'm still engaged. Not to mention the fact that just the thought of the two of us anywhere near each other upsets my parents tremendously."

Sam's glance hardened. "So what are you saying?" he asked abruptly, looking as unhappy as Kate felt about the decision she'd had no choice but to make.

"One, what happened last night is not going to happen again," Kate said firmly. "And two, as soon as you find my replacement, I'll be out of your life."

Chapter 15

"Are Brad and Riley in trouble?" six-year-old Kevin asked late Monday afternoon as he and Kate walked back from the hospital where she'd faxed her preliminary proposal to the Graham Foundation.

Kate looked at Kevin in surprise. Although he'd begun to talk a little more each day she had been there, going from no answers to single words to sentences, this was the first time he had initiated a conversation instead of just replied to something she or someone else had asked him.

"Yes, honey, they are."

"How come?" Looking uneasy, Kevin's hand tightened in hers.

Kate inhaled a breath. "Saturday night, while you and Lewis were still out at the ranch, Brad and Riley decorated three girls' houses with toilet paper."

"Why did they do that?"

Easy, Kate thought. "Well, it's sort of complicated."

Kevin thrust out his chest importantly as he looked up at Kate. "I'm big enough to understand."

Maybe he was, at that, Kate thought tenderly. "Brad was trying to date three girls at the same time and he hurt their feelings, so they sprayed him with perfume and put lipstick on his face. Toilet-papering their houses was Brad and Riley's way of getting back at the girls. Unfortunately, they made so much racket they woke one of the girl's parents, who called your dad. He made them clean it all up and then he grounded them."

"But Will's not grounded anymore, is he?"

"No, he's not," Kate said. Although you'd never know it from his increasingly surly behavior.

"Well, I'm not gonna get grounded," Kevin promised.

Kate smiled down at him and squeezed his hand reassuringly. "That's good."

"I almost got in big trouble once, though," Kevin confided as they turned onto the sidewalk that led up to the front porch of Sam's rambling Victorian. "It was when I fell off the roof. I knowed I wasn't s'posed to be up there, but I was, anyway."

Kate put her briefcase and purse down, and delayed going inside the house for a few minutes. She turned to Kevin, who had the remnants of his lunch in the hospital cafeteria—hot dog with mustard—on his shirt. "How come?" Kate asked as she and Kevin sat down on the wicker settee on the front porch. Kevin fell silent.

"It's okay," Kate said gently, not about to push him to do anything until he was ready. She ruffled his dark hair and thought about how much he looked like Ellie. "You don't have to tell me."

A look of unbearable sadness in his eyes, Kevin slid across the seat and climbed onto her lap. He wrapped one arm around Kate's shoulder and rested his head on her chest. "It's 'cause I wanted to see my mommy," he confided soberly.

Kate wrapped her arms around him. She rubbed his back, seeking to comfort him in any way she could, even as she tried to understand. "And you thought your mommy would be on the roof?"

Kevin shook his head. He reared back to look at Kate. "No, silly." He looked at her as though she was a complete dope. "I know she's in heaven. I just thought I could see her better from the roof. You know, if she's way up there in the clouds. So that's why I climbed out there. To find out if I could see her from up high. Only I couldn't." Kevin's face fell as he remembered his disappointment. "And so I looked and looked and then I fell." He stared at the tiny floral pattern on Kate's shirt. "I thought my dad would be mad, but he wasn't. He was just scared."

"That's right." As Kevin once again rested his head on Kate's chest, she continued to rub his back. "He doesn't want you to get hurt."

"Well, I'm not going to do that again. 'Cause it didn't work, anyway." Kevin sighed and said thickly, "But I sure wish I could see my mommy."

Recalling what it had been like to lose her brother, to know she would never see him again, never hear his voice, or share a laugh with him, Kate swallowed around the knot of empathy in her throat. Loss was such a hard thing to deal with, even when you were old enough to understand the randomness and sheer unpredictability of life. Kevin wasn't. "You have pictures of her, don't you?" she asked, knowing the good memories could help supplant the pain in his heart.

Kevin nodded, admitting this was so, even as he looked all the sadder. "I got one in my room, but…" He paused. Unable or unwilling to go on, Kate couldn't be sure which.

"What, honey?" Kate prompted gently.

Kevin shrugged his little shoulders as tears brimmed over and slid down his face. "I can't remember what she sounds like anymore," he whispered, as if he had just spoken the most dreadful, guilty secret in the world. "And I wish I could. I wish I could just hear her calling me to come in for dinner or something, like she used to, you know."

Able to feel and see the depth of his grief, grief that up until now had been pretty much locked away deep inside, Kate's heart went out to him. She had to take a long breath to keep from crying herself. "I want to see one of the videotapes that has Mommy on it. Can you help me use the machine?"

"Sure. Just show me where the tapes are kept." Kate didn't recall seeing any.

Kevin stood and took Kate's hand, already pulling her along. "They're in my dad's room."

Sam had told Kate when he'd first showed her the house to stay out of there, and she had. But with Sam at the office and Kevin in such distress… Kate decided to heck with Sam's rules on that particular subject. She'd tend to Kevin's needs first and deal with his father later. She felt a little guilty and a lot uncomfortable as they opened the door to the master bedroom and walked inside. It was a lovely room, furnished with a big cozy canopy bed that harkened back to another era. There was a large armoire and a highboy in the same beautiful cherrywood, and a pair of chairs and a table set in front of a fireplace provided a small, cozy conversation area. The vanity was still set with Ellie's things: hairbrush, perfume, makeup. None of it had been removed. The large walk-in closet was half filled with Ellie's clothes; it still smelled of her fragrance.

Deliberately ignoring the deeply romantic aura of the room, a room that radiated Ellie's loving presence more than any other in the house, Kate followed Kevin into the walk-in closet. There on a shelf was the video camera and case and boxes and boxes of film, all labeled in Ellie's neat hand. Family picnics. Ball games. Christmases. Everything they'd had and lost. Everything every one of them wanted still.

"First things first," Kate told Kevin as they'd gathered up what they needed and taken them downstairs. She had to make dinner for the family. But as soon as they'd eaten, she'd assured him, they would settle in the family room and make memories come to life. Once they had cleaned up the dishes, she and Kevin got right down to it.

"What are you doing?" Brad and Riley wandered into the family room where Kate, Lewis and Kevin were viewing the tapes.

Kate hooked up the video camera to the TV. "Kevin wanted to see some of these home videos."

Will, who was passing by, took one look at the picture of his mother on the TV screen and, his expression unerringly grim, backed out of the room. He had a sleeping bag in one hand, a cooler full of goodies in the other. A small canvas duffel bag was slung over one shoulder. "I'm leaving," he announced from the doorway.

Kate had earlier helped him get everything he needed for the camp-out with the football team. "Have a good time."

"Yeah. Whatever." Will looked exceedingly bored, while Brad and Riley exchanged looks Kate couldn't quite interpret. "I'll be back tomorrow morning, after football practice. All right?" Giving her no chance to say anything else, Will strode through the hallway and slammed out the back door.

Lewis turned to Kate with a sympathetic look and explained, "Will can't bear to see any videos of Mom and neither can Dad."

"That's not surprising," Kate said gently, while Kevin, enthralled at the pictures of his mother and the sound of her voice, sprawled next to Kate on the floor. "Most people tend to react in one of two ways. The home movies and pictures and such either comfort them so much they want to watch them almost continually, or they can't bear the sight of them because any reminder makes them so sad, and they don't want to be sad. As time passes, you eventually get over either stage. You either need to look at the stuff less, or you begin to be able to look at it without crying."

Riley slouched on the sofa. "How do you know all this stuff?" Riley looked at Kate curiously. "Is it because you're a grief counselor?"

"That's part of it," Kate said cautiously, "but I've also been through it myself."

"When?" Brad looked over at her.

"My brother Pete died when he was seventeen and I was twelve," she told them quietly.

Abruptly the room grew hushed. They all looked stricken, upset by what she had just revealed. "What happened?" Lewis asked.

"He was out with the other football players on the high school football team. They were drinking beer, and he got behind the wheel of a car, and ran off the road, down into a ravine. The car flipped over and he was killed instantly."

Brad took a long, slow breath. "Were you sad for a long time?"

"Yes." As Kate looked at the boys she didn't try to hide the depth of the loss she'd felt. "And so was your dad. Pete was his best friend."

"How'd you cope?" Lewis asked.

Badly, Kate thought, as she rested her arm on her upraised knee. "Well, I was one of the people who didn't want to look at anything that reminded me of my brother." Which had been hard, given that her parents had turned Pete's room into a shrine. "I missed Pete so desperately. He was my only sibling, my big brother. But at the same time, every reminder

I had of him just made me feel all the pain and the grief all over again. So I mostly tried to bury it and pretend everything was okay," Kate concluded.

"Even when it wasn't okay," Lewis said sadly.

Kate nodded. "So I didn't really come to terms with Pete's death until I finally went off to college and started taking psychology classes. When I began studying grief, I realized I wasn't over losing Pete, not by a long shot, so I joined a grief group and got some help."

Silence fell as the boys thought about that. "What do you do at a grief group?" Lewis asked curiously at last.

From her perch on the floor, Kate leaned back against the sofa. "Mainly, you sit around and talk to people who have been through similar tragedies and loss. You can talk if you want to, or just listen. They always have a counselor there to help. But mainly it's just a safe place to go, where you know you can say whatever is on your mind, and know that everybody else there is going to understand what you're going through."

Riley made a face. "Do people get all weepy and hysterical?"

"Yes," Kate admitted freely, wanting them to know that crying was nothing to be afraid of. "But it's the kind of crying that makes you feel better," she said.

"Crying always makes me feel stupid," Brad lamented.

"That's true," Kate admitted, "in the short run." She looked at the boys, commiserating gently, "No one likes having red, puffy eyes, a runny nose, or those weird hiccupy sounds coming out of your chest. Or even worse, the feeling that you couldn't stop the tears coming out of your eyes if you tried. But in the long run crying actually makes you feel better. Because when you get upset or worried or you're grieving there's a buildup of certain chemicals in the brain and a depletion of others. Your emotions build up, and that in turn affects how you feel. The physical act of crying releases those emotions, your brain chemistry alters, and then you start to feel better."

"What happens if you don't let yourself cry?" Lewis asked.

"Then the emotions stay locked up in the brain, creating havoc with your moods and your brain chemistry, and you continue to feel sort of lousy or vaguely unhappy or angry without really knowing why. Which is what happened to me," she admitted quietly as she looked at the boys one by one. "I was so busy trying to be strong and brave that I didn't really deal with any of the emotions I was feeling at the time, and then, when I least expected it…when I was in college, they all came back with a vengeance and I realized I had never really gotten over losing Pete at all," she concluded quietly.

Riley studied Kate thoughtfully. "Are you over it now?"

Kate let out her breath slowly. "I'm always going to miss him. And there's a part of me that's always going to hurt when I think of how his life was cut short. But I think I've come to terms with my loss. And, really, that's the best you can do, sort of accept what happened, because you never really get over the loss of a loved one, you're always going to miss that person, and wish he or she was here."

Brad looked at her with new respect. "Is this what you do in your grief group, explain this kind of stuff to people, so they sort of understand?"

Kate nodded. She felt proud of what she had accomplished in that regard. "When I was growing up, we didn't have grief groups at the hospital or anywhere in Laramie. That's why I came back and eventually got one started here. So that there would be immediate, accessible help for people who've suffered trauma, grief and loss."

Riley studied Kate. "Does Dad know all this…about what you do, I mean?"

"Sort of," Kate said cautiously, aware they were headed

into dangerous territory. "It's not the kind of thing he's really wanted to talk to me about just yet."

Lewis adjusted his glasses on the bridge of his nose. "Would you mind if I went to one of your groups?"

"I'd love to have you," Kate said warmly but cautiously. "But you'll have to get permission from your dad first."

Downcast expressions all around. "Well, that's just it," Lewis said with a troubled sigh and a discouraged look at Kate. "He's not going to want me to go."

Sam got home Monday evening a little after eleven. The lights on the second floor were out. The house was quiet, except for what sounded eerily like Ellie's voice. The sound hitting him like a blow to the heart, Sam put his briefcase down and headed for the source. It turned out to be the family room television, where Kate and four of his boys were busy transferring video camera film to videocassette.

Oblivious to his presence, the boys laughed softly as they watched a shuddering Ellie reluctantly hold up a channel catfish they'd caught on a fishing trip. He and the boys hadn't looked at any of these since Ellie had died. He'd figured it would be too painful. But obviously that wasn't the case for his four youngest children. To his amazement, they seemed comforted by the taped memories of their mother. Not sure how much of this he could take without feeling their loss acutely all over again, Sam walked into the room. They swiveled around to face him in surprise. They looked as if they'd been caught doing something they shouldn't. "What are you doing?" Sam asked casually.

"Watching videos with some of our favorite Mom stuff on them." Pausing only long enough to adjust the glasses on the bridge of his nose, Lewis stood and gave Sam a hug hello.

Sam hugged him back, then sat on the sofa. Lewis sat beside him, staying unusually close to Sam's side.

Kevin uncurled himself from Kate's lap and moved to Sam's. "I couldn't 'member what Mommy's voice sounded like. Does that ever happen to you?"

"Sometimes," Sam said.

Sam continued cuddling his youngest son close and turned his attention back to the screen, where the action had shifted to the hilarious setting up of tents at the campsite.

"Where's Will?" Sam asked.

Kate stood and pushed down the legs of her trim white jeans, where they'd ridden up. "He's camping out at the lake with some of the guys on the football team."

Since it was too late to veto the arrangement, Sam supposed he would have to accept that.

"Do you think you could give me a hand with the garbage and the recycling?" Kate asked Sam casually. "I forgot to set it out next to the curb."

Able to see that what Kate really wanted was to speak to him privately, Sam said, "Sure." He shifted Kevin off his lap and, leaving the kids to enjoy their videos, followed Kate out to the garage where the bins and cans were kept.

As they came face-to-face in the yellow glow of the outdoor lights, Kate got straight to the point. "Lewis wants to go to one of my grief groups to see what it's all about. I told him I'd ask you."

Sam knew Kate was very tied to what she did professionally, that she believed in it with all her heart and soul, but he was still stunned she had betrayed his wishes this way. He'd thought—erroneously, obviously—they'd had an understanding about this. He regarded her grimly, knowing if she'd been anyone else he would have hauled her out then and there. "You pitched this to them when I wasn't home?"

Kate tilted her chin at him. "They had some questions about what I did at the hospital."

"And that just came up, out of the blue?" Sam returned sarcastically. He didn't buy that for one minute.

"As a matter of fact," Kate said, glaring right back at him and mocking his icy tone to a T. "It did."

Careful to keep his voice down, lest the boys overhear a ruckus and come to investigate, Sam advanced on her, not stopping until they were toe-to-toe. "You really expect me to believe that?" he demanded.

"You know what?" Kate pressed her lips together firmly and gave him a withering glare. "Given your ridiculously narrow-minded attitude about what I do for a living, I don't care what you believe."

He caught her by the shoulder before she could spin away. He knew he never should have made love to her. Doing so had changed things, made everything between them intensely personal, even when they were doing their best to keep a safe physical distance from each other. "You owe me more of an explanation than that."

"Okay." Kate folded her arms in front of her. She considered him impatiently, not about to give up or to give in no matter how much he tried to intimidate her. "You want to know why Kevin was on the roof that day he fell?" she said in a taunting whisper that arrowed straight to his heart. "He was trying to see Ellie in the clouds. He thought he'd have a better view of heaven from up there. He missed his mother so much he couldn't bear it. He didn't tell anyone because he didn't want to be made fun of."

For a moment Sam was so taken aback by what she told him he could barely take a breath. "He told you that?"

Kate nodded, her expression as grim as his. "As well as how sad he was that he couldn't seem to remember what Ellie looked like or how she sounded," she said sadly, her eyes turning even more compassionate. "Which is of course why I broke one of your cardinal rules and went with him into your bedroom to retrieve the videotapes. Because I didn't think he should have to wait a moment longer to hear his mommy's voice or to see her face if that's what he needed to feel better."

"How did the other kids get involved?" Sam asked gruffly, unable to remember when he had felt so completely ticked off.

"They saw Kev and me watching the tapes and they came in and joined us. There was no big conspiracy, no deliberate plot to supersede your wishes."

Sam understood what had happened, but only to a point. "Then why does Lewis suddenly want to go to one of your group therapy sessions?" Sam demanded sternly.

"Because he is obviously still having trouble dealing with Ellie's death and he thinks it might help him to feel better. Unfortunately, he's also convinced that you'd never allow it. I saw how disappointed he was and volunteered to talk to you, to see if I could change your mind."

Sam studied her, aware the more they stood there, alone like that, the more he wanted to take her to bed and make wild, hot, passionate love to her, which defied all reason and convention. But since he couldn't do that, shouldn't do that, he held on to his anger, knowing that would work well to continue to keep them apart. "Did you promise Lewis you would be able to manage it?" he demanded, wondering just how far her betrayal of his wishes had gone.

"No," Kate said coolly, looking him up and down in the same thoroughly encompassing manner he regarded her. "But, for the record, I don't see how you can reasonably deny any of your boys whatever comfort they might seek, whether it meshes with your particular way of handling things or not."

The derision in her voice stung. Worse, he knew Ellie would probably have agreed with her. "And what is my way?" Sam demanded.

Something flickered in the depths of her eyes. Kate regarded him with the same contemptuousness he had shown her earlier. "You want an honest answer?" she asked in a low tone that fired him up even more.

"Nothing but," he challenged.

Kate inclined her head to the side, her look becoming almost distant, clinical. "Your way is to keep everything to yourself."

Sam just looked at her. *What in blaze's name was wrong with that?*

Kate threw her arm out to the side, in the direction of the house. "All of Ellie's stuff is in your room. Shut away. Unfortunately, no matter how much you try, you can't keep Ellie alive that way. Not in your bedroom and not in your heart. You can't keep living in the past that way. It's not good for you, and it's not good for the boys."

Bristling at her no-holds-barred attitude, he crossed his arms over his chest as a red veil descended over his eyes. "Is this a professional opinion, Ms. Marten?"

"As a matter of fact," Kate admitted, leaning closer still when what she really should do is run, "it is. The way your bedroom is right now, Sam, when you go in there and see all of Ellie's stuff still around, it's like she's away on a trip instead of gone."

Sam stepped back, grabbed a garbage can in each hand and hauled them out to the curb. "You are out of line, Kate!"

Kate merely looked at him as she carried out the recycling container for aluminum cans. She stopped just short of the curb, dropped the container, and planted her hands on her hips. "I'm not saying you shouldn't remember the good times, Sam," she said gently, her face looking even more angelically pretty in the glow of the overhead streetlights. "I think you all should remember as much as you can, as often as you can, and you should cherish those memories with all your heart and soul. But you've also got to move on, however painful a process that is."

"Easy for you to say," Sam flung back before he could stop himself, hating the lecturing quality of her tone almost as much as the validity of her argument. He grabbed her by the shoulders and shook her lightly, his fingers sinking into the softness of her skin. "You don't know what it's like to be married to someone for seventeen years." His voice caught as he let her go every bit as abruptly as he'd grabbed her. "To build a life and a home and a family. And then she's gone. And you're just supposed to carry on—" His voice broke. He couldn't go on. Not without breaking down himself. And that he sure as hell wasn't going to do.

Kate reached out for him, all soft, sympathetic counselor now. "I'm sorry, Sam."

Sam swore. No, he was the one who was sorry. He knew it wasn't her fault, even if he kept acting as if it was. Struggling to stop acting like someone Kate should pity, Sam said, "Look, I know I've been a bastard..."

"No one's saying you don't have a right to be upset." Kate regarded him, the gentleness in her eyes almost worse than the derision. "But you still have to move on. And one of the first steps is to sort through her things."

"I haven't had time to deal with it," Sam said gruffly.

"Except you do deal with it on a daily basis," Kate argued. "Because you see Ellie's things every time you walk into that room."

Like, he didn't know that? Sam thought impatiently. "I get the message," Sam said, irritated she wouldn't just let him do things in his own way, in his own time, like everyone else.

Before Kate could reply, the back door opened. Brad stuck his head out and looked down the curb. He was holding the cordless receiver in his hand. "Dad! Phone—for you!"

* * *

Sam came out the back door. Even in the glow of the outdoor lighting, Kate could see he looked very unhappy. "Are you sure Will was camping out with the team tonight?"

Kate didn't like the way Sam posed that question. "That's what he said," she told him cautiously. "Why?"

"That was Amanda Sloane's father. Apparently she was supposed to be spending the night at a girlfriend's house tonight. They just called to check on her and found out she wasn't there, and wasn't supposed to be. They think she's out with Will. And that they're intending to spend the entire night together."

Kate held up a silencing hand. "Wait a minute, Sam. There's no way the coaching staff on the football team would allow girls to be at this camp-out," she said firmly. All Laramie high school functions were very well chaperoned.

Sam regarded her steadily. "So maybe he's not with the rest of the team."

"And maybe," Kate said slowly, realizing too late she had been duped, "there's no team camp-out."

Leery of burdening her father with unnecessary stress given his current still-untreated health problems, Kate called Gus Barkley to check, while Sam sent the rest of the boys on to bed. She returned to Sam, embarrassed at how easily and thoroughly she had been duped. "There's no camp-out."

Sam swore. "You think they're out at the lake?"

Under the circumstances, Kate hated to speculate, especially when, because she was the "adult" on duty, she was at least partially responsible for this happening. She met Sam's eyes. "He definitely took a lot of camping gear with him," she said.

"All right." Sam went to get a flashlight, his cell phone and keys. "I'm going out there."

Remembering how surly Will had been when he left, Kate
hurried to catch up. "I'll go with you," she said, the look she
gave him brooking no arguments. "We'll find them a lot
faster if there are two of us looking." They told Brad and
Riley where they were going. As they got into Sam's eight-
passenger SUV, Kate asked, "What did you tell Amanda's
parents?"

"That I'd call as soon as I located them." His hands tightened on the steering wheel. Frustration tightened the line of
his mouth. "I don't understand why Will would do such a
thing. Will's never been so defiant. Or at least he never was.
Ellie would have never stood for it."

Kate inclined her head to the side.

"She knew what those boys were thinking and feeling almost before they did," Sam continued.

Kate figured that was so. Ellie had been remarkably sensitive and perceptive. It didn't explain why Sam, who also
shared many of the same qualities, at least when it came to
building his business, sometimes seemed so clueless about
his own kids. "And you don't?"

Sam's expression turned brooding and conflicted. "You
have to understand. She was the one who took care of them.
She knew I was busy building the business, and she wanted
me to concentrate on that, without worrying about any of the
little things, like whether or not the kids got their homework
done. As long as she was there, I didn't have to worry about
anything. I knew she'd handle it."

"So when she got sick…"

"She still handled everything—emotionally," Sam said.
"And she and the kids both wanted it that way. They wanted
to turn to her with their problems and dilemmas. She said
knowing they still needed her, despite everything, was what
kept her going, even when the cancer had robbed her of just
about everything else."

But what about you, Sam? Kate thought, her heart going out to him. *Didn't you feel shut out of your own kids' lives?* "It had to have been devastating when she died," she said gently.

Sam looked as if he wouldn't go back to that point in his life for anything. "You're not kidding." He looked at her with a wealth of feeling. "I never knew how many crises there could be in a single week. But with five kids, there's always something going on, always someone in trouble, or having a tough go of it, or needing extra time and attention."

An understatement and a half, Kate thought as Sam guided his SUV through the entrance into the lake and slowed to a crawl, so they could visually search every potential campsite for Will's Jeep. It took a good two hours, searching all the nooks and crannies around the lake, but at 2:00 a.m. they spotted Will's two-person pup tent. Sam cut the motor on the truck and they walked through the trees.

"Will?" Sam's voice echoed in the silence of the night.

There was a rustling-around sound and swearing from inside the tent. A girl's soft voice. A lot more rustling. And then Will came stumbling out, wearing only his jeans.

Chapter 16

"What the hell do you think you're doing?" Sam asked, not sure when he had ever felt as disappointed in one of his children as he did right now.

Will glared at him as if he were the one in the wrong, and said nothing.

"Since when do you start lying about where you're going and with whom!" Sam continued, his temper heating up all the more.

"Like you'd ever know the difference," Will muttered.

"What's that supposed to mean?" Sam demanded sharply.

"It means, Dad…" Will countered, an edge of belligerence creeping into his voice, "that all you care about—all you've ever cared about—is your stupid company."

Sam recoiled with hurt. "That's not true and you know it."

"Oh, yeah?" Will's shoulders slouched and he slid the tips of his fingers into the front pockets of his jeans. "Then how come you're never home?"

"Because someone has to earn the living that puts a roof over your head and clothes on your back and pays for your Jeep and the four-plus years of college ahead of you. Not to mention all the other expenses."

Sam provided a damn good lifestyle for his kids. Up until right now he'd thought they had all not only appreciated his efforts but had been proud of his hard-won success.

"Whatever," Will exhorted sarcastically.

Realizing this was a discussion that should be continued at home, Sam nodded at the still-closed flaps on the pup tent and the muffled sounds of someone moving around inside. "I take it that's Amanda in there."

Abruptly, Will's expression grew protective though no less surly. "Let's just leave her out of this, okay, Dad?" he said shortly. "This is between you and me."

To their left, another figure stepped through the trees.

Sam swore silently. Amanda Sloane's father was the last person he wanted to see at this moment. Roger Sloane looked at the pup tent. "Amanda, get out here right now."

Amanda slipped out through the flaps of the tent. She was fully dressed and looked braced for the worst. Roger just looked at her and shook his head. "Get in the truck."

"I-it's not as bad as it looks," Amanda sputtered.

"I'll be the judge of that," her father said grimly, glaring at both Will and Amanda.

"We just wanted to spend the night together!" Amanda continued.

"That's obvious."

Sam looked at Amanda's father, hating the fact any of them was in this situation. "I apologize for any part my son played in this," he said stiffly.

Roger's jaw shot out pugnaciously. "You damn well should."

"I can guarantee you it won't happen again," Sam continued, with a stern look at Will.

"You're right about that, too, because she will never see him again." Roger took Amanda by the elbow. Amanda mouthed *I'll call you* at Will, then flounced off, shoulders back, head high.

Sam turned back to Will. "Damn it, Will, you know better than this."

Will shrugged and continued to look at Sam as if he were a stranger. "You're a fine one to talk, considering the fact you got Mom pregnant before you were married."

Sam had known this would come up someday, given the fact Will had been born seven months after he and Ellie had married. "I don't want you making the same mistakes your mother and I did." He didn't want his son having his youth and freedom taken from him before he was even eighteen.

Will studied him with resentment. "So what are you saying, Dad?" he demanded quietly. "That you wouldn't have married Mom if she hadn't been pregnant with me?"

"No," Sam returned evenly, wanting to make it clear about this much. "I'm saying your mother and I would have gotten married—eventually—but we would not have run off and eloped in secret when we had both just turned eighteen. We would have waited until we were old enough to take on such a big responsibility."

"Did you regret sleeping with her?" Will grabbed his shirt and shrugged it on.

"No," Sam said firmly. Nor did he regret marrying her. He'd had a responsibility to Ellie and he'd met it.

"Then what makes you think I'm going to regret what happened here tonight with Amanda?" Will retorted coolly.

Sam frowned at the smug know-it-all-quality of Will's tone. This rebellious side of him hadn't been there when Ellie was alive. "The situations are entirely different, Will," Sam said, hanging on to his temper by a shred. "I grew up with your mom. I had been dating her for three years when we first made love."

"So?" Will snarled. "Amanda knows the score. She knows two people don't necessarily have to be in love to make love."

"But they should be, Will," Sam said heavily.

Will arched a sardonic brow. Offered another insufferably smug smile. "Oh, really, Dad. Is that what you tell yourself and Kate?"

Shocked silence fell at the campsite. Even though she was standing on the perimeter, Sam could see that Kate's face had tightened in the flickering firelight. "Where did you get an idea like that?" Sam demanded.

"Come on, Dad." It was Will's turn to look impatient. Angry. Resentful. "I see the way you look at Kate."

"You're out of line, Will," Sam warned, knowing whatever had happened between him and Kate was their business, not Will's.

"No. You are." Will glared at Sam and sneered. "With all your 'Do as I say not as I do' moralizing. All I'm doing here is the same thing you're doing—using some girl to help me forget all the lousy things that have happened to me this past year." His voice rose emotionally. "And the truth is, right now, only two things make me feel even halfway decent, one of them's playing football, and the other's being with Amanda. And for your information, we haven't gone all the way—yet. I sure as hell would like to, but she's been holding me off."

Sam shoved both hands through his hair, not sure whether to be relieved or distressed by what Will had blurted out. "Ah, Will."

"Look—" Will shrugged at him, more belligerent than ever "—you wanted the truth, you got it. Now can we go home or not?"

Will was barely in the door of the locker room the next morning when Coach Marten singled him out with an icy, disapproving look. "McCabe. Get your butt in my office. Now!"

Every eye turned in Will's direction.

Great. After last night, this is just what I need. Will tried to look cool as he set his duffel down next to his locker.

"Bring that with you," Coach said.

With every eye in the room still on him, Will picked it up and followed Coach Marten down the hall.

Coach had barely shut the door when he turned to Will with a censuring glare and said, "You're off the team."

Will blinked, sure he hadn't heard right. This could not be happening.

Coach nodded at a cardboard box in the corner. "I've already cleaned out your locker."

Will stared at Coach nonplussed. He knew he hadn't been doing that great at practice, but as far as he knew he hadn't done anything to deserve this kind of humiliation. "Why are you doing this?"

Coach folded his beefy arms across his chest and continued to look at Will as if he were some half-rotted piece of trash. "To protect the integrity and reputation of the team."

Will blinked. Was this a dream? A nightmare with no end? "What do I have to do with that?" Will said, his voice dropping back to its usual surly register.

"Everything, as it happens." When Will still didn't get it, Coach elaborated, "Amanda Sloane's father called me last night after Amanda got home. He was pretty darn upset. And with good reason."

Despite his decision to show no emotion in this dressing-down, Will stiffened with resentment. He met Coach Marten's glance. "What happened between me and Amanda last night is no one's business but ours."

Coach shook his head, sadness coming into his eyes. "That's simply not true, Will," he returned, almost kindly.

"Everything you say and do as an individual reflects back on this team and this school. And you have only to open up a newspaper to prove it. Don't believe me?" A challenging expression on his face, Mike picked up a stack of laminated newspaper articles on his desk and handed them to Will. "Read the headlines to me."

Now he felt as if he were in first grade. Will read rotely, "'Six Football Players Kicked Off Southern High Team.'" Will scanned the article quickly. "They were caught breaking into houses and stealing stereos." Will looked up. "But I didn't do anything like that," he protested.

Mike merely lifted his brow. "Read the headlines on the article underneath it."

"'Three Basketball Players Arrested on Rape Charges.'" Will felt a flush start in his chest and move up his neck into his face. "I didn't do anything like that, either."

"Then you're telling me Amanda Sloane is not underage? And that she had her father's permission to be camping out with you last night?"

The heat in Will's chest and face intensified. He looked at Coach. "I'm underage, too."

"It doesn't make any difference in the eyes of the law, Will. If her father wants to press charges for statutory rape, you can be tried as a juvenile."

Will swallowed. "But we didn't go all the way..." How many times was he going to have to repeat this?

"You don't have to go all the way with an underage girl to be charged for sexual battery or molestation."

Will wet his lips, beginning to panic. "Is Amanda's dad going to do that?"

"He was." Coach Marten sighed, looking grimmer than ever. "Until I talked him out of it."

God. All they'd wanted to do was to have a little fun. Get away from their folks for a while. Will tried again to explain this really wasn't such a big deal, everyone did not need to get all bent out of shape about a little making out in a tent. Especially when what they had done was tame by other standards. "Kids our age have sex all the time, Coach," Will said.

Mike's glance hardened. "So in other words this kind of behavior is nothing new for you," he assumed, still glaring at Will.

"Yes. No. I…" Will fell silent. He didn't care what happened, what anyone said. No way was he admitting to Coach or anyone else that he was still a virgin.

Coach leaned toward Will earnestly. "Listen to me, Will. I don't care what it's like in Dallas or anywhere else for that matter. I expect every player on this team to be of good moral character. And that means doing the right thing no matter what the circumstances. Encouraging some underage girl you barely know—never mind love—to sneak out with you and sleep with you, is not a commendable action."

So his dad had said—repeatedly—on the drive home last night, while Kate sat beside him, silent, tense, and—for Counselor Kate—way too quietly. Which made Will wonder. Had he inadvertently hit the nail on the head with his wild accusations? Will couldn't imagine his dad with any other woman, not after he'd been married to Mom for such a long time. On the other hand, Kate was there. She was extremely good-looking. Kind. Sweet. And she was there…in the same way that Amanda was handy…

Aware Coach was still waiting for Will to say the magic words that would get him out of such deep trouble, Will took another breath and said, "No one was supposed to find out about last night, Coach."

"So what are you telling me, that you're only going to demonstrate integrity when someone is watching you?" Coach waited, letting his words sink in before he continued, "Or are you going to be the kind of man this team and your family can be proud of all the time? The truth...behaving with integrity...should be the basis of all that you do, on and off the field. And until you can demonstrate to me that you not only understand this, but agree to live by it, you've got no place on my team. Now get out of here and go on home." Coach shooed him away.

Will watched as Coach sat behind the desk. Dangerously close to tears, his voice shaking with a mixture of hurt and rage, Will warned, "If I leave, I'm not coming back."

Coach looked at Will as if he couldn't care less. "That's up to you."

Will swallowed around the lump in his throat, unable to believe this was really happening. "You'd really let this team continue without a quarterback the entire year?"

Coach shrugged, indifferent. "I've got other quarterbacks."

"Not as good as me," Will said.

"Maybe not as gifted," Coach Marten agreed, looking Will straight in the eye, "But they have their heads on straight. And right now that's what I want to see." Coach dismissed him with a nod.

Will's temper flew out of control. "Bull."

Mike lifted his head in surprise. "Excuse me?" *No one* spoke to him like that.

"You've been looking for an excuse to kick me off this team since the first day I started," Will accused emotionally. "And the *truth* is, Coach, that it has nothing to do with anything I've done or not done, on or off the field. It has to do with a twenty-year-old grudge you have against my dad and the fact you're pissed off because my dad lived and your kid died the summer before his senior year."

Coach Marten's face turned white, then red. "You're right." He zeroed in on Will with lethal anger. "I do hold your father accountable for my son's death."

"My dad wasn't even in the car when your son was killed!"

"No, he wasn't. But he knew Pete was drinking a lot that summer and he should have either stopped it or come to me and told me what was going on so I could have stopped it."

Will shook his head, outraged. "You can't seriously expect that my dad should have ratted on your kid!"

Again, that deadly glare, generated by years of resentment. "If it saved Pete's life…yes, I do. Because that's what a true friend, what a person of character, would have done."

Will shook his head, as disgusted at Coach's blindness as at his lack of fairness. "You're just looking for a scapegoat so you don't have to feel guilty for your part in his death."

"My part," Coach echoed, incensed.

Will kicked at his duffel bag. "If your son and the rest of the team was drinking that summer, it's probably because you drove them to it!"

"You're wrong about that."

"Am I?"

"A lot of things happened that year that brought dishonor to the team," Mike continued. "And none of it had anything to do with how strictly I ran my team or how much peer pressure there was to run wild—that's there every year. It was the *leadership* of the group of kids involved, their disregard for the rules, that set the tone of the entire year."

Will had only to flip through his parents' high school yearbooks to know that Sam had been one of the leaders of their high school class as well as the football team. "So, now what?" Will said contemptuously, guessing where this was all going. "You want to hold me responsible for my dad getting Mom pregnant, too?"

"And reneging on a college football scholarship he had already accepted, yeah."

"So first there was Pete's death, then Ellie's pregnancy

with me, then the ditched scholarship." Will ticked off the transgressions on his fingers one by one.

Coach's glance hardened. "That about sums it up."

"Three strikes and you're out," Will continued.

"Yeah."

"And now you've completed the cycle of What Comes Around Goes Around by shifting the blame for my dad's actions to me."

Coach shook his head. "I blame you for your actions, Will."

"Yeah, well you just keep telling yourself that," Will turned for the door, duffel bag in hand.

"I have not been unfair to you," Coach said as Will reached the door. "And if you think about it, you'll know that."

"I'll tell you what I know," Will snapped angrily. He turned, his hand on the doorknob. "My dad was within his rights to turn down that scholarship if he didn't want to play. His turning it down gave someone else a chance, and he made it through college and made a success of himself, anyway. As for what happened between him and my mom, that was their business, not yours, not the team's. And as for your son? Pete's drinking was his problem. Pete was responsible for his actions that summer. If Pete drove drunk, and died because of that, then his death was his fault. Not yours. Not my dad's. Not anyone else's." By the time Will finished, he was crying openly. Coach was as red in the face as a lobster.

"Get out," Mike barked.

It was all Will could do not to turn around and punch him. "Gladly."

Sam was just getting ready to leave for the office when Will stormed in the door a little after eight and slammed his athletic gear to the floor. "What are you doing back so soon?" Sam asked.

Will threw his keys down on the front hall table. "I got kicked off the football team."

Kate came out of the kitchen, where she'd been busy preparing breakfast for Lewis and Kevin. She looked as surprised as Sam felt. "Why?"

Will turned to glare at Kate. "Because Amanda's father called your father and told him what happened last night. That's why."

Kate looked as stunned by the latest turn of events as Sam was. "What about Amanda?" Kate asked softly. "Is she going to get kicked off the cheerleading squad?"

"Worse. She's being shipped off to an all-girl's boarding school in Virginia later this afternoon."

Sam frowned. "That's awfully quick." Almost too quick.

"Not in this case. Her aunt is the headmistress there," Will reported glumly.

Having recovered from the shock, Kate asked Will gently, "How do you know all this?"

"Because," Will replied in frustration, "I just came from Amanda's house. I went over to apologize to her father about last night, and he told me never to come by there again. He doesn't want me anywhere near Amanda, ever again."

"Well, that can hardly come as a surprise," Sam pointed out grimly, sorry Will was having to find out the hard way there were stinging consequences to his actions. "Given the fact you've only been dating her a few weeks and you've already gotten her into enormous trouble."

Will swung around to face Sam as he defended himself hotly. "It wasn't all my idea."

"You still should have known better," Sam said.

Silence fell between them. Will sank down onto the bottom steps of the staircase. He put his head in his hands and muttered, "Forget that. What about football? How am I going to get back on the team?" He turned to Sam to bail him out.

"Don't look at me." Sam shook his head in escalating disapproval. "You got yourself into this mess. You're going to have to get yourself out."

The pleading look in his eyes faded as Will gaped at Sam. "You're supposed to be on my side!" he said angrily.

I am on your side, Sam thought. *That's why I'm doing this.* "Actions have consequences, Will," Sam said firmly.

"So what am I supposed to do now?" Will stormed, leaping to his feet. "Just give up football? Not even play my senior year?"

As much as Sam wanted to give Will an easy solution to his problems, he knew he couldn't do it. The only way Will would learn anything from this was if he had to figure out how to bail himself out of the trouble he'd gotten himself into. "I'm sure when you think about it for a while, you'll figure it out."

Will looked at Sam as if he hated him with every fiber of his being. "If Mom were here, I wouldn't have to even try." Tears in his eyes, Will dashed up the stairs. Sam turned to Kate, who looked every bit as disappointed in him as Will had. "I can't believe you picked now to try a tough love approach with him," Kate said.

"Why not?" Knowing the other kids did not need to hear any of this, Sam took Kate's arm and steered her into his study. He shut the door behind them. "Nothing else has worked."

Kate stepped away from him. She looked as if she didn't relish being alone with him any more than he wanted to be alone with her. "You haven't really tried anything else," she said.

"How would you know?" Sam challenged, irritated to discover Kate finding fault with him, too. "You've only been here a few weeks yourself." He went over to his desk and began stuffing papers into his briefcase.

Kate took a deep breath and said, more gently still, "I just think you ought to try talking to him, that's all."

"No," Sam said, wanting them to be clear about this much. He looked Kate straight in the eye. "You think I ought to try to bail him out. And I'm not going to do that. I'm glad Will went to see Amanda's father. It means he is starting to try to take responsibility for his actions. But as for the rest... This is between Will and your dad. The rest of us need to stay out of it." Kate was wrong to think otherwise.

Kate frowned. She looked at Sam as if he weren't doing nearly enough and said curtly, "What about Amanda?"

Sam shrugged. "Starting this afternoon, she's out of the picture." And for that Sam was glad. Amanda and Will were not a good combination. For whatever reason, they seemed to bring out the worst in each other.

"Sam." Kate rolled her eyes heavenward, as if praying for strength. "Just because Amanda's being sent away doesn't mean everything is suddenly going to be okay."

But as far as Sam was concerned, that was exactly what it meant.

"I thought you might come over," Joyce said when Kate walked in later that afternoon.

"Where's Dad?" She figured he might be around. In the summer he usually went home for lunch and a brief rest before returning to the school to run the evening practice.

"He's outside on the patio."

Kate walked outside.

Mike took one look at her face. "You heard." He picked up his glass of iced tea and took a long thirsty gulp.

"Yes." Kate had expected Mike to defend his actions hotly. Instead he looked as upset and depressed as Will. Well, that was something, she guessed as she sat next to him, knowing someone had to make the peace here, for all their sakes.

"Did I drive Pete to drink?" Mike asked Kate.

Stunned, Kate looked at him. Where had this come from? "What are you talking about?" she asked cautiously. The last thing she wanted to do was to give her dad another attack of indigestion or chest pains.

Mike scowled. "Will McCabe said if Pete was drinking that summer it was probably because I drove him to it," he said. "I want to know if you think that's what happened, too."

Kate swallowed. If ever there had been a moment of truth, this was it. Aware Mike was waiting for her answer, knowing whatever she did or did not say had the potential to make things that much worse, she said carefully, "I know that Pete felt a lot of pressure that summer. He didn't want to let you or the team down."

Mike folded his arms across his barrel chest. "Do you blame me for your brother's death?"

Kate loved her father too much to lie to him. "I blame all of us, Dad," she said softly. "We didn't talk about things."

"What do you mean?" Mike said, blustering. "We talked every night."

"About what was expected of us," Kate said, remembering those carefully scripted dinner table conversations well. "Not about what might be bothering us."

Mike regarded Kate with exasperation. "I wasn't going to coddle you."

Joyce walked out, carrying a tray of iced tea and lemon cookies. "Kate, please don't bring this all up." She set the tray down on the patio table and poured Kate a glass. "Your father is upset enough already."

Now that she was finally making some headway with her dad, getting him to face the past, Kate wasn't about to let her mother smooth things over the surface again. Like it or not, they had to deal with Pete's death in a more honest manner so they could all come to terms with it and move on without the lingering angst and guilt. Inwardly blessing Will for his courage, Kate said, "Tell me then when would be a good time? Tomorrow? Never?"

Her mom gave her a warning look. "Rehashing the past won't change anything," Joyce countered.

"Except," Kate said heavily, "maybe the future."

Mike had to hand it to Kate. She had guts, that little girl of his. He turned to her again. "Is that the way you really feel?"

"Yes, Dad, it is."

A strained silence fell as Mike thought about that. He had tried so hard to be a good parent. It hurt, knowing he had failed at the thing he had wanted to do best. It hurt even worse, thinking he might have been the driving reason behind Pete's unprecedented recklessness that summer. He had always prided himself on knowing his players' hearts, how to teach them to be the kind of men the community could be proud of, and to get the very best out of them. And yet he had failed so utterly when it came to his own son. How was that possible? And more important, why had it occurred?

Suddenly Mike had to know, if for no other reason than to prevent it from happening again. "I know you were only twelve at the time. But you've had a lot of time to reflect on the past. Tell me what you think happened, Kate." When she didn't reply right away, Mike pressed her. "I'm man enough to take the truth, Kate." If he could dish it out, well by God, he could take it. And if this helped prevent him from making the same mistake again…then any hurtful things said would be well worth it.

Still looking wary, Kate said, "I think you put too much pressure on Pete to be the best football player Laramie had ever had."

Mike immediately felt his dander go up. "Pete never complained to me. Not once. I tried to make it fun for him. That's why I always included Sam in our drills, from a very young age. I wanted it to feel like a game to them, instead of work."

"I know that, Dad." Kate's glance turned compassionate as she reached over and touched his arm gently, reassuringly. "And it was fun for both of them, for a long time, until Pete and Sam reached their senior year and then the pressure to perform—Pete's desire to please you, to make you proud—just got to him. So instead he internalized it, and when that got to be too much, he drank and behaved recklessly."

Mike sat back in his chair and numbly tried to digest what Kate was telling him. "Your brother told you this?"

Kate sat back in her chair, too. "Not in so many words, but I overheard him and Sam talking about how vital it was for them both to get big-time football scholarships one afternoon. Sam seemed to be taking the pressure in stride, but Pete was pretty stressed out about the scouts coming to see him. He was worried he would freeze up under pressure. Sam kept trying to reassure him it would be okay, but I don't think Pete really believed that."

Pete hadn't, Mike thought. And possibly for good reason. In crisis situations, no matter how well prepared he was, Pete'd had a tendency to freeze up. It had been Sam who had kept his cool. And more than once, with quick thinking and the courage to ditch the plan and follow his instincts, saved the day, and managed to score, anyway.

"When did Pete's drinking start, do you know?" It bothered Mike to admit he had never seen any evidence of it. Because he hadn't wanted to see it?

"It's hard to know." Kate lifted her hands helplessly as Joyce continued to pace nervously, wringing her hands all the while. "I never saw any evidence of it until that summer, when I saw him come in drunk twice, when you and Mom weren't around. Both times, he said it was just a senior thing that all the kids were doing, and he swore me to secrecy. I didn't want him to get in trouble, so I never told what I'd seen and heard. If I had…" Kate's voice caught and tears welled in her eyes. Joyce teared up, too, as the guilt and sadness that had weighed on them all for years came back to hit them full-force. "Well, it might have had a very different outcome. So you see, Dad," Kate continued, wiping away her tears, and looking Mike straight in the eye. "All this time you've been blaming the wrong person for not coming to you in time to prevent Pete's death."

Mike knew Kate had kept a secret this powerful and damaging to herself all this time for only one reason. She'd been afraid he would not be able to forgive her any more than he'd been able to forgive Sam. He grimaced, realizing he hadn't just failed Pete, but Kate, too.

Joyce grabbed Kate's hand. "Honey, you are *not* responsible for what happened to your brother," she said fiercely.

"Pete is," Mike said in a voice leaden with pain.

Kate and Joyce turned to him in shock.

Mike knew it was past time he put his own need for exoneration aside and faced the truth it had taken a belligerent kid like Will McCabe to get him to admit. "Pete was aware it was against the law for him to be drinking. He certainly knew better than to drive drunk," Mike concluded sadly. "He did it, anyway. And more than anyone, paid the consequences."

Chapter 17

Will stared at the message Kate handed him, then looked up at her. "Is this a joke?" he asked suspiciously.

Kate shook her head. "No. I talked to my dad myself. He wants you to go over to the field house to talk to him at four this afternoon."

"What about?" Will demanded, following Kate into the laundry room.

"That," Kate replied carefully as she began sorting a pile of dirty clothes, "he didn't say."

Will glared at Kate, trying to figure out her hidden agenda. "Why should I go? He already kicked me off the team." When Kate said nothing in response, Will pushed on, still angry not just at Kate and her dad, but the whole world. "Did you have anything to do with this?" Will asked.

"I talked to my dad on your behalf," Kate replied calmly, looking him straight in the eye.

Will stalked farther into the laundry room, doing his best to intimidate her. "I don't need you trying to protect me."

"I know that," Kate said calmly.

"So why did you?" Will demanded, wishing like hell Kate would mind her own business, for once.

Kate advanced on him, the fire of her convictions in her eyes. "Because I thought someone needed to, Will. I don't want to see you crash and burn, and I think, if someone doesn't do something, that's right where you're headed."

Will's eyes burned. Leave it to Kate to give it to him straight, whether he wanted to hear it or not. "This isn't going to make me like you any better, you know," he warned.

Kate sighed. "I know." For a second she was both hurt and saddened by his deliberate cruelty. Composing herself quickly, she said, "I might be out of your hair sooner than you think. Your dad is interviewing fifteen housekeepers in Dallas today. If one of them fits the bill, he'll be bringing her home with him, and I'll be out of here today."

Will paused. This, he hadn't expected. He didn't want to have to break in another housekeeper. He studied Kate. "You can't be happy about that."

Kate offered him the kind of cool, professional smile he figured she gave her patients at the hospital. "On the contrary, Will," she said, "I'll be relieved if your dad finds someone who can take care of you boys on a permanent basis."

"I thought you wanted to do that," Will said accusing.

Kate looked away—a sure sign, Will thought, that she was hiding her feelings—and went back to loading laundry into the machine. "You know as well as I do that my helping out here was only a temporary thing."

Will didn't know why, but he couldn't rattle her. Any of the other housekeepers they'd had would have been screaming at him in frustration by now. Not Kate. She kept her cool with him and his brothers, no matter what. It wasn't fair.

Kate leaned against the washing machine, folded her arms in front of her and regarded him gently. "Look, Will, I know you're having a rough time of it. And I'm sorry for that. I really am. I wish I could do more for you."

"I don't want you to do more for me!" Will retorted angrily.

"Believe me, I am all too aware of that," Kate said, a hint of irony creeping into her voice before she turned serious once again. "But it doesn't change how I feel. I still wish you'd let me help. In the meantime, think about keeping that appointment with my dad. If you're as smart as I think you are, you'll at least want to hear what he has to say."

Will told himself a million times he didn't have to go. He wasn't going to go. Coach Marten had already reamed him out quite enough, thank you very much. But in the end, curiosity won out and he found himself heading over to the L.H.S. field house at three forty-five, anyway. Not because he wanted to grovel to Coach Marten. But because without football, his life was truly wrecked. And if there was even a chance—he didn't care how it had come about—he could get himself back on the team, he had to take it.

Coach was sitting in his office when Will walked in a couple of minutes before four. He looked up at him, no expression readily identifiable on his face, and gestured to a chair. "Sit your butt down, kid. I want you to see something."

Not sure whether he was more ticked off than nervous, Will reluctantly sat. Coach picked up the remote control for the VCR and pressed a button. Will turned toward the TV and watched what Coach wanted him to see—play after play of Will messing up during practice. He shook his head and sighed. "Okay, I get the picture," Will said grimly. "I've been screwing up out there—a lot."

Mike frowned and looked at Will as if he were the biggest dunce in the world. "That's not what I want you to look at," he said gruffly. "I want you to listen. What do you hear?"

Aside from the thuds and grunts and groans and the whistle blowing shrilly at the end of every play? Will shrugged.
He didn't have a clue what Coach Marten wanted from him,
but maybe that was the problem—he never had. "The only
other thing I hear is you yelling at me," Will said, exasperated.

Coach nodded. And for a moment Will could have sworn
he saw sadness come into his eyes. "Exactly, kid. It embar-
rasses the heck out of me to admit it, but I gotta face facts,
even when I'd prefer not to. All I did from the get-go with
you is yell. And I shouldn't have, especially when I saw it
wasn't working as a motivational tool."

Will turned back to the screen. The apology was nice,
if unexpected. But he was more interested in what was appearing on the TV. Despite his earlier conviction to never
give Coach Marten another moment's peace as long as he
lived, he was beginning to understand why Coach was such
a fanatic about videotaping practices as well as games. You
could learn a lot from watching a tape. Will shook his head,
unable to tear his eyes from the TV. "Man," he whispered,
"I knew practices weren't going well for me, but...I had no
idea I was this bad."

"Then that makes two of us. I had no idea I was yelling
that much at you, either, until you pointed it out to me and I
took a good look at these tapes." Coach clicked the remote
again. The TV screen went blank. Will had no choice but to
look at Coach as he turned back to Will. "I need to explain
a few things to you about the way I coach. You got time to
listen?"

He was asking—not telling. Amazing. Will wondered just
what Kate had said to her father to get him to come to his
senses and ease up. It must have been something to cause
such a change as this... Given the way he'd treated Kate,

Will admitted silently, he was amazed she'd even bothered. "Sure," Will said.

Mike met Will's glance in a man-to-man stare. "Gus and I work a lot on plays and drills over the summer. But my entire focus during preseason workouts is to try to get to know all the kids and to figure out who they are and how I can best coach them. It really burns me to admit I didn't do that with you, kid. I started out with a preconceived notion of who you were—and that wasn't fair to either of us. I expected you to give one hundred percent to me at every practice, yet I wasn't willing to give the same to you."

Will nodded. He couldn't believe Coach Marten was being this frank with him. But now that he was, Will felt he owed it to him to be just as honest. "I think we both could have done a lot better," Will admitted grudgingly, encouraged by the relief in Coach Marten's eyes. "'Cause you're right. I wasn't giving one hundred percent effort, either. I didn't know my plays as well as I should have, and I kept screwing up because I was nervous. Instead of working harder to overcome that and to fit in better with the rest of the team…" Will's face reddened in embarrassment despite himself. "I just tried to forget about it."

Mike leaned forward and looked him straight in the eye. "The thing is, Will," Mike continued, all the mind games and anger forgotten, "I could have helped you make the transition from your old team's way of doing things to ours, but I didn't. And looking back at the past couple weeks, I'm ashamed of that." Mike put a beefy hand over the center of his chest. "I love football with all my heart. And I love to win. I became a coach because I'm a teacher, and I think sports is one of the best ways to teach kids about courage and teamwork. When you play football, you learn how to work hard and how to dedicate yourself and persevere even in the face of great adversity. You learn how to lead and how to follow and how to work your way through crises, both over the long haul and moment-to-moment. But so far this season I haven't been teaching you or any of the other kids any of that. Instead, I've been thinking about myself and my own personal losses, and taking them out on the players. Especially you. And that's not right, Will. Not when you and I have a chance to be a part of something bigger than ourselves, and neither of us has taken advantage of that."

Mike stood and held out his hand. "I've always believed a man should own up to his mistakes as soon as he realizes them. I have not been a good coach to you thus far this season, and for that I'm sorry. I want another chance to do right by you and the team, if you'll give it to me."

How many times had Will wanted the chance to start over with Coach, to earn his respect instead of his wrath? Will stood and took Coach's hand. It was the first time anyone had treated him like a man and at the same time made him want to be better than he was, the man Coach Marten seemed to think he could be. "I won't let you down this time. I promise." *No more stupid mistakes, on or off the field.*

"Good." Mike clapped his other hand on Will's shoulder, understanding, even empathizing. "It's important that we both learn from situations like this. Now that we have, we move on."

"I don't see why you have to go so soon," Lewis complained as he and Kevin helped Kate carry her belongings out to her car.

If Kate had harbored any doubts about the woman Sam had brought home, she would have found a way to stay on indefinitely, helping to ease the transition. But she had only needed to talk to the petite, lively woman with the silver-gray hair and kind blue eyes to know Sam had found a real gem. Evelyn Roundtree was a fifty-five-year-old former schoolteacher and mother of two, had a sparkling sense of humor, an intimate knowledge of growing boys and the problems they faced, and a genial, can-do attitude that would bring more calm to Sam's household than Kate's stay had wrought. Kate had not a single qualm about leaving the boys in her care. Sam had been right to hire her and bring her home straight away.

"Mrs. Roundtree needs the room."

"So? You could sleep in my bed," Kevin offered desperately, wiping the chocolate off his mouth with the back of his hand. "I'd sleep on the floor in my sleeping bag. I don't mind."

Kate paused to ruffle his hair affectionately. "I know you don't, honey, and it's really nice of you to offer, but it's time I went back to my own apartment and back to work at the hospital."

"I think he's trying to say he'll miss you," Riley said, as he came up to join the group.

"We all will," Lewis added.

Although it suddenly felt more as if she was leaving home instead of going home, Kate feigned an air of nonchalance. "You guys have my home phone number and also the one at the hospital. If you need me or want to talk, just call me up or come over and see me. In the meantime, you're going to have your hands full helping Mrs. Roundtree get settled in here. So do your best to make it easy for her, instead of initiating her to your ways, okay?" Kate gave them a stern but knowing look. The boys grinned mischievously, recalling what they had done to her, and she to them, then promised they would not do the same to Mrs. Roundtree. "And give your dad a break, too," Kate continued firmly, "'cause he's really trying to be around more."

"We know," Riley said.

Kate smiled, knowing her work here—to get the family

back on an even keel—was done. Yet at the same time, even knowing the kids were being left in good hands, she felt as if her heart were breaking. Maybe everyone was right, she admitted reluctantly to herself. Maybe she had gotten too involved here, under the circumstances. Determined to be upbeat for the kids' sakes if it killed her, Kate plastered a cheerful smile onto her face and hugged them good bye, one after another.

The misty looks in their eyes triggered an answering ache in her throat. Knowing she was going to cry if she didn't hurry, she turned and got into her car. "Aren't you going to wait until Dad finishes talking on the phone?" Lewis asked anxiously.

Kate shook her head as she put her key into the ignition and started her car. The unexpected three-way call with Sam, the California company and his Dallas office that had come in a few minutes ago could take a long time. "Just tell him I'll catch him later, okay?" And on that promise, she drove away.

Deciding the best thing for her sinking spirits would be to return to work as soon as possible, Kate changed into business clothes and headed over to the hospital to lead a grief group. She had just finished the evening session and had returned to her office to catch up on her mail when Sam arrived. He, too, was wearing business clothes, but she could swear he'd had a haircut and a shave since she had seen him last.

His glance covered her from head to toe as he rapped on the door frame and—not waiting for permission—sauntered in. "You left without saying goodbye."

Kate shrugged. "It's not as if we're never going to see each other again," she replied calmly, doing her best to pretend her heart hadn't just skipped several beats.

Sam circled around to where she was sitting. He thrust

his hands into his pockets and lounged against her desk. "If you'd hung around, I could have told you the good news. We got the contract with the California company to build their new Web site."

"Congratulations," Kate said. Was it her imagination or had it suddenly gotten very hot and close in here? She leaned back in her chair and crossed her legs. "I know how hard you've worked to earn their business."

"It means a lot to me," Sam conceded. He paused. "Almost as much as what you've been able to do for my boys, and me, getting our lives back on track."

Kate struggled to maintain a professional demeanor. "That's my job."

Sam shook his head in disagreement and gestured at the room around them. "No, this is your job," he said with studied nonchalance. "What you did for us was an act of friendship and genuine caring, and for that," he continued solemnly, looking deep into her eyes, "I will always be grateful."

"Is that why you came over here?" Kate asked, her heart suddenly pounding. "To thank me?" *To be nice to me? To tempt me to fall into your arms all over again? Because it could happen. So easily....*

Sam shook his head and looked straight into her eyes, his regard for her as innocent as it was sexy. "I was hoping we could go somewhere and talk about where you and I go from here," he told her, "now that you're no longer working for me or living at the house."

Kate's hands began to tremble. There was no mistaking what that meant. Or what he wanted here. Her. In bed with him. Again. She pushed back her chair and leaped up, nervously moving around her office, checking a plant that needed watering, adjusting the blinds so they were open not closed. "I thought we'd covered that."

Sam shook his head, straightening, and followed her to

the window. "You had your say," he said, casting a glance out at the darkened visitor parking lot with its dwindling supply of cars. "I have yet to have mine."

Kate inhaled a jerky breath and turned away from him, aware nothing essential had changed, despite how much the vulnerable part of her wished it would. "I don't think that's wise," she said in a low, strangled voice. She was looking for love. He was offering her sex.

Sam gripped her wrist before she could move away and held her eyes with his steady, probing glance. "We can't pretend it didn't happen, Kate."

Oh, really, Kate thought as footsteps sounded in the hall outside her office, because that was exactly what she wanted to do.

Kate shook her head and pulled away from Sam. And Major Craig Farrell, resplendent in his blue air force uniform, walked in.

For a second Kate couldn't breathe. And then Craig was beside her, his handsome face sporting a wide, welcoming grin, his arms open wide. "Surprise!" he teased, lifting her up and swinging her around jubilantly before kissing her firmly on the lips and lowering her ever so slowly to her feet.

Ignoring her stunned response, Craig turned to Sam and reached for his hand. "Good to see you again, Sam," Craig said warmly.

Recovering, Sam shook Craig's hand and said cordially, "Good to see you."

Which was, Kate knew, a complete lie. Sam wasn't any happier to see her fiancé crash their first truly intimate conversation, than she was.

"I'm really sorry about Ellie," Craig told Sam, his low voice radiating a laudable depth of compassion. Craig slid a possessive arm around Kate's waist before continuing. "But

I'm glad Kate was able to step in and help you and the boys out."

Sam nodded, abruptly looking as uncomfortable as Kate felt. And for that, Kate couldn't blame Sam. She didn't want to be here, either, pretending her farce of an engagement was okay when it clearly wasn't. But short of telling Craig here and now that it was off, there was nothing she could do but suffer through it.

"We really appreciated her help."

Craig turned back to Kate. "I hate to rush you out of here, but your mom and dad are hosting a big party for us over at the Lone Star Dinner and Dance Hall."

"Tonight?" It was all Kate could do to not groan. It was hard enough now, pretending everything was okay, when she knew damn well it wasn't. To have an audience looking on…

"You and all your boys are invited, too, Sam." Craig grinned, tugged Kate closer still, and pressed an affectionate kiss to her cheek, before turning his attention back to Sam. "Just don't count on stealing a dance with her," he added with a friendly wink. "I've been away from my woman for a long time and I'm not letting her go tonight. Even for a minute."

To Kate's chagrin, no sooner had she and Craig entered the dance hall and greeted her parents, who looked very happy to be welcoming their future son-in-law home again, than Craig took Kate's hand and dragged her up to the bandstand.

"Man, it's good to be back in Texas," he drawled as the entire dance hall erupted in applause. "I know some of you were disappointed when I didn't make it home a few days ago. Especially Kate." Craig paused to plant an affectionate kiss on her cheek, which prompted another round of cheering and applause. "'Cause we were supposed to set our wedding date. But I'm here now. And this time—" Craig whipped a small notebook out of his pocket "—I've got my calendar!

So, enough dawdling. Right here and right now, Kate and I are going to pick a date."

Kate stared at him. This was her worst nightmare come true. Not only were her parents and all the friends she'd grown up with here, so were Sam and his boys. She'd never been a good liar. She was an even worse actress. And she hated Craig for making them a spectacle this way. Especially after the cavalier, uncaring way he had treated her. But then again, maybe that's why he was doing this, because he knew his behavior had been unforgivable. Determined to not let his actions humiliate her, Kate merely smiled and said, "Why don't we just keep that our secret?"

"Actually…" Craig interrupted, something in his eyes hardening decisively. "Why don't we give them a hint?" He turned to the crowd and determinedly waved his pocket calendar. "Starting November first, I've got twenty-one days' leave. That's plenty of time for a wedding and a honeymoon, don't you-all think?" Hoots and hollers accompanied Craig's joshing. "So, what do you say, hon?" Craig persisted, running her down like a bulldozer. "The first Saturday in November?"

If there had ever been a chance to get even with him, this was it, Kate thought. The trouble was, she thought, spying a grim-faced Sam out of the corner of her eye, she didn't want to get even with anyone. She just wanted to end their engagement, quickly and quietly, with as much dignity as possible. As much as she wanted to, she couldn't do that here or now.

Anger flickered briefly in Craig's eyes. It was quickly replaced by incredulity. "What do you know, folks, I do believe she's speechless!" he teased lightheartedly, prompting more chuckles from the crowd. "And those of you who know Kate know that's a first."

Determined to end this before she inadvertently gave away her true feelings, Kate grabbed the microphone and took control of the situation—and by extension, her life. "Sorry, folks, but you're just going to have to wait."

Still playing gregariously to their audience, Craig looked deep into Kate's eyes. "Is the groom going to have to wait, too?"

She nodded.

Knowing not just when he had been bested but when Kate was truly miffed with him, Craig shrugged. "Then there's only one thing to do." Craig turned to Greta McCabe, who was manning the sound system. "Maestro, our song?"

The worried look in her eyes matching the sinking feeling in Kate's heart, Greta complied. Seconds later, the foot-tapping strains of Tim McGraw's "The Trouble With Never" erupted from the sound system. Still looking as if he had the world on a string, Craig guided Kate onto the dance floor. And soon they were joined by everyone else.

"Well, don't you look like the dog ate your last shoe," Wade McCabe drawled, joining Sam for a bottle of Lone Star beer.

Sam grimaced. The only thing worse than a comment on his love life or lack thereof from John and Lilah, was a commentary from one of their sons. He turned to his cousin and said drolly, "Cute."

"I'm serious." Wade pushed back the brim of his black hat. "I know it's been a rough year for you and the boys, but you really look glum tonight."

That was because he felt glum, Sam thought. He hadn't expected to come to depend on Kate in such a short period of time. But he had. And so had his boys.

"Especially given the fact that your company just landed one of the biggest e-commerce deals going right now," Wade continued with the same business savvy that had made him a multimillionaire by age thirty.

"How'd you hear about that?" Sam asked, raising his voice to be heard above the music. So far, he hadn't told anyone but Kate.

Wade, a phenomenal investor and businessman in his own right, replied, "The CEO gave a heads-up to the Dallas and San Francisco papers. They're both running it on the front pages of their business sections tomorrow morning. I imagine you've got messages right now from reporters, needing quotes from you on the deal."

That was probably true, Sam thought.

Wade paused to study him thoughtfully. "You wouldn't by any chance have developed a thing for Kate while she was bunking at your house and helping you out with the boys, would you?"

His gut tightening with a mixture of jealousy and resentment, Sam watched as Craig two-stepped Kate around the dance floor. Even as his emotions rose, he schooled himself to cool it. "Kate *has* a fiancé."

"So?" Wade shrugged as if that were of no consequence. "She's not married yet."

Sam had promised himself he was never going to love again because he didn't want to be hurt. Yet, here he was, not sure what he felt for Kate, only knowing he didn't want to lose it, whatever it was.

Wade's glance turned compassionate. "If you want her the way I'm guessing you want her, cousin, you better go after her."

Because it was a week night and everyone had to work the next day, the party broke up around midnight. Craig and Kate thanked her folks for the party on their behalf and headed back to her apartment for some necessary time alone.

"You were awfully quiet tonight," Craig remarked as they walked through the door.

With good reason, Kate thought. It hadn't been easy pretending everything was fine in front of all those people when she knew, better than anyone, that it wasn't.

"I guess you're just tired. It's been a long day for both of us. Maybe we should try to get some sleep and talk about the wedding tomorrow," Craig said.

Kate blocked Craig's path before he could head toward her bedroom. "That's not it…" she hedged.

It isn't going to get any easier, she told herself. *Just say it.* "I can't marry you."

Abruptly, Craig's face relaxed into a coaxing smile. "Kate, honey, you don't mean that."

Kate looked Craig straight in the eye. "Yes," she said firmly, never more sure of anything in her life. "I do."

Silence fell between them. Craig's geniality began to fade. "You're not yourself tonight," he repeated, decisively. "We'll talk tomorrow." He took her arm and tried to steer her into the bedroom.

Kate shrugged off his calming grip. "There is no reason for us to talk tomorrow, Craig. I know what I want and don't want. And I don't want to marry you."

Silence fell between them. Craig's patience vanished. "What's going on here?" he demanded, piqued. He unbuttoned his uniform jacket and jerked it off. "You've been as cold as an ice cube all night long. If it's about last weekend… I couldn't get back—"

"Couldn't," Kate countered before she could stop herself, "or just didn't want to?"

He looked at her impatiently. "Kate. Come on. I explained why I canceled my trip." He spoke as if to a five-year-old.

"Yes," Kate agreed. "You did."

"So why are you still ticked off?" He strode toward her, arms outstretched. "You've never been mad before when something came up and I couldn't make it home."

"But I should have been," Kate replied tightly, refusing to let Craig take her into his arms again. "It should have bothered me a lot the way you put us second at every opportunity. The bottom line is, I don't think we have what it takes to make this marriage work."

Craig's jaw tightened. "Are you speaking for both of us," he asked quietly, retaining his military bearing, "or just you?"

Kate swallowed. She had known he would argue. Arguments could get ugly. She didn't want it to end ugly, but he wouldn't be satisfied, he wouldn't give up on them, without a reason or an honest accounting of the problems. "Look, it's not just one thing," Kate said in frustration. "There are other reasons, too."

"Such as?"

Kate shrugged. "The fact that you couldn't be bothered to set a date or come home and plan our wedding, no matter how much I pleaded with you to do so. The fact that you not only had no idea how to describe your feelings about me to others, but had no desire to do so, either. The fact that our relationship is nowhere near the top of your priority list!"

"Those are all things that can be fixed, Kate."

Hurt Craig was dismissing her concerns as irrelevant, Kate shot back emotionally. "Yeah, well, some things can't!" She met his eyes with difficulty and forged on quietly. "We have to face it, Craig. The passion just hasn't been there for us— ever—not the way it should be if we're going to get married." Surely he could accept that. Surely he felt it, too.

Craig stared at her as if seeing a stranger. "I don't believe this. Now you're complaining about our sex life?" He was astounded. And furious.

Kate reddened and moved away from him. "Damn it, Craig, we both deserve to have real passion in our lives. The kind that makes it absolutely impossible for us to stay away from each other for months and months at a time!"

Craig relaxed again. Abruptly he looked as if it all made sense to him. "You're upset about the time we've had to spend apart, aren't you?" he asked gently.

"That's part of it," Kate conceded reluctantly. The only problem was, she swiftly realized, he wouldn't accept that their engagement needed to be called off. Not at all.

"It's not as if this was some big surprise, Kate," he told her reasonably, coming closer once again. "You've known for years I was career military. You knew that there'd be long separations. So did I. It's just part of life in the service." Jaw hardening resentfully, he glared at her as if this were all her fault. "You told me you could handle it."

"And I could have, Craig, if things were different when we were together! But they're not," Kate snapped, suddenly beginning to lose control of her emotions, too. "And I can't pretend that everything is going to be all right anymore, when it just isn't!"

"So what do you want, then?" he asked resentfully. He grabbed her hand and tugged her against him, length to length. "More hot and horny lovemaking the moment I walk in the door?"

Kate pushed him away, frightened by his aggressiveness. "Let go."

Craig grabbed her again and shoved her against the wall, pinning her there with his weight. "I thought this was what you wanted."

Kate turned her head to the side before he could kiss her. It was just this kind of ugliness she had wanted to avoid. "Don't."

"See?" Craig taunted, releasing her as abruptly as he had grabbed her. He stared at her, hands jammed on his waist, breathing hard. "You're not as passionate as you thought, after all."

* * *

Sam told himself he was just going to drive by her apartment to make sure she was all right. If Craig was there…if things looked peaceful, he'd go on home. On the other hand, if there was any sound of discord coming from the apartment, he wouldn't hesitate to step in. After all Kate had done for him, he owed it to her to see that she was all right. He had just turned the corner when he saw Craig's rental car zooming off.

He parked and took the steps two at a time to the entrance of her apartment. Knocked. The first thing Sam noticed when she opened the door was that, except for the tears streaking down her face, she was fine. The second was that she seemed very glad he was there. "I told him it was over," Kate said stonily.

"I'm guessing he didn't take it well."

Kate let out a soft, bitter laugh, as if that were the understatement of the century, and looked at Sam miserably. "He didn't believe me. He said I was just angry at him for not coming home to see me more often. So I told him the truth. That our relationship wasn't going to stand the test of time."

Going with his instinct, and against what her body language seemed to be telling him to do, he went to her and took her into his arms. "Did he hurt you?"

"No," Kate said, wincing when he touched her arms. She pulled away from him.

Sam looked down at her hand and noticed that she was no longer wearing her engagement ring. "Are you sorry you ended it?"

"No."

But there was *something* troubling her, Sam thought.

Kate turned her glance back to him. "I'm worried what he's going to say to my folks." Now that it had actually happened, Kate was afraid what news like this would do to Mike's health.

For all their sakes Sam tried to formulate an action plan to curtail the damage. The last thing Craig needed to do was to compare suspicions with Kate's dad. "Where did Craig go?"

"I don't know. Maybe one of the bars. Or a motel. It's too late for him to drop in on my folks tonight—"

"I'll find him."

"Sam—" Kate caught his hand and looked up at him. She let out a shuddering breath. "Thanks."

And the next thing Sam knew, he was kissing her again. And once he had started, he couldn't stop. His lips fused with hers and his hands were in her hair, crushing the soft, silken strands, guiding her head beneath his. Over and over he stroked her tongue, tasting the sweetness of her lips mingled with the salt of her tears. Whimpering low in her throat, much the way she had when he'd made love to her, she wrapped her arms around his shoulders and pulled him against her.

And that was when the door opened. And Craig Farrell walked in.

Chapter 18

"So your dad was right," Craig said grimly as Kate and Sam moved apart and Kate pressed a hand to her damp, tingling lips. Craig looked at Sam, venom in his eyes, his hands balled into fists. "You were out to steal my girl all along."

"That's not the way it happened," Kate said anxiously, moving to step between them.

"Then what the hell would you call this?" Craig sneered as he pushed past her and went nose to nose with Sam.

"None of your business," Kate warned firmly, desperate to do or say whatever she needed to, to prevent violence from erupting between the two men, "since the two of us are no longer engaged."

"And what about you, McCabe?" Craig grabbed Sam by the shirt. "You may have been kissing Kate, but I don't hear you making any great pronouncements of love here."

Looking as though it was taking every ounce of self-control he had to not react in kind, Sam clenched his jaw and said, "Why don't you and I just take this outside?"

"The hell we will," Craig said. He charged at Sam, like a bull, plowing into him headfirst and knocking him backward into the table. It crashed into the wall as Kate hurried to get out of the way. Sam swore. Craig's fist flew, catching Sam just beneath the jaw. A second hit against him squarely in the mouth. A third caught him across the face. And then Sam was up and grabbing Craig by the front of his shirt and knocking him to the floor. They rolled, scuffling, swearing, punching.

"Stop it, both of you!" Kate screamed as a lamp hit the floor, the bulb and base shattering into a hundred tiny pieces. Sam's mouth was bleeding, there was a jagged cut beneath his chin, and Craig had a nasty cut across his cheekbone.

As they struggled to get up, her phone began to ring. "Get out. Both of you. Now!" she said. With a warning look at each of them, Kate went to answer it. "Hello?" She braced herself for the inevitable complaint about the noise. But it wasn't one of her neighbors. It was her mother…

"What happened?" Kate asked her mother as she rushed into the emergency entrance at Laramie Community hospital. Joyce was wearing slacks and a sweater. Her hair was a mess, her face ashen and streaked with tears. The only time Kate had seen her look more disheveled and upset was the night Pete had died.

"They think your father had a heart attack."

A chill went through Kate, followed by a sharp stab of fear. The scene at her apartment forgotten, she led her mother over to a chair and pushed her into it. "When?"

A fresh flood of tears flowed down Joyce's face. "He woke up with chest pains about half an hour ago. His whole arm was numb and he was so pale and sweaty. I phoned Luke Carrigan right away and he called the ambulance. Oh, Kate…" Joyce grabbed Kate's hand and squeezed it like someone in extreme pain as she broke down in sobs. "What are we going to do if something happens to your father?"

Kate wrapped an arm around her mother's shoulders. She felt as though she were caught in a nightmare from which she'd never waken. "Nothing's going to happen to him, Mom," Kate said calmly, willing it to be true.

"You didn't see him. His face was such an awful color and he was in such terrible pain." Joyce burst into tears all over again.

Fighting back sobs, Kate wrapped her mother in her arms and held her while she cried. She tried her hardest to be strong, to be calm. But before Kate knew it, she was crying, too.

"What in God's name happened to you?" Jackson McCabe demanded after Sam had routed him and his pretty wife, Lacey, out of bed.

"Can the lectures," Sam warned his cousin, still pressing the bloody towel to his mouth and chin, trying to not notice that it looked as if he had interrupted some hot-and-heavy lovemaking. "And just stitch me up."

Jackson ushered him in, still staring at him as if Sam were some alien who had just landed on his doorstep in the middle of the night. "Have you been fighting?" he asked incredulous.

Sam grimaced from the pain radiating up through his chin. He hadn't been in a brawl since—he didn't remember when. High school? Junior high? "Either that or I walked into a door, chin-first." Sam didn't even want to think how much fun it was going to be trying to explain this to his sons, their new housekeeper Mrs. Roundtree and the people who worked for him.

Jackson led him into the kitchen and, hand to his shoulder, guided him into a chair. Carefully he pried the pale pink towel, with the KJM monogram, out of Sam's hands. "Let me see. Man. What do you think, Lacey?"

Lacey had already retrieved Jackson's medical bag. At Jackson's behest, she tilted her head for a better look. "Seven stitches?"

"Maybe eight," Jackson decided as he pulled on a pair of latex gloves and ripped open a package of sterile gauze to apply to the wound. "Not exactly the look for a CEO of one of the hottest young companies in Dallas."

Sam glared at him as Lacey filled a syringe.

"Why didn't you go to the emergency room?" Jackson asked as he gave Sam a shot that quickly and blissfully numbed his chin.

Sam scowled at Jackson and leaned his head back the way his cousin directed. "Because you're like a brother to me and you'll do it for free."

"Yeah, but I'm not a plastic surgeon..." Jackson countered as Lacey slid some clean towels beneath Sam's chin and he irrigated the wound.

"You're a general surgeon, which is plenty good enough, and if you couldn't do it, I figure Lacey could. As a pediatrician, she's probably had plenty of practice stitching people up."

"True." Lacey grinned, preparing the sutures. She slanted Sam an amused glance. "Although most were far younger than you. So, what happened?" she continued curiously. "Or are you determined not to tell us?"

"Obviously he was in a fight," Jackson said. "The question is with whom."

Lacey tensed. "Not one of your kids, I hope."

"Nope." Sam winced as Jackson began to stitch him up. He couldn't feel much, but he could see it, and for some reason, that disturbed him. Sam closed his eyes. "Although I wouldn't blame them if one of them had taken a swing at me, the way I was neglecting them earlier."

Jackson sighed. "Glad you finally owned up to that."

Sam opened his eyes, wanting them both to understand this much. "God knows it wasn't deliberate. I just was so deep in my grief…" If it hadn't been for Kate, charging in, waking him up despite his resistance, demanding he change…

"I know exactly what you're talking about," Lacey said, touching his shoulder sympathetically. "I lost my dad as a kid, and my mom and I had a hard time communicating for a while after. Not because we didn't love each other, but because we did."

"Things seem a lot better now, though," Jackson said. Finished with the suturing, he applied a thin layer of antibiotic cream, then a bandage. "The kids all looked happy at the party for Craig and Kate tonight."

Sam nodded. He sat up slowly, aware he felt a little woozy. "They are a lot happier since Kate came into their lives."

"What about you?" Jackson asked, ripping off his latex gloves. He sent Sam a knowing look as he put them and the used medical supplies aside. "Are you happier, too?"

"Jackson…" Lacey warned as she went to the fridge.

Grinning mischievously all the while, Jackson shrugged. "I've got a right to find out what happened. After all, I got hauled out of bed in the middle of the night to stitch this guy up. With not an explanation to be found. Not that I really need one. It's perfectly obvious who hauled off and punched Sam a good one. One can only hope Craig Farrell didn't get in the only punch. And what kind of shape is he in, might I ask?"

Sam grimaced. "He's got a cut on one cheek, maybe a bruise under one eye, but nothing that's going to need medical treatment."

Jackson looked disappointed as he concluded, "So you went easy on him."

Sam shrugged, admitting, "I didn't want to hit the guy at all, but after he bloodied my mouth and split open my chin... well, someone had to end it, and it's clear it wasn't going to be Kate."

Too late, he realized he should have omitted that detail in his storytelling.

Lacey's eyes widened with interest as she handed Sam a glass of apple juice. "She was there, too?"

Sam sipped. "Unfortunately, yes."

Jackson pulled up a chair and sank into it backward. "Where did this brawl take place?"

Sam figured he might as well spill it all. He needed to talk to someone about what happened. And despite the ribbing he was taking, he knew he could trust Jackson and Lacey to be discreet. "Her apartment."

Jackson shot Lacey an I-told-you-so look. "And what were you doing there, dear cousin?"

Sam took another sip of juice and sighed, glad the wooziness was beginning to pass. "Checking up on Kate to see if she was okay."

Lacey frowned as she sat, too. "Why wouldn't she have been?"

"Because she told me she was going to end things with Craig as soon as he got back to Texas," Sam admitted. "And I was worried Farrell would not take it so well."

"Obviously, he didn't," Jackson said, deadpan.

"So it's true," Lacey mused with another look at her husband before turning back to Sam. "There is something going on between you and Kate."

Sam tensed and put his glass aside. "Who said there was?"

"Just about everyone who's seen you together recently."

Sam released a baffled breath. "I don't know where they'd

get that idea. Because we never… It's not as if people saw us holding hands or something…"

"You don't have to hold hands with someone to look at them like you're in love with them," Lacey said gently. "Which is exactly the way you were looking at Kate tonight when she was with Craig. Everyone at the party noticed."

Sam sighed. Swore. Ran a hand through his hair.

"Are you in love with her?" Jackson asked.

Sam hung his head and studied the pattern on the floor. "I don't know," he said. Part of him wanted to be. The other part still felt as though he'd never love anyone the way he had once loved Ellie. And he knew that wasn't fair. And yet at the same time, he couldn't bear being apart from Kate. Couldn't bear to see her with anyone else. Couldn't wait to hold her in his arms again.

Jackson scowled his disapproval. "This isn't good, cousin. Kate Marten just broke up with her fiancé on account of you."

Sam lifted his head, determined to set the record straight about this much. "She broke it off because they weren't right for each other."

"And you had nothing to do with it." Jackson didn't believe that for a second. Nor did Lacey.

Sam was silent. They were right. He'd had everything to do with it. Had he talked Kate into staying with Craig, forgiving him…had he simply walked away from her…maybe Kate would have changed her mind and the two of them would be together now. But he hadn't. He had encouraged her to leave the bastard. But, damn it, she deserved better.

"Well, if you weren't in trouble before, you're in one hell of a mess now," Jackson said cheerfully. "Because come tomorrow morning, when people get a look at you and Craig, and find out he and Kate broke up, there's not one person in Laramie who is not going to be talking about this. Hell, given your status in the business community, you'll be lucky if it doesn't make the gossip columns in the Dallas papers."

Bad publicity, gossip, Sam could handle. It was tragedy he was worried about. The fear that this time Coach Mike Marten was not going to walk away from his neglected health problems unscathed.

"That's the least of our worries right now," Sam said, consulting his watch. Briefly, he explained about the phone call Kate had gotten, her insistence she go to the hospital alone, without Sam or Craig. Figuring enough time had elapsed for an assessment and diagnosis to be made, Sam said, "I need one more favor. I need you to call over there and find out how Coach Marten is doing…if there's anything Kate and Joyce need. And then I need to make sure you get it to them."

He would have done it himself, but Kate had insisted that the best thing both Sam and Craig could do was stay away. And they'd had no choice, under the circumstances, but to agree.

It was five o'clock in the morning before the tests had been completed, her father stabilized, and his cardiologist, Dr. Fletcher, came to talk to them. "Mike had a heart attack tonight. He's been moved to CCU—the coronary care unit— and we're going to have to keep him there until he's strong enough to have surgery."

"Will we be able to see him?" Kate asked.

"You can go in for short periods—maybe five minutes or so—no more than once every hour. And no stress when you do talk to him. Don't be telling him that the car broke down or the house went up in smoke or anything else that might be upsetting to him. By the same token, don't project any worries you might have about the surgery on him. He needs you to be cheerful, calm and optimistic. Everything else can wait until he has recovered. Got it?"

Kate and her mother nodded.

"Any more questions?" Dr. Fletcher asked with a reassuring smile.

"Yes," Joyce said, still clutching Kate's hand tightly. She took a wavering breath and looked Dr. Fletcher in the eye. "Just how dangerous is this surgery?"

The unchecked optimism on Dr. Fletcher's face faded to be replaced with a realism that was, in a way, almost as frightening as Mike's heart attack had been. "There are risks inherent with any surgery," he told them seriously, "and we'll go over those with you in depth a little later. But he's a relatively young, very strong man with a fierce will to live, and that will count for a lot."

It would have to, Kate thought, tearing up as her mother broke down and began to cry again. Because she and her mom couldn't lose her dad, too. They just couldn't.

As news of Coach Marten's heart attack spread, people began stopping by the CCU waiting room, to talk to Kate and her mother and see if there was anything they could do for them. For the most part there wasn't—at least at that point— but Kate did talk Joyce into letting Lilah McCabe take her home for a shower and some sleep.

And it was at that point, when the waiting room had finally cleared out of all but Kate, that Craig showed up.

He was in civilian clothes this time. In jeans and a short-sleeved sport shirt, a cut on his bruised cheek, he looked more like the caring and thoughtful college kid she had once thought she loved than the cocky, self-absorbed military pilot he had become. "I'm sorry about your dad."

Kate knew he was. No matter what had happened between her and Craig, Craig had always been good to her dad and vice versa. She had no doubt the two of them loved each other the way a father-in-law and son-in-law should. But they were no longer going to be related by marriage. Kate couldn't—wouldn't—pretend to Craig that they ever would.

Craig looked away a long moment. He was still hurt, but he also understood she was not going to budge. "What are we going to tell people?" he eventually asked.

Kate shook her head, aware she had never felt so unbearably weary in her life. "That we both wish it had ended some other way but that we're still going to be friends." At least, she hoped that was the case.

Craig's jaw tightened. "Is that what you want?"

"Yes." Kate took his hands in hers and waited until he faced her. "You were a lousy fiancé to me, Craig. But you were a great friend. We just never should have tried to be anything but pals." Kate let go of his hands and sat back.

Craig sighed. "Maybe you're right about that."

Silence fell between them, less awkward now. Craig looked over at her, "Have you told your folks what happened?"

"No. And I can't until my dad has recovered from his surgery to be able to handle the news. His doctor said absolutely no stress."

"Where's Craig?" Joyce asked around suppertime when she returned to the hospital. In a sky-blue dress, jewelry and heels, she looked strikingly pretty and a lot more composed. Both were good signs, in Kate's opinion. Her mom was pulling it together.

"He was here earlier, Mom, while you were home sleeping," Kate told her gently. "He and I went in to see Dad, briefly, before he went on to Corpus Christi to see his folks."

Joyce settled into a chair and pulled her needlepoint from her bag. "Will he be here for the surgery?"

"I'm not sure." Kate pretended to concentrate on the magazine she'd been reading. "He might have to go back to Italy straight from Corpus Christi."

Joyce stopped threading her needle and looked over at Kate. "Just tell me what's going on, Kate. Don't make me drag it out of you."

"Craig and I called off our engagement."

Joyce was silent, thinking. "Are you sure this is the right thing to do?"

Kate nodded, relieved to finally be able to tell her mother the truth. "Very sure," she said softly.

"Is Sam McCabe the reason?"

Kate flushed self-consciously at her mother's unabashedly interested look. "We're not seeing each other, Mom. I'm not even working there anymore."

Joyce let her hands fall to her lap. "That's not what I asked. Do you have feelings for Sam? Does he have feelings for you?"

"I don't know," Kate said. They had passion unlike anything she had ever felt. She wanted to be with him. And it was clear, from the way he had come after her last night, twice, that he wanted to be with her. But beyond that...

"How is Craig taking this?" Joyce asked, still studying the confusion on Kate's face.

Kate shrugged. "He doesn't like it, but he understands it's for the best, and wants to try to be friends again when things cool down."

Joyce nodded approvingly. She began to sew with slow, steady strokes. "Your father would like that."

"I know."

"I'm not sure he'll like you hooking up with Sam," Joyce continued.

Kate sighed. "I know."

* * *

"Looking good, Dad." Kate breezed into the room with a bouquet of sports magazines in her arms. She winked at her mother, who was sitting in a chair beside Mike's bed, holding hands with her husband, then bent to kiss them both hello, and get kisses back in return.

Mike Marten grinned, watching as Kate pulled up a chair and perched beside her mom and dad. "I'll tell you one thing. It feels damn good to finally get out of the CCU and into a regular room."

Kate was happy about that, too. For the first day or so after coming through his heart surgery, her dad had been intubated and unable to speak. It had been frightening to see him that way, hooked up to all the machines, barely able to communicate, and not even able to breathe on his own. But then things had begun to improve, just the way the doctors had predicted they would. The doctors had been so pleased with her dad's progress that on the second post-op day they had extubated him. And on the third morning, they had moved him to a monitored bed. He still had heart monitors attached to his chest, a nasal oxygen tube to help him breathe and an IV attached to his arm, but he was no longer in critical condition and for that reason they were all very happy.

"Dr. Fletcher and Dr. Carrigan were just in. John McCabe and his son Jackson stopped by, too. They all said your dad is doing great," Joyce reported.

Mike grinned. "They're even going to let me get up and walk a little tomorrow."

"Way to go, Dad," Kate said, impressed but not surprised about the determined way her father was going about his recovery.

Mike turned to Joyce. He lifted their entwined hands to

his lips and kissed the inside of her wrist. "Why don't you go on home tonight, and sleep in your own bed? You look awfully tired."

Kate agreed there. Her mom had barely left the hospital since Mike had suffered his heart attack. Joyce was so afraid something would happen to Mike if she wasn't there, it was a struggle to get her to sleep or eat. Kate knew how her mom felt. She harbored the same misgivings herself. But she also knew that being there wouldn't stop anything bad from happening, and that they needed to stay strong and healthy so they'd be able to take care of her father once they got him home again.

"I'll be here, Mom."

"But just until Gus and John McCabe arrive," Mike stipulated, checking his watch. "Then I'm kicking you out, and watching the first 'Monday Night Football' of the season with my pals. No women allowed."

"Who's playing?" Kate asked, glad to see her dad returning to his old bossy, irascible self.

"Dallas and Denver, in Colorado. It's the first preseason game and it looks to be a good one, so we don't want any chatter about sewing or fashion going on while we're trying to watch the game."

"Did your cardiologist say this was okay?" Joyce asked, frowning.

Mike nodded. "Dr. Fletcher not only approved it, he said he might stop by and catch some of it with us."

"Well, then, I guess I will go home." Satisfied, Joyce stood and kissed Mike tenderly on the cheek. "I'll be back first thing tomorrow morning. Anything you want me to bring you?"

"Yeah. Some of your home-cooking," Mike replied with a lusty appetite that seemed to encompass more than food as he looked lovingly at his wife. "This hospital food is for the birds. How they can expect a man to get his strength back on salt-free, fat-free broth, and Jell-O, I sure as hell don't know."

Joyce rolled her eyes at Mike's good-natured but heartfelt complaining. "You know very well they're switching you over to a soft diet tomorrow morning."

"I can't wait." Mike smiled sickly with anticipation. "Cooked cereal and salt-free, gravy-free mashed potatoes. Yum."

"Behave yourself," Joyce admonished affectionately. It took another five minutes of chitchat and warnings and tender kisses for that to happen before Joyce finally headed out the door. After she had gone, Kate took the chair her mom had vacated next to her dad's bed. She looked over at him fondly, hardly able to believe how swiftly he was recovering. "Your color is so much better tonight, Dad."

"I feel better, too." He switched off the TV, then turned to her. "So, tell me, how are you?"

"I'm fine," Kate said automatically. *Especially now that I know you're going to be okay.*

"And Craig?" Mike shot a pointed look at Kate. "How is he?"

Suddenly aware she was no longer wearing her engagement ring, which was stupid given the doctor's orders that her father not have any stress until he had fully recovered, Kate curled her left hand into a fist and put it upside down in her lap. Damn, but she hated keeping something as important as this from her dad. She needed his blessing, his understanding, of what she'd done. "He's fine, too," Kate said noncommittally, recalling the doctor's edict of absolutely no stress.

Mike nodded and continued to look at Kate intently. "Back in Italy already, hmm?"

Kate swallowed and pretended an insouciance she couldn't begin to feel. "You know these hotshot pilots, Dad. They're always in demand. He headed straight back to Italy from Corpus Christi."

Mike watched her face carefully. "Craig's a good man."

"Yes, he is." Despite their difficulties, Kate had never doubted that. She just hadn't been the right woman for him, that was all.

"But it takes more than a good man, or a good woman for that matter, to build a marriage," Mike continued meaningfully.

Kate tensed, and knowing she had to pretend another reason for the edginess she felt, propped one hand on her hip and demanded playfully, "Are you getting ready to lecture me?"

Mike narrowed his eyes at her affectionately. "Maybe," he allowed, as if that were something she was just going to have to take. "Of course," he teased gently, "I wouldn't have to do that if you'd ever played on one of my teams. I impart all life's lessons to the kids on my teams."

Kate warmed at the love in his eyes. "So I've heard."

Mike took Kate's hand in his. "The one that's hit home to me the most during the past few days is that you never know what's going to happen tomorrow. In fact—" he turned and looked at Kate steadily, as if it were vitally important to him that she understand this much "—if there's a rule of thumb, it's that life changes when you least expect it to."

A shiver went down Kate's spine at the slightly fatalistic note in her father's low tone. She froze, not sure what was happening here, just knowing she didn't like it. "Why are you talking like this?" she asked in a voice that was less steady than she would have liked.

Mike's gaze gentled as he looked her square in the eye. "Because," he continued seriously, his voice rasping a little because of the oxygen tube in his nose, "it takes a hell of a lot of commitment and love to make a marriage, Kate. It's an all-or-nothing proposition, you can't just do it halfway. So if you don't feel what you think you should feel, Kate…if you don't love Craig the way you and I both know you need to love him to make this work, then you need to call this marriage off and find yourself someone you can feel this way about."

Kate looked at the understanding in her father's eyes. Relief poured through her as she realized he approved of what she had done. "I broke it off the night you had your heart attack."

"I had a gut feeling that was the case. I'm sorry it took me so long to realize he wasn't the one for you, after all."

"But…?" Kate prodded, sensing there was more.

"This…whatever it is…with Sam McCabe has happened awfully fast," her dad stated, concerned.

"I know that, Dad. But it feels so right."

"Then I hope it works out for you," Mike said. He squeezed Kate's hand, hard, and looked deeply into her eyes. "Because I want you to have everything you deserve," he told her emotionally. "I want you to have the kind of marriage your mom and I have."

"I want that, too," Kate answered hoarsely.

"Just make sure Sam can give that to you." Mike held up a hand before she could interrupt. "I know he's a good man, Kate. I'm through disputing that. But he's been lonely and hurting, and so have you."

Kate tensed as the uncertainty she'd felt earlier came back to haunt her. "You think that's all it is, a sort of misery-loves-company thing?" *Brought on by the fact Sam was missing Ellie and she was looking for a way out with Craig?*

Mike shrugged. For that, he had no answers. "Time will tell." He gave her another stern look. "Just remember your mother and I love you and support you no matter what."

The ache in Kate's throat grew. "I love you, too, Dad. So very much." Tears flooded her eyes as she stood and, careful of the wires and tubes, gave her dad a hug.

"You just do what you have to do," Mike said firmly as they pulled apart. He looked at her with such trust and confidence Kate found herself tearing up again. "When all is said and done, your heart will steer you in the right direction. If I'm sure of anything, I'm sure of that."

The only thing Kate wanted to do was to see Sam. As it turned out, she didn't have far to go. He was standing by the information desk in the lobby, talking to the person behind the desk, when she stepped out of the elevator. As soon as he saw her, he immediately cut short his conversation and made his way across the tile floor toward her. He looked as if he'd had as little sleep the past few days as she had; no matter, her heart leaped at the sight of him. "How's your dad doing?" he asked, concern in his eyes.

"Much better," Kate said, marveling at how good it felt to just be standing near Sam, absorbing his strength and the innate tenderness he tried so hard to hide. She tilted her head up, drinking in the sight of him, as she smiled and said, "In fact, he's upstairs right now watching 'Monday Night Football' with Gus Barkley and John McCabe."

Sam grinned, knowing as well as Kate what a good sign that was. At last, it seemed her dad was really and truly on the mend. They could all begin to relax. Sam slid his hand beneath her elbow and walked with her to the automatic doors. He paused to let her pass through first. "Have you had dinner yet?"

Kate turned to him as they walked to their cars. "No. You?"

"Nope." Sam shook his head and didn't take his eyes from her face. "Which means you're in luck."

"Oh, really, how's that?" Kate asked, thinking what a relief it was to be able to flirt with Sam a little, free and clear.

Your heart will steer you in the right direction, her dad had said. *If I'm sure of anything, I'm sure of that.*

Sam's hand slid from her elbow to her waist as he led her over to his truck instead of her car. "You've been taking care of everyone else for weeks now." He lowered his head, took her face in hand, and kissed her tenderly on the lips, in plain view of anyone who might happen by. "It's time someone took care of you," he told her, his dark gaze intent. "And tonight that's exactly what I plan to do."

Chapter 19

They'd intended to stop by her apartment just long enough for Kate to change clothes. But the second the door was shut, Kate turned to him and closed the distance between them. And once Kate was in his arms, Sam found he could no more stop himself from making her his than he could the first time they'd been together. Reeling from the wonder of it all, he matched her kiss for kiss and drank in the sweetness that was Kate. She moaned, soft and low in her throat, the softness of her breasts pressing against his chest, the scent of her perfume and the softness of her skin inundating his senses.

They made their way to the bedroom, kissing hotly all the while, and stretched out on the bed. Sam didn't know quite how it had happened, but she had become so much a part of his world it was impossible to not imagine her in it. "It's been hard as hell staying away from you the past few days," he told her, wondering how it was possible for one woman to bring so much serenity to his life. But she did. She gave him hope that everything would be okay again, that he could be—and was—happy again.

And then she was on top of him, straddling him, pulling off his shirt, while he tugged off her jacket and unzipped her dress. They kissed and undressed, caressed and kissed, savoring every moment of pleasure. When they were finally naked they came together once again. He wanted to remember her just this way, with her honey-blond hair all mussed, everything she felt for him on her face, for him to see. "I've missed you so much," he said.

"I've missed you, too." Kate whispered as he shifted her so she was beneath him. He didn't know what it was about her, he just knew he never wanted to let her go. "Maybe we can make up for it now?" she whispered, kissing him again.

And she did. Arching beneath him. Sighing softly. Whimpering. Every touch, every kiss, every caress elicited a soft sigh, a quiver. By the time he found her, she had surrendered to his will completely. It wasn't long before her body had yielded, too, shuddering uncontrollably.

"Now?" Sam asked, aware he couldn't wait to be buried deep inside her.

"Now," Kate whispered, letting him know she was lost in the pleasure, the wonder, of being together again, too. He lifted her hips and then they were one. Completely. Irrevocably. Climbing higher, faster, harder. Sweeter, slower, until the world fell away, and it was only the two of them.

Sam left—reluctantly—at one, and Kate fell into a deep, peaceful sleep. She felt rested and refreshed when her alarm went off at six. She didn't know what her future held, but she knew Sam would be in it. And for now, that was enough.

Joyce was already out in the hall when Kate arrived at the hospital. Noting her mom looked happier and more relaxed than she had since the ordeal had begun, Kate walked up to her. "How's Dad this morning?"

Joyce shook her head in obvious exasperation. "Chomping at the bit. Not surprisingly, he wants out of this hospital. They're getting him up to walk a bit for the first time now."

Kate handed Joyce the sack of pastries and coffee she had brought from Isabelle Buchanon's bakery. "I'm sure he's liking that."

Joyce smiled as they went to sit in the waiting room at the end of the hall. "You're right about that. He wanted to do this yesterday. But they wouldn't let him. They said he wasn't strong enough yet."

Without warning, there was a crash from down the hall, followed by yelling and people running. Kate had worked in a hospital long enough to recognize a code blue situation when she heard one. What she wasn't prepared for was the sight of the code blue team running into her own father's hospital room.

As they realized it was Mike's life the staff was trying to save, Kate's heart lurched and Joyce stumbled to her feet in a panic. The cup of coffee she was holding in her hand dropped to the floor with a thud and splattered everywhere as the lid flew off. The next instant they were both racing down the hall in the direction of Mike's room. Mike was on the floor, not breathing or moving, his skin an awful bluish gray. Half a dozen doctors and nurses were bent over him, working hard to revive him. Joyce's face crumpled and she let out a low keening wail as two more staff rushed in to assist.

Kate stared at all the activity around her father's motionless body as she gripped her mother tightly. "He's going to be okay, Mom," she said firmly as the team transferred Mike to the bed and began to intubate him once again. Mike had to be. He was strong. He was vital. He would overcome what-

ever this setback was, Kate told herself firmly as they fran-
tically worked to "shock" Mike's heart back to life.

Joyce began to sob. "Oh, God. No...no..." she moaned as
the first effort failed.

Her heart thudding heavily in her chest, Kate held her
mom all the tighter, aware if ever her parents had needed her
to be strong and in control it was now. "Dad's going to be
okay," Kate repeated, moving her mother away from the door
and all the frantic activity inside her father's hospital room.

He was going to be all right. He had to be.

Sam had just stepped out of the shower when the phone
rang. Whistling, he went to get it. "Oh, God. Sam," Kate
said, obviously crying on the other end.

Sam sat down on the edge of the bed. He strained but
couldn't understand a single word she said. "Where are you?"
he asked, every protective instinct he had coming to the fore.

"The hospital."

Knowing Kate wouldn't have called unless she had wanted
him with her, Sam said, "I'll be right there."

Two minutes later he was dressed and on his way out the
door. Ten minutes later, he was headed up to the room where
Mike had been the night before. The door to the room was
shut. Joyce was seated in a chair in one of the family-doctor
conference rooms opposite the reception area. John and Lilah
McCabe were hovering over her. Their backs to him, they
hadn't seen him come in. Instead of being with her mother,
Kate was standing alone in the reception area, at a bank of
windows overlooking the hospital parking lot. She had her
arms folded tightly in front of her, a tissue crumpled in one
hand. Sam could see she was still crying. Hoping this wasn't
as bad as it looked, Sam crossed to Kate's side. "Kate?" he
said softly, touching her shoulder.

Kate turned and looked at him. "Oh, Sam," she said, and burst into tears.

Instinctively he put his arms around her and cradled her close. "What happened?" he asked. He had called the hospital upon rising that morning to get an update on Mike's condition, and he had been doing fine, after a good night.

Tears flooded her eyes. She looked up at him, her expression disbelieving, her fingers clasping the front of his shirt. "He was fine when I got here."

"And then...?" Sam asked, remembering without wanting to how quickly and unexpectedly Ellie had gone downhill at the end. Even though they'd known for months her condition was terminal, her death had caught them all unawares, left them reeling and in shock, left them looking the way Kate was looking now. Mike hadn't been terminal. Mike had been recovering.

Kate shook her head. New tears flooded her eyes and without warning she began to sob, harsh, racking sounds that seemed to come from her very soul as she laid her head against his chest. Her grief was so intense and devastating, he knew what the outcome had been even before she told him. "It happened when they got him up to walk..."

Sam had the difficult task of rounding up all five of his boys, taking them into the family room, sitting them all down on the sofas, and telling them what had happened to Kate's father. Will stared at Sam as he shot to his feet. "This is some sort of sick joke, right?"

Sam understood their shock. He still could hardly believe it himself. His four younger sons would and did feel for Kate, but they hadn't really known her father. Will had. And despite all the friction that had gone on between Will and Mike Marten, Will was taking it hard. Sam stood and moved toward Will, his arm outstretched. Putting his arm around Will's shoulders, Sam repeated as calmly as possible, "Coach Marten died this morning."

Will backed away from Sam, angry and upset. "He was supposed to be all right! Gus told us at practice yesterday Coach Marten's surgery went great!"

"It did, but…" Sam paused, not sure how to explain a fate no one had anticipated. He looked at the stricken expressions on his sons' faces. They'd all thought, for the time being, anyway, that death was behind them. "There were complications," Sam said finally, feeling himself begin to choke up, too. The autopsy might tell them more, but right now all the doctors knew for certain was that Mike Marten's heart had abruptly begun beating very fast and then given out entirely. The medical team had done all that they could to revive him, but nothing could bring Mike back. He was gone, and his wife and daughter, and indeed the entire community, were devastated by the loss.

Lewis rubbed at his face with the back of his hand and looked at Sam anxiously. "Kate must be really upset."

Yes, Sam thought, she had been.

"Did you talk to her?" Brad asked, concern on his face.

Again, Sam nodded. "She called me this morning, after it happened, and I went over to the hospital to see her."

"Is she there by herself?" Riley asked, concerned.

Sam pushed away the mental image of Kate's devastated face. "She's with her mother and family friends." It had been hard as hell leaving her, but she had insisted he go and tell the boys what had happened while she and Joyce began to deal with the formalities of Mike's death.

Kevin wrapped his arms around Sam's waist. "Are we going to go to the funeral?"

Sam hugged his youngest close, able to guess what he was recalling. "You don't have to go to this one," Sam promised quietly, smoothing Kevin's hair away from his face.

But as it turned out, Kevin wanted to go. He wanted to be with the rest of the family and to see Kate. So Sam let him. He knew it would help his family to be together at a time like this, and also probably help Kate to see them all there, supporting her, the only way they knew how.

Kate saw them come in. Lewis first, looking hesitant but determined. Brad and Riley next. They caught her glance, gave her sad looks and encouraging nods, and then, heads bent respectfully, followed Lewis into the pew. Will was next. Even in the midst of his family, he somehow seemed to be apart from them. Emotionally. Mentally. And the look on his face worried Kate. As usual, Will was holding far too much in. Sam followed, holding Kevin by the hand, his face tense, stricken with sadness.

Their eyes locked. And Sam's strength seemed to reach out to her from across the room. His understanding was all the fortification she needed. With a sigh, she turned back to the front of the church. Kate thought about how ironic it was that one of her dad's last acts had been to encourage, in his own blustery way, her relationship with Sam. *You knew I loved him, didn't you, Dad?* Kate thought as her mother reached over and squeezed her hand. *But that didn't stop you from worrying.*

And that worry was a stress Mike hadn't needed.

"Where's Will?" Sam asked hours later when he went into the family room to check on the boys. Although they had all done their best to hide it, they were all pretty upset. He knew how they felt. It had been hard, seeing Kate and her mom suffering that way.

Lewis looked up from the movie they were watching. "He went upstairs a few minutes ago. He said he was going to bed."

Sam glanced at his watch. "At eight-thirty?"

Brad and Riley shrugged. They had no idea what was on Will's mind. They did know enough to not bother Will when he was in one of his darker moods. "Can we go out for a while?" Riley asked, already getting restlessly to his feet.

"Yeah. Some of the kids were gonna meet down at the pizza place tonight and talk about what happened and stuff," Brad said.

Sam figured it would help them to get out of the house for a while and be with their friends. "Just be home by curfew."

They nodded and took off. As soon as they left, Lewis looked at Sam and said, "I think Will was kind of bummed out about everything that happened today."

Kevin tugged on Sam's shirtsleeve and looked up at him. "He looked like he was gonna cry. Only he didn't."

Sam nodded. Maybe Will just needed some time alone. It was understandable. He'd give him some time to vent his emotions in private and then go up and check on him later. Kevin tugged on Sam's sleeve again. "I want you to come upstairs and stay with me till I go to sleep," he said.

"I can do it," Lewis volunteered quickly.

Sam knew he could. So did Kevin. That wasn't the point. Sam turned to Lewis. "You've been pinch-hitting for me quite a lot lately, haven't you?" he said quietly.

Lewis shrugged and looked at the floor shyly. "I know how it feels to be one of the youngest."

Judging from the expression on his face, that meant undervalued and overlooked. And it was time that changed, too, Sam thought. He clasped Lewis's shoulder in a one-armed hug. "I appreciate the offer as well as everything you've done for me lately. But I've got it covered tonight, okay."

Lewis nodded, pleased his effort had been recognized, relieved not to be responsible for Kevin. "Okay. I'm going to go play on my computer and then go to bed."

"Good deal," Sam said, turning off the TV.

"Can you read me a book?" Kevin asked as he and Sam headed for the stairs, after Lewis.

"Sure," Sam said, wondering how long it had been since he had done that for Kev—if he'd ever done that for Kev. He'd done it for Will, maybe even Brad. After that, it was always Ellie who had read for the kids.

Three chapters of the Winnie The Pooh book later, Kevin was asleep. Sam looked in on Lewis and found him sacked out, too. He climbed the stairs to the third floor, and knocked on Will's door. There was no answer. Eventually he opened the door and went in. The room was dark. Sam made his way over to the lumpy figure in the center of the bed. The bedcovers were pulled up all the way over the pillows. Odd. Will never slept with the blanket over his head. But he had tonight, and when Sam pulled the bedcovers back, he understood why.

Will wasn't in his bed. Probably never had been.

Sam sat on the edge of the bed, stunned. He'd thought Will had learned his lesson. He certainly wouldn't have figured Will would pick tonight to pull anything. Unless this was more than just a ruse to stay out all night without permission. Unless Will was running away. Swearing, Sam turned on the light and headed straight for Will's closet. It was the usual mess, with belongings piled on top of belongings, with little actually hung up, and stuff crammed in every inch of available space.

His suitcase was still there, Sam noted with relief, as appeared to be most of his clothes. The only thing that looked to be out of place was his duffel bag, which was sticking out from beneath a stack of magazines and books and athletic gear. Sam went to push it back and heard the clink of glass upon glass. Frowning, Sam unzipped the bag all the way. And swore at what he saw.

He took the stairs down two and three at a time. Riley and Brad were just coming in. They looked in much the same glum mood as they had when they'd left. Which meant, whatever trouble Will was up to, he wasn't sharing with them. "Did you guys see Will?" Sam asked hurriedly.

"No." Brad and Riley traded perplexed glances. "Should we have?"

"Is his Jeep out front?"

They went to the window to look out. "Uh, no, it's not, actually. Guess he went out."

Sam checked the board for messages, and found no notes from Will.

"How come you're so upset?" Riley asked.

"I'm worried about him," Sam said. "So I'm going out to look for him. If he comes home in the meantime, I want you to make sure he stays here until I return. Got it?"

Brad and Riley nodded in unison.

Sam headed out to his truck. He couldn't believe he had missed all the signs. They'd been right there in front of him. He should have suspected what was going on, but he hadn't. And now Will was out there, driving, probably alone, and quite possibly drunk. Damn. Damn, damn, damn!

Will drove around for hours, wanting to be alone, unsure where to go. He hadn't been this depressed since his mom died, and all he wanted was for the sadness and the sense of futility to go away. That had happened for a while, with Amanda.

Okay, so it was mostly the sex—or more accurately, the possibility of it—that had kept him from dwelling on the mucked-up mess his life had become the past year. But it had still been something to look forward to, the hours alone with his girl.

Since she'd been sent to boarding school, he didn't even have that.

And now this. Will pushed away the memory of Coach Marten's funeral, lifted the bottle to his lips, and took a long, numbing sip.

If he were lucky, by morning, he wouldn't feel a damn thing.

Sam checked every restaurant in town, the movie theater, the putt-putt place. He drove out to the lake, and spent an hour there, cruising around, looking for Will's black Jeep. Nothing. It wasn't at any of the campsites, or the place where the popular kids hung out. And all the while, he had one sharp image in his mind. Will, lying somewhere, drunk or dead. For the first time Sam had an inkling of what it had been like for Mike and Joyce Marten when they had lost Pete in a car crash, and knew, as a parent, just how they had suffered. To lose a spouse was hard enough. To lose a child...

Please, he prayed, *let it not be too late. Let me find him...*.

Will was seated at the top of the bleachers, half a bottle of whiskey in him, when he saw the headlights of an approaching vehicle move across the high school parking lot and then shine through the chain-link stadium fence onto the football field. He smiled crookedly as whoever it was passed right on through the double gates, just as he had, and drove along the hard surface of the running track until they were dead even with his Jeep.

His smile faded as he saw his dad climb out of the vehicle and head for his Jeep. Finding it empty, he watched as his father turned in the direction of the stands, and saw Will sitting in the shadow of the press box at the top.

Will swore as his dad mounted the steps two at a time. Unlike Will, who couldn't wait to change into jeans and a

T-shirt once they'd all gotten home from the church, Sam still wore his black suit pants and starched white shirt. He'd loosened his equally austere tie, but hadn't bothered to take it off. There was just enough light from the moon up above, and the lights in the high school parking lot for them to see each other clearly. "I've been looking all over for you," Sam told Will grimly.

Will tilted his head at Sam, not knowing why he was so angry now, just knowing that he was. "Too little, too late, don't you think?" Will asked sarcastically.

Sam's lips thinned and hurt glimmered in his eyes. "What's that supposed to mean?"

"I mean it's too late for you to be playing the dutiful father." Will lifted his whiskey bottle at Sam in a silent go-to-blazes toast. "Go back to work. Go back to Kate. Go wherever the hell you want, but leave me the hell alone."

"That's enough, Will," Sam said firmly.

"You may think so. I don't."

Will uncapped the bottle and, still holding his father's eyes rebelliously, took a sip. "You can't all of a sudden care what happens to me."

The frown lines on either side of Sam's mouth deepened. "That's not true and you know it. I do care about you. I care about all of you boys."

"Okay," Will said as the whiskey burned in his stomach, "how many times have I missed curfew since January?" He tensed at Sam's blank look. "See, that's the difference," Will pointed out, sadness flooding him again. "Mom would have known everything I'd done right and everything I'd done wrong on a moment's notice, whereas you, Dad, don't have a clue."

Sam stiffened. As he stared at Will, he seemed to be struggling for patience. "I don't keep score about things like that."

"Wrong again," Will corrected, his disappointment in his

father deepening. Couldn't he be honest once—even with himself—about this? "You know all sorts of things off the top of your head when it comes to your work. You just don't know stuff about us kids because we don't matter to you the way your company does." Tears burned his eyes. Furious at the display of weakness, Will pocketed his bottle of whiskey and rubbed the heels of his hands against his eyes.

Sam closed the distance between them and reached over to touch Will's shoulder gently. "We can talk about this at home, Will."

Will shrugged off his father's hand. "I don't want to go home."

Sam braced his hands on his hips. "You sure as hell can't stay up here, drinking."

"Yeah?" Will glared at his father and shot to his feet. "Who's going to stop me?"

"I am."

They tussled over the bottle. It fell through the bleachers and crashed to the ground below. Sam looked stunned at the violence, but Will shrugged. "Plenty more where that came from." Unfortunately, he'd have to go down to his Jeep and reach beneath the seat to get it. He started down the steps. To his surprise, his legs were none too steady and now that he was up and moving, his head felt a little light and fuzzy, too. Holding on to the railing that separated the reserved section from the student section, Will moved unsteadily toward the bottom row of bleachers. Sam was right behind him as they crossed the track to his Jeep.

Will felt better, just knowing another drink was close at hand. He smiled drunkenly as he fished the keys out of his pocket. "Well, nice seeing you, Dad."

Sam clamped a hand on Will's shoulder before he could open the door, and spun Will around toward his vehicle. "You aren't driving anywhere," Sam said.

Will dug in his feet as they reached Sam's truck, successfully slowing their forward motion. "Well, I'm not going home with you," he said, beginning to struggle against his father's pushiness.

Sam reached around Will to open the passenger side door and ordered in a voice as relentless as his grip, "Get in the car, Will."

Will held himself stiff, refusing to bend his head, even in the slightest. "You just try and make me," he threatened darkly.

Sam put one hand on the middle of Will's spine, kept the other on his shoulder, and tried to shove Will into the SUV. So full of fury he could barely see, Will rammed his forearm into his dad's stomach and spun away. Before his dad could regain his grip on him, Will threw a punch, catching Sam squarely in the gut. Swearing his frustration, Sam grabbed at Will again. They tussled, both of them cursing, Will kicking and shoving and yelling, and Sam gripping him and telling him to calm down. Will swung out again as hard as he could. Only this time, Sam was ready for Will, and he ducked and stepped neatly aside.

His target suddenly gone, Will tried to change direction and pull back, to regain his balance, but his body was not responding to his brain's cues. He took a nosedive toward the truck door. Will had a brief impression of cold hard metal coming up to greet him before all went totally, blissfully black.

Sam managed to catch Will before his head slammed into the open car door, but he could do nothing to stop him from passing out. Nor could he rouse him from his drunken stupor—Will was out cold. Knowing there was no time to spare, he lifted him into his truck and drove straight to the emergency room at Laramie Community Hospital. The first person he saw as he parked beneath the covered portico was Jackson McCabe.

"What happened?" Jackson asked as he dashed out to Sam's truck.

Sam explained while Jackson checked Will's vital signs and shone a penlight into his eyes. "If he's had as much whiskey as you think, we're going to have to pump his stomach," Jackson said as an orderly rushed out with a stretcher.

"Do whatever you have to do," Sam said, dashing the tears from the corners of his eyes. He'd never forgive himself if anything happened to Will.

Jackson went with Will and the nurses to a treatment room while Sam talked to the admitting clerk and gave his insurance information. Then there was nothing to do but wait. As he sat there, thinking about all the ways he had failed his kids, Sam wished he could call Kate. But he knew he couldn't. She had just buried her father. She had enough to deal with without taking on his problems, too. Beside, this wasn't her crisis, Sam thought fiercely. It was his. And it was high time he started dealing with it the way he should have from the very first.

An hour later Jackson came out to tell Sam what was happening. "He's going to be okay."

"Thank God," Sam said, his whole body sagging with relief.

"But this could've had a very different outcome," Jackson continued sternly, "if you hadn't found him when you had and brought him in."

Sam swallowed around the hard knot of emotion in his throat. No one had to tell him Will could very easily have died tonight, either from alcohol poisoning, or a fall. No one had to tell him what would have happened had Will gotten behind the wheel of his Jeep, and driven off, just seconds before he passed out. Sam's eyes stung. "I'll make sure he understands that," he said hoarsely.

Jackson took Sam aside, acting as much family now as Will's doctor. "I want you to do more than that. I want Will to undergo alcohol counseling, and because he's under age, the program requires you, as his parent, to take the classes with him."

Feeling too choked up to speak, Sam nodded his consent. He didn't care what he had to do. He just wanted his family happy, healthy and whole again. That wasn't going to happen unless he made it a priority and took the necessary steps.

"I've already talked to Will about the foolishness of his actions, but you need to speak with him, too, Sam."

Jackson took Sam back to the treatment room. Will was lying in his hospital bed. He had an IV in his arm. Tears streaked his face. His gown was stained with the charcoal solution they had pumped into his stomach. He was pale and sweaty and his hands were shaking. "We're going to release you in a few minutes," Jackson said.

"I don't feel very good," Will said.

Jackson looked as if he had expected as much. "You're not going to feel too great tomorrow, either. You're going to have a headache, an upset stomach and cramping in your arms and legs from dehydration." Jackson looked from Will to Sam and back again. "I'll let you and your dad talk while I fill out the paperwork so you can go home."

Jackson shut the door to give them some privacy and Sam pulled a chair up next to Will. "You really scared me, Will."

Will refused to look at Sam. Tears leaked from the corners of his eyes.

"I found the duffel bag in your room. I know you've been drinking for some time. Is it because of Mom dying?"

"It's everything. It's her. It's Coach Marten. I don't understand why this stuff has to happen. It's not fair."

"No, it's not. But that doesn't give you or me permission to self-destruct. We've got to stop running away from the painful stuff and be there for each other. Do you think you can do that?" Sam asked.

He wanted Will to say yes. Instead, there was only silence.

Sam rose and perched on the edge of Will's bed, and forced him to look at him. "Listen to me, Will. I couldn't bear it if anything happened to you. I love you and I want to help you. I know I haven't been the kind of dad you wanted or needed this past year. Hell, maybe I've never been there for you the way I should. But it's not too late—"

"Yeah, it is," Will said, crying.

Sam took Will by the shoulders, forced him to look at him, and tried again. "Don't you understand if I lost you it would break my heart? I love you, and I want to help you. But you've got to let me."

Will gripped Sam, hard, and broke down in his arms. His body shook with harsh, racking sobs.

"Do you hear me?" Sam said, hugging Will all the harder. "I love you. And starting now, I am going to be there for you every day, every night." Sam didn't know how, he didn't care how long it took, but his son was never going to feel this alone again.

Chapter 20

"Tell me you're not back at work already," Meg Lockhart-Carrigan said when she ran into Kate in the corridor outside Kate's office.

Kate carried her briefcase into her office and set it on her desk. "I'm back at work."

Meg hovered in the doorway, obviously wanting to offer Kate what comfort she could. "Everyone thought you'd take at least a week off," she said gently, "not just a few days."

Kate sorted through the stack of mail on her desk, the sheer routineness of the action making her feel a little better. "I know," she replied absently. "I had a call from the hospital administrator urging me to do just that."

Meg shut the door, ensuring them some privacy. "Then why don't you?"

Because I need to feel useful. I need to get my life back to normal. If it would ever get back to normal without her dad, Kate thought. "I just needed to be here," Kate said finally.

Meg nodded. Having lost both her parents when she was in her early twenties, she understood what was going through Kate's heart and mind as only someone who has also been through it themselves could. "How's your mom holding up?" Meg asked softly.

"As well as can be expected," Kate said. "She's got a lot of friends, and that's helping. Plus, we did everything we needed to do related to Dad's death." They had hosted a wake at the house after the funeral services. They had met with the family attorney and financial advisor. Cleaned out Mike's office at the school, and sorted through his belongings at home, giving some thing to charity and others to friends and keeping the most personal items for themselves and any children Kate might have someday. They'd even established a scholarship fund in Mike's memory, and accepted civic and education awards bestowed on him posthumously, knowing the actual ceremonies of such awards would come later. Through it all, Sam had called Kate often and done what he could to help her and her mother out, given the responsibilities he had at home. But now, Kate thought, it was time for her to move on and resume her life again.

Meg rummaged through the file folder she was carrying and handed Kate a sheet of paper. "Well, as long as you're in, here's a list of counseling referrals. Some of them have already made appointments with your office. Some will be calling."

Kate scanned the list, perusing who needed grief counseling, checking the trauma victims. She stopped at the name referred for alcohol counseling. Read it once and then again. "Will and Sam McCabe signed up for alcohol counseling?" Kate asked, stunned. She didn't personally handle this—someone from Alcoholics Anonymous would—but the arrangements were made for hospital patients through her office.

Meg nodded. "I never thought I'd see Sam agree to any kind of counseling period, for him or his boys. But after what happened with Will…"

"What happened with Will?" Kate asked in alarm. "Damn it, Meg. Tell me."

"Will drank enough whiskey to kill himself the night of your dad's funeral. Sam found him at the football stadium and brought him to the ER. They had to pump his stomach. I thought surely, given how close the two of you seem to have gotten recently, that Sam would have told you."

So would have Kate.

Will was sitting on the front porch when Kate drove up and got out of her car, some sort of book in her hand. He couldn't say he was surprised. He had been expecting her to come over to see him and his brothers for days, although he understood all too well why she hadn't. Losing Mom had been horrible. It couldn't have been any easier for Kate to suddenly lose her dad.

She walked up the steps and headed straight for him. "Hi," she said softly, looking down at him.

Will could tell by the way she was looking at him that she'd learned what he had done. He sighed, wondering when his humiliation was going to end. "You know, don't you?" he said, dispiritedly.

She nodded and gestured at a chair. "Mind if I sit down?"

Although he didn't particularly want company, Will didn't have the heart to tell her, not after all she'd been through herself the past couple weeks, with her broken engagement to that hotshot pilot, her dad's illness, surgery and death. He shrugged. "If you want."

Kate spoke in a soft, business-like tone. "I wanted to tell you someone else in my office is making the arrangements for you and your dad."

Will didn't know what to make of that. He'd sort of gotten used to Kate butting into their lives and trying to help. "They said at the ER that you were going to do it."

Kate shrugged as if it were no big deal. "I figured you'd be more comfortable with someone else."

"I gave you a pretty hard time when you were living here," Will said.

Kate looked at him, letting him know it was all water under the bridge. "I know you didn't mean it."

Will tilted his head. He wondered how she had gotten to be so understanding. Especially when she'd had to put up with so much stuff from him. "I sure acted like I did."

"You were hurting," Kate countered, nothing but gentleness in her eyes. "You would have lashed out at anyone who happened to be near. I was just a ready target, that's all."

Will breathed in deeply through his nose. He didn't know what it was lately. He hadn't been able to cry the whole time his mom was sick. And now, about all he wanted to do *was* cry. Despite the calm way she talked to him, Kate looked really sad, too.

"I never had a chance to thank you for talking to your dad that way," Will blurted, unable to help himself. "It really made a difference. If he hadn't—" *Died,* Will was about to say. "Well, we had worked things out, and he gave me another chance to be on the team." Will paused. "He was a good guy."

Kate smiled through her tears. "Just kind of rough around the edges."

Will nodded. "Yeah. He was that, all right. But all heart on the inside."

Kate picked up the book on her lap and handed it to him. "This belonged to my dad. It's a book about the greatest football players ever. I thought maybe you'd like to have it."

"Thanks." The ache in Will's throat grew.

"Well…" Kate stood. Abruptly she looked as if she were trying hard to not cry.

Will swallowed, looked away, afraid if she did, he'd lose it, too.

After a moment Kate pulled it together, reached into the pocket of her jacket, and handed him a small white business card. "If you ever need anything…"

"I'll call you," Will said. And to his surprise, he could see himself doing just that.

Chapter 21

Sam caught up with Kate at her apartment early that evening. She was wearing a pretty blue dress but her hair was rumpled and her eyes, empty. When Sam started to hug her, she turned her glance away and remained rigid and unyielding in his arms.

Realizing he'd been right to think something was very wrong, and had been getting more so ever since her father's funeral, Sam dropped his hold on her and stepped away. Wondering what was making her so tense and ill-at-ease in his presence, wondering what he had done to make her pull away from him this way, he leaned against the wall. "Will said you stopped by the house today to give him a book that belonged to your dad." Sam figured they had to start somewhere and it might as well be with that. He looked at Kate steadily, taking in the blue-gray shadows of fatigue beneath her eyes, the vulnerable set of her mouth. "From what I gathered, he appreciated both the gift and your concern for him."

Looking ready to flee at the first available opportunity, Kate perched on the edge of the armchair. She folded her arms tightly in front of her and continued to regard Sam warily. "Good, because I do care about him, Sam," she said gently but impersonally. "I care about all your kids."

Sam tensed at the cool civility in her low tone. She was treating him as though he was someone she barely knew. As though they'd never made love or spent the night together, wrapped in each other's arms. "And they care about you, too," he said quietly. He paused, then continued seriously. "So do I."

Silence fell between them, more awkward than before. Sam wished he could do something to extinguish her hurt. He wished he could hold her in his arms. Hold her while she cried. But she didn't want him touching her and she didn't want to confide in him. She wanted him to keep his physical distance, just as she was keeping hers. All he could do was coax her to tell him whatever the problem was, and go from there. "I know it's been a rough time for you," he said after a moment.

Kate looked at him, curious now. "Is that why you didn't tell me what had happened to Will?" Her voice was flat, expressionless.

Sam had known excluding her that way was a risk, given all they had been through together, but at the time he'd had no other choice. She'd had all she could do, just coping with her father's death. "You've been handling a lot," he said gently. "I didn't want to lay anything else on you. I figured it could wait until you were feeling better."

Kate sent him an angry, impatient glance. "I don't need you to protect me, Sam."

Sam didn't need a crystal ball to see she was spoiling for a fight. Anything that would give her a chance to push him away from her and out of her life. He knew, because he'd been where she was, and felt what she was feeling, in the weeks and months after Ellie died. He hadn't wanted anyone to understand him. He hadn't wanted anyone to get close to him or to pull him out of his misery and grief. When that was exactly what he had needed. "I can still be here for you," he told her calmly, remembering the way she had barged into his life and kept at him until he'd begun to live again, his feelings about the matter be damned.

Kate turned away from him, but not before he saw the tears in her eyes.

"No, Sam," she told him in a low choked voice as she stood and began to restlessly move around the room. "You can't. Not after the pain and heartbreak our being together has caused others."

As he heard the guilt in her voice, fear stabbed at him, sharp and real. "What are you talking about?"

Her eyes filled with tears and she spoke with such sadness and self-condemnation it broke his heart. "Like it or not, we have to face the facts and own up to what happened and why. If I hadn't insisted on moving in with you, over my parents' objections…if I had just listened to them…my dad might be alive today."

"You didn't cause your father's heart disease, Kate."

"But my relationship with you did cause him enormous stress, and that stress precipitated his heart attack." Kate's voice broke and the tears she'd been holding back streamed down her face. "Don't you see, Sam? If his heart hadn't suffered so much damage in the heart attack he had the night Craig came home…if he'd been able to have the surgery before it got to that point, then he might have lived."

Sam didn't want to hurt her, but the alternative was to let her sink deeper into despair. "Then again," he countered bluntly as he took her by the arms and held her in front of him, "your dad might have gone on ignoring his symptoms, refusing to get medical treatment, and then had a massive coronary during a particularly exciting football game. There's just no way to tell, Kate. No way to change fate. It just can't happen. We don't have that kind of power. No one does. Things like this are out of our hands. The most we can do—the best we can do—is accept it and go on treasuring each other and living each day to the fullest. Looking back, wishing things had turned out differently, is futile." Sam's voice broke and he had to force himself to go on. "I know. Because I spent damn near six months doing just that, and all I did was hurt everyone close to me. Don't make my mistakes, Kate," he told her urgently. "Don't shut me out."

"And don't you ask me to give you what I can't," Kate retorted with a numbness that was painful to see.

"So what's the solution?" Sam said, angry at how she was pushing him away after all they had been through together. "You shut yourself off from the world? Refuse to accept any comfort anyone might offer?"

"I'm not doing that," Kate retorted stiffly. Her blue eyes were filled with anger. "I'm going to work. I've been spending time with my mom and family friends."

"Just not me," Sam concluded, hurt. *Not anymore.*

Kate swallowed and there was no pretending for either of them that she hadn't been holding him at arm's length since her father's funeral, because she had. Now he finally knew why she had seemed to drift further and further away. She was hell-bent on punishing herself for her father's death, and that punishment primarily included cutting herself off from him and the love they had discovered. But that wasn't what Mike Marten would have wanted. Sam was sure of that. Mike had wanted Kate to be happy, cared for, loved.

"I need time alone, Sam," she said evenly, looking as if she were struggling to not cry. "Time to figure things out. Time to recover. You can't help me do this."

Yes, Sam thought fiercely, he could, if only she would let him. Once again, he tried to get through to her. He stepped closer then watched in frustration as she backed away. "I understand how overwhelming your grief is," he said gently, "and I know you need your space to work through it. But you need to understand something, too, Kate." He waited until she looked him in the eye before he continued sternly. "My feelings for you are not going to change. I don't care how long it takes. I don't care how you test me or what you put me through. I'm going to be right here waiting for you," he promised. "And when you're ready, I'm going to marry you, and give you the kind of life you've always wanted, and certainly deserve."

"You can't wait for something that might never happen," Kate told him sadly.

And right now, Sam thought with equal parts helplessness and resentment, she didn't see how they could, or would, ever get past this. For the first time Sam knew how Kate must have felt when she had confronted him that night in his study weeks ago, when he was so mired in grief he'd lost all hope of ever being happy again. He hadn't given her a single indication that her efforts to help him were anything but futile, but she hadn't given up on him then. And he wasn't giving up on her now, he vowed. Kate needed him. He wasn't walking away.

As soon as Sam left Kate cried until she had no more tears. Kate fell into bed, still telling herself it was for the best. They couldn't turn back the clock and redo the events that had led to such disaster, and they couldn't build their happiness on someone else's suffering. Sam was better off without her. And certainly the boys didn't need to be around her, with her falling apart the way she was, from the inside out. Life would go on. Somehow she would survive this. They all would.

The next day a beautiful sterling-silver clock was delivered to Kate's office with a cryptic message from Sam. "Time is on our side." Wednesday, she received a calendar of all the McCabe family events for the next year filled in, and a beautiful bouquet of yellow roses. Thursday, Lacey Buchanon McCabe popped in, needing to know her ring size, and then popped right back out again. And sometime during the day a framed photo of Sam and the boys appeared on her desk.

Friday, Kate received a beautiful teakettle with the name Kate Marten McCabe engraved on it, and a dozen misshapen but delicious cookies baked by Sam and his boys. The moment she tasted one, she began to cry, but to her surprise they were sentimental tears, tears of gratitude, not grief. Saturday morning, she woke to find a thermos of her favorite fruit juice on her doorstep, and an invitation to Sunday dinner at Sam's tucked inside her newspaper.

The message was clear. Sam knew what he wanted and he wasn't giving up. *Your heart will steer you in the right direction,* her dad had said.

There was only one place Kate's heart wanted her to be.

And that meant there was only one thing to do. So Kate showered and put on her shorts, sneakers and a pretty cotton sweater perfect for a sunny late-summer day, and drove over to Sam's. She had no idea what she was going to say or do, she just knew she had to see him. And the boys, too.

To her surprise, a furniture store van was parked in front of the house. Workers were unloading a rolltop desk and swivel chair of the highest quality. Though where Sam was going to put that, Kate didn't know. He already had a fine desk in his study and there was one in every bedroom, including his. Figuring that little mystery was the least of her problems, Kate headed for the door.

Brad was first to catch sight of her coming up the front steps, onto the porch. He about broke his neck leaping over the sofa in the living room to greet her. "Oh, man. You're not supposed to be here," he said, looking very worried.

Will shouldered his way through the front door. He squinted at her thoughtfully, then picked up where Brad had left off, demanding suspiciously, "Or are you?"

Lewis shoved his scrawny shoulders through the well-muscled frames of his older brothers. Pushing his glasses up on his nose, he said, "You know what the deal was. Dad said Kate wasn't supposed to find out any—"

Brad clamped a hand over Lewis's mouth, cutting him off in midsentence, and gave him a warning look not to be argued with. "Why don't you come inside, Kate?"

"But..." Lewis sputtered anxiously, shooting a nervous glance behind him.

"Never mind what Dad said before, Lewis. I'm sure he can handle this," Brad said in a voice laced with double meaning.

Beside him, Will and Riley remained skeptical.

Unable to contain either her curiosity or her eagerness to see Sam and make amends with him a second longer, Kate stepped inside the house and saw the disaster zone it had become. She knew Mrs. Roundtree was away for the weekend—Lilah had said something about it at the hospital—but this was ridiculous. The interior of the house looked like a college dorm on move-in day.

"Hey, Kate's here!" Kevin dodged the clothes and books and toys all over the front hall and ran up and gave her a hug. "I missed you."

Kate hugged him back, loving the feel of his small sturdy body in her arms. "I missed you, too," she said thickly. In fact, even though it had only been a week since she'd seen them, she had missed them all tremendously.

Sam's voice thundered from up above. It was more than

a little irritated. "Guys, I told you not to disappear before the job was done!"

Kate turned her glance to the furniture piled up in the hall on the second floor. It looked as if the boys' rooms had exploded, their toys, games and athletic gear landing at random places all over the house.

"We're never going to get finished," Sam continued grumpily, threading his way down the stairs, "unless you—" Sam broke off at the sight of her, then continued his descent, his eyes locked with hers, not stopping until they stood toe to toe. Kate felt her breath catch in her chest.

Clearly, Sam had been working very hard at whatever he was doing here. Sweat dotted his dark brow and clung to the roots of his hair. His T-shirt was damp with sweat. It molded to his taut, strong body as well as his tight, worn jeans. Clearly, he hadn't shaved for at least a day. The stubble lining his face added a dark, dangerous aura to his handsome profile. Just being near him again made Kate's spirits rise and her heart take on a slow, thudding beat.

Before either of them could say anything else, the guys with the furniture store logo on their shirts tromped down the stairs. The one who looked to be in charge handed Sam a piece of paper and a pen. "You're all set up there, Mr. Mc-Cabe."

"Thanks, guys. I appreciate the quick work." Sam scrawled his signature. When they'd gone, Sam took Kate's hand and led her through the front door and around to the side of the house, to a deserted corner of the wraparound porch. He guided her into a wicker chair and pulled one up next to her, so they were sitting knee-to-knee, face-to-face. "I wasn't expecting to see you today," he said.

Chapter 22

"Oh, man, he is screwing this up so bad," Will said from his vantage point behind the next-door neighbor's hedge. The way things were going he was almost sorry he'd let his brothers talk him into monitoring the situation.

"Have you ever seen anyone who has less talent with the opposite sex?" Brad complained, shaking his head. "Even a complete moron knows you should shower and shave and put on some nice-looking clothes before you get close to your woman."

Riley agreed wholeheartedly as he peered through the leafy green leaves of the Buford holly bushes. "You'd think he would learn from his mistakes and try laying on a little charm before he gets to the serious stuff."

"It's probably our fault, for letting her in at all," Will said, spreading some of the branches for a better view. "We should have made her leave before she saw him looking all hot and sweaty. And not sent him back out onto the field until he had a better game plan."

"Will you stop with the football metaphors," Riley said. "Not everything in life relates back to some stupid game."

"You'd be surprised how much you can learn from sports," Will countered.

"Yeah, well, Dad's problem isn't sports," Lewis observed with near-clinical wisdom as he adjusted his glasses on the bridge of his nose. "It's showing Kate how much he wants her to come back to us. And from where we're crouched now, it doesn't look like he's being very successful."

Six-year-old Kevin sighed and shook his head. He sat, put his elbows on his knees and rested his chin on his propped-up hands. "I sure hope he doesn't make her cry."

Kate knew she should have put this conversation off until later. Until she had figured out exactly how to make amends to Sam. But now that she was here, there was no turning back. She inhaled a bracing breath. Stood. Knowing if she was going to keep her head and say everything that needed to be said, the way it should be said, she needed some physical distance from him. She strode several steps away from him and turned to face him, knowing better than ever how very much depended on her getting this right.

"You were right, Sam. I should never have shut you out the way I did." She swallowed hard around the growing lump in her throat. "I wanted love to come under perfect circumstances, without any conflict or risk or family difficulties. But that's just not the way it works. Love comes when you least expect it. It disrupts your life and wreaks havoc on your plans. But love is the one thing in this life worth living for," Kate said, the tears sliding down her face as she realized she no longer cared how it had come about or why or when, it was enough just knowing that the passion, the tenderness, the caring between them existed. And it did—in spades. "And I know my dad would *not* want me to go the rest of my life without it."

Sam stood and swiftly closed the distance between them. "What are you saying, Kate?" he asked gruffly as he took her all the way into his arms.

"That I've stopped being afraid to take a chance on us. I'm through putting up roadblocks to keep us apart." And she knew now that's all they had been. "Because I love you, Sam," Kate confessed emotionally, "more than I could ever say." And to make sure Sam knew it, felt it, wondered and reveled in it, she kissed him. Long and passionately. Slow and gentle. And every way in between. When they finally pulled back, they were both trembling.

"I love you too, Kate." Sam brushed her tears away as her heart thundered crazily inside her chest. "When you barged into my house and told me you were single-handedly going to help me get over my grief, I didn't think it was possible. I didn't think I could ever get past it, never mind want to love again. But I did. And I do. To the point I can no longer imagine my life without you in it."

Tears spilled down her cheeks as Sam continued to regard her tenderly. "I meant what I said the other day when I told you I wasn't going to let you—let us—go. We're a part of each other now, Kate, a big part, and we always will be."

He tightened his arms around her protectively and kissed her again, not stopping until she was filled with the most wonderful peace, the kind that only came from being with him.

Trembling, too, he pulled back. "I want to spend the rest of my life with you," he said in a rusty-sounding voice. "And to make that possible—" Sam took Kate by the hand, guided her back inside the house "—the six of us have undertaken a very necessary reorganization."

His hand linked confidently with hers, Sam led Kate to

the second-floor master bedroom. Gone were all of Ellie's belongings and the furniture. In its place were bunk beds and what looked to be a lot of the boys' stuff. Sam turned to her, his brown eyes darkening seriously, and continued in a way that let her know he'd given it a lot of thought. "The guys and I had a family meeting and agreed if you were going to be a part of our lives—and we all wanted that very much—we had to make some changes around here. We didn't want to sell the house—it belonged to my parents and had too many memories. So we decided to do what Ellie and I did when we inherited the place from my folks—transform it. We spent last night sorting through Ellie's things, keeping the items that were of sentimental value, and carting off the rest to charity where they could be put to good use. We moved Brad and Riley and Will down to the second floor, so that all four older boys will be on the second floor."

Looking more determined than ever, Sam led her up the staircase to the top floor, continuing to explain all the while. "Mrs. Roundtree will still occupy the first-floor guest suite. I'm moving up to the third floor and taking over the largest bedroom up here." Sam stopped in the hall to show Kate the new Southwestern-style furniture he had put in his bedroom. "Kevin gets the second largest one across the hall. And we're turning the storage room into a combination office-sitting room for you because we all know how crazy it can get in a household of six men, and we figure there might be times you're gonna want a refuge of your own. Although it could eventually become a nursery…if you think…" There was no doubt what he wanted. "Just in case I'm not being clear here," Sam continued, all the love he felt for her in his low, husky voice. "I'm asking you to marry me, Kate, as soon as possible."

Kate looked into Sam's eyes and saw their future stretching out happily in front of them. She'd had doubts before. She had none now. She knew he was the man for her, the only man for her. Her dad had been right—her heart was telling her what to do. "Oh, Sam." Kate's heart filled with joy as they kissed. Contentment unlike anything she'd ever felt before swept through her, and her soul filled with optimism for the days and weeks and years ahead. She knew there would be hard times. But she also knew there was nothing they couldn't handle as long as she and Sam were together. Smiling, she told him exactly what he wanted to hear. "My answer is yes."

Epilogue

The Thanksgiving weekend football game at the McCabe Ranch was in full swing. Sam and his five boys had teamed up against John and Lilah McCabe's four sons and their offspring, resulting in one of the most hilarious games ever. Kate and her mother, who'd come over to join in the holiday festivities, lounged on the porch with Lilah and Annie. Out on the lawn, Josie and John McCabe refereed the game. The only one missing was Jackson's wife, Lacey, who'd been the pediatrician on call at the hospital all day. But she was due to arrive soon, and would no doubt see the second half of the McCabe vs. McCabe game.

"You seem awfully deep in thought today," Lilah noted as Will passed the football off to Riley, who handed it to Kev.

Joyce nodded in agreement as Kev raced, laughing, down the field. "Are you sure you're feeling okay?" Joyce asked Kate with motherly concern as Kev was tagged just short of the goal line. "You looked awfully pale this morning."

"I'm fine, Mom," Kate said, trying not to flush.

Joyce and Lilah exchanged looks. Annie, who was the mother of triplets, grinned speculatively, too. Kate knew what they were thinking. She and Sam had been married almost two months now. It was possible there was a very good reason for her unexpected but short-lived queasiness. Which was why Kate wanted Lacey to hurry up and get to the ranch.

As if on cue, Lacey's car turned into the lane. Jackson jogged over to give her a kiss and a hug as she got out of the car, then trotted back to the field to rejoin his teammates.

Smiling, Lacey headed for the porch. Kate had only to look at Lacey's expression to know the answer she had been waiting for. As Lacey nodded, confirming it to be true, Kate couldn't help it—she broke out into a spontaneous grin of pure joy. It was all she could do to not let out a big "Yee-Haw!" Who said dreams didn't come true?

"Okay," Sam said, catching sight of the look on her face. He called a time-out and then jogged over to the edge of the porch. He looked from Kate to Lacey and back again. "What's going on, you two?" he demanded.

Kate took Sam's hand. "If everyone will excuse us for a moment, I'll fill you in."

Speculative looks were exchanged all around as Kate led Sam away from the others. "So what's the big secret?" he demanded as soon as they had disappeared behind the latticework arbor decorated with Lilah's prize-winning roses.

"The best kind of all." Kate stood on tiptoe and went easily into Sam's strong arms. "You are going to be a daddy again."

Grinning, Sam swept her against him and delivered a heartfelt kiss that swiftly had Kate tingling from head to toe and would have lasted a heck of a lot longer if not for the muffled giggles behind them. Reluctantly, they pulled apart. Kate and Sam turned to see all five boys watching them. The rest of the McCabes were not far behind.

Riley frowned. "Gee, Dad, we're trying to have a football game here. We're inches from making another touchdown, and you're back here making out with Kate!"

Will elbowed him. "I think it's a little more than that," he told his younger brother seriously.

"Yeah, like what?" Brad frowned impatiently.

Sam wrapped his arm around Kate's shoulders. "Kate and I just found out we're going to have a baby."

At his announcement, there was a brief stunned silence followed by whoops and hollers all around. "Way to go, guys!" Riley said enthusiastically.

"We could use another player for our team," Brad agreed.

Kev tugged on Will's jersey. "But what if it's a girl?" he asked.

"Then we'll teach her, too," Will reassured him gently.

"When's the baby going to be born?" Lewis asked.

"July," Kate said as she and Sam accepted hugs and kisses and congratulations from Joyce and the rest of the McCabes, too.

As it turned out, Sam and Kate did have a baby girl. She was born on July sixth, and was just as beautiful and darling as everyone knew she would be. They named her Laurel McCabe. And Sam immediately became as protective as everyone knew he would be. "She's not dating until she's thirty," he told everyone who stopped by to see the newest addition to Sam and Kate's family.

Not that his sons, or even Kate, agreed with him on that. "Come on, Dad, she ought to be able to date when she's sixteen," Will said.

"Just go on the dates with them," Brad explained.

"That way nothing romantic can go on," Riley agreed.

"Or better yet, we'll set up a computerized action-cam and follow her on her dates," Lewis said. "That way Laurel can be on her date and you can watch everything that's going on while you and Kate are still at home."

"Yeah," Will said, getting into the spirit of things with a teasing wink, "just put one of those electronic bracelets, the kind prisoners wear, on both Laurel and her date, and no problem, they won't be able to get away with a thing."

Kate rolled her eyes.

Everyone laughed.

Kevin patted Laurel's foot. "It's not easy being the youngest," he said. "But don't worry, little sis. I'll keep our big brothers from giving you too hard a time."

As if on cue, Laurel let out an indignant cry.

"See?" Kate said as she went to pick her up. "She's protesting at all this overprotectiveness from the men in the family already!"

Sam looked down at their still-loudly-complaining baby girl. Just as he had suspected, she had Kate's eyes and smile, and was every bit as beautiful, to boot. Which cost Sam no small amount of sleep. How on earth was he going to keep the boys away?

Sam comforted Laurel by patting her back. But, like her mother, once Laurel had made up her mind to be heard, she wasn't easily silenced. "I have a feeling she's going to be a handful." Sam grinned.

All five of their sons guffawed at his remark. "Like that's a surprise?" Will quipped.

"Dad, she's a McCabe," Riley pointed out.

Lewis nodded. "She's supposed to know her own mind."

"If she were easy to raise, it'd be more than a surprise," Brad added knowingly, "it'd be a first."

"Yeah," Kev chuckled. "She's got a tradition of orneriness to uphold."

Sam and Kate laughed at all the teasing. Kate handed Laurel to Sam as she went to get a diaper. By the time she got back, Laurel was curled up against Sam's chest, cooing sweetly, and enjoying the adoring glances and soothing murmurs of all five of her brothers. "One thing for certain," Kate said softly, tears of happiness filling her eyes as she thought about how Sam and his boys had made all her dreams come true. "There's no shortage of love in this family."

"Nor," Sam said, giving Kate a warm glance that encompassed her, their daughter and all five of their sons before continuing solemnly, "will there ever be. And that's a Texas-size vow we all mean to keep. Because there's nothing more important, more satisfying in this life than love and family. Right, guys?"

Will, Brad, Riley, Lewis and Kev all nodded. Abruptly, there were tears glistening in their eyes, too.

"I love you guys," Kate said thickly, hugging them all one by one.

They hugged her back in a way that let her know she would always and forever be a part of their hearts and lives. "We love you, too."

Kate changed Laurel's diaper, then the boys took turns holding their new baby sister while Sam and Kate looked on. Sam wrapped his arms around Kate. Holding her close, he pressed a kiss on her head. "We really have it all, don't we?"

Kate nodded, loving the way his arms felt around her, so warm and strong and right, loving the vows they had made and kept with all their heart. "And then some," she said.

* * * * *

FAMOUS FAMILIES

YES! Please send me the *Famous Families* collection featuring the Fortunes, the Bravos, the McCabes and the Cavanaughs. This collection will begin with 3 FREE BOOKS and 2 FREE GIFTS in my very first shipment— and more valuable free gifts will follow! My books will arrive in 8 monthly shipments until I have the entire 51-book *Famous Families* collection. I will receive 2-3 free books in each shipment and I will pay just $4.49 U.S./$5.39 CDN for each of the other 4 books in each shipment, plus $2.99 for shipping and handling.* If I decide to keep the entire collection, I'll only have paid for 32 books because 19 books are free. I understand that accepting the 3 free books and gifts places me under no obligation to buy anything. I can always return a shipment and cancel at any time. My free books and gifts are mine to keep no matter what I decide.

268 HCN 9971   468 HCN 9971

Name _____ (PLEASE PRINT)

Address _____ Apt. #

City _____ State/Prov. _____ Zip/Postal Code

Signature (if under 18, a parent or guardian must sign)

Mail to the **Reader Service**:
IN U.S.A.: P.O. Box 1867, Buffalo, NY 14240-1867
IN CANADA: P.O. Box 609, Fort Erie, Ontario L2A 5X3